The INKLINGS DETECTIVE AGENCY

PRAISE FOR

The INKLINGS DETECTIVE AGENCY

"As a lifelong fan of C. S. Lewis and J. R. R. Tolkien, I could not have guessed that the book I most needed to read was an amazing yarn of Jack and Tollers turned detectives. This multiverse adventure is imaginative, intriguing, and wildly satisfying. The premise seems, at first, almost zany—yet, as the narrative develops through richly drawn moments and pitch-perfect dialogue, the Inklings' destiny as sleuths becomes inevitable. Because the book includes a cast of who's who from early twentieth-century British literature and a brilliant framework, the reader will experience these titans of storytelling in an marvelously fresh way. It is now possible to believe that the Inklings of our world squandered their true potential."

—JOHN HENDRIX, *New York Times* bestselling illustrator and author of *The Mythmakers: The Remarkable Fellowship of C. S. Lewis and J. R. R Tolkien*

"*The Inklings Detective Agency* by John R. Kelly is a delightful achievement. Part literary homage, part historical fiction, and part detective mystery, Kelly's work invites readers into the world of Oxford at one of the richest moments in literary history. Fans of Lewis and Tolkien, Doyle and Sayers, will find much to admire here as this novel inhabits their personalities and allows readers to see them not only as towering literary figures but as friends working together. I admire this work of imaginative re-creation, and I enthusiastically recommend it."

—CHRIS PALMER, PhD, dean and professor at Barnett College of Ministry and Theology, Southeastern University

"John R. Kelly's *The Inklings Detective Agency* is a brilliant and fascinating novel that will delight and move readers that are admirers of J. R. R. Tolkien, C. S. Lewis, Charles Williams, Dorothy Sayers, and Agatha Christie. This book conveys how goodness, beauty, and truth triumph over darkness, and it is a great contribution to the Inklings canon of literature!"

—JUSTIN WIGGINS, author of *Surprised by Agape* and *Tír na nÓg*

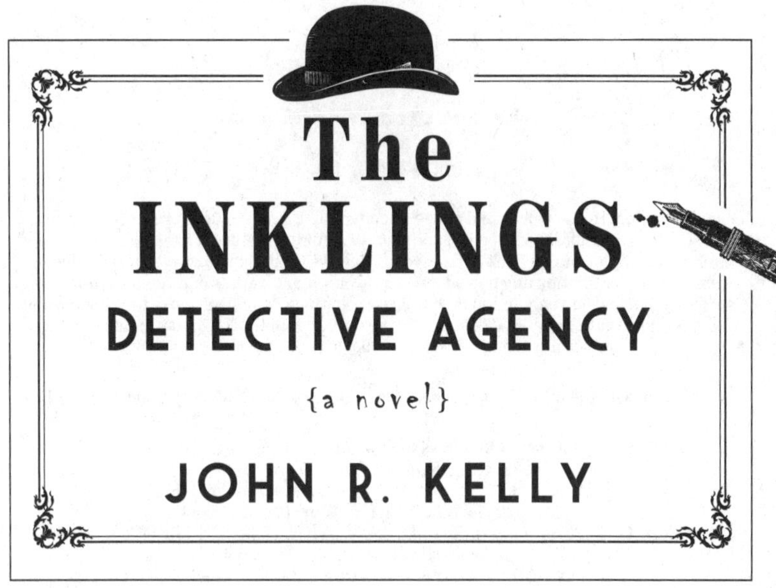

The INKLINGS DETECTIVE AGENCY

{a novel}

JOHN R. KELLY

WATERBROOK

WaterBrook

An imprint of the Penguin Random House Christian Publishing Group, a division of Penguin Random House LLC

1745 Broadway, New York, NY 10019

waterbrookmultnomah.com
penguinrandomhouse.com

A WaterBrook Trade Paperback Original

Library of Congress Cataloging-in-Publication Data
Names: Kelly, John R. (John Richard), author
Title: The Inklings Detective Agency : a novel / John R. Kelly.
Description: New York, NY : WaterBrook, 2026.
Identifiers: LCCN 2025040658 (print) | LCCN 2025040659 (ebook) | ISBN 9798217151981 paperback | ISBN 9798217151998 ebook
Subjects: LCSH: Inklings (Group of writers)—Fiction | LCGFT: Detective and mystery fiction | Novels | Fiction
Classification: LCC PS3611.E449243 I55 2026 (print) | LCC PS3611.E449243 (ebook)
LC record available at https://lccn.loc.gov/2025040658
LC ebook record available at https://lccn.loc.gov/2025040659

Printed in the United States of America

1st Printing

The authorized representative in the EU for product safety and compliance is Penguin Random House Ireland, Morrison Chambers, 32 Nassau Street, Dublin D02 YH68, Ireland.
https://eu-contact.penguin.ie

BOOK TEAM: Editor: Jamie Lapeyrolerie • Production editor: Laura K. Wright • Managing editor: Julia Wallace • Production manager: Jane Sankner • Copy editors: Whitney Bak, Tracey Moore • Proofreaders: Bailey Utecht, Rachael Clements

Interior art from Adobe Stock: DESIGN BOX (frame), lynea (hat and vintage pen)

Book design by Diane Hobbing

For my family.

Author's Note

This novel is a work of historical fiction. While it draws inspiration from real people, places, and events, I have taken certain creative liberties with timelines, historical details, and character portrayals in service of the story. Any deviations from the historical record, whether they involve condensed events, imagined dialogues, altered chronologies, or fictionalized interpretations, are entirely intentional and my responsibility alone.

These choices were made to enhance narrative clarity and serve the story, rather than to serve as a definitive account of history. I encourage curious readers to explore the historical context further and to view this story as one entertaining interpretation, not a substitute for historical scholarship.

Thank you for stepping into this version of the past with me.

—John R. Kelly

The INKLINGS DETECTIVE AGENCY

{1} The Bird

Thursday, December 10, 1936
Oxfordshire, England

> I was talking aloud to myself. A habit of the old: they choose the wisest person present to speak to.
>
> —J. R. R. TOLKIEN, *The Two Towers*

The wiry-framed fellow looked the part of a typical Oxford don: stylish and elegant in a burgundy vest and pressed trousers, topped with a tailored tweed jacket, perfectly cuffed with monogrammed links. He spoke out loud to himself as he walked the worn cobblestones in a late evening drizzle, passing the Martyrs' Memorial on his left with a quick salute. He pulled the jacket tight around him, but the blustery wind did not relent in biting and chilling him to the bone. John Ronald Reuel Tolkien paid it no mind. He was deeply lost in thought, speaking quick phrases and languages, some known only to him. He often shared unrefined ideas with himself. Thoughts of hobbits, orcs, dragons, a place called the Shire, and whatever else swirled around his strange and restless mind. Passersby would think him mad if they didn't understand his genius. But soon, those who paid the handful of shillings for his next book would be allowed to peek behind the curtain to see the wizard, if only just a little.

The words flowed faster with each hastening step, though everything Tolkien did was done at speed. He spoke fast, walked fast, read fast, and ate fast. His fellow Oxford colleagues joked he also slept fast. As Tolkien continued north on St. Giles', past the Ashmolean Museum on his left, and St. John's College to the right, he glanced down at his pocket watch and gasped. He was never late. Tolkien again quickened his pace, the heels of his shoes clacking like a metronome, and soon drifted back to acting out a dialogue, playing the dual role of quarreling elf and dwarf. The thunder cracked and roared overhead, and soon the rain came down in full sheets. A nearby evergreen tree, decorated for Christmas, sat short and wide, its lowest boughs nearly touching the ground under the sudden weight of water.

"Oh blast!" Tolkien said as heavy droplets splashed off his hat and narrow shoulders and filled the cracks of the cobblestone. He realized he'd forgotten his umbrella, but forged ahead on his trek, head bowed low with shoulders scrunched forward into the wind. There was no need to step into a nearby shop or wait under an awning for the rain to subside. Tolkien set his sights on the familiar pub ahead, less than a block away now. He pulled a handkerchief from the left breast pocket of his jacket, which was now, along with the fedora, nearly soaked through. He set his mind on the joy of a pint of warmed cider, which brightened his mood even more on this dismal evening. Tolkien stepped over the granite curb, waited for a passing motorcar, which splashed water onto his shoes, then walked across the wide cobbled road exactly where he usually did. He glanced up at the familiar round sign dangling and swinging in the wind, dripping rainwater on any who entered beneath it.

The sign depicted a giant eagle flying across a golden sky with a young child in its talons, a nod to the story of Ganymede, the legend of the boy carried off to Olympus by one of Zeus's eagles to serve as cupbearer to the mythical gods. Whether the boy went by choice or against his will, Tolkien could not remember at the moment, though he did like the look of the huge eagle.

Tolkien worked the latch and pushed open the wooden door of the Eagle and Child, more affectionately known to locals as simply the Bird and Baby or even just the Bird. He heard the tinkling of a bell above his head as he stepped inside and set about stomping the water from his shoes and shaking out his hat. He placed the hat gently on a well-worn peg jutting from the mortar in the wall, then stood for a moment; he usually needed time to let his eyes adjust but now realized it had already been dark outside and his eyes were well adjusted to the low-lit room. He sneezed and wiped at his beak-like nose with his wet handkerchief before shoving it into his hip pocket with a snort.

Scanning the room, he noticed the crowd at this time of night were mostly unfamiliar to him and then remembered he was already late and began moving toward the Rabbit Room at the back with renewed purpose, his long legs carrying him quickly past tables. Candles and electric wall sconces cast a dim light throughout the public house. The dark oak paneling on the walls and ceiling didn't help any to lighten the place, but the locals seemed to like everything as it was.

The Bird was long and narrow, barely wider than a railway car, and Tolkien often felt as though he were jostling down a train's center aisle as he made his way to the caboose.

Tables and booths lined either side as passengers watched the professor pass by. Some coupled patrons spoke in hushed tones and others sat alone, nursing a pint of something dark or golden colored and smoking one cigarette after another.

Tolkien inclined his head to an older regular. The man frowned, swayed in his bench seat, and grunted back, clearly at the end of a long day spent drinking. A copy of *The Times* lay spread out before him on the table, yet the man was no longer in any state to read it. Despite its being upside down for him, Tolkien read the bold headline, which featured a continued story from the front page, something related to King Edward VIII staying at Fort Belvedere in Surrey and swirling rumors of his possible abdication of the throne. Another booth's bench was filled with men in uniform—British RAF on leave, speaking boisterously of heroic deeds, either feats from the past or what they would do tomorrow if given the chance and enough bullets.

Tolkien felt a release of tension when at last he stepped into the familiar back room of the Bird. The rear of the pub was theirs, a home away from home for him and his like-minded friends, known to one another as the Inklings. They were naturally drawn to gather around the already-roaring fireplace, which was near a back door—an exit that was rarely used but still there should the need arise.

"Sorry I'm late, old man," Tolkien said. He gestured to a seat opposite his good friend and colleague Adam Fox and sat in a weary huff. "I have a lecture Saturday at Pembroke on linguistics and got caught up at my office going over notes. Didn't notice the time. I hope I haven't missed anything of interest."

"Pay it no mind, John," Fox answered with a friendly smile

and wave of his hand. "Relax and dry yourself off. Nothing of note can happen until the Bird closes. We have time to kill, and besides, we're still waiting on Lord Cecil." He checked his own pocket watch, a silver piece with a scrolling *F* etched onto the back, and took a small sip from the honeyed ale in front of him.

Fox, the dean of divinity at Oxford's Magdalen College, was the eldest of the Inklings, and though he was older than Tolkien by only nine years, all saw him as a friendly uncle or wizened mentor. Tolkien sighed before peering around the space for the first time to see who else had arrived at this specially called meeting of minds. Off in the corner booth sat Nevill Coghill and Hugo Dyson, leaning toward each other and speaking intensely about God knew what. So lost in passionate conversation they could be the only two in the entire pub for all they cared.

"Is that all?" Tolkien asked. "Just the five of us, then, with Cecil? Where are Jack and Warnie?"

Adam Fox chuckled and smoothed his wispy white hair. "Professor Lewis and his brother got the sniffles. It's going around, I hear. They opted to stay at the Kilns and let their lovely nanny make them chicken soup instead of making the trip to Oxford."

Tolkien frowned. "Why exactly are we here? Tell me you know. Surely not for an emergency manuscript reading?"

"I haven't the foggiest," Fox said with a shrug. "This is all Cecil's work. I had nothing to do with it. Our resident royal has a surprise for us, and all I was told is that it is incredibly important, sensitive, clandestine, and that lives may very well be at stake."

Tolkien couldn't help but snort and laugh out loud. "Are you serious? That sounds like our Lord David Cecil, as melodramatic as ever. Always someone about to die or suffer unimaginably in the direst of circumstances. He's told us that given his health, this could be his last year for . . . what has it been, the last five years?"

"He'll outlive us all," Fox said, followed by his signature deep, hearty laugh that caused his shoulders to bounce.

After a momentary pause, both men burst out laughing again just as Charles Blagrove, the aproned proprietor of the Bird, arrived and set down a warm cider in a thick mug for Tolkien and a fresh ale topped with foam in front of Fox.

"You gentlemen going to be reading tonight?" he asked politely with his warm smile. "I sure did enjoy hearing what I could of the last chapter, Professor Tolkien. Though I only got it in bits and pieces. I made as many excuses as I could to make my way back here."

"I don't believe so," Tolkien said slowly, eyeing Fox, who also shook his head. "At least I hadn't prepared to read anything. Tonight is a meeting of another sort. Besides, I think if Hugo over there had to listen to me read aloud about hobbits and elves twice in one week, he may have an aneurysm or go jump in the Thames."

All three men chuckled together. This was how it had always felt back at the start. Men talking about literature or the news of the day, sharing a smoke and a pint of their favorite drink, and, most important, jesting together about some part of life, faith, or work. That was where the Inklings had begun, as an informal meeting of comrades from the outside world. There were no preplanned agendas, no minutes taken, no club officers or stated goals of any kind; the friends spent the time talking, laughing, sharing, and encouraging and learning from one another. But lately, underneath the rosy surface and academic façade, the Inklings were becoming something entirely different.

"If you're not reading, sirs," Charlie began. He squinted and moved his blue-eyed gaze back and forth conspiratorially between the two men. "Then is tonight about you-know-what? The other side of the Inklings. Because if it is, I can roust out these old drunks and close up shop in two snaps so you men can get down to business. You can count on me." He pointed his thumb at his puffed-out chest and raised a brow.

"We can wait until midnight," Fox reassured him with a gentle smile. He leaned back in his creaking chair. "Though, when the time comes, Charlie, if you could double-check and make sure no one has fallen asleep under a table or in the lavatory, that would be much appreciated. Prying ears and all that."

"Oh, absolutely," Charlie Blagrove said with a salute. "Anything I can do to help the cause." He leaned in close and lowered his voice. "I know what important work you all have started to do, both in the public eye and outside of it. Should you need anything, anything at all, I am your man." He again hooked a thumb in to his chest, winked with a flash of a smile, pivoted, and was off, back toward the bar, wiping tables and whistling "Rule Britannia" as he went.

Fox raised his glass and toasted with reverent somberness, "To those who did not make it through." Tolkien held his glass high and nodded solemnly before sipping the delightfully warm liquid.

More laughter echoed from the booth where Hugo and Nevill traded compelling tales. Hugo's curls bobbed up and down as his face turned red with laughter and he pressed down on his stomach. "Tollers," Hugo called loudly, his first acknowledgment that anyone besides the two of them existed. "You need to hear this. Nevill here was just telling me about Michaelmas term and a precocious student in his Middle English course who felt the need to plagiarize—"

Hugo's words were cut short when Lord David Cecil entered the room. He looked agitated, even thinner and paler than usual, and his eyes were wide. "We'll need to move a few things around," he decided quickly, tapping his finger nervously on the tabletop and flicking his eyes about the space. "Can you all help? Our guest should be arriving soon."

"Who is arriving?" Hugo asked, getting to his feet. "What's with all the secrecy? I thought we were on the inside . . . brothers and all that. Spit it out, man!"

"You'll understand soon enough, Hugo," Cecil replied, glancing at the nearest occupied booth outside the Rabbit Room to make sure the Bird's other guests were out of earshot. "I want to make a good first impression, so be on your best behavior."

"We always are," Fox said with a smirk. "Or at least, we try to be."

Cecil frowned. "I'm not worried about the two of you, or even the brothers who I hear won't be making it—that is, unless the elder drinks too much." He lowered his voice. "It's those two who lack verbal filters and certain manners. I don't want to offend or scare off our special guest; not tonight, please dear God."

"Good heavens, man," Nevill said, walking over and helping to turn a chair around to face the fireplace. "I don't know how much more suspense we can take. Is it the King?"

Cecil flashed a grin. "Better," he answered before again lowering his voice. "Much better."

Hugo placed his hands on his hips and scowled. "Better

than the King of England?" He furrowed his bushy brow. "I'm not sure that's possible, Cecil. You realize what country we're in, don't you?"

Lord David Cecil went through the motions of taking an ornate golden watch on a chain from his pocket before returning it, only to repeat the action a few seconds later. "It's nearly midnight," he noted, flexing his right hand. "He should be arriving soon."

The pub closed. The couples, drunks, and singing merry-makers made their way reluctantly out into the stormy night as approaching lightning flashed in the distance. Charlie blew out candles and turned down the electric lights even further, in all except the back room. After throwing two more dry logs on the fire, he made his exit reluctantly, and a hush fell over the space. Five men now sat silently, facing the fire in a semicircle. Tolkien noted how very different and strange all this was indeed.

"I think we're ready," Cecil said finally, nodding his head and once again checking his watch.

Hugo grunted. "Are we having a séance?" he asked, his prominent brow now raised. "Because if we are, I'm leaving."

"In a sense, we are," Cecil responded. "But it's not what you're thinking. Please stay, Hugo. Mind your manners." He stood and walked to the back entrance.

Tolkien fiddled with his unlit pipe before striking a match in the silence and holding it to the pipe's bowl. The smell of cherry and walnut wafted and mixed in the air as he heard a door open and close and low voices speaking in the hallway's shadows. Cecil soon emerged alone without expression and took his seat. Behind him, a man walked out of the dark hallway, and Tolkien felt the breath pull from his lungs. The man was of average height and build. He wore a dark wool coat with a bowler hat and held a glossy black cane. He walked over and warmed his hands by the fire, then took up a place standing in front of the hearth, facing and eyeing the seated Inklings one at a time before finally speaking.

"Yes, yes, I know," he said with a placating gesture of his hands. "I should be a dead man. I died on July 7, 1930, in Crowborough, Sussex, and was buried in my rose garden at Windlesham Manor. But that is nothing more than nonsense, misdirection, and farce. Something I know a bit about. My name is Sir Arthur Conan Doyle. As you can see, I am very much alive, and I need your help in solving a heinous murder."

{2} The Writer

When you have eliminated all which is impossible, then whatever remains, however improbable, must be the truth.

—ARTHUR CONAN DOYLE, *The Case-Book of Sherlock Holmes*

The legendary author stood larger than life before the Inklings. Tolkien puffed absently on his pipe as Doyle smoothed the hair that had become ruffled after taking off his bowler hat to set it on the warmed mantel. The whole scene felt dreamlike. Doyle's hair was a shade whiter than it had been in the photo used for his obituary. He otherwise looked healthy, especially for being a dead man walking. Doyle looked dressed for a funeral, with his black woolen coat that fell to his knees, matching black vest, and black silk tie over a crisp white collared dress shirt.

"I've been led to believe here sits the greatest buzzing hive of literary minds in all of Great Britain," Doyle said slowly and deliberately while allowing his gaze to settle in turn on each of the five men seated before him. His wide gray mustache was twisted at both ends and bounced up and down as he spoke. "Is that correct?" He arched a bushy silver brow. Doyle's bright blue eyes were surprisingly gentle, yet they held a somberness that seemed to convey a mild sense of disappointment in whomever his gaze settled on.

The four shocked members of the Inklings glanced curiously at one another while Lord Cecil stared intently at a smudge on his dark polished shoes. Tolkien puffed his pipe, unwilling to affirm or deny such a bold statement and still not entirely certain what he was observing was real life and not just some fantastical vision of his often-overstimulated mind.

"I don't know if I would say that, sir," Nevill Coghill finally responded. "We do our best, but . . ."

"I may have exaggerated a bit," Cecil blurted out. His normally pale face showed a tinge of red.

"Wouldn't be the first time," Dyson added under his breath, before leaning back in his chair and crossing his arms over his broad chest.

"Never mind all that, gentlemen," Doyle said, waving them off. "Beware the man who agrees too heartily with accolades, I say." He cleared his throat. "For the better part of this past year, I've been observing your little writing cohort from a distance and have worked up a dossier on each of you. I believe you have great potential to be the exact men I've been looking for." Doyle paused and frowned, gripping the lapel of his coat with both hands. "Where's C. S. Lewis?" he asked, shifting his weight as he pursed his lips. "I've heard a great deal about him."

"I'm afraid Jack is under the weather," Cecil said sheepishly. "As well as his brother, Warren. And if you care to know, Owen Barfield is on a trip to America at the moment. But you can be assured, Sir Arthur, that any relevant information will be passed along promptly to all Inklings posthaste."

Sir Arthur frowned again but nodded, as there was nothing to be done about it. "Not a good first showing," he said. "I would have liked to meet Professor Lewis especially. Another time, perhaps?"

Cecil nodded vigorously as his left hand shook.

"As I was saying," Doyle continued, "I also know all about one John Tolkien." He inclined his head to the seated professor, who puffed intently and blew gray smoke out of the side of his mouth before forcing himself out of mild paralysis to raise the stem of his pipe in affirmation to the roll call.

Doyle tilted his head and stared at Tolkien as he spoke from memory. "A professor of Anglo-Saxon at Pembroke College; a philologist with an active imagination and head for linguistics." Doyle shifted and eyed Hugo and Nevill. The former did his best to look only mildly interested. "These two, Dyson and Coghill if I'm not mistaken. You gentlemen could have an important role in all this as well. You may not even realize it, but God has blessed you with remarkable minds, molded to be researchers, puzzle solvers, and mystery revealers. You make what is unknown in this mad world known and possess the character to not let slithering evils go unchecked. At least that is what I suspect and hope."

"You spoke of murder, sir," Adam Fox said, an uncharacteristic waver in his otherwise steady baritone voice. "I am not sure we Inklings are quite right for that type of thing. We've never worked out a murder before. A robbery once, and a simple case of fraud this past year—quite by accident, I might add—but never a murder. This may be better handled by Scotland Yard."

"No, no, no," Doyle said, shaking his head briskly while

gripping the top of his cane with both hands. "You'll soon understand why police presence cannot be involved in this matter in the slightest, nor can they ever catch wind of it, which is precisely why I am here to recruit you."

"So, what exactly do you expect us to do?" Fox asked.

"I expect you to catch a killer," Doyle answered with a flash of his teeth. "Nothing less will do. And I might as well get on explaining the case to you." He rapped his slender cane on the wood floor two times as a sort of exclamation point, like a judge's gavel, and began. "I have given a folder to Lord David Cecil here with all the relevant information. Names, dates, witnesses, and even a few grisly images you'll want to look at sparingly if you enjoy your sleep. Lord Cecil, and he alone, will know how to reach me should the need arise or when means, motive, and mystery have been solved. By week's end the number of people who know I am alive will have risen to three dozen." Sir Arthur frowned and placed both hands on the brass ball of his cane. "Can't be helped, and I'm placing my trust in you fine gentlemen that you won't go blabbing to *The Times* about it. For all intents and purposes, I am dead. I died in 1930 of a heart attack, and I would prefer to remain dead."

"Why exactly is that?" Dyson questioned. Tolkien recognized the frown on his face as conveying deep skepticism. Dyson waved a hand. "Why give up your fame and everything you worked so hard for?"

Doyle took a deep breath as if remembering it all himself. "If you must know, at the time I had been commissioned to investigate a serious crime, and it became clear certain people in positions of considerable power were involved and wished me dead. Before said villains could harm me or my family, I staged my death to buy time and move about freely in the shadows. After the resolution of a successful case, I did not feel the need to reemerge publicly into the spotlight and make my presence known to the world. Remaining clandestine has served me well, giving me time to read, write, research, and do what I must to oppose the growing evils in our little corner of the world."

"How very interesting," Fox said. "It must be strange to know most everyone believes you are dead and buried."

"I've gotten used to it." Doyle walked over and pressed his finger onto the manila envelope sitting in front of Cecil. "Nearly two weeks ago, on November twenty-ninth, an old friend of mine, Lord Roger Pennington, was murdered. I will not bore you with the details of the murder, though they are intriguing. I would expect whoever takes the lead in this case to go themselves and speak with the witnesses and those who found the body. The facts of his death are strange, to say the least." Doyle shuddered before continuing.

"The family, I suppose you could loosely call them, wishes to keep the true nature of Lord Pennington's death secret for reasons you will soon find out. Word made its way to me through my colleague, who will remain anonymous for now, and I approached those concerned to offer my services, which is what brings us here today and to my offer for you." Doyle looked to where Nevill Coghill sat with his hand raised just over his head. "You have a question, Professor Coghill?" Doyle said with a slight air of annoyance. "I would hope you have many, my good man, but I would ask that they be held off until the end of my little speech."

"It's not about the murder," Nevill said, his voice faint and small in the presence of a man he had admired as an author for so long. "Though I do have questions about that as well."

Doyle raised a bushy eyebrow and sighed. "Go ahead and ask, then, though I cannot linger here long."

"Why you?" Nevill asked, tilting his head. "I understand you have a mind that likes to solve mysteries and puzzles and all that. Reading one chapter of *A Study in Scarlet,* we could all see that. But why investigate murder?"

"Why not?" Doyle replied. "If God created me with a gift, who am I to refuse its use? I don't mean to sound arrogant or like a braggadocio to you men, but Sherlock was ever only as brilliant as his author. And I am not the only one. It's not as far-fetched as you might think. Throughout history, the minds of literary geniuses and the practical science of detection have walked hand in hand."

Dyson snorted. "You're saying many writers have also investigated murders?" He didn't hide the cynicism in his voice.

"That is exactly what I am saying. We writers invent adventure stories in our minds, and we crave it in real life. We think of motive and plot in our sleep. We possess imagination, and we desperately need it to solve these mysterious puzzles the world puts before us."

He paused and again raised a brow. "This would not be the first time writers were called upon in situations like this. Just to the north, on the University of Cambridge campus, a club was launched some seventy-five years ago by men not so different from you sitting before me today. The club was known affectionately as the Ghost Club, and it remains the oldest paranormal investigation organization of its kind. What started as simply a group of academics and professors sitting around talking about apparitions, mysteries, and paranormal activities soon became an effective group of men and women who solved real murders, and quite successfully, I might add."

"You've got to be joking, sir," Dyson said as he shot a sidelong glance toward Tolkien, whom he also knew to be a skeptic.

"I do not joke," Doyle responded. "Some of the members of the Ghost Club were none other than Charles Dickens and W. B. Yeats. Throughout history, writers have been among the best investigators, though that remains to be said about you. I do see promise in you gentlemen; otherwise, I would not present you with this test."

"But us"—Fox pointed to his chest—"solving real murders. Isn't it dangerous?"

"Of course it's dangerous," Doyle agreed. "That's what makes it so addictive. How dull and boring is a life of predictable safety anyhow?"

"I quite like my safety," Nevill said with nervous laughter.

Doyle frowned, set his jaw, and scrutinized the five men. His right fist was now balled up and jammed into his hip. "Up!" he practically yelled. "Follow me." With that, he turned on his heel and moved quickly to exit the way he'd come. The line of six men soon spilled out into the darkened alley while lightning flashed overhead, followed by rolling thunder that rumbled and rattled the windows of closed shops.

The confused Inklings followed at Doyle's heels, Tolkien taking up the rear as they turned out of the alley and began walking south on St. Giles' the way Tolkien had come not long before.

"Where exactly are we going?" Dyson called out as he fumbled with the buttons on his overcoat. It had stopped raining, but now a blustery wind whipped about and fluttered Doyle's coattails as he paced out in front with purpose.

"You'll see soon enough," Doyle said as another bolt of lightning split across the sky like white-hot skeleton fingers.

After a minute of brisk walking, Doyle stopped and looked up at a familiar statue. It was one Tolkien had walked past thousands of times, but now it looked somehow different in the flickering flares of distant lightning and the orange glow of burning streetlamps.

"What is this?" Doyle asked, pointing up at the Victorian Gothic limestone spire that featured a series of alcoves, each housing the figure of a different robed man. The statue always appeared to Tolkien as if it had been lopped off the top of a cathedral and stuck in the ground with only a bit of mortar to hold it in place.

"It is the Martyrs' Memorial," Fox said confidently.

"Yes, but why is it here?" Doyle prodded. "What is the reason for this memorial? What is the story? Who will impress me?"

Tolkien cleared his throat. "It commemorates three sixteenth-century Oxford martyrs: Hugh Latimer, the bishop of Worcester; Nicholas Ridley, the bishop of London; and Thomas Cranmer, the archbishop of Canterbury. They were convicted of heresy for their Protestant beliefs and burned alive after failing to publicly recant."

"As a staunch Catholic," Doyle said with a smirk, "how does that make you feel, Professor?"

"Mistakes were made," Tolkien responded.

"Hmm," Doyle said. "The point is that these men were martyrs. Men willing to put themselves in the line of fire for what they believed was right. They did not seek a life of safety or comfort. Neither did those who fought in the Great War seek to stay away from the front lines. They chose to put themselves in harm's way because they believed in something bigger than themselves. In the same way, I am asking each of you gentlemen a similar set of questions here tonight.

What do you believe in? What are you willing to die for? What are you willing to expose yourself to the risk of danger for?"

Doyle paused and turned to meet the eyes of the other five men in turn, his burning passion evident to all. He held up a finger and pointed it at each. "Murder has taken place," he declared firmly. "What will you do about it? The only thing needed for evil to flourish in this world is for good men to simply stand idly by and do nothing. So, I ask you again: Will you stand aside when you know very well you could do something? Will you only write stories about heroes, or will you be a part of something truly heroic and significant yourselves?"

There was a long pause, filled with the distant sound of thunder and the rising patter of rain splashing on the cobblestones. Doyle's shadow stretched long from the light of a nearby gas lantern and seemed to Tolkien to be dancing.

"I suppose you are right, Sir Arthur," Fox said, almost ashamedly. "We'll do what we can."

"I need more than that. I need to hear it from your soul!" Doyle nearly shouted. "I also need you to know what exactly you are agreeing to. You must work together. Do not simply go about this investigation on your own and play the hero. That is how men die foolishly, and a true hero cannot also be a fool. A collective mind is far superior to any one individual, no matter how observant or meticulous they are. There is a flow of logic and reason paired with creativity, problem-solving, and soul within a hive mind of a club like yours, and these are the ingredients necessary to solve the most difficult and ghastly of mysteries. Together, you are men who can tell fact from fiction from fantasy, and as we know, the truth lies somewhere in between." Doyle stood straight and lifted his chin. "What will it be, gentlemen? Are you in it together, or do I need to find someone else?"

"Oh, we are very much in," Fox answered with a smirk and a snort. "You had us as soon as you walked through the door back at the Bird, though I suppose the theatrics were helpful. The hair on my neck is standing on end."

Doyle smiled widely as the others nodded in affirmation. "Good, good," he said. "Then the game is afoot. Up until this moment, you were mere amateur sleuths. But today, you Inklings have stepped into something much greater. You will either sink or swim, and I leave that to you. As I have said before, 'Mediocrity knows nothing higher than itself; but talent instantly recognizes genius.' I will resurface in one month, just after Christmas but before the next full moon."

Tolkien pulled the pipe from his mouth and raised the stem. "Just one question, if you don't mind, Sir Arthur. Do you already have an idea who may be responsible for this murder?"

Doyle shrugged as he plopped his hat on his head. "I haven't an inkling."

A bolt of lightning lit the sky close above, followed instantly by a bark of thunder that caused the men to flinch and turn toward it. When they looked back, Doyle was gone, disappeared like a ghost into the Oxford night.

{3} The Agency

All we have to decide is what to do with the time that is given us.

—J. R. R. Tolkien,
The Fellowship of the Ring

Within the hour after Doyle's disappearance, Tolkien had already used a brass skeleton key retrieved from his office at Pembroke to enter the Bodleian Library through a back entrance. The professor was now wide awake, driven to uncover answers to a mountain of questions bouncing around his restless mind. If he was going to find any satisfaction, he knew this ancient library with more than one million printed items was his best chance, even if it took all night. There was no use going home and expecting a good night's rest, Tolkien had reasoned. His brain simply would not let him find peace until questions about Doyle had some resolution.

Hugo Dyson followed reluctantly at Tolkien's heels, torn between his desire for a blackberry brandy nightcap followed by a comfortable bed and his natural skepticism of everything Doyle had said, coupled with a stubborn craving to prove the man a fraud. The two men had the expansive library to themselves, their hard-soled shoes echoing off the marble floors as they paced up and down the countless stacks looming overhead like shadows of giants in the darkness.

Both men set to work independently, searching the library's vast collection of periodicals and newsprints, meticulously organized and categorized by date and keyword indexes filed away in small drawers that pulled out the length of a man's arm. Whenever one of them found something of interest concerning Doyle, they brought the item to a lamplit central table and splayed it out for easy viewing.

"We want his personal life," Tolkien called out into the darkness, "not a summary of *The Hound of the Baskervilles*. Hugo, do you hear me?"

"Yes, yes," Dyson called back. Minutes later, when the two men happened to meet at the same time at the table, he asked, "Are you certain we're allowed to be here, Tollers?"

"I do have a key," Tolkien noted while arranging faded articles chronologically.

"That is not what I asked," Dyson stated with a knowing frown.

"It would be wise not to mention this to many people and also for us to clean up and have left well before the librarians come at dawn."

Dyson nodded. "Wisdom is knowing one should never upset a librarian if it can be helped."

After not finding anything noteworthy, Tolkien took up a search for Charles Dickens. It was another hour before the men returned to the table for a longer second look at their collection of articles and biographies. They pored over faded documents with a magnifying glass for the better part of three hours, setting aside anything of interest for further examination and returning items of no interest to keep their workspace as clean as possible.

Dyson had just retrieved a copy of a lesser-known biography on Doyle when he eyed Tolkien curiously. "Did you know the Bodleian is supposedly haunted by a ghost?"

"I didn't," Tolkien said, pulling his eyes away from text for the first time in hours. "I've heard a few ghost stories about places around campus, but nothing concerning the library."

"Well, you first. Which are those?" Dyson asked eagerly. He loved a good story.

"Let me think." Tolkien blinked, grateful for the momentary distraction. "There is supposedly a haunting near Merton around Dead Man's Walk. Another shade haunts a staircase at University College, and another the altar in the chapel at St. John's College." Tolkien nodded, then held up a finger. "I almost forgot, there is still another alleged haunting in the dining hall of Wadham College. This place is rife with ridiculous ghost stories."

Dyson beamed. "Well done, Tollers. But you left out one of the best, and it is connected to the very library we are in right now. King Charles the First resided at Oxford during the English Civil War, even setting up a palace of sorts at Christ Church College to hold parliament. Charles was eventually captured and executed under orders from Oliver Cromwell, but while here at Oxford, even though he was king, he was banned from borrowing books. So as an act of rebellion in his afterlife, it is said the ghost of King Charles pulls books from their place and drops them on the floor for librarians to find in the morning."

Tolkien smiled and shook his head. "How devilish of him. I suppose we should leave a few volumes on the floor before we go. Just to keep the whole thing going."

Dyson grinned. "You've read my mind, Tollers."

A faint glow had begun to pour into the library from the upper windows when Tolkien finally leaned back in a creaking wood chair and rubbed his reddened eyes with his thumb and forefinger. He then noticed the lightening of the sky and made a face as though he'd sucked a lemon.

"Oh no, I've done it again," he lamented, a roughness to his voice.

"Done what, exactly?" Dyson asked, glancing up from a book he'd been perusing. He took his reading glasses off and began cleaning them with his handkerchief.

"I've stayed up all night." Tolkien chuckled wearily. "I get lost in all of it and don't realize the time. Usually happens in my home office."

"Well, let's make it count, old boy," Dyson said with a half smile. "What did you find?"

Tolkien answered slowly, "From what I can tell—and you're not going to like this—Doyle's words are true and trustworthy."

"Balderdash!" Dyson practically shouted into the sprawling library before lowering his voice. "Forgive me if I remain skeptical, Tollers. You believe the gibberish that Doyle actually investigated murders and what he said about the Ghost Club and Dickens and all that?"

"I'm beginning to," Tolkien acknowledged. He looked down at the well-worn library table where their collection of newsprint was strewn in a half circle, lit by a single green-shaded lamp. "Here." He pulled out a copy of an article from *The Times*. "It's right here. One incident, the Staplehurst rail crash, as it became known, took place on June 9, 1865. Many people died in the derailment, and it was reported that Dickens was on the train but survived." Tolkien removed his glasses and studied Dyson. "That isn't an average day for a writer."

"Are you saying the derailment was intentional?" Dyson questioned. "A way to cover up a murder?"

"Yes, it could have been," Tolkien said. "Or an attempt by killers to rid themselves of the man investigating them. In this case, it would have been Dickens, though he lived."

Tolkien withdrew another article, this one from the *Daily Herald,* and traced his finger down the small print. "And look here," he said when he found what he had been searching for. "In 1912, Doyle himself was named in the paper as being connected to a case involving a man named Oscar Slater. The man was released from prison, it says, after being wrongly convicted of the murder of an eighty-three-year-old woman. A reporter for the *Herald* saw Doyle at the scene of the crime with an investigator from Scotland Yard and snapped a photo. Here it is."

Dyson leaned over and looked at a faded black-and-white photo of a much younger and wide-eyed Doyle standing next to the investigator. "Circumstantial," he countered, waving his hand dismissively. "He could have just as easily been researching a book."

"That is exactly what the article says," Tolkien said. "I imagine Doyle thought the pop of that flashbulb would mark the end of it all, but his publicist turned it into a whole campaign for his next Sherlock Holmes novel, with further stories about how Doyle had been consulting with Scotland Yard."

"It does make a bit of sense," Dyson admitted. He scratched

at his chin. "If it were true—and I'm not saying it is—Doyle might have been able to question people about murder because he wrote about murder. He could have quelled any concerns raised by saying he was simply researching a book. If his case notes were discovered, they would be dismissed as background and due diligence for a story."

"Not only that," Tolkien added, raising a finger, "but a known celebrity like himself or Dickens gains access where others do not. They could have meetings with royals, dukes, lords, and Gilded Age business magnates and no one would think twice about it. There would have been an unspoken understanding of expected privacy among these men and women of high society that none would dare question."

Dyson flipped open a book in front of him to a bookmarked page. "I found something out about Doyle as well," he said, almost reluctant to share anything that didn't prove Doyle a fraud. "Doyle did in fact establish a club in London in 1903 called the Crimes Club. It is well documented in more than one biography."

Tolkien smiled. "Speaking of clubs, I forgot to mention I found some conspiratorial whispers hinting that members of the Cambridge Ghost Club were even brought in to consult on Jack the Ripper. Imagine that. Hard to believe, but it sounds as though you are starting to, as am I."

Dyson frowned. "I'll admit, I believe his story more now than I did a few hours ago. Though I remain skeptical of any man with an overactive imagination. We writers can be the worst of liars."

"How true," Tolkien agreed with a crinkle at the corners of his mouth. "Though sometimes we may not realize it or do it maliciously." He looked at the upside-down book in front of Dyson. "I suppose it doesn't need to be said that this Crimes

Club would have also been a front. Men pretending to be a group of writers discussing ideas for fake crimes when in actuality they were investigating real ones."

Dyson sighed. "I suppose Doyle sees something similar for us. Though I'm not certain we're up to it."

"So, we believe him enough to move forward then?" Tolkien prodded.

Dyson pursed his lips. "For now, though not everything he said was accurate. He did say something about us being mankind's only hope."

Tolkien laughed. "How wise can the man be if he's been surveilling us all this time and still thinks us capable of anything more than getting dressed in the morning and fixing a proper cup of tea?" Both men chuckled before the empty library again grew silent.

Tolkien looked toward the window where the sky continued to lighten. He shivered and rose to his feet. "I should get home before Edith wakes up. She may not realize I didn't come to bed last night."

"Margaret prefers I stay out," Dyson remarked, also standing to stretch. "She says not seeing me very often is what makes ours such a happy marriage." Dyson's usual booming laughter echoed across the library before his smile faded, as if he had just felt a great weight placed on his shoulders. "I have a strange feeling all our lives are about to change dramatically."

"Yes, I sense it too," Tolkien said, with a sense of soberness. "Though I'm not certain how to feel about it yet. I suppose it is also a historic night, and if I weren't so tired, I would like to celebrate."

"Celebrate Doyle, back from the dead?"

Tolkien stretched his sore back with a twist. "Not only

that, but tonight we witnessed the birth of the Inklings Detective Agency."

"Hmm, I suppose we did, didn't we?" Dyson said, smirking and raising a thick brow. "I like the sound of it. And what exactly do you suggest we do now?"

Tolkien plopped his hat on his head and slid his arms into his jacket sleeves. "Well, I would think it only makes sense that we should clean up, then crack on with solving a bloody murder."

{4} The Kilns

Friday, December 11
Headington Quarry, Oxfordshire

I am looking for someone to share
in an adventure that I am arranging,
and it's very difficult to find anyone.
—J. R. R. TOLKIEN, *The Hobbit*

Later that morning, after a hard-boiled egg and mug of Earl Grey tea, Tolkien said goodbye to his wife, Edith, and the two of his sons who were awake. He took three deep breaths of cold December air and blinked away the tiredness from his eyes, then mounted the bicycle he had walked from the garage to the street and began the four-mile journey from his home at 20 Northmoor Road to the home of Clive Staples (whom they all called Jack) and Warren Lewis.

The Lewises' home lay just outside the city limits to the east of Oxford proper in Headington Quarry. Tolkien ventured this far only if the occasion was serious enough and the weather allowed. Today was such a morning. He pedaled his way farther from the residential areas, eastward over the River Cherwell via a narrow stone bridge to Marston Ferry

Road, which brought him south on a slight incline toward Headington. From there, Tolkien knew of a trail off the main road. Upon entering the trail, he pedaled slower and caught his breath. Tolkien didn't like to sweat if he could avoid it.

The redbrick façade of the home caught Tolkien's eye as he crested a gentle slope and pressed along the final stretch, past a line of elms whose lower limbs drooped over a white fence into a pasture. When the trees had leaves, goats would strip the branches they could reach, leaving them bare like bony fingers reaching toward the dirt. Tolkien imitated the sound of a goat, then smiled and pedaled on. He couldn't help but imagine the tallest of the trees coming to life and speaking to him in a low, rumbling voice.

The name given to the Lewises' home, the Kilns, was inspired by the two old, funnel-shaped brickmaking kilns that were still located on the property, though they had not been used in decades. The bricks that formed the reddish walls of the home had been fired on-site—a point of interest that the Lewis brothers or Janie Moore, Jack's dear friend's mother who lived there, offered to any first-time guest. The home was modest but came with a brick-drying house converted into a garden shed, a rarely used earthen tennis court, a peaceful wooded area, and a small pond with a well-worn trail winding around it. Best of all, the Kilns was secluded and private yet close enough to Oxford that it was accessible by foot should the need arise.

As Tolkien drew closer, he saw something strange that he had never spotted on any previous visit to the Kilns. In the front drive, hoisted up on blocks, sat a boat. Tolkien squinted as he continued toward it before pulling up, dismounting, and walking the bike the remainder of the way. It was a small vessel, wood-bottomed, with badly chipped paint and what looked to be holes you could poke a finger through.

"By chance, are those bullet holes?" Tolkien asked when he was close enough. The boat rocked, and up stood a barrel-chested man with a short brown mustache and receding hair. He had a pipe in his mouth, unlit at the moment, and a knowing smile on his face. Warren was three years older than his brother, shorter, and wider, but he still carried his former athletic build. His loose-fitting gray sweater was full of oil stains, and his pants were pulled up high on his belly, cinched tight with a tan woven canvas belt.

"Tollers, you old rascal," Warren said. "I thought I might see you here." Warren grunted as he heaved himself over the side of the boat and thumped onto solid ground. "What do you think?" He gestured with his hands toward the wood-paneled canal boat as if it were a prize. "I bought it. Can you believe it?"

Tolkien didn't want to hurt the man's feelings but also felt he should always at least try to be honest. "You've always been impulsive," he noted with a faint smile, then squinted in mock inspection. "She's a bit ugly, I have to say. But I'd imagine that underneath the barnacles and grime, there lies a worthy seafaring vessel. Tell me, Warnie, why exactly did you buy it? I hope it didn't cost too much."

Warren beamed. He placed his balled fists on his hips and bent at the waist to proudly examine the boat's underside. Running one hand gently along the chipped wooden railing, he looked at the boat the way a doting husband would his new wife. He nodded as he pulled a small flask from his back pocket and took a swig in satisfaction, all while Tolkien looked on patiently. "It's a relic from the war," he finally explained. "A real beauty." He nodded to himself. "And yes, those are bullet holes. Browning automatic rifle, I would suspect. She was the bargain of a lifetime; I really couldn't pass it up. A real beauty indeed."

Tolkien furrowed his brow and shifted his weight from foot to foot. "Not the exact words I would use, Warnie, but I suppose that's why the 'beauty' was delivered here to Oxford and not to a marina or some nearby river."

"Yes, quite right, Tollers," Warren barked. "*Bosphorus* doesn't exactly float at the moment." He glanced over at Tolkien. "That's what I've named her. Every good boat needs a good name, don't you think?"

"After the strait in Istanbul?"

"That's right. Don't ask me why. It just sounded right." Warren shrugged. "There are some repairs that need to be made, but I've picked up books on the subject from Blackwell's. They have an impressive nautical and carpentry section if you can find it. I should be able to figure it all out." He threw up his hands. "How difficult can fixing a boat be? Besides, I don't know where I want to float her yet. And once you choose a canal or river, it can be a whole jumbled mess to get a boat moved again elsewhere, and costly to boot."

"I take it you're feeling better," Tolkien stated, amused by the whole turn of events.

"Oh yes, quite," Warnie replied quickly. "I was down for a couple of days but woke up this morning feeling better than ever. And just in time too. Jack is a day behind me." He pointed toward the house. "Dr. Havard is in there with him now, though I told him calling the doctor here was unnecessary. He's probably prescribing some quackery of a remedy. I told him it was just a common cold and will pass like it always does. This is the time of year for it, after all. But he listened to Janie on this one. She's always so worried about 'her boys.' Jack even more than me."

"We've got a case," Tolkien said, taking a step toward the house. "A big one. I've come to talk it over with your brother. Are you interested in being part of this one?"

Warren shrugged. "I'm sure Jack will find some way I can contribute. Talk it over with him. I'll catch up later after I've scraped *Bosphorus* free of old paint."

"Don't breathe it in," Tolkien warned.

He turned toward the house when he heard a noise. A man had exited the creaking front door and headed down the steps to a stone-slab walking path. A stethoscope hung around his neck, and a cracked brown leather bag dangled from one hand. Dr. Robert Havard was a tall man, handsome and athletic, with a full head of hair that had once been red but now was speckled with silver.

"Hello, Professor," he said, smiling. "Good to see you again."

"And you." Tolkien shook his hand briskly. He had met Dr. Havard on a few other occasions since the doctor had set up his medical practice in Oxford two years prior. "Is it safe for me to enter?" Tolkien questioned, inclining his head toward the house with a faint smile.

"Quite so," Havard responded. "No quarantine necessary. He'll be fine. He let his imagination run wild again, in a less constructive way. I suppose Professor Lewis only wanted someone to talk to, but now that you're here, that, too, will be remedied. He likes you most of all."

"I'd better go in and see him then," Tolkien said as he tipped his tan hat.

The front door was painted white, and white shutters bordered the windows, contrasting nicely against the brick. Ivy grew up the wall in places, even in the winter, though now it was no longer green. The front yard also featured a garden, usually filled with a healthy array of flowers thanks to Ms. Moore, but now all was brown and dead and in need of a good winter's cutting back. A kitchen garden peeked out of the side yard, usually full of herbs and vegetables but now also barren and awaiting spring. It seemed to Tolkien that this winter would surely drag on forever, and it hadn't even technically begun.

Jack sat in his usual chair in front of the fire. A haze of tobacco smoke drifted in the air in front of him, revealed in the rays of morning sunlight streaming in from a nearby window. Lewis wore a tattered red flannel robe. Both pockets of the robe were full of tissues to the extent some had begun spilling out onto the floor around him. Lewis's nose was tilted down into a book, as it usually was. He sneezed, wiped his reddened nose with yet another tissue, and readjusted his glasses.

"You can come sit, Tollers," Lewis said evenly, setting the creased paperback on the side table next to an ashtray and morning newspaper. "Robert says I'm not contagious." Jack spoke in a deep resonant voice, firm but friendly. His usually amiable face instead reflected his annoyance at his malady.

"You don't look so grand, Jack," Tolkien observed, finding the opposite chair, one much less worn, and sinking into it with a sigh. The fire felt good on his face as he realized the extent of the ache in his muscles. Pedaling in the cold always took more effort than in the springtime or summer.

"My brother gave me whatever he had." Lewis picked up his lit cigarette from the ashtray and pulled gently on it before coughing. "Then he woke up this morning and was perfectly fit as a fiddle, outside tinkering away with his boat. And I feel like death. My mind is foggy. Whatever I've written has ended up in the wastebasket. I could barely sleep a wink last night. Another blasted dream about a faun in a snowy wood. I woke up shivering despite the extra blanket."

"Chin up, Jack. Hopefully by tomorrow you'll be right as rain and back to yourself. I promise it will be a good morning."

"Hmm. I feel better already now that you're here." Lewis spoke the words with a feigned smile. He rubbed at the dark circles under his eyes, then folded up his glasses and set them down next to his book. "No greater joy than good friends, good conversation around a fire . . . and a case to solve."

Tolkien frowned. "How do you know there is a case?"

"You're here, aren't you?" Lewis answered, a raised eyebrow creasing his broad forehead. "Pedaled all this way. You don't usually stop by for nothing. And Cecil hinted as much when I told him I would not be able to make it. You should have seen the disappointment in that poor, rich man's eyes. Dark pools of deflated misery. It was as if I stole his lolly and threw it in the Thames."

"Well, you may have missed the single most important meeting of the Inklings Detective Agency that we have ever had."

Lewis frowned. "Detective Agency, eh? And how so? What is this case we've been handed? Why all the secrecy?"

"A very important one, or so we've been led to believe. It's all hush-hush. We are helping to solve a rather brutal murder." Tolkien lowered his voice on the last word and flicked his eyes toward the kitchen.

Lewis held his frown, then raised a brow again when he realized Tolkien wasn't joking. "Seriously, a murder? I don't know that we're quite up to—" He broke off at the sound of porcelain rattling on a tray. Janie passed from the kitchen into the library, the silver tray in her hands. Lewis looked up and smiled at the woman as the conversation paused. Tolkien took the cue and sat in silence, using the moment to remove his pipe and accoutrements and set to the work of lighting it.

"It's chamomile with eucalyptus for your throat; it's sore—I can hear it in your voice from the kitchen." She scrutinized Lewis and Tolkien in turn, perfectly aware they were discussing a case. "The professor is welcome to it as well. I made a full pot, and the doctor didn't have any." Janie Moore was visibly growing older but remained healthy and strong, though more irritable now than ever before. The lines around her eyes and mouth were much deeper than when Tolkien had first met her a decade earlier. It was easy to tell she had always been attractive and was aging gracefully.

"Thank you, Ms. Moore," Tolkien said, preparing his tea with honey.

They waited until she had gone before resuming. "It seems as though we've been chosen to spearhead this one, Jack," Tolkien explained, "then call in the troops and deploy them as we see fit."

"Isn't that normally Fox's role?" Lewis drank his tea and set it back down on the saucer with a clink. "Have you been promoted?"

Tolkien shook his head. "The wise dean is traveling to Paris and then on to Berlin for a conference and family reunion. He'll be in and out of town for the next few weeks. Rang me early this morning with the news. He was apologetic to be sure, but it couldn't be helped. So, I drew the short straw instead."

"Nonsense," Lewis countered, his eyes brightening. "It's an adventure, Tollers. A puzzle to solve and minds to sharpen. This is the best news I've had in weeks, and just in time for Christmas. It is the best gift I could have received."

"Sounds like you want in," Tolkien said, amused. "If you're up to it, you can join me. I'm to go and interview key witnesses tomorrow in London. They also happen to be the ones bankrolling the investigation."

"London!" Lewis exclaimed, looking suddenly more dour. "You know I hate going to London. Too many people and loud noises."

"A short walk, a short train ride, another short walk," Tolkien replied evenly. "It won't kill you to get away from Oxford for half a day. You have no Saturday lecture tomorrow; I've already checked. And I've already canceled mine."

"Hmm." Lewis gulped his tea and sighed. "If you can endure the Somme, I suppose I can endure Piccadilly."

Tolkien shook his head, then slapped down a manila folder on the coffee table in front of him. "I've brought the case file with me as homework for you to review before our meeting. I imagine you have time and nothing better to do. There is also a note tucked in from yours truly with some added information from our special guest last night. You'll want to read that," he emphasized, tapping his finger on the folder. "Our new patron and benefactor is a man brought back from the dead."

"You don't say?" Lewis eyed the folder. "My mind is a bit foggy at the moment. I'll get to it later after breakfast. I do hope it's not written in Elvish."

Tolkien smirked. "Didn't you already eat breakfast?"

"Yes, but not yet second breakfast."

"You and I both know that as soon as I leave, you will begin at once to devour the folder's contents. No puzzle can go left unsolved in your vicinity, Jack."

"Maybe so," Lewis conceded. He smiled faintly and took one final puff of his cigarette before snuffing it out. "I only hope I can be of use on this one. I'm not back to my full self."

Tolkien drank his tea down to the dregs, then stood up and buttoned his tweed jacket. "As I said, I do not doubt that by tomorrow you will be right as rain, and it will be a wonderful Saturday in the city. Who knows what adventure awaits us as soon as we step out the door?"

{5}
The City

Saturday, December 12

What wonderful adventures we shall
have now that we're all in it together.
—C. S. Lewis, *The Lion, the Witch, and the Wardrobe*

Lewis set out early Saturday morning just before sunrise. The walk to Magdalen College in the early-morning gray could be done easily in under an hour, depending on whether he was in a hurry or in a mood to take in the vivid sights and sounds of a casual stroll. He cut through foggy pasture-lands that soon gave way to a smattering of closely situated thatched-roof homes from which morning dew dripped onto the walking paths below. The trek to Oxford was slightly downhill and always more enjoyable than the return. Lewis crested a rolling ridge, and there below him lay the tangle of towers, spires, and stone cathedrals of the multitude of Oxford colleges he had fallen in love with so many years ago.

From there it was a short downhill across the River Cherwell to the stone walls of his Magdalen College. Lewis took the most direct route to his office. After twisting a skeleton key in the lock, Lewis went to his desk and collected a well-worn dog-eared book along with a few papers, which he shoved together into a cracked leather briefcase before pulling the straps tight and buckling them. Once outside, he glanced up at the clockface on the Great Tower and hastened his steps across the quad toward the train station where he was due to meet Professor Tolkien for the nine-twenty to London.

He walked down the High Street westward, passing the Queen's College, All Souls College, Radcliffe Square, and Brasenose College before switching over to the cobbles of Queen Street. From there, he kept straight ahead instead of his usual right turn toward the Bird and passed St. Peter's College and finally Nuffield College before crossing over Castle Mill Stream via the arching bridge and huffing the final stretch to Oxford station.

"I've got us two tickets." Tolkien said, looking down his nose at Lewis in a genuinely concerned way. "How are you, Jack? You look pale."

"I felt better . . . when I woke up," Lewis answered, catching his breath and dabbing at the sheen on his forehead with a cream-colored handkerchief. "The walk this morning seemed farther than usual and all uphill. I suppose I'll need a moment to rest or I may be sick."

"Plenty of time to rest on the train." Tolkien slapped his old friend on the back before adjusting his bow tie while squinting up at the platform numbers to get his bearings.

The train from Oxford to London was fifty miles, and it would take slightly over two hours before they arrived at Paddington station. The men sat opposite each other in green padded seats. Only a handful of other passengers occupied the car, all of whom sat half a car's length away. Lewis appreciated the privacy as he needed to speak to Tolkien about something.

"Don't be cross with me, Tollers," Lewis began over the rattling jostle of the train, "but I've invited a guest to join us today on our London adventure."

Tolkien frowned and folded *The Times* in his lap, tearing himself away from an article containing the latest information on the King's abdication. "I don't think I need to remind you, Jack, of how delicate and sensitive this case could be."

Lewis waved him off. "It will be fine. I read the case file you left yesterday, and Charles Williams is exactly the man we need for this sort of thing. As decent a chap as I've ever met. Besides, he doesn't need to know everything about you-know-who, just consult on a few select items related to his expertise."

"Charles Williams, you say?" Tolkien unfolded the paper and glanced back absently at the headline. "You're a fan of his, if I remember. A fine writer from what I've heard, although a bit obscure and niche. Editor at Oxford University Press for nearly the last thirty years?" Tolkien folded down the page and peered over. "That part of his résumé is far more impressive if you ask me."

"You're one to talk." Lewis chuckled lightly before coughing into his handkerchief. "Calling other writers 'obscure and niche.' You couldn't be more of a hypocrite." Lewis smiled, and the corners of his eyes crinkled upward. "Charles is a special talent and a bit peculiar, I'll admit, but to our benefit. He's an expert in theology, hermeticism, religious history, as well as the spiritism movement and all things eschatological and supernatural. I find the man fascinating. He also happens to already be in London on press business. It took a bit to track him down via his secretary and ring his hotel, but in the end, Charles was thrilled to be invited and will be meeting us at the station."

The train rocked as the tracks switched. Both men swayed back and forth to the rhythmic movements. Tolkien sighed and rolled up his paper, seeming to give up reading—at least until they reached a long, even stretch of track.

"Charles was a member of a mystical order himself for over a decade," Lewis continued. "A secret society that called themselves the Fellowship of the Rosy Cross."

"The Fellowship," Tolkien repeated absently. "I do like the sound of that. What exactly was it?"

"An offshoot of Rosicrucianism," Lewis explained. "Which I know you to be familiar with as a devout Catholic." Lewis saw a spark of recognition play over his friend's face. "They are Christian, or at least claim to be, though any Christian practice intermixed with mysticism and secrecy is suspect if you ask me. I suppose that drift toward Gnostic thought is what finally drove Charles away. From what I know of him, he's as devout and pious as they come, almost saintly some say, but not before being as skeptical as they come."

"Even more than Hugo?" Tolkien asked.

Lewis nodded. "Possibly. Charles once joked to me that Thomas the doubter was his patron saint."

Tolkien barked out a laugh. "Sounds a lot like yourself, the most doubtful and reluctant convert of them all."

"We have a lot in common," Lewis agreed, as the train passed into a tunnel. "Another reason to give the man a chance to prove his worth."

For the next hour, the two sat in silence, watching through the window as the countryside morphed into industrialization. Single stories became multi, and green pastures turned to a gray mishmash of roads, lots, and concrete graveyards.

For Lewis, the trip to London always contained a mixture of excitement and subtle, pained dread. With a howling release of pressurized steam, the train came to rest, and the passengers shuffled onto the platform.

Charles Williams sat on a bench outside the station with his nose in a book. He wore round wire-framed glasses and a gray overcoat that covered a smart-looking suit, if not a size too small for his already slight frame. Lewis, on the other hand, preferred his suits a size too large, with room in the chest and waist. Charles looked up as Lewis and Tolkien approached. His mouth naturally rested in a frown, but he forced an awkward smile and eagerly shook both men's hands with both of his.

"I was very pleased to hear from you, Professor Lewis," Charles stated after introductions were made. "Though I'm still not exactly sure how I can be of service to you gentlemen."

Lewis rested his hand on Charles's shoulder and faced him. "I will put it plainly. We are investigating a crime," he said solemnly, "though that is not public knowledge. Today, we are set to interview two people at White's—potential witnesses with information about said crime. I'd like you to join us for this interview. However, I need you to understand that there is an element of danger to what we are doing today, as a criminal is very much on the loose and may be aware of an investigation." Lewis paused and let the words sink in.

Charles nodded once. "I think I understand. But how could I refuse such a puzzle? It's all very medieval."

Tolkien, standing a few steps off, let out a hearty laugh. "Thick as thieves. You two are perfect for each other."

Lewis flicked his eyes over to Tolkien, gloating a bit at his choice, before continuing to Charles, "We'll get a late lunch afterward and talk it over. But for now, I'd like you to go into this interview with an open mind, without knowing much more than what I've already said. Ask questions you think are relevant. You'll soon know why I've requested your presence. This is an area you have some background in and an element of expertise far beyond our own."

White's gentlemen's club was located on St. James's Street, a short cab ride from the station past mobs of scurrying and overdressed Christmas shoppers. The marble façade loomed over the heads of the trio as they stepped out of the shared cab and approached the front entrance. The building was not nearly the tallest on the street. It wasn't even the biggest gentlemen's club on the street, though it was the oldest, most exclusive, and most well known to the average London gentleman.

"We're here to meet Lords Percival Beckworth and Robert MacDougall. We're a bit late." Tolkien spoke the words politely to the thin, mustached man behind the polished mahogany desk. The attendant took one look at Lewis, then at Williams, and finally back at Tolkien, who continued smiling widely.

"The gentlemen are waiting in the third-floor belvedere cardroom," he responded with a practiced air of pomp. "I'll have a boy walk you up."

The boy, named James, turned out to be an energetic young man, polite but eager to display his hospitality and knowledge. "The club was founded in 1693 as a factory for making chocolate," James narrated, glancing back over his shoulder. For some reason, he appeared to assess Tolkien as his greatest chance of earning a sizable tip and focused his speech on him. "It was called Mrs. White's Chocolate House originally. That's where the name comes from." He opened a mahogany door and ushered the three men up a set of wide stairs carpeted in a dark forest green. "In the 1700s, the building mainly served as a gambling house—a place where English nobility could misbehave discreetly." He smiled knowingly, then caught himself. "I'm not allowed to tell any particular stories, though I've heard a few about people whose names you'd know. We pride ourselves on discretion here at White's."

"I'm sure you do," Tolkien said.

They reached the landing and passed into the third-floor hallway, lined with ornately framed art depicting fox hunts and portraits of past European royalty who had been treasured members.

"Later, the building was a political headquarters for the Tory Party," James continued enthusiastically, "as opposed to the club down the street, that will not be named, which housed the Whigs." He paused for effect. "Today, we boast a fine dining room with all the modern luxuries—a billiard room, a library with an impressive collection of rare books available to members, several cardrooms, and smaller conference rooms for intimate groups and business meetings . . . which brings us to the belvedere room."

James stopped at a taller-than-normal varnished ebony door and straightened his tails. He knocked three times before someone opened it from the inside, and all four men were ushered in. Tolkien slipped a bill into James's sweaty palm, and the boy backed out of the room, bowing as he went.

The belvedere cardroom was dark, the windows thickly curtained, with the only light coming from two green-shaded banker's lamps hovering over matching desks. A square card table had been pushed to one side and replaced with a low and long oval table surrounded by four club chairs and a tufted leather chesterfield. One far wall was lined with shelves of leather-bound books while the opposite boasted what looked to be a fully stocked dry bar.

Two men stood, extending their hands as the newcomers approached. Lord Percival Beckworth was tall and slight of frame. His smile revealed thin, yellowish teeth that were crooked on the bottom, and he sported a dark patch of hair under his bottom lip but no hair elsewhere. His eyebrows were all but gone, and the top of his head was so bald it looked as though it had been wax-polished to a high shine like a billiard ball.

"It is so good to meet you." Beckworth shook their hands with long, slender fingers. "I have heard so much about these learned professors and also the Inklings as a whole. It seems as though you are a staple in the whispers of events I attend." He pivoted and raised an invisible brow to the man next to him.

Lord Robert MacDougall was undoubtedly Scottish. His plaid kilt displayed his clan designs proudly and gave his heritage away from across the room. MacDougall was much shorter than Beckworth, muscular and barrel-chested with a thick red mustache and a beard that ran down his neck under his too-tight collar. "And I am pleased as pie tae meet ye as well," he said in an expectedly thick accent. He bowed low and squeezed each man's hand in turn until he came to Williams.

"This is an Oxford colleague of ours, Mr. Charles Williams," Lewis supplied. "He will join us for our interview and can offer a unique perspective."

Beckworth narrowed his eyes but nodded. "Tell me," he asked with a burst of enthusiasm, "where does the name Inklings come from? I am so fascinated by what you men do at your little brainstorming gatherings. The whole thing is so incredibly intriguing, especially for one who enjoys a good clandestine society."

Tolkien took the lead. "The name is a bit of whimsy, actually, a pun on those who dabble in ink—writers—and also those of us who may have only an inkling of what we intend to write about when we begin a project, which is usually the case."

"Fascinating," Beckworth murmured. "I love how these things come about. Diving in before you have everything worked out."

"Yes, much like what we are doing here today," Tolkien went on. "An earlier version of the group was called the Kólbitar, an Icelandic word that means 'coal biters,' because the members sat so closely around the fire discussing Old Norse literature that they were likely to bite a piece of coal."

MacDougall let out a belly laugh at that, though no one else seemed amused. Beckworth flashed a look of annoyance at his Scottish friend, who quickly lowered his eyes as his face grew even redder.

Lewis's gaze drifted toward the back of the expansive cardroom. A previously unseen figure sat in a wing chair in the shadows. The task lamp over his head had been switched off. He simply watched and listened in silence, not moving and, from the looks of it, barely breathing.

The five other men sat facing one another after drinks and cigars were passed around. They exchanged more pleasantries until a pregnant silence hung in the air and signaled that the time had come to shift to more serious matters.

"I appreciate your discretion in this investigation," Beckworth began. "Lord Pennington was a dear friend of ours."

"Aye, he was," MacDougall added, a faraway look on his face. "A better friend and brother a man cannae have."

"We'd known him since we were at university together," Beckworth continued. "Seems a lifetime ago now. He was a good man, despite his vices. He will be missed and, I believe, avenged as well. His spirit has called out to me strongly these weeks since his passing."

"Tell me . . ." Tolkien pulled a small pad of paper from his inner jacket pocket. "Before we go over details surrounding the night of Lord Pennington's death, the file I received makes mention of an order and that somehow it may be centrally involved in this series of events."

"Oh yes." Beckworth took a small sip of scotch from a heavy glass and swished its remaining contents in a clockwise motion. "The Order of the Golden Dawn. *Ordo Hermeticus Aurorae Aureae* in Latin. We were and still are an order devoted to the study of hermeticism and metaphysics. Harmless enough—more of a social club in reality." He glanced up and smiled faintly. "Those in our order pursue the study of thaumaturgy, ceremonial magic, divination, astrology, and geomancy as we fancy it. Are you familiar?" He tilted his head and inspected Tolkien.

Charles Williams leaned forward but said nothing. Lewis noted how his left leg began to bounce.

Tolkien flicked his eyes at Lewis and shrugged. "Somewhat, though I'd imagine we have a lot to learn. Perhaps you could enlighten us."

"Ah yes, 'enlighten.' An apt choice of words." Beckworth nodded. "It's become a bit of an addiction for me, I must admit, the pursuit of it all. The chase of what has eluded humankind for millennia."

"Tae me as well," MacDougall added, shifting his weight in his chair and downing a large swallow of a smoky, peat-smelling whiskey.

"So, you're spiritual men?" Lewis asked, looking slowly from Beckworth to MacDougall. "In pursuit of a higher truth?"

"I suppose you could say that," Beckworth answered. "I would think we all are to some extent. No matter your religion or lack thereof."

"Very true," Lewis conceded. "Though not all roads lead to the same place; some are wide and some narrow." He watched the dark figure still sitting in shadow at the back of the room. An orange glow appeared as the man sucked a cigarette, then faded again.

Tolkien extracted a pen from his breast pocket and prepared to write. "Can you tell me what you saw, both of you, that night . . . last Sunday?"

"Our records were in the file." MacDougall pointed toward the table. "Were they nae clear?"

"Yes, I've read your statements," Tolkien assured him, "but it's good investigative practice to hear directly from the sources. Perhaps to jostle up new details and fresh memories."

"Very good. I like a job done thoroughly as well." Beckworth sat up straight. "We were supposed to meet here at the club, just after dark, for a drink. We are known to do that quite often."

"Who is 'we'?" Tolkien questioned.

"Men from the Order," Beckworth replied. "A handful, though I'd rather not say exactly who." He glanced to his left at the man sitting in shadow, then quickly flashed a toothy smile. "I hope you understand."

"About how many members of the Golden Dawn are there?" Lewis interjected.

"Not certain I should say that either," Beckworth responded. "At least not an exact number . . . discretion and all."

"Hundreds?" Lewis prompted. "Thousands?"

Beckworth looked again toward the shadow, and the silhouetted head moved down almost imperceptibly. "Here in London, dozens," he said briskly. "We are an exclusive club. Growing but very selective. Only the finest pedigrees are allowed in our ranks."

"What were your plans that night?" Tolkien asked. "The night of Lord Pennington's death."

"We had other places to go after White's," Beckworth recounted. "Mostly drinks, cards, conversation, at local establishments of the finest taste."

"Only Pennington ne'er showed," MacDougall put in, raising both of his thick reddish brows.

"Yes, we waited here for him," Beckworth affirmed. "In this very room even. We drank and talked for hours, stalling for time until it was decided, in a bit of a stupor, that we should go to his home and see what had happened. Perhaps the liquor decided for us. It's not far from here. Only a handful of blocks at most."

When neither Lewis nor Tolkien interrupted, Beckworth continued, "So, we all went over, singing bawdy songs and making fools of ourselves on the way. There were witnesses, even a beat officer from the Yard. It was a well-lit night, so we were seen clearly. MacDougall here pounded on the door, though by that time it was after midnight. We'd lost track of the time. A housekeeper at the residence answered our knocking with wide eyes in her nightdress. She reasoned that Pennington hadn't been feeling well of late and had most likely stood up his friends and gone to bed. But at our insistence that we would not be turned away into the night without speaking with him, she went to fetch him for us . . . and that's when we heard the scream."

"Are you certain of the time?" Lewis quizzed.

"Not completely," Beckworth admitted. "But later, as we stood in the foyer, we all saw the grandfather clock chime at one in the morning, and I'm fairly certain we'd been there at least half an hour at that point."

MacDougall nodded in affirmation and took another large swallow.

"Tell us about seeing the body," Tolkien said. "Who went up?"

"Once we heard the sounds of hysteria," Beckworth answered, "MacDougall and I went up right away after Ms. Cornish. That is the maid's name, if you want to write it down—a Ms. Sarah Cornish." He paused while Tolkien noted the name. "The fact MacDougall and I went up the stairs is precisely why you are now speaking with us and not other members of the Order who were also present that night. Our names could not be avoided in the inspector's report, and so here we are." He flashed a placating smile before continuing, "He'd not been dead long, as far as I could tell. I'm no doctor, though I've always had a fascination with death." He grinned sheepishly. "When we found Roger lying on the floor of his bedroom, he was still warm, yet his face was strangely colored. He looked horrible. Blotchy and red, his eyes wide with horror and shock. And it looked as if he had pulled patches of hair from his own scalp. Terrible really. Ghastly. I dreamed about it for the next three nights. Woke up in a cold sweat each time. Something in those eyes of his was not right." Beckworth paused as he recalled the scene. He shuddered and sipped from his glass.

"What then?" Tolkien urged, squinting down at his notes.

"We contacted Scotland Yard, obviously," Beckworth said. "The room was cordoned off. Photographs taken. We were all questioned initially, though only MacDougall and I were detained until well after the sun had come up, without biscuits or a break for Earl Grey, I might add." He frowned. "Scotland Yard declared Pennington had died of acute self-inflicted strangulation. At least that was what came out a few days later."

"The police did not think Pennington was murdered?" Tolkien pressed. "They claimed he killed himself? How again exactly?"

Beckworth sighed. "He strangled himself with a leather belt. Which was wrapped around his neck and pulled tight. A simple case of suicide by asphyxiation. Horrible, I know. I don't like speaking of it, though I know I must." Beckworth took a drink but held up his pointer finger to indicate he had more to say on the subject. "His staff, upon questioning, agreed that Pennington had been depressed of late, not feeling or looking quite himself. A man prone to drinking and indulgence who had hit some sort of emotional wall and decided to end it all. But obviously, we don't buy that story. And that is why the Order used our contacts to connect with Sir Arthur, which led to you gentlemen being sent here today."

At the mention of Doyle, Charles Williams flicked his eyes over to Lewis, surprise flashing over his otherwise stoic face. Lewis didn't react. He only lit a cigarette and shifted his gaze once again toward the man in the corner. There was something off about their hidden observer, like darkness hiding within a shadow.

Tolkien furrowed his brow, glancing down at his jumble of shorthand notes, then back up at Beckworth. "I'm a bit confused. What makes you think Pennington was murdered and didn't take his own life as the police say? Why do you not buy the assertion that he wrapped a belt around his own neck and died of asphyxiation?"

Beckworth exhaled slowly and looked over at MacDougall. "Because . . . I was the one who put the belt around his neck and pulled it tight."

Tolkien gasped. "You murdered him? You admit it freely?"

"No, no!" Beckworth exclaimed, waving his hands in front of his narrow face. "I could never. He was a dear brother. The man was already dead, and I had nothing to do with it. It was a moment's reaction to a looming problem—and it turned out to be the right decision, I might add. I'd do it all over again if it came to it."

"You must explain yourself." Tolkien's pen hovered over his pad of paper. "I must be missing something. Why in God's name would you do that?"

"Because murder investigations invite more attention and curiosity than a simple suicide." Beckworth spoke the words firmly, then paused. He held up his hands in mock surrender. "I knew this was coming. There are a few things you need to understand. First of all, Pennington was not the type of man to kill himself. If you knew Roger, you would know the man loved life. He loved living. In fact, he would have done just about anything he could have to go on living forever, if it were possible. He was also a very careful man, so his death was not some horrible accident either. No, it was obvious to me, and MacDougall as well upon entering the room, that Pennington had been the victim of foul play."

Beckworth sipped his drink before adding, almost reluctantly, "I also noticed something strange when I entered the room and saw him lying there that caused my own heart to almost burst forth from my chest. It was what he was wearing when we found him, a certain robe of our order, the

Golden Dawn. I don't want to spend too much time on this, but trust me when I say it was a ceremonial robe he should not have been wearing at that time and place."

Lewis could see Beckworth was growing agitated at this particular point of the story. Beckworth fumbled for and flipped open a silver case of cigarettes and pulled one out. He lit it with a slight, almost imperceptible tremble in his hand.

"What did the Yard's inspector say about the robe?" Tolkien continued the line of questioning.

"That's just it—the inspectors never saw the robe," Beckworth responded with a faint smile. "We took it off him before they arrived. We'd sent the housekeeper away to go fetch a blanket to cover the body. When she was out of sight, upon my request, MacDougall pulled a plain dressing gown from Pennington's closet that looked similar, at least in color, to the robe he was wearing, and we put it on him. That was also when I retrieved a leather belt from his dresser drawer and slipped it around his neck. We convinced the maid it had been there the whole time when she returned. She believed us. Two confident witnesses repeating a lie in a distressed person's ear over and over will lead them to believe just about anything."

"You again admit to interfering with an investigation." Tolkien's words were firm, his mouth in a line.

Lewis could tell the professor was growing angry, but he kept silent and observed the interaction with great interest. The man in the corner also watched.

"The police would start asking too many questions," Beckworth rejoined. "We couldn't have officials and the press poking their noses into things they can't understand. It was for the good of all, you must know. To raise doubts about an accidental death or suicide would mean revealing sensitive information best kept secret. The Order of the Golden Dawn would have been embroiled in scandal, placed under a microscope, and cast into the public eye. These are all things we hope to avoid. You see, the robe Roger wore is used in certain ceremonies that may . . ." Beckworth hesitated. "That may not seem acceptable to those not part of the Order. Even though everything is aboveboard. Are you familiar at all with ceremonial magic?"

"We've heard of it." Tolkien glanced over at Charles Williams, who remained silent but leaned even closer. Williams's leg still shook, and he rested his palm on his knee to still the movement.

Beckworth was breathing harder as he finished his glass. "We believe Lord Pennington was killed in the middle of some sort of ceremonial ritual. It is absolutely ludicrous he would be involved in something like that without us, at the wrong place and time, and—"

"I may be able to shed more light on this situation," a voice called from the far side of the room, cutting Beckworth off mid-sentence. The figure sitting in shadow stood up and walked into the light. He was imposing in his double-breasted blazer, his eyes wide and piercing, his head large and bald like a giant egg. Something about him set Lewis's teeth on edge—the cold feeling continued to grow as he approached.

"I didn't want to interrupt but felt I must." The man spoke slowly and deliberately with a lightly held half smile. "I'm very pleased to formally meet you all. My name is Aleister Crowley."

{6} The Magician

We must conquer life by living it to the full, and then we can go to meet death with a certain prestige.

—ALEISTER CROWLEY, *The Diary of a Drug Fiend*

"Do you know who I am?" Crowley asked. He tilted his head to one side and continued holding a faint smile that reminded Lewis of a hyena standing over a fresh kill.

Williams spoke for the first time since arriving. "I do, Mr. Crowley. I have studied your body of work to an extent, along with that of many other occultists—Helena Blavatsky, Alice White, Yeats, and Randolph. In my study, I have concluded you are depraved, warped, vile, and insane. You have made a career out of shameless corruption in pursuit of wanton evil."

Crowley grinned, revealing his large white teeth. "I like an honest man. And such a colorful vocabulary. However, I prefer to think of my life's work as a pursuit of my own truth."

"There is no such thing as your own truth," Lewis interjected. "There is only *the* truth. All else is counterfeit and hollow."

"We've all had our own spiritual awakenings, Professor Lewis." Crowley's gaze flicked around the circle and came to rest on him. "I was 'born again' in a way very different to your own experience." He glared down at MacDougall, who quickly stood and moved from his chair to the couch. Crowley unbuttoned his gray pin-striped blazer and slumped lazily into the center chair facing Tolkien. The whites of his eyes looked like frothy pools with dark centers that bore into one's heart. Lewis felt the sensation of bugs crawling under his skin.

"Gentlemen," Tolkien broke in. "While I would love the opportunity to proselytize the leader of the mystical scene in Britain, we do need to remember why we are here today. To discuss a murder and try our best to solve it."

"Murders, plural," Crowley corrected, without averting his gaze from Tolkien. All eyes rested on Crowley. He stopped speaking for a moment, basking in the undivided attention. "Another of our order was killed," Crowley began, almost lightheartedly. "A man named Baron Huxley. Drowned in a bathtub. Slipped and fell on All Hallows' Eve during a full moon, hit his head on the edge of his copper bath, and lights out—that's all she wrote. Or at least this version of the story is what his doting wife and adult children were led to believe."

Crowley smiled faintly. "The truth is that Huxley was murdered as well. I found him myself. Perhaps I was supposed to be the one to find him. It was like a waking dream, walking in and seeing him like that—naked and pale in water tinged red with blood. Like a reverse baptism. Huxley was no doubt murdered, and before you ask, no, I did not kill him, or

Pennington for that matter. I was home alone in my flat all that night."

Tolkien shifted uneasily in his seat. He apparently felt the eeriness too.

Crowley smiled again, the expression never reaching his cold eyes. "Why on earth would I kill two of my most ardent supporters and financial backers? Those men were true believers. Men who have made my life, which you call one of indulgence and depravity, possible."

Tolkien flipped his writing pad to a new page, but Lewis beat him to the next question. "How do you know for certain this man Huxley was murdered?"

"He had a cut on his hand. The left palm." Crowley held up his own very large hand, with the faintest hint of his own scars. "Scotland Yard thought it simply an accident in the kitchen. Insignificant and without meaning or connection to his death. But I saw the wound up close. I knew what was carved into his flesh." He paused and surveyed the men slowly from left to right, seeming to relish the fact that all eyes remained on him.

The man was like a performing magician in the spotlight. Lewis hated to give him the satisfaction, yet he did need to know what this man knew, no matter how he made Lewis's spine tingle.

"What was it?" Charles Williams asked, his eyes squinting. He, too, had been drawn in by his own curiosity. "A pentagram? The Star of Remphan? A swastika?"

Crowley shook his head. "Astute guesses, my friend, but no. Simply the number 418. It means a lot more to me than anyone else."

Lewis put out his cigarette. "Are you going to tell us what it means, or do we have to read your mind?"

Crowley's tone was placating. "I'm getting to it, Professor. Building up the tension to a frenzied crescendo. Did you know I am a writer too? Published a book this year in fact. It's called *The Equinox of the Gods*. Perhaps I can join you Inklings and read it aloud, though it's surely not as exciting as Mars or Middle-earth." He flicked his black, beady eyes back to Tolkien.

Williams cleared his throat. "I've heard you're a bit of a hack when it comes to writing."

Crowley glared at him, then let his expression melt into a practiced smile. "We all have our audiences. Mine are just more fun than yours."

"The number," Tolkien said impatiently. His fingers tapped on the arm of his chair. "Let's focus so we can get on with it."

"The number 418 is significant in gematria," Crowley responded quickly. "Do you know what gematria is?"

Williams recited, "Gematria is the practice of assigning a numerical value to a name, word, or phrase by reading each word and the letters in the word as a number. It is essentially a hidden mathematical language found within most ancient languages: Greek, Hebrew, Aramaic, and even Latin to an extent."

Crowley raised a faint brow. "That is precisely correct, though my real love is the study of the ancient Egyptian languages. My, you are a bright one. I know now why you were brought along." He turned to Tolkien. "Though not as impressive as the professor here. I hear you've created your own languages. You might not know it, Professor, but fae languages and myth culture are a great love of mine. Very magical creatures indeed. We have a lot more in common than one would think. I, too, was raised by Christian parents. I suppose gematria might be right up your proverbial alley."

Tolkien frowned. "I've never been good at math."

Crowley blinked, then continued, "I won't bore you with the details of my pursuit of higher knowledge, though they are intriguing." He let out a small laugh as if remembering some past conquest. "Within this study of gematria, certain words hold unique power. I realize this may sound strange to the uninitiated ear, but I took a special interest in the word *Abrahadabra,* with an *h.* When all values are added up, the number 418 is assigned to this word and has since become a cipher of the Great Work. My forthcoming book explains more about this; I'll send you a copy."

"Very interesting," Lewis said evenly. "Though how does the number relate to this case?"

Before Crowley could answer, there was a knock on the door. The young man James entered with a tray of tea sandwiches. Beckworth used the moment to stand and help himself to another drink while MacDougall sat stoically, his eyes glued to Crowley, hanging on every word his master spoke. Charles also stared at Crowley, but with a wary look, like a wounded bird eyeing an approaching snake. Lewis shot a sidelong glance toward Tolkien, but his friend held his best poker face, not revealing what Lewis knew to be a strong desire to tell Crowley how much of a fool he was.

Once they had privacy again, Crowley unfolded his hands and held up his palm once more. "There are five unique letters in the word. Each letter represents not only a number but also a vital part of a magical ceremony where great supernatural power is released into our physical realm. The letter *A* is the crown; *B* is the wand; *D,* the cup; *H* is the sword; and *R,* the rosy cross. In essence, the number 418 is delightfully and intrinsically linked to the release of significant magic, which, as you are aware, is a great pursuit of mine." He looked around at his audience, likely expecting confusion, but was met with a level of understanding from the three guests.

"It's only a smoke screen, though, isn't it?" Lewis demanded. "Just a way to pursue your fleshly appetites and assign some moral spiritual significance to it."

Crowley smirked. "Of course it is," he said, but Lewis didn't believe him. This man was playing a game on both sides. He was either a true believer in things better left alone or a fake wizard like that of the Emerald City.

Lewis then asked, "Do you believe the murderer was another member of the Order of the Golden Dawn?"

Crowley's eyes snapped toward Lewis. "What an incredibly perceptive question." He sounded amused. "It would make sense, yes. Who else would know the ins and outs of my teaching besides a disciple? Who else understands the number 418? Who else knows our ways, our ceremonies, and other hidden, higher knowledge?"

"Was Huxley killed as part of some ceremony?" Lewis wondered.

"You're asking all the right questions, Professor," Crowley commended. "It could be that both Huxley and Pennington were killed in some form of magical ceremony. Whether by their own design and volition or someone else's, I do not know. But I am certain someone with knowledge of our clandestine inner workings is surely responsible and still at large and as dangerous as ever."

"Do you have a suspect in mind?" Tolkien questioned, scrawling shorthand as he spoke.

"Yes, I do." Crowley nodded as if this was where he had wanted the conversation to land. "Though only one member of the Order is living in the area, I cannot openly reveal or give introductions to any beyond these two here today. That would be a breach of trust. I hope you understand. However, I can point you in the direction of a former member who is no longer under my protection and guidance. He became disgruntled many years ago at the direction our order was taking. Threats were made—threats this man is more than capable of acting on. His name is Mortimer Doolittle. Your fellow Inkling, Lord Cecil, will know of him quite well, along with how to make contact."

Crowley stood and buttoned his jacket. He was apparently at the end of what he wanted to share. "Do you see the pattern yet?" he asked, eyeing Lewis and Tolkien in turn.

"The full moon," Lewis noted.

"Yes." Crowley's brows rose in surprise. "Tell me more."

"Huxley was killed during a full moon. All Hallows' Eve. So was Pennington twenty-nine days later. That is why Doyle mentioned the upcoming full moon. He'd put it together as well."

Crowley nodded slowly. "All of life is a pattern, so it makes sense that all of death is also a pattern. Gentlemen, let me put this plainly," he stated firmly. "Someone is targeting us. Members of my order. And if they are not stopped, I believe another will die on the next full moon, which is only a little more than two weeks from today, on Monday, December 28. This means you and your merry band of mischief-makers have two weeks to solve two murders and to prevent a third from happening. I, for one, am skeptical, but I hope you prove me wrong. I think enough time has been spent here. Finish your drinks and then it's best you get to work."

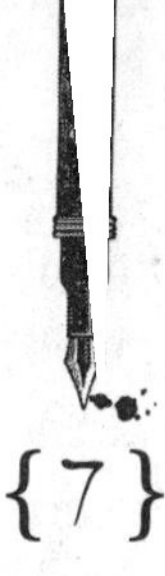

{7} The Sabbath

> Hypocrisy is folly. It is much easier, safer, and pleasanter to be the thing which a man aims to appear, than to keep up the appearance of being what he is not.
>
> —Lord David Cecil

The three men crossed the street, walking westward from White's in an air of heavy silence. Eating a late lunch was the furthest thing from their minds as each pondered and replayed different parts of what had been revealed to them. They walked toward the cabstand two blocks over that would take the trio to the train station. Tolkien pulled up at the next crossing to fill his pipe while overdressed Londoners shuffled past in the brisk air. He puffed the ember to glowing.

"I feel as though I need a bath," Lewis muttered. "To get the dirt off."

Tolkien nodded. "I feel it too, Jack. It's a dirty business, murder."

"I believe he was referring to Crowley," Charles Williams interjected. "A darker stain, if you ask me."

Tolkien nodded again. "I agree. The man is a certain type of disagreeable. Gives me the creeps to my core."

"Of course he does," Williams said sharply. "He is a pagan occultist and worshipper of Lucifer. He is the opposite of everything good and decent in this world."

"Even still . . ." Lewis paused to light his own cigarette and pressed his eyes closed. Now was as good a time as any to debrief. "He is loved by God the same as any of us. But I strongly believe in my spirit that somewhere in Crowley's depraved mind is the key to this entire mystery. We will need to talk to him again before this whole story has played out."

"I'd rather not if it can be helped," Tolkien remarked.

Lewis turned toward Charles. "I think you might have some further insight into all of this that you're holding back. Would you care to share it while we walk?"

Charles looked around impatiently. He adjusted his glasses. "I do, but it will have to wait."

"What do you mean it will have to wait?" Tolkien demanded, mildly flustered.

"I need to go to my office at the press. It's not far from here, but in the opposite direction. I have some research material there I want to look at."

Lewis tilted his head. "And when will we hear your analysis?"

"Soon, soon," Williams replied, bobbing his head. "I'll catch the early train to Oxford tomorrow and visit the Bodleian." He gazed at Lewis through thick lenses that magnified his eyes. "The college library should have any other resources I need. Drop by tomorrow evening after evensong if you are free. By then I should have more clarity for you."

He pivoted to Tolkien. "You are obviously welcome as well, Professor."

With that, Charles Williams waved and darted across the street back in the opposite direction.

"Strange man." Tolkien frowned and clicked his teeth. "As if his mind were somewhere else."

Lewis snorted and stared at the London skyline. "You're one to talk, Tollers—usually walking around Middle-earth somewhere with a hairy-footed hobbit or elf. Speaking of walking, I think I may stick around in the city for an hour or two to clear my mind." He turned to look at his friend. "You don't mind returning alone?"

Tolkien shrugged and palmed the walnut bowl of his pipe. "Fine by me. You know I prefer a quiet train." He raised a brow. "Sorry I can't dillydally. I need to get back. Edith is making a roast tonight, and I promised Christopher and Michael I'd take them to the Covered Market before dark." He lifted his arm to hail a cab that slowed and pulled up to the sidewalk. "Though I am interested to hear what Charles has to say, I'll leave that lead to you, Jack. I think I'll look into Lord Pennington and his housekeeper. I'll come back here to London on Monday and see if I can't track down this Ms. Cornish and ask her a few questions."

"Very good." Lewis snuffed out his cigarette on the sole of his shoe as Tolkien slid into the cab. "I'll talk to Cecil about this Doolittle chap and recruit Dyson to do some digging on the first victim, Baron Huxley. He'll want something important to do. We'll all compare notes Tuesday morning at the Bird."

After Tolkien and the cab were out of sight, Lewis sighed and walked a few blocks in silence. He then looked for a nearby open park bench near Whitechapel. He had started to feel nauseous for a variety of reasons, one of them being the location's reminder of Jack the Ripper, and felt he needed a minute to catch his breath and right himself. The thought of a cab ride followed by a train ride set his stomach to roil and his head to throb. Lewis sat in a deflated heap and spent the next half hour watching a slice of London pass by through a swirling haze of cigarette smoke.

Later that evening, Lewis took a ragged deep breath, coughed, and looked up at the impressive front entrance of Lord David Cecil's home. He reluctantly climbed the wide steps to the glossy black door, grabbed the brass knocker, and rapped three times. The oversized door swung inward to reveal the family butler in a crisp, newly pressed, and starched uniform. The butler was a slight man with wispy white hair, a sharp nose, and a continual frown—a man who, Lewis remembered just in time, was called Morley.

"Hello, Morley. I'm here to see Cecil. I'd expect he is in."

"He is home," Morley confirmed slowly, his face dour as usual. "However, my lord's nurse is with him now. He is taking his medicine. You can wait in the library, Professor Lewis, and I will come and fetch you when Lord Cecil is ready to see you."

Lewis followed the small man into an impressive library off the foyer and took a seat on a tufted bench, which was backed with ornate wooden scrollwork covered in gold leaf. Lewis closed his tired eyes as he smelled leather, paper, and binding glue. He'd always loved the aroma of an old library, and Cecil's family had curated a fine collection over the years.

"Can I get you anything, Professor Lewis?" Morley inquired.

"Very kind of you, Morley, but I'll take my tea with Cecil when the time comes."

"Very good, sir." Morley departed, his feet making no sound on the veined-marble floor.

Lewis gazed around at the portraits on the walls, including a life-sized, framed depiction of Cecil's father, the fourth Marquess of Salisbury, above the large fireplace.

"He will see you now," Morley announced.

Lewis was startled, as he had not heard the soft-footed butler reenter the room. He quickly stood and followed Morley back through the central foyer space, down a checkered-floor hallway to a first-floor room that had been converted into a bedroom. Cecil had been unhealthy since he was a young man and was told the constant use of stairs would strain his already fragile constitution.

Cecil lay in bed, as he did every Saturday, propped up by pillows in what had once been the family's formal dining room. The space was warm as the fire blazed in the hearth on this mild day. Cecil smiled when he saw Lewis, then set his glass of juice on a nearby tray and pulled himself upright with the help of two overstuffed pillows. He was wearing pinstriped pajamas and looked to have just finished a meal.

"Come to visit me on my deathbed?" Cecil asked.

Lewis shook his head. "You'll outlive us all." He didn't really believe his own words, however. Cecil appeared thin, with dark circles under his eyes and the pallor of one who was not long for this world. Though, in his defense, Cecil had been sickly for as long as Lewis, or any of the Inklings, had known him. Still, Cecil did not let his poor health slow him down the other six days of the week, even teaching at Wadham College for many years, though not currently and not for any financial need but simply because of his deep love of history.

"What brings you to this cemetery of a home?" Cecil

wondered. His eyes had brightened and revealed his respect and adoration for Lewis. "Do you have news? I do hope so. Winter days here grow tedious at times, especially today."

Lewis approached the bed. "As it happens, I was on my way back from London and I thought I'd stop by. I knew you'd be home."

"Of course I'm home. I take my Sabbath quite literally. And there is no need to lecture me on the new covenant. What happened in London?"

Lewis spotted a copy of a Jane Austen novel on Cecil's nightstand and smiled. "We interviewed Lords Beckworth and MacDougall at White's. Thank you for arranging the meeting. I'd never been there before. There was something interesting—" Lewis cut off when a young woman entered the room, carrying a tray. She wore a stark white uniform, which nearly matched the paleness of her skin.

"Did ya take yar medicine?" the nurse asked. To that, Cecil grabbed two small pills and washed them down with an audible gulp of juice. She frowned and eyed Lewis. "Make sure to keep his pulse low—no unnecessary excitement."

Lewis held up his hands in mock surrender. "I would do no such thing. You have my word." The nurse smiled faintly.

"Professor Lewis, this is my capable nurse Beth, short for Elizabeth." Cecil gestured toward Lewis. "And my dear Beth, this is Professor C. S. Lewis, a close friend and colleague."

"Cecil told me 'bout ya." Beth's thick accent indicated she was from the Birmingham area. "In fact, I don't think a shift has gone by he hasn't said something 'bout ya or these other Inklings."

Lewis bowed slightly. "It's a pleasure to meet you."

Nurse Beth inclined her head before gathering some used towels and making a hasty exit.

Cecil watched her leave. "She's not exceptionally bright," he confided in a lowered voice, "but I like this one better than the last. Doesn't say much, but a good listener, and quite pretty."

"Cecil, behave yourself," Lewis admonished.

"Yes, yes. Of course you're right, Jack," Cecil replied. "Tell me about the interview."

Lewis looked toward the door. "Give it a moment. We'll wait for tea." He grabbed the arm of a nearby chair and pulled it toward the bed before slumping down onto the worn buttery leather, thankful to be off his aching feet.

Cecil tapped his finger on the empty glass. "Fine. Small talk then. I know how to do that. Are you glad Michaelmas term is finally over? I remember how those eight weeks could seem an eternity. At least to me it did when I was teaching."

Lewis nodded. "Only minor obligations remain for the ninth week. A few sputtering students in need of extra credit, which they will not receive. I'm glad to have a new focus now that should steal my mind through the end of the year."

Cecil flicked his eyes toward the door and regained his pout. "You're building up tension on purpose, Jack, making me wait to hear." He rolled his eyes. "This is torture, and you are a cruel man. Did you hear the latest on the abdication this morning?"

Lewis smiled faintly and shook his head. "It's happening, I know that much. The chair won't stay empty long enough to get cold. Beyond that, I'll admit my ignorance of anything sounding like drama or gossip."

Cecil frowned. "You'd be a great gossip if you put your mind to it, Jack. People always tell you their deepest and darkest. When are Owen and his father getting back from the States? Barfield and Barfield has been shuttered for weeks.

Lord knows the other solicitors cannot pull the weight without the principals for long."

"They will be back next week, in time for Christmas," Lewis answered. "I received a letter from Owen just a few days ago. Roosevelt won reelection in a landslide." Lewis shrugged. "Maybe one day I'll go across the pond and visit."

"No, you won't." Cecil laughed. "Warren, yes, but you'll stay here in Oxford your whole life. We all know it. You'll die in your chair in front of the fire."

Lewis sighed and crossed his right leg over his left. His gaze drifted far away. "There are many things Owen and I said we would do in life as younger men, but it's turned out much different, hasn't it?"

"It has," Cecil agreed, his tone soft. "How is Janie?"

"As feisty as ever. And your Janie?" Lewis inclined his head toward the well-worn copy of *Pride and Prejudice* on the nightstand.

"As feisty as ever," Cecil returned with a sly smile.

The tinkering of tea on its way stopped their conversation. The men sat in silence until Morley left and the room was theirs again.

"We interviewed Lords Beckworth and MacDougall today," Lewis began again.

Cecil's eyes brightened as he straightened up in bed. "Thank God. What did you think? Tell me your impressions."

"They were interesting characters." Lewis studied Cecil. "Aleister Crowley was also there. He told us about a second murder that happened only a month prior, on All Hallows' Eve."

Cecil narrowed his faint brow and set down his tea. "I wondered if Crowley would show up. He's been suckling at the underbelly of London for too long, if you ask me. Only met the man once and that was enough, though he does have a certain unexplainable charisma."

Lewis continued, "Crowley believes a former disgruntled member of the Order of the Golden Dawn may be targeting current members. He suspects a man named Mortimer Doolittle."

Cecil grimaced. "I know of him. A horrid man. Hungry for power and as greedy as they come. I, for one, wouldn't put murder past him. Every other vice and deadly sin are part of his repertoire. Why not murder?"

"You sound like Crowley," Lewis remarked.

Cecil shook his head. "I don't like the sound of that. Though Doolittle would be more likely to hire a contract killer than do it himself. Certainly has the money and connections, and if premeditated, he'd have found a way to distance himself."

"Either way," Lewis told him, "I plan to make contact. Would you happen to know where I might find him?"

"Be careful, Jack," Cecil cautioned, a look of concern growing over his face. "I am serious when I say I don't know what Doolittle is capable of. I've heard rumors of his past business dealings. Troubling to say the least."

Lewis nodded. "I don't plan to accuse him to his face."

"You should bring your brother," Cecil suggested quickly, before biting into a biscuit.

Lewis squinted. "For . . . protection?"

"That too," Cecil said as if just remembering that point, "but also because Doolittle is an avid fan of French history—Warnie's area of expertise. He's on a few museum boards, the Ashmolean being one. That could be a way to question the man while keeping his guard down."

Lewis took note. "I don't think a direct interrogation is the right approach for now. I was looking to track him down so that one of us Inklings could follow him for a few days or even the entire week. See what he's up to, where he goes, who he talks to . . . anything suspicious. Just observe and report."

"Well, I could do that," Cecil volunteered. "At least until next Saturday. I'd love to, in fact. You know how I love watching and studying people. Add in a murder mystery and I'm as hooked as a cod." Cecil brightened further. "If he catches me, I'll just say I may be planning to write a biography of his fascinating life. He's a vain man. He'll buy it." Cecil fell into a coughing fit, which soon brought his nurse back with a glass of water mixed with honey and lemon.

"I think it's perhaps time for a nap." Beth the nurse glared at Lewis as if the coughing had been his fault.

"That's my exit cue." Lewis stood to his feet but suddenly sat back down, lightheaded.

"Are you well?" Cecil's face showed concern again. "You look like my mirror."

"Can I get ya anything, Professor Lewis?" Beth asked. "Ya look as though ya could use a bit of rest of yar own."

Lewis stood again and pressed his eyes closed. "A touch dizzy is all. I may have put too much strain on myself today. Could be needing my own Sabbath tomorrow."

"One thing before you depart . . ." Cecil sat up even straighter. "Will you pray for me, brother?"

Lewis smiled. He put his hand on Cecil's shoulder, bowed his head, and prayed, as he always did, for the health of his dear friend. Despite the fogginess of his mind, the words flowed easily as Lewis threw in a little prayer for himself, as well as for Elizabeth the nurse, that she would have patience in dealing with Cecil and that God's guiding hand would rest on her.

{8}
The Library

Sunday, December 13

> You are speaking . . . as if the pleasure were one thing and the memory another. It is all one thing. . . . What you call remembering is the last part of the pleasure.
>
> —C. S. Lewis, *Out of the Silent Planet*

The low winter sun had been set for hours by the time Lewis went through St. Mary's Passage into Radcliffe Square. The circular stone structure of Radcliffe Camera lay in front of him with the south-facing gray stone façade of the Bodleian just beyond. Lewis had stopped by the Queen's Lane Coffee House for tea and a biscuit and ended up staying in a private corner nook reading a well-worn George MacDonald novel for nearly two hours before realizing it was dark outside and time to go to evensong and afterward to track down Charles Williams at the Bodleian Library.

Thanks to an encouraging Christmas-themed sermon earlier in the day, Lewis was able to push the thoughts of murder and macabre images away for most of the day. He preferred to stay clear minded and not mentally weighed down before his conversation with Charles, which, if he knew the man, would be intellectually heavy. There would be time to dwell on and ponder the intricacies of the grave mystery later while sitting, toes splayed, in front of a glowing fire with a cigarette and snifter of brandy.

As he made the short trip to Christ Church Cathedral and pulled his bike into the rack, Lewis felt a shiver pass down his spine. He spun on his heels and looked out, his gaze passing over a variety of students, locals, and tourists alike milling about the outer walking paths and inner quads, some sitting on nearby benches illuminated by gaslight or perched on low stone walls and still others bundled up, making their way to nearby shops to finish holiday shopping. He'd had the strangest foreboding, and though it was difficult to name, with every fiber of his being he felt as though he were being watched. After an uneventful minute, his heart slowed to normal. Lewis shoved his hands into the pockets of his oversized wool jacket, entered the half-filled cathedral through propped doors, and slid into a pew near the back.

The evensong cathedral choir, arranged in the loft, quietly practiced the "Hallelujah" chorus from Handel's *Messiah* while Lewis sank into borderline paranoid thoughts. He turned, startled again, when he heard a sound behind him, yet it was only an elderly gentleman who made his way up the central nave with the help of a twisted cane. A young man in maroon robes closed the door with a creak to signal that the singing was set to begin.

As voices echoed, rising and falling from the barrel-vaulted ceiling, Lewis contemplated, reasoned, and rationalized, like he always did when faced with some problem he did not fully understand. If indeed he were being watched by someone, as he felt in his spirit, who could it be? Perhaps Doyle, his mysterious unnamed colleague, or Crowley on behalf of the Golden Dawn. Or maybe it was the unknown murderer. Lewis shuddered at the thought. How horrible to be watched by someone with such nefarious evil and darkness in their heart. More likely, it was all in his mind and there was no one and nothing to fear. Lewis wondered what would be worse—to be certain of his feelings or to be uncertain and not know if he was going mad.

Needless to say, Lewis did not enjoy the evensong concert as he usually did. When it was done, he checked his pocket watch, stood, and abruptly exited without applauding. Lewis felt the strange sensation again as he left the church, a wave of cold that could not be quantified, measured, or named, only experienced and swallowed up. He looked out into the dim Oxford night while he hastily took the stone steps two at a time. A group of students laughed as they playfully shoved one another. Under a gas lamp, an elderly couple huddled against each other for warmth while walking presumably homeward. A woman fiddled with her overfilled gift bags. Could she be a killer?

Lewis walked his bicycle out to St. Aldate's, keeping his eyes and ears open while concealing the absurd panic he felt rolling over him. He was in England, after all. It wasn't until he passed Tom Gate, which led back into the spacious Christ Church quadrangle, that the feeling slowly began to fade like a lifting fog. He breathed deeply, mounted up, and pedaled north toward the Bodleian Library, determined not to be thrown off his schedule as the cold wind turned his exposed cheeks a shade of red.

After one final look over his shoulder, Lewis entered the library and instantly felt what was left of the tension release and slide off him, like dirt in a hot shower. Something about the smell of old books and whispers put him at ease, turning him into a young boy crawling into the safety of his blanket fort or a wardrobe filled with furs. He was in a new world now. A world made of books.

Lewis walked down the central aisle, his soles tapping on marble, surrounded on either side by a wall of tens of thousands of academic tomes. Above him, an upper walk displayed a second façade of colorful volumes stretching skyward toward the vaulted ceiling. The highest shelves required a ladder to reach, of which there were many, wooden and creaking with each elevated step.

Lewis knew the general location of where Charles would make himself at home, and he set off in that direction. He passed a booth where a gray-haired librarian sat, her eyes briefly flicking up as she stamped a book before returning to her ledger. Lewis was no threat. This was his home away from home after all.

He passed through an arched doorway into an even grander wide-open space that went on just as far as a nearsighted eye could see. The stacks alternated with a section of circular tables and chairs between each, serving as semiprivate study spaces for sleep-deprived students.

Lewis heard the echo of muted whispers and the flutter of flipping pages as he walked to the very end of the great room to the last stall, where, as suspected, Charles Williams sat with his nose in a leather-bound book. Another half dozen volumes, some quite old from the look of them, were splayed in front of him on the table in a wide half circle as if they were an orchestra and he their conductor. He looked up only when Lewis slid a chair out and sat near, but not too close.

"What time is it?" Williams asked. His voice sounded hoarse. He pulled his thin wire-framed glasses off with his thumb and forefinger and rubbed the reddened bridge of his nose with the other hand.

"It's nearly eight o'clock," Lewis replied. "The library has been closed for some time, though I've arranged for us to stay as late as we need—the perks of being an Oxford fellow."

"An hour should do, I suppose," Williams said evenly. "I'll catch the late train back." He yawned. "I've been here all day. Since they opened the doors. Waited out front to get in."

Lewis arched a brow. "I, too, love research, Charles, but that many hours straight is a lot even for me. Are you hungry?"

Williams grunted and shuffled some of the papers in front of him. "I packed a sandwich; suppose I ate it at some point." He eyed his notes, as did Lewis. Charles had jotted down script in a strange sort of shorthand that Lewis couldn't make out with only a glance.

"No need for pleasantries, Professor. Shall we crack on? Where to begin?" Williams twisted his neck from side to side, satisfied with a series of pops and cracks.

"Wherever you'd like," Lewis offered, then amended, "perhaps with Crowley."

"Yes. A wise place." Williams shuffled some notes around until he pulled what was on the bottom back to the top. He had drawn a few symbols on the paper. Lewis spotted star constellations and what appeared to be Egyptian hieroglyphics.

Lewis considered the notes curiously. He then shifted and angled his chair so he could glance back over his shoulder the way he'd come. "Before you begin, I should let you know I think I may have been followed."

Williams lifted his eyes and squinted as if his mind needed

a moment to readjust to the present reality and comprehend what he had just heard. "Are you quite sure?"

"No, not sure at all actually," Lewis admitted. "I didn't see anyone, just had a feeling I couldn't shake. Most likely nothing at all."

Williams laid his page back down on the table. "Trust your instincts, my brother, whether spiritual or physical in origin."

Lewis nodded solemnly. "Quite right, Charles, but I'd prefer to believe it was all in my head. It will help me sleep at night, and I need sleep more than the average man."

Williams murmured his assent, then said, "I might as well go in chronological order so I don't miss anything, though I most certainly will." He adjusted his glasses to read. "Yesterday, I pored over what resources I had at my office in London. I focused first on Crowley himself, writings with him as the subject and also his own disappointing works. From there I branched out to other affiliations, known associates, then Thelema itself."

"What is Thelema?" Lewis asked, though he had a vague idea of it already.

"It's a religious system of belief Crowley seems to have invented under dubious circumstances. Quite kabbalistic or Gnostic in nature, with Far East flavors, but I'll get to those origins shortly." Williams perused his papers. "For now, we agree—Tolkien as well—there exists some connection between these murders, the Order of the Golden Dawn, Crowley himself, and some happening in the past."

"Logically, there has to be," Lewis concurred. "One does not simply murder two people in the way they were murdered without a deep animosity driven by some past wrong."

Williams nodded. "A soul was stained, and we need to find out how and why."

"Whatever happened in the past," Lewis added, processing out loud, "will invariably lead us to why these present events are occurring. Find the connection, find the killer."

Williams consulted another page of his notes. "As for Crowley himself," he recounted, "the man is no doubt unsettling, manipulative, highly intelligent, and perhaps even brighter than the great literary minds you hold in your own circles, though I hate to admit it and would never say it to the man's face. He is also very evil."

"I take it you greatly dislike the man." Lewis smiled.

"For good reason. Throughout most of his adult life, Crowley has been dabbling in the occult in one form or another: a conjurer of spirits, a spiritual guide in witchcraft, sorcery, necromancy, divination, sensual magic, and other pagan carnal delights. His notoriety, or infamy, has risen steadily across Europe and even America over the past three decades."

"The man is a con artist," Lewis said evenly. "He puts on a show for his admirers. He gives them what they want to see and reaches into their pockets while it's happening."

Williams shook his head. "I think this goes beyond the common charlatan." He shivered before continuing. "Crowley has a way of warping reality around him. You felt it. The stories he tells—whether true or not—tend to blur the line between the living and the dead, from what is real and what is myth, as if he exists on some other plane entirely."

"So, he's a very good charlatan," Lewis remarked, lighting a cigarette.

Williams adjusted his glasses again, but his fingers lingered on the frame for a moment too long. "I've seen things, Lewis," he confided hesitantly. "Dark things. Some of it could not have been faked. He's tasted power, and it's hard to walk away after that." He pointed at his own chest. "If not for wise people in my life, I, too, may have strayed down a shadowy path, pursuing those same corrupt spiritual appetites." Williams breathed deeply, his own words seeming to stir up troubling memories, perhaps even feelings he'd thought dormant. After a moment, he came back to himself and forced a smile. "I may be wrong. Perhaps all Crowley desires is notoriety, money, and sex—not too uncommon in our twisted world."

"And not necessarily illegal either," Lewis added. "I am a believer in the supernatural realm, but I also am good at spotting a fraud."

Charles Williams paused and sighed. "Fraud or not, he is, at his core, simply an immoral man who has cast aside all restraint and gained a loyal following of many like-minded hedonists in the process."

"Is it enough of a motive for murder?" Lewis blew smoke out the side of his mouth.

"That's the question," Williams conceded. "But what is different about Crowley from millions of other arrogant men is the way he goes about it. He walks a left-hand path, so to speak. He espouses evil as good and immorality as a noble and moral pursuit. I know you may disagree, but I find him truly devoted to darkness."

Lewis squinted. He tapped his finger on the table. "I remain unconvinced by him, Charles. He strikes me as an atheist, as I once was, and all this act is one big publicity stunt. If the man has sold his soul, it was just for a headline or two." Lewis tilted his head. "I wonder what he would say if confronted about it."

Williams shrugged. "If asked publicly, he may make theater out of the inquiry, declaring Satan to be only a symbol of rebellion and independence to be followed as a model or example but surely not worshipped or even venerated. But I've studied his work; his own words give him away at every turn. They describe very real incantations and ceremonial magic."

"Though again, Charles," Lewis pointed out, "this only means he's read a book or two. It does not make him a magician, a murderer, or even a criminal."

"I can still dislike the man," Williams argued coldly. "Respect his calculating intelligence, yes, but still disdain who he has become and his influence on those impressionable."

"So, what of his past?" Lewis asked, putting out his first cigarette before sliding another from his brass case.

"Born Edward Alexander Crowley in Leamington Spa in 1875. Crowley was born into wealth, but he rejected the Christian fundamentalist beliefs of his parents to pursue mythology and esoteric interests in his school-age years."

"Perhaps we do have more in common than I thought," Lewis said, amused as he pictured an adolescent Crowley.

"I believe you two had very different college experiences." Williams glanced at his notes. "At Cambridge, Crowley was known to enjoy the company of women, especially women of the night. It was even reported he caught syphilis." Williams looked over his glasses at Lewis, who only shook his head faintly. "Much more could be said about those years, I'm sure, but you get the idea. It should be noted that it was at Cambridge that Crowley met some of his more long-standing men of the Order, those who would later become his disciples."

"Yes," Lewis confirmed. "Pennington, Huxley, Beckworth, and MacDougall have that in common. Though there would be others, including Doolittle."

"Crowley graduated with honors," Williams continued.

"He was married in 1903, to Rose Edith Kelly, and they soon moved into the home he had purchased a few years prior—Boleskine House, on the shores of Loch Ness. Some minority reports say the marriage was one of convenience; others say the two soon fell in love and experienced if but a moment of true marital bliss. There was a specific incident early on I wanted to bring to your attention. On their honeymoon in Cairo, a little more than thirty years ago, Crowley claims to have been visited by a spiritual being for three nights in a row in his rented room."

"Like the Dickens novel," Lewis interjected, in an almost amused way.

"Yes." Williams looked up and smiled faintly. "You caught that little tidbit as well. If indeed the occurrence was faked, he may have had inspiration from *A Christmas Carol*. Only this ghost or spirit simply spoke to him from over his left shoulder. The entity was called Aiwass, a name that in gematria also adds up to 418. Crowley claims that this, what he calls his guardian angel, dictated to him what would become *The Book of the Law*, which would go on to serve as the foundation for the religion of Thelema."

"Tell me more about this made-up religion," Lewis said.

"Gladly," Williams responded. "The book proclaims that humanity has entered into a new Aeon and that Crowley will serve as the prophet of this new age. It states a supreme moral law is to be introduced in this Aeon—'Do what thou wilt shall be the whole of the Law'—and that people should learn to live in tune with their will." Williams's eyes brightened as he remembered something, then he shuffled and searched for another specific piece of paper. "I jotted down an interesting note about this encounter. Here it is." He pulled out a scrap with a pencil sketch and an abundance of small shorthand scrawled on it. "Crowley and Rose arrived in Cairo, claiming convincingly to be a prince and princess. Crowley set up a sort of temple room in an upscale apartment they had rented and began invoking ancient Egyptian deities. What's even stranger is that according to Crowley's later accounts, Rose would fall into trances and deliver strange messages like 'The equinox of the gods has come' and 'They are waiting for you.' "

"Reminiscent of the title of his latest book," Lewis recalled.

"Oh, that's right." Williams raised his brows. "I had forgotten he'd said that." He pulled another sheet full of dense writing to the top of the stack. "The couple had a daughter the following year. The girl, called Lilith, died of typhus when she was very young. Crowley blamed his wife for the death of their first child, saying she had become neglectful and was not able to shrug off the casual use of substances as her husband did. Crowley claimed her neglect indirectly caused the care of his daughter to be lacking in her sickness. Eventually, the child's tragic death pushed the couple apart, even after a second daughter was born, and they were soon divorced in an ugly affair. Rose's life spiraled downward from there until she was committed to an asylum for alcohol-induced insanity."

"It's a shame." Lewis folded his hands in his lap. "So many lives have been impacted by one man's twisted path."

"It's despicable," Williams stated before continuing. "Crowley himself didn't mourn long. He couldn't be held down, even by grief. He was a traveler, mountaineer, teacher, and spiritual guide to his various disciples, some more devoted than others. The man has surely smoked his weight in opium over the years, chasing the dragon in more ways than one."

Lewis smiled at his friend's turn of phrase.

"There were rumors he was approached by the British secret service," Williams went on, "because of his vast network of international contacts and proclivity to use people as assets. No matter what Crowley went through, he came out of it unscathed."

Lewis mused, "A conspiratorial mind could be persuaded to believe that a bit of governmental protection helped with that fortuitousness."

Williams sighed and took off his glasses. "There is much more, but in all, there is far greater depth and mystery to the man than meets the eye. We could discuss him for hours, I'm sure. But at the end of it, he is a man who has made for himself many admirers as well as adversaries who would love to see him humiliated or deemed a failure in the eyes of the men who look up to him."

"Hmm. That is something I didn't think of." Lewis leaned forward. "If Crowley cannot protect his disciples from this threat, why would they trust him with anything? They will soon turn on Crowley and abandon him, which means all his money will dry up as well."

Williams affirmed, "He has an even greater interest in finding the killer and stopping this chain of events than we do."

"Or that is what he wants us to believe. He has no alibi for himself in either case." Lewis shifted his weight in his chair, trying to wrap his mind around this new information. "Regardless, I feel as though all of this, in a sense, is pointing back to him. Like a punishment or retribution for something Crowley did in the past. He seemed so sure of himself when we spoke at White's, yet I had the sense that it was a façade and that he, too, was perhaps a little fearful. And why not? If he is innocent in all of this—and that would be a strange idea indeed—something is happening outside of Crowley's control that he doesn't have answers to. Someone else is pulling the marionette strings, and Crowley does not like it one bit."

Williams noted, "Yet some aspects remain very much under his control. Surely it was Crowley who initiated contact with Sir Arthur, and the Inklings were brought in."

Lewis nodded. "Yes, and Beckworth and MacDougall did not speak a word in their testimony to us that Crowley hadn't preordained."

Williams tipped his chin in agreement, then added, "I had one more thought about the murders, or rather a question I found myself asking: Why Huxley and Pennington? Of all the members, what do these two have in common besides being students of Crowley's?"

Lewis rubbed at his chin. "They both have, or have had in the past, a thirst for power and greed. That could account for something."

"I'm certain Professor Tolkien will learn something new about them in the next few days." Williams sounded hopeful.

"Their killer would also have deep knowledge of their rituals," Lewis commented, continuing the trail of thought. "From what we've seen and heard, it sounds as though the murders themselves were some form of ritual—the bodies, the markings, the robe."

Williams's eyes brightened. "That's just it. The Golden Dawn does not have any sort of ritual like that, at least not in their public documents."

"Well then"—Lewis frowned in contemplation—"I'd say it was another ritual. There are many secrets yet to be revealed. But what all this tells me is that Crowley, Beckworth, and MacDougall were not only withholding information from us but also freely giving information that might not have been trustworthy. Why they would mislead us, I do not know, other than to cover up greater involvement in some way." Lewis furrowed his brow. "Perhaps they told us only what they thought we wanted to hear."

"But what has been withheld or twisted could be the key to this whole puzzle," Williams said emphatically. "And these men may not even realize it."

"Then we'll have to find the truth another way." Lewis mulled it over in an extended pause while both men's minds raced. "Charles, would you perhaps be interested in coming back to Oxford this coming Tuesday or Thursday? I'd love for you to join us at one of our literary meetings. There are a handful of people I want to introduce you to."

{9} The Perfect Day

No one ever told me that grief felt so like fear.
—C. S. Lewis, *A Grief Observed*

In near silence, Lewis, Warren, and Janie Moore ate an uncharacteristically late dinner consisting of leftover kidney pie from the night before, salted cabbage with dill, potatoes that had been boiled in water with mint leaves, and rice pudding to finish it off. Though the food was excellent despite no longer being hot, Lewis spent the meal replaying the conversation with Charles Williams in his mind, ruminating over what he'd learned and how it fit together. He felt like a man working on a puzzle only to have another box of loose pieces dumped in front of him. The pieces were there; he needed only to put them together correctly.

Warren glanced up from his plate occasionally, seeming to recognize that his younger brother was lost in thought. He'd once commented that whether Jack's thoughts were academic or imaginative, the familiar faraway look and the resulting distance remained the same.

When they were enjoying the rice pudding, Janie finally spoke up. “I went to the Covered Market with Florence yesterday,” she said lightly. “One shop had just received a delivery of fresh oysters and salmon. Whole boxes of them shipped straight from the ocean. Devon, I think. That might be a nice change for Christmas this year, a seafood menu. Don’t you think? I’ve heard it’s wonderful.”

Jack didn’t reply.

“I’d prefer to stick to tradition,” Warren said dryly. “You can’t always believe what people tell you.” He poured ale from a swing-top bottle into a glass. “We’ll stick with some roasted bird—a duck, turkey, or chicken, depending on the number of guests—with a thick brown gravy poured over whatever it is. That’s the ticket.”

Jack looked up at his brother and squinted, a seed of a thought taking root in his mind.

Janie acquiesced. “Very well. We’ll need to chop a few new stacks of firewood soon.” She inspected Jack. “What we have surely won’t last through the winter. It’s very cold, and I hear the winter in the new year will be especially harsh.”

“I’ll take care of it,” Warren assured her. “I just want to get the boat a little further along before the first deep freeze.”

“What if it was Crowley?” Jack suddenly blurted out.

Startled, Janie placed her hand on her chest.

“What was that?” Warnie raised a brow.

“Oh nothing.” Jack flashed a quick smile. “I was thinking about a project I am working on.”

“You always are,” Janie replied, but Jack was already drifting away again.

"What was that?" Jack asked a few moments later, coming back to himself and wondering if either of the two had asked him a question. "Sorry. I'm at sixes and sevens presently."

"Nothing," Janie responded. "Nothing at all. We were only commenting on the chill in the air."

"I'll stoke the fire." Jack poked at his pudding. "It's going to be especially frigid tonight. It may be time to put the bicycle in the garage until spring."

"Nonsense, Jack," Warren countered. "You love the cold. You'll ride in the snow and dunk yourself in a nearly frozen-over pond."

Jack smiled faintly and looked out the window at the sky beyond. A sliver of the moon shone through the bare tangle of branches, its face like the mostly hidden clock ticking down to zero.

"How are your classes?" Janie prodded, keeping him from drifting off again. "Isn't the term nearly over?"

"Yes," Jack affirmed with a quick grin. "A bit of tutoring in the morning tomorrow. Finals are Wednesday through Friday, though a proctor will be asking my questions. I'll only need to finish grading some papers and post the grades, but after that . . . I'll be mostly free until Saint Hilary day."

"You're never quite all the way free, are you, Jack?" Warren quizzed with a knowing glance coupled with a sly smirk. "Always another project in the works. Something to fill the empty spaces."

"You'll have to tell us all about it," Janie said, suddenly excited.

"Yes, you will." Warren's half smile reached his eyes as he arched one brow excessively. "I feel left out and would love to know more."

Jack shot his elder brother an overtly annoyed look.

"Is it that book you're working on that takes place on Mars?" Janie asked.

"Malacandra," Jack answered slowly, emphasizing each syllable. "It is Mars in Earth's history. But, yes, in the new year I plan to finish my manuscript. At least a rough draft of the first volume. I also have a handful of letters of reply to write."

"Don't become so busy you forget about us," Janie warned.

"Never," he replied honestly.

After stoking the fire and making a pot of Irish herbal tea, Jack nestled into his favorite worn chair and surveyed his nearest bookshelf, noting well-admired titles like *Essays of Elia* by Charles Lamb and *The Anatomy of Melancholy* by Robert Burton, among others. He settled on a lighter read, one he'd enjoyed as a young man, and drew the tattered copy of *Sir Nigel* by Sir Arthur Conan Doyle from its perch. Recent events had brought the novel and its author back into the forefront of Lewis's mind, and he had a curiosity to get lost in it once more.

He scanned the first page, then realized his mind was elsewhere and read it again. Though he felt the warmth on his face from the fire and everything was as it should be, he found he could not bring his brain into focus. Lewis reached for the nearby brass cigarette case and popped it open. Still, even in the haze of tobacco smoke, flashes of the murder scene coupled with the wild eyes of Crowley popped up in his mind's eye and would not relent. It was difficult to concentrate on anything else. Lewis concluded there was no hope of finding peace and joy in any other distraction until this maddening puzzle was solved and set behind him and nagging questions about Crowley and his disciples were answered.

His earlier thought returned, and Lewis muttered the same query as before: "What if it was Crowley?" It sent an anxious chill down his spine. He bit his thumb and reasoned that if a man couldn't be trusted to tell the whole truth and nothing but the truth, who knew what else that depravity might set him to. Murder? Cover-ups? False leads? "How would he have done it?" Lewis whispered. "And why bring in us Inklings?"

"I need to measure you," a voice said. Lewis looked up to see Janie standing over him, one hand holding a measuring line and the other on her hip. "It's for a Christmas present. Don't ask any questions." She flashed a knowing smile as she wrapped the string around Jack's neck and pinched it off. "I'm sure it won't be much of a surprise, but I'd rather get the measurements right than not."

Lewis chuckled and flipped to the next page of the book he only just realized was still in hand.

"Paddy loved Christmas," Janie reminisced without prompting. "It was his favorite time of year."

Suddenly, Jack was totally present. With only a few words she'd brought him back from staring into the abyss. He looked up at the woman who had become like a mother to him. She was so much more human in this moment—not just a figure he was sharing the same space with. Her eyes glistened, and she wiped them with the back of her hand before smiling quickly.

"I miss him every day," Jack said evenly. "As I'm sure you do in abundance. Paddy was a good friend and an even better son."

Janie nodded vigorously. She couldn't speak, fighting hard to keep her composure. She gripped Jack's shoulder, turned, and made her way back into her sewing room.

It was then, while alone and in the glow of the evening fire, Lewis realized that, by all accounts, today had been a nearly perfect day. The only exception was what had happened deep in the recesses of his mind. From an outside view, he had slept well, awakened in good spirits, and eaten a fine breakfast before bicycling to church to sing and hear an above-average sermon. From there he had drunk good, strong tea; read for hours from one of his favorite novels; and listened to choirs singing his favorite Christmas hymns before spending time with a friend in a much-loved historic library that felt like a second home.

Then he had returned home for a hearty meal and an evening in front of the fire with a warm drink in hand. To all observers, it would appear to be a glorious and perfect Sunday. But in his own mind, he could enjoy none of it as he should. His joy had been stolen—a surprising thing because it happened so rarely. He had fought long and hard to find it and would be hard-pressed to let it be taken from him again.

A sudden indignation arose within his spirit. His resolve steeled, Lewis made his way to his bedroom where he sat at his desk and began to do what he always did, to employ the method with which he always solved puzzles, righted wrongs, and put sense to all sorts of mystery—by not just thinking about things but taking pen in hand and writing it all down.

{10} The Housekeeper

Monday, December 14

Magick is the science and art of causing change to occur in conformity with the Will.
—ALEISTER CROWLEY, *The Book of Thoth*

The high walls of plank-supported earth seemed, in the blink of an eye, to move inward. Tolkien narrowed his eyes and watched intently, his lower lip quivering. He was sure he'd seen it. His heart pounded in his chest as a series of bullets whizzed overhead, hissing their warning to keep one's head down. A skull-rattling bomb detonated farther down the line, sending a shower of dirt and debris into the trench. Tolkien heard a distant cry of pain, followed by a whistle and an officer's orders shouted into the black night. The young soldier gripped his rifle until his knuckles went white, pressing his eyes closed before looking down at his mud-caked boots. With a crack of rolling thunder, the sky opened up and a shower of rain began to fall. Tolkien was already wet to the bone, cold, and shivering with only faint dreams of English home fires to keep him warm.

He felt it again—the walls of the trench began squeezing together, slowly, one bit at a time. He tried to dig his boots into the earth to stop it from moving, but instead they scraped and slid uselessly along the slick mud. The wall at his back pushed him forward and would not stop. Tolkien brought his legs up toward his chest and pushed the soles of his feet against the far wall with as much effort as he could muster. He was not going mad or seeing an illusion; the walls of the trench were truly closing in from both sides with a mind to crush him. Tolkien felt the choking claustrophobia as his knees pressed hard into his chest. He wiggled free and fought to stand to his feet, gasping and frantically searching for a ladder to escape into another sort of danger. Finding no exit, Tolkien pressed his back into the wall as the trench continued to squeeze in on him. Feeling hopelessly alone, he turned his head to the side and felt his metal helmet begin to turn askew and press into his skull at the same moment the air was squeezed from his lungs.

Tolkien awoke suddenly, his breath coming quick and shallow. Edith sat up in bed and turned on the bedside lamp, casting a worried look at her husband as she noticed his wild eyes.

"I'm all right," Tolkien reassured her, rising from the bed. While the frantic pictures replayed and flashed through his mind, he forced himself to slow his breathing and come back from war to reality. His white shirt was nearly soaked through, and he pulled it over his head. The early gray of morning was already glowing through the edges of the curtain.

"Was it a dream?" Edith asked once, then again. "Darling, was it a dream?"

Tolkien turned at the doorway and nodded. It had been nearly a decade since he'd last dreamed of the Somme, though the horror of the trench was not a thing one forgot no matter how many years had passed. Maybe it was this recent violent darkness that had caused such a vivid dream. Either way, he would get no more rest tonight.

"Go back to sleep," he murmured softly. "I might as well get dressed."

Tolkien didn't have a scheduled class at Pembroke College until later in the afternoon, so after making a few phone calls, he took the early train southwest from Oxford to Bristol, intending to get off at the station nearest Bath. He held his unlit pipe between his teeth, a now-steady pencil poised over his sketchbook as he scrutinized his latest drawing. Something about the train's movement had stilled his trembling hand after the images of war from his nightmare had faded. The sketch before him was a landscape of an otherworldly place that existed entirely in his thoughts. The railcar rounded a wide corner and jostled from side to side as Tolkien flipped to a blank new page, and before he even realized what he was doing, he scrawled the number 418 and circled it.

A young boy answered the door of the country row home at half past nine. He had smudges of dirt on his face and looked to be of an age that he should be in school. Tolkien glanced into the interior of the modest suburban dwelling and smiled at the boy when he saw no one else was coming.

"I'm looking for a Ms. Sarah Cornish. I was told she was staying here. Do you know if she is around?"

The boy said nothing but hung on the handle of the door,

his light eyes wide and staring up at the professor. He suddenly turned and bolted down the hallway and out of sight, leaving the front door ajar. Tolkien glanced to his right and left from the stoop, not sure whether he should close the door and knock again or simply step over the threshold. He'd nearly come to a decision when he saw a portly woman approaching from down the hall. She wiped her hands on her apron as she waddled.

"I'm coming, good sir. That boy will get my backhand, he will." She glanced up and caught the gaze of the finely dressed gentlemen before her. He noticed a flash of surprise in her eyes. "He knows not to answer the door, and he surely knows not to leave a guest unattended without so much as a word."

Tolkien smiled, hat in hand, feeling sorry for the beating the boy was sure to receive on account of him. "No worries, ma'am. My name is John Tolkien," he said, extending his hand. "I'm here to see a Ms. Sarah Cornish."

The woman snorted and scowled. "Third visitor this week." She turned and walked away. "Come inside," she called over her shoulder. "Sarah is my younger sister, out back getting some laundry done on the washboard. I'll call her and tell her another inspector is here to see her."

"Oh, I'm not . . ." His words faded as he was soon alone. Tolkien walked into what seemed to be some sort of sitting room, though clothes and books were piled on most of the seating. He moved a nursing blanket and nestled onto a floral embroidered couch, holding his hat between his knees.

"You don't look like the other inspector." A woman—presumably Sarah—spoke from the doorway. She wore a simple utilitarian blue dress with an off-white linen apron over the top on which she dried her hands, and her hair was pulled up in a bun under a fabric wrap. She looked to be nearly a decade younger than her sister, if not more. A handsome woman, with a strong frame, striking features, and light green eyes.

"I'm not with Scotland Yard," Tolkien explained, maintaining a cordial smile as he rose to standing. "That should be made known. I'm a professor. However, I would like to ask you a few questions about the incident with Lord Pennington, your employer."

"Former employer," Sarah corrected with a scowl. She tilted her head in a way Tolkien interpreted as warranted skepticism. "I was placed on leave and told my services in the Pennington household were no longer needed." She shook her head. "Makes no sense. It's still a house that needs to be kept tidy, isn't it? The man is dead, that is true, but there is still dust to be wiped and dishes that need to be cleaned through the holiday. The residence won't have new owners at least until after the new year or, more likely, spring."

"The house is being sold?" Tolkien asked, narrowing his brow.

She nodded. "Sure it is. His son came, took one look around, and put it on the market right after the reading of the will, even before the funeral. A bit coldhearted, if you ask me."

Tolkien pulled out a small notepad and made a record of that. He underlined the word *will* three times. He would need to check with public records about the listing and try to learn more about the contents of said will.

The woman frowned as she stepped all the way into the room and again wiped her hands on her apron. "Who did you say you were? A professor?"

"Yes, I work at Pembroke College of Oxford. I have some questions for you if you can spare a moment to talk."

Sarah shook her head. "Scotland Yard asked loads of questions already. I don't think I should make any statements to anyone else, especially a teacher. You sure you're not a writer for *The Times*? You look like a writer, come to think of it."

"In fact, I am a writer," Tolkien responded with a smile, "though not for the newspaper. I write many types of books, and it just so happens I am writing a book. A sort of mystery in fact, and I thought the former Lord Pennington's death would be excellent material for said novel."

The woman squinted, a look of confusion washing over her face. "It was all so horrible. I don't think I want to speak about it anymore. Why don't you ask Scotland Yard? I'm sure they would—"

"I'd really like your personal perspective," Tolkien interrupted quickly, then added, "from someone who was there and who knew the man. I've already talked to Lords Beckworth and MacDougall and just need your story to bring it all together."

A faint, troubled look of doubt flashed across her face.

"Of course, I would pay a small fee as compensation for your time," Tolkien went on. "A consultant fee is common for those who give valuable insight for a published novel." Suspecting that the woman might need the money if her employment had dried up, Tolkien had saved this tempting tidbit as a last resort to prevent being ushered out the door empty-handed.

And, indeed, the news seemed to remove the last of Sarah's reservations. She nodded and stepped closer. "Ask me your questions then." She swept a pile of clothing from a chair onto the wide-planked floor and sat. "Though I can't talk long. I need to help my sister with lunch if I'm going to earn our keep."

Tolkien flipped back a page in his notebook, resumed his seat, and read out the first question. "How long did you know Lord Pennington?"

"I was in Lord Pennington's employ for nearly a decade," Sarah answered, her green eyes looking up and right as a person's gaze often does when recalling memories. "His first name was Roger. Not sure if you knew that. It's not right that his son just cast me aside like he did with no warning. Lord Pennington would never have done that if he were still alive, or stood by and let it happen."

"I'm sure he wouldn't have," Tolkien commiserated. "How many children did Pennington have? Other than the son you mentioned."

Sarah narrowed her dark brow. "Just Francis, from what I know of." She hesitated slightly. "That is the son's name, Francis. Lives in Brighton, I believe. He'll inherit it all. Though I've heard stories. Perhaps Roger might have more." She paused and glanced up. "Forgive me, sir. I shouldn't speak that way of the deceased."

Tolkien smiled faintly but decided to press. "Are you implying Pennington may not have been a wholly moral man in his younger years?"

Sarah sucked in a breath through her teeth. "I shouldn't have said anything. He had a lot of good qualities as well as vices," she said firmly. "As we all do. Some are well balanced, and others aren't."

"How was the relationship between father and son?"

Sarah shrugged. "I heard them argue, Mr. Pennington and his son. A couple of times, actually, just in the past few months. They were in the private study, behind closed doors, but still I could hear the tone of their voices." She glanced up to meet Tolkien's eyes. "I didn't linger. I'm not the type to eavesdrop on what doesn't concern me."

"Of course," Tolkien acknowledged, though not buying it fully. "But you wouldn't happen to know what it was they argued about, would you? Simply from the tone?"

"I know he asked for money the first time." Her eyes almost brightened as she remembered. "I saw Francis holding a folded check with a smile on his face as he passed through the foyer."

"What about the other time?" Tolkien questioned as he jotted a note.

"I suppose that was about money as well. Only the second time, he left in a huff, with no check in sight and not a smile either."

"Perhaps Lord Pennington turned down his son's request for financial assistance?" Tolkien wondered.

Sarah nodded faintly. "I suppose that makes sense. I didn't like him." She clasped her hands on her lap and rubbed them together. "Francis, I mean. He treated the staff, me, and the cook like rubbish. He once shouted that his tea was too cold and to take it away, though it was perfectly warm."

Tolkien nodded along. He wanted to build a sense of trusting rapport with the woman. "Tell me about the final two weeks of Lord Pennington's life. I understand his behavior became somewhat erratic in November."

"Yes, that's right." Sarah swallowed and took a few shallow breaths, then continued. "A good friend and associate of Lord Pennington's had just passed away, and I think it hit him really hard. Might be that Roger—Lord Pennington—came to grips with his own mortality. He kept saying he would be next and he deserved it for what he'd done. I overheard him crying one night in his room with the door locked. He spoke strange things at times. He said he had done and been a part of things that would surely send him to hell. He said he could already feel the flames burning his feet. I told him that was nonsense and that he'd done a lot of good things as well." Sarah looked up and met Tolkien's eyes. "Did you know Lord Pennington was a philanthropist? He supported many charitable causes around London. He was as good a father as he could be. He did his best."

Tolkien had written down a few additional notes as she spoke. "Did he see a doctor?" Tolkien asked when her words finally trailed off to stillness.

She nodded. "Yes. A doctor came, and then another a few days later. But there was nothing to be done. Both the first and second said he was otherwise healthy. He was tested for various ailments, and all came back negative. A nurse was sent over to help care for him, and I overheard the doctor saying to the nurse that he thought it was all in his head—a disease of the mind." Sarah paused and held on to that thought, as if weighing it in her own head. "Lord Pennington was just fine for a few days, mostly on bed rest. Then he went back to work, and it happened again. This time it got so bad he pulled out his own hair. I was frightened to be in the same house as him, and so were the other staff."

When she caught Tolkien's gaze, he saw fear now reflected in her eyes. "I thought certainly he was possessed by a devil or going mad," she admitted. "Turns out that thought wasn't far off from the truth. He took his life a few days later." She shook her head. "What a horrible way to exit this life. I wish I could have done more. I really do."

After scribbling a few more notes, Tolkien looked up and

noticed that the woman was crying. She wiped at her reddened eyes with her apron. In the doorway that led out to the hall, the young boy who had initially opened the front door peered around the frame, green eyes wide, until he saw Tolkien spot him, then bolted away back into hiding.

{11} The Tutor

> Man without art is eyeless; man with art and nothing else would see little but the reflections of his own fears and desires.
>
> —Hugo Dyson

Lewis arrived at his office at Magdalen just before eight o'clock, and by the time he'd set his briefcase down and placed his jacket and hat on a hook, there was already a knock at the door. Lewis sighed. He'd wanted to make tea before the first of three back-to-back tutoring sessions with wide-eyed students eager to finish the term with honors and spend the holiday, at home or abroad, in peace.

For most of the morning Lewis listened as, one by one, his three tutees presented their findings and insights into a literary figure chosen for a research paper due by the end of the week. The first was a tall, wiry boy named George with a badly pockmarked face who laid out his haphazard research on Thomas Aquinas with reservation. The next, Lionel from Leeds, was confident until Lewis poked holes in his research on Geoffrey Chaucer with a few simple questions and helpful advice for polishing. Finally, Patrick, a young man with red hair and freckles, almost instantly began to pepper his tutor with a laundry list of questions about Augustine. What Lewis liked best about Patrick, apart from his insatiable curiosity, was that the boy was from Ireland and, more particularly, an area just outside Belfast near the shipyards—not far from where Lewis himself had grown up watching as the *Titanic* was being built. Patrick reminded Lewis a bit of himself at that age.

When Lewis had finished his professorial responsibilities for the day, he put his wool jacket and hat back on, leaving his leather briefcase behind, and set out north from Magdalen up the meandering street called Queen's Lane. He walked first past the high walls of the Queen's College on his left, then New College and its many spires on his right, before passing under the Bridge of Sighs, which connected two parts of Hertford College otherwise separated by the ancient street. From there, his destination, the octagonal Sheldonian Theatre, lay straight ahead.

Lewis entered the auditorium and slid into the thin wooden seat nearest the door. He let his gaze survey the half-filled hall before settling on the stage, where Hugo Dyson paced from side to side, waving his arms wildly to portray the passion of the dynamic rise and fall of Macbeth. "The soul of William is anticipation of what will come next," Dyson stated loudly, pausing to allow his words to take hold. "Take this phrase for example: 'By the pricking of my thumbs, something wicked this way comes.' Not only does it rhyme"—Hugo's smile showed his large teeth—"but there is anticipation. What is coming?" He raised a brow. "Something wicked!" he shouted. "We don't know exactly what it is or when, but we know it is coming, and we know this wicked thing is of our own making." Dyson reached the left end of the stage, pivoted, and started back the other way. "Or take this phrase: 'Fair is foul, and foul is fair.' We can anticipate now that something good and beautiful will soon be corrupted, and something broken will soon see some form of redemption."

Dyson stopped again, his bushy brows rising as he peered at the nearest row of captivated students. "The key to good writing is the building of tension that is to be released in an ever-so-climactic way. A collective release of held breath." Dyson inhaled deeply before letting it out in a dramatic rush. His gaze floated up to the higher rows, catching Lewis's. Jack sat silently, his right leg crossed over his left, watching his friend.

Hugo raised his arm and pointed. "Your very own Professor Lewis is in our audience today." All eyes turned and looked at him.

Lewis smiled sheepishly and gave a protracted wave. He hated when Hugo did this.

"Here is a man who knows a thing or two about anticipation," Hugo went on with a sly grin. "A skilled writer in his off-hours, Professor Lewis has been building tension little by little over many months with a new book he has been writing, an otherworldly tale I have been privileged to hear bits and pieces of. Don't give away the ending too soon. Don't reveal what is in the shadows until the reader is primed. We don't know what is coming and from where and at what time, but mark my words—when it comes, you'll know it, and there will be goose bumps covering you from fingertips to toenails."

The students soon filed out the doors, excitedly conversing while bundling up to face the frigid blast, which was noticeably less severe by now. Lewis moved against the current of exiting students and made his way down to the floor near the stage. Dyson had already descended from the platform and was vigorously shaking the hand of one of the deans of Merton College, an older gentleman who never smiled but seemed to take a liking to Dyson. Everyone liked Hugo. The man had an almost supernatural gift of making friends and putting people at ease, if he wanted to, wherever he went.

"I didn't expect to see you in the crowd, Jack," Dyson greeted him when the two were finally somewhat alone. "Imagine my pleasant surprise. I hope I didn't embarrass you back there. I'm not supposed to be seeing you until tomorrow morning at the Bird. To what do I owe this honor?"

"First of all," Lewis said with a smile while shaking Hugo's outstretched hand, "a fine lecture, despite my lukewarm feelings about the subject matter."

Dyson chuckled, his shoulders bouncing as he took his gray flannel jacket from the back of a chair and slid his arms into the sleeves.

"I wondered if you might care for chowder at the King's Arms and a quick walk along Addison's. I'd love to hear from you before the hubbub of the Bird in the morning."

Dyson frowned. "It's quite frigid outside, Jack."

"Nonsense. A brisk walk will get your blood pumping. I may even take a dip in the pond later."

After a lunch of clam chowder and biscuits, Lewis and Dyson set off on foot toward Longwall Street. As they turned south, Magdalen's Great Tower jutted upward toward the heavens like a beacon guiding their steps. At points, the open quad of New College and the church of St. Peter-in-the-East could be seen through wrought iron gates or in gaps between tightly packed buildings.

"Do you know why I like Shakespeare?" Hugo quickened his pace to walk shoulder to shoulder with Lewis.

"I know you'll tell me whether I say yes or no."

"There are few elves, dwarves, or orcs in any of his writings," Hugo quipped. Both men laughed.

"Yes, but," Lewis began, holding up a finger, "in Shakespeare, there are witches, cauldrons, and magic systems, no?"

The corners of Hugo's eyes crinkled. "Tastefully used, but I see your point, Jack. Lord knows if I hear another phrase spoken in Elvish, I'll join you in walking into that freezing pond."

Both men laughed again. It felt good, like an internal weight being lifted if only for a moment. And Lewis did not feel guilty in their conspiracy, because these were words Dyson had often spoken, only partly in jest, to Tolkien's face.

"You've always been a good friend, Hugo," Lewis acknowledged. "You've helped me to both process my scattered thoughts and sort everything in its proper place. I must admit I haven't felt myself as of late, in my body, mind, and spirit. I suppose I just need to talk and listen and get a fresh perspective on a few things so they can stop their incessant bouncing around in my jumbled mind. I thought of no other person than you and no other place in which to see things set right in the world than where we are going, despite the cold."

Hugo nodded briskly. "It sounds as though this case has quickly taken root in your mind."

"Yes, it has," Lewis confirmed. "Like a weed or a bramble."

"Pleasant," was Hugo's brief response.

"What do you know of secret societies?" Lewis asked. "Especially those operating here in Britain?"

"Oh, not much more than you, I'd expect." Dyson looked down at his boots as he kept pace. "I know they've existed as long as secrets have. Egyptians, Babylonians, Greeks, and Romans—every civilization has had powerful people with secrets, and powerful people with secrets want the option to contain those secrets and to flaunt anything they wish to be made public. It's a balancing act. If it's too secret, it goes extinct, and if it's not secret enough, it goes extinct."

"That's one way to look at it," Lewis agreed.

"But just because something is secret doesn't mean it's wrong, immoral, sinful, or illegal. The early persecuted church met in secret. You could say in a way that early Christianity was a secret society in and of itself."

"Hmm," Lewis mused. "Yet none of Christianity's core tenets were hidden or secret. The gospel was and is for all. Only the members and locations of meetings were kept secret."

"One could make a similar claim of Jesuits, Freemasons, Illuminati, Rosicrucians, Ordo Templi Orientis, or even the Inklings." Hugo smirked. "As with all generational secrets, some aspects are passed down, and others die with the previous generation. I suppose one generation may slip deeply into the occult, and the next may treat pagan ceremonies with disdain or disbelief, as if only a plaything or make-believe. Magic to be laughed at or entertained by, but not to be taken seriously."

"Then there is the very real realm of the supernatural," Lewis put in. "One of the greatest tricks the devil ever pulled was to convince those fallen that he was and is only legend and myth."

Dyson nodded. "I cannot argue with that, Jack. And I suppose at the root of these two murders that we have dived headlong into, there is something very sinister and spiritual in nature, even if only influenced and driven by the internal spiritual longings and hunger of the guilty party. I would assume the murderer to be guilty of great sins in both a physical and spiritual sense."

Lewis pondered his friend's words. There was a depth of truth to them that he had not yet fully considered. The murderer, as with all murderers, would most likely be driven by deep wrath. A deadly sin that may have started small, as only a thought in the mind, but grew into something huge and ugly, perhaps over many years or even decades, before the monstrous beast was finally unleashed.

The men followed the road around through a large black double wrought iron gate, which was wide open. They descended a few steps off icy pavement onto the frozen ground of the well-worn path affectionately known as Addison's Walk. The path ran a circuit around a small island in the middle of the River Cherwell. It was here, on a walk five years earlier, that Lewis's life had been forever changed. Lewis, Dyson, and Tolkien had taken a stroll one late night in an intense discussion that would continue into the early hours of the morning. When Lewis returned home the following day, he had become a changed man from the inside out.

The usually full deciduous trees had long since dropped their leaves, providing a good view of the tower and bridge through their naked branches at any point in the circular stroll. Lewis frequently looked up and gazed at the landmarks, which ever faithfully helped lead him back home.

"Tell me about Baron Huxley," Lewis finally said, after a minute of watching a family of ducks cross the trail ahead.

"Tolkien told me you would look into the first victim. I know it's only been a short time, but have you learned anything of use so far?"

"I did learn something interesting." Hugo smiled and used the pause to build anticipation. "I did something quite unlike me," he continued, jamming his gloved hands into his pockets. "I made a friend."

"I want to hear it all," Lewis prompted, feeling a narrative story brewing.

Hugo sucked in a deep breath. "Through a simple search of a months-old newspaper obituary, I found out Huxley hailed from Coventry. It was where the funeral was held in early November, followed by a simple graveside service, which I would later learn was attended by only a few people. Yesterday, I took the midmorning train north to Coventry and went to the local Anglican church just as Sunday mass was being let out. Out front, I found a pair of gossiping old ladies and befriended them. I told a bit of fiction and said I had wanted to come to the funeral to pay my respects to old Huxley. They knew the family name, and I knew I was in the right place. I told the pair that Huxley and I were old college friends but that I had missed the ceremony because I'd only just heard of his tragic death. I asked where I might find some more of Huxley's old friends. They told me they weren't sure he had any real friends of late, at least not in Coventry, but suggested the local watering hole closest to the Huxley estate."

Hugo flashed a sidelong glance to make sure Lewis was still following. "I then went to the Golden Cross, ate some fish and chips, and told my story a few more times without much success. Eventually, I was directed by a sympathetic bartender to one of Huxley's old mates from college, a local who had just come home for the holiday. After a fruitless conversation with that man, since he hadn't seen Huxley in more than a decade, I was thankfully directed to the home of another man, who had served in the war with Huxley. I dropped by his work in the afternoon. He's a foreman at a manufacturing factory. I told my story again, and when I learned that this new man, called Reginald, had seen Huxley just this past summer, I said I'd love to take him out for drinks on me if only he'd share a story or two of my dear long-lost friend for old times' sake. He was hesitant at first, but soon we were on our way back to the Golden Cross."

"Dear Lord," Lewis interjected. "You have an uncanny gift, Hugo. I fear I would have had the door slammed in my face and caught the next train home."

Dyson laughed. By now they had reached the midway point of the circular walk and had begun their return leg back toward the bridge and Magdalen. Lewis could feel that his toes would soon be going numb.

Dyson cleared his throat and continued the story. "There was much nonsense and throwaway banter at first. But once Reginald was a bit, shall I say, loosened up with ale, he did mention two tidbits I found very interesting, and I think you will as well."

"Good chap," Lewis praised. "What were they?" He could feel his heart suddenly speed up as his walking pace slowed.

"The first is that this man Reginald said Huxley had complained he hadn't been feeling well toward the end. He grumbled about growing old and said that he was sore and losing his hair. Reginald put him at ease by lying and saying this happens to all men at a certain point in their lives, but he remembered the conversation well because it struck him as strange. The second interesting nugget was that, apparently,

Huxley was in some sort of financial trouble. He had a serious debt and even asked Reginald if he might be able to spare some money. Reginald gave him some, but not nearly enough to cover the whole amount spoken of. The most interesting part was who Reginald told me Huxley owed the money to. After further inquiry and careful prodding, I found out it was none other than . . . the late Roger Pennington."

{12} The Rabbit Room

Tuesday, December 15

It cannot be seen, cannot be felt,
Cannot be heard, cannot be smelt.
It lies behind stars and under hills,
  And empty holes it fills.
It comes first and follows after,
  Ends life, kills laughter.
  —J. R. R. Tolkien, *The Hobbit*

Tuesday morning, though warmer than the previous day, was still damp and foggy to the point Lewis could see only one block ahead of him at a time. Because of the limited vision, he had kept the bicycle in the garage. Despite walking for nearly an hour, with renewed energy since his stroll the day before, Lewis was still the first to arrive at the Bird and Baby. The bell jangled overhead as he unwrapped a striped woolen scarf from around his neck and carefully pulled off his gloves by the fingers. The public house was nearly empty, except for an older man reading *The Times,* whom Lewis knew to be mostly deaf, and a young man who was carefully counting out coins at his table, preparing to leave.

Lewis made his way directly back to the Rabbit Room, glancing quickly at the outward-facing front page of the newspaper. It featured a picture of the royal family in the wake of the abdication and, below that, pictures of the blackened remains of the recently burned Crystal Palace, which had stood so elegantly in Hyde Park and Sydenham Hill for nearly a century.

Speaking of fires, Charlie had already prepared one, which roared and crackled in the hearth, much to Lewis's delight. He loved feeling the warmth on his face as he walked closer and closed his eyes. Charlie had also put the meeting space back in its usual arrangement since the Inklings had met last Thursday night, when Lewis was under the weather and all this mystery had sprung forth like Pandora's jar. A long, familiar wooden table full of scuffs, scratches, and dents from decades of hard use now filled the center of the room, making the space feel much tighter.

Lewis pulled out a chair in his favorite spot, where the fire was closest, and warmed his backside through the ladder-back slats. He reached into his inner breast pocket and fetched his brass cigarette case. He tapped the butt against the case and lit a match generously provided in a small wooden box in the middle of the table. Lewis hadn't even taken his first pull when Tolkien entered like a hurricane.

"Good!" Tolkien exclaimed. "I hoped you'd arrive before the others. What news do you have? I have some of my own."

Lewis laughed and then coughed. "I have far more to talk to you about than a few measly minutes will give us before this room is drowned in cherry smoke and Dyson's laughter."

"I suppose that's true." Tolkien sighed. "I've written notes, a log of sorts." After sitting down opposite Lewis, he slid a notebook across the table. "I'll need that back," he added, pointing to the leather-bound copy. Another journal-type book lay in front of Tolkien, but he kept it to himself.

“Is it written in Elvish?” Lewis thumbed the proffered journal open a few pages from the front. It looked as though it contained notes from Tolkien’s interview with the housekeeper, which Lewis was interested in, especially now that it sounded as though his friend had learned something of use.

Tolkien ignored the jest. “What of your meeting with Williams?” he asked, after finding and pulling a small pouch from his hip pocket that contained his pipe among other accoutrements.

Lewis grabbed a wad of haphazardly folded papers from his jacket pocket and handed them over. “You can keep those. I learned some useful information about Crowley, which I’ve taken to heart, as well as the first chap who died, Baron Huxley, though I’m not sure what to make of it all yet.”

“I wonder if a Thursday night meeting in your rooms at Magdalen might be in order?” Tolkien caught Lewis’s eye. “A bit more private. Perhaps a full chalkboard session like we did for the kidnapping. What do you say?”

Lewis nodded. “There is only so much we can openly discuss here. I’m finding the Bird to be more of a front anyway. A public face for a private endeavor.”

Tolkien raised a brow. “A book cover,” he said, before smiling at his clever joke and scratching a pair of matches.

Nevill Coghill and Adam Fox were the next to arrive. Nevill appeared disheveled. He rubbed his reddened eyes and ordered a strong coffee, which was unlike him. He was in the midst of directing a many-weeks-long stage production through the Oxford University Dramatic Society, and it seemed as though the long nights and lack of sleep were catching up to him.

Fox took a chair next to Tolkien, and Coghill sat next to

Lewis, a man with whom he had shared a special bond since their school days at Oxford, due to their both being Irish.

Lord Cecil came next, followed closely by Warren, who had stopped by the wooden bar top on the way and now carried a tray of ciders, which looked darker than usual in color and closer to a lager.

"I feel better than I have in years," Cecil told the group as he took his seat.

"And why is that?" Fox wanted to know.

Cecil shrugged. "I haven't the foggiest. Though perhaps it is because my new nurse is actually good at her job."

Hugo was the last of the seven to enter. Instead of immediately sitting down and apologizing for his lateness, he walked around the table and loudly greeted each man, shaking hands and clapping them on the back in turn. And just like that, the Rabbit Room had transformed from early-morning stillness to buzzing chatter and fullness of life. Dyson had this almost supernatural effect of energizing and animating every room he walked into.

"We have deep and mysterious waters to delve into this morning," Fox broke in, motioning with his palms for all to be seated. "I was out of town for the weekend, and I'm excited to hear about the progress. Now, normally, we would have readings from manuscripts, but as you are well aware, there are other, more pressing matters to discuss."

"You mean we don't have to hear about another bloody elf?" Hugo asked playfully. All the Inklings laughed at his comment, including Tolkien himself.

"We'll get back to regular programming soon," Fox responded with a smile. "No doubt you'll get your fill of hobbits and dwarves in the new year."

Hugo rolled his eyes and glanced down at a paper that

was being handed around, which contained some notes Tolkien had written.

"Until then," Fox continued, "let's see how the other project is coming along." He looked pointedly at both Tolkien and Lewis before his gaze settled on the latter.

Lewis smiled and rose from his chair in mock formality. "I would like to take this opportunity to invite you all to my rooms at Magdalen on Thursday night at the usual time. I feel as though the bulk of the information I would like to both share and discuss would be better suited where we could speak more openly, using real names and locations. I spoke to Tollers about it just a few moments ago, and he feels as though a chalkboard session is in order."

All eyes turned to Tolkien, who nodded. "I think it would be prudent. We need to be careful of curious eyes and ears. There is also a very real possibility that we are being watched. By whom or why I do not know, but we need to be aware of it and take precautions when sensitive material is shared."

A sudden chill fell over the room, and a moment of pregnant silence ensued.

Fox nodded. "Very well. We can wait that long, I suppose. Each man should continue their area of inquiry until said meeting."

"I would also like to invite Charles Williams to join us," Lewis added. "If it is all right with all of you. He is aware of the case and has valuable insight to offer."

Heads nodded again as Fox eyed Tolkien. "I suppose your briefing will wait as well?"

"Some of it, yes," Tolkien answered.

Lewis interjected. "There is a matter regarding Cecil that is a bit more timely." He looked to Cecil, who took the hint.

"Yes," Cecil began, a bit awkwardly, "I suppose this can't wait. I was tasked with keeping an eye on and investigating a man named"—he lowered his voice—"Mortimer Doolittle. He was mentioned as a possible person of interest by those who were closest to the slain. I used my contacts to find out everything I could about Mortimer. Yesterday I spent much of the day following him. Then late last night, I reached out by telephone and set up a dinner meeting with him for tomorrow evening in Wolvercote."

"Are you mad?" Fox demanded, taken aback. "You did what? Why on earth would you do that?" Fox then glanced around and lowered his voice to a near whisper. "He is suspected of murder. You know my view on any sort of surveillance. We only follow, gather information, observe, and report. Not invite the man out for dinner."

Cecil hesitated and looked to Tolkien and Lewis for support, though he only received blank stares. "It wasn't done on purpose per se," he explained. "I followed him into his home club in the city, and he must have turned back, because he bumped into me in the lobby. I panicked. I wasn't sure if he had spotted me prior. He is a possible murderer after all. But I quickly regained my composure and made up a story on the spot that I was highly interested in donating to the Ashmolean. I left it open-ended as to whether the donation was a relic, art piece, or monetary gift, though I don't believe I possess any historical relics they would be interested in."

"Dear Lord in heaven." Dyson held his palm to his forehead.

"What happened then?" Fox asked.

"Well, after I introduced myself and he realized who my family was, Doolittle was all ears, like a snake who'd just spotted a hatching egg. At that point I could no longer continue to follow him, so I returned home, defeated in one sense. Later, perhaps unwisely, I made a phone call and was put through directly to Doolittle. That's when I set up a dinner at the Trout Inn tomorrow evening to further discuss the donation. I figured it would be the best way to question him under a guise and the day would not be a total loss."

"Cecil, you've put yourself at unnecessary risk," Tolkien admonished. "It would be better at this point just to make a generous financial contribution and walk away. We'll put someone else on him to observe his movements."

"I agree." Fox bobbed his head enthusiastically.

"Warren and I will join you," Lewis said, "at your dinner, I mean. Not officially, but we'll just so happen to arrive at some point during your meal. You'll need to come up with a reason to invite us to join you."

The room fell silent as all eyes looked from Cecil to Fox to Lewis.

"Why me?" Warren sipped his ale and wiped the foam from his upper lip.

"Because," Lewis replied, "Cecil told me that Doolittle is a bit of a French history buff. Your job will be to butter his bread and get the man to talk—about what I do not yet know, but just enough to find some opening to either count him as a valid suspect or rule him out. I'll know it when I hear it."

{13} The Trout Inn

Wednesday, December 16

The world is so much larger than I thought.
I thought we went along paths—but it seems
there are no paths. The going itself is the path.
—C. S. Lewis, *Perelandra*

The Trout Inn was a favorite of Lewis's, and he was glad Cecil had chosen it. The watering hole overlooked the River Thames, which flowed just outside the window, meandering on its way toward London where the river would grow to meet its full potential. The modest two-story tavern and lodging house sat a ways outside normal walking distance, which led the brothers to reluctantly hire a car.

Jack and Warren got to the establishment just after dark, only to exit the vehicle and stand outside in the cold, several steps back from the entrance, waiting patiently for Doolittle to show. Cecil came first, giving a slight incline of his narrow chin as he passed them. Jack looked up to the roofline of the Trout Inn, whose chimneys on either end were billowing smoke, as to be expected on a frigid December night. He closed his eyes and pictured himself walking up to the radiating hearth and splaying his chilled hands toward the inviting warmth.

When he heard the rumble of an engine, he opened his eyes. Doolittle, fashionably late, arrived in style—in a Cadillac V-16 Phaeton, dark green and luminous in the flickering gas lanterns that stood sentinel outside the inn's main entrance. The car sputtered and stopped, and out stepped Doolittle, his icy glare inspecting this quaint establishment and most likely finding it not up to his London high-society standards. Lewis shivered.

"That's a very nice car," Warren muttered under his breath.

The two brothers stepped further back, under the boughs of a nearby pine tree, until Doolittle had passed by. He looked to be a bit older than they were, more than likely of a similar age to Crowley since they had attended Cambridge together. To cope with his slight limp, his large hand gripped a bentwood cane that had what looked to be a crystal skull attached to the top. He was of above-average height with a thick barrel chest, a close-cropped beard flecked with silver, and an overall air of pomp and privilege. He sniffed the air as if the Thames had offended him by allowing the smell of fish or algae to invade his nostrils.

Jack instantly disliked the man, and he sensed that Warren felt the same. Jack let out a deep sigh and shivered again as he checked his pocket watch. "Give them time to be seated," he said reluctantly. "We don't want to be too obvious." He gazed out over the flowing waters and listened as the current bubbled under a nearby walking bridge.

Ten long minutes later, Lewis and Warren entered and walked toward the table where Cecil and Doolittle sat. Cecil had specifically chosen one with four chairs that was well out of the way, near the farthest back corner.

"Is that you, Cecil?" Jack called loudly from still a ways off. He smiled as widely as he could and approached, his hand extended and his mouth agape. Cecil stood, and the two shook hands vigorously.

"It's so good to see you, Jack!" Cecil exclaimed. "What a surprise! It's surely been too long. It really has. And Warren is here with you. Let me introduce you to my new friend, Mortimer Doolittle." He turned toward his companion, who had unenthusiastically extended his hand as if Lewis was supposed to bow and kiss his ring. "Lord Doolittle, Lewis is a professor at Oxford. He specializes in medieval and Renaissance literature. And his brother, Warren here, is a renowned scholar of seventeenth-century French aristocracy. I've seen some of his notes on the Sun King, Louis the XIV. Very intriguing work."

At this news, Mortimer's eyes lit up. He stood, stepped closer, and shook Warren's hand with a renewed sense of vigor. "That is very interesting indeed, Mr. Lewis. I consider myself a student of royalty and the aristocracy. I see so much of myself in those types of people, past or present."

"Sorry to bother you both." Jack backed away. "We've only just arrived to have a few pints and pass the time."

"Why don't you join us?" Cecil invited enthusiastically, without first looking at Doolittle.

"Oh, we don't want to be a bother," Warren objected.

"Nonsense." Doolittle waved his hand toward the two open seats. "You can sit here. I have a few questions for you . . . Warren, is it?" Mortimer pulled out the chair nearest to himself for the elder Lewis, who graciously accepted.

They ordered rare meat and pints of dark ale all around,

and for the next half hour, the Lewises and Cecil focused on putting Mortimer at ease by appealing to his interests and vanity. It was clear that his favorite subject, even above that of history, was himself. When Warren was given the chance to share, he spoke of French royalty and details of Versailles, which thrilled Doolittle, who responded with a rambling tirade. Cecil broke in and spoke of art his family was looking to find a home for in a qualified museum. He listed off all the museums he'd visited recently and shared stories of his father, which also delighted Doolittle, who pivoted to tell embellished stories of his privileged bloodlines. Cecil twice hinted that a museum Doolittle was on the board of was in the running to receive the art, but that his family was hesitant, wanting instead to find somewhere that would display their name on a placard over a doorway or grant them naming rights for a new medieval art wing. Doolittle fought off a look of annoyance at this yet seemed to become more determined to win over Cecil, who was clearly of higher rank and station.

Jack remained mostly silent but, when called upon, drew from his knowledge of Arthurian legend and poetry. Although Doolittle found this somewhat engaging, soon he turned back to ask Warren another series of questions and make a poorly veiled pitch to Cecil. After three beers each and half a dozen cigarettes, the four men sounded as though they were old friends from university getting together over summer break to paint the town red.

Cecil called for another round of drinks from the eager waiter, then flashed a look at Jack. "I was just at the National Gallery over the summer, and you would not believe who I saw there." He paused for effect, and Doolittle leaned toward him. "It was the occultist," Cecil continued, with a raised brow. He snapped his fingers as if the action would help him recall the name. "It's the one who writes the books about all his exploits and tells everyone that they should do whatever they want. What's his name?" He snapped his fingers again.

"Crowley," Doolittle inserted, with an almost visible grimace. He downed the lower third of his glass and set it on the table with a thud. "I absolutely loathe that man."

"Oh? Why is that?" Jack asked as if the news were a surprise.

"Yes, why?" Cecil echoed, nestling his chin on the back of his hands.

"No reason in particular," Doolittle said dismissively. "I just find him dull and crude. A man of low station and quality."

"I think he's quite fascinating," Jack countered. "I was pondering using him as an expert source for a book I'm thinking about writing."

Doolittle narrowed his eyes. "And what book is that?"

"I wrote a book that was published just this year called *The Allegory of Love*. I'm thinking of doing something similar about an allegory of good and evil—temptation and virtue and man's perspective of both."

"Which one is Crowley? Good or evil?"

Lewis smiled. "That's just it, isn't it? From my worldview, Crowley symbolizes a certain zeitgeist that is felt by many—the ability to flaunt openly what is normally hidden away in the dark recesses of our hearts. In this new world, in which good becomes evil and that which is evil becomes good, Crowley would be seen by a new society as being a moral man, a hero even. One who simply wants what is best for everyone, not withholding anything. Like the serpent in the garden, he only wants to free us from the shackles of authority and the definition that has been cast upon us."

Lewis examined Doolittle and drank from his pint. The man's eye twitched, but Jack continued, "It is a struggle we all wrestle with to some degree, is it not? To convince ourselves that what is dark in our hearts is right, good, and justified in our own eyes and that we are within our right to see it revealed. Crowley is simply doing what millions of others would like to do, and to some degree, I can't help but applaud him for it."

Doolittle clenched his jaw. "I would caution against using Crowley as a source," he responded slowly. "The man is more likely to use you than you are him. He'll twist your words, your motives, and your mind. And I know from experience that Crowley is a small, petty, and spiteful man." Doolittle's tone emphasized his disdain. "He is not fascinating or interesting or worthy of applause in any sphere of society. He is no more than a common charlatan, showman, and fabricator of lies."

"It sounds as though you know him personally," Cecil remarked. "Do you?"

"I do, in fact," Mortimer confirmed, as another pint of ale was set in front of him. "He and I were at Cambridge together decades ago. This was back when he was known by his real name—Edward Alexander Crowley." He drank and wiped his mouth. "I was the one who introduced him to Rose Kelly, the woman who would later become his wife before she went insane and drank herself into oblivion. A shame that was, and what a waste of a beautiful young woman." He drank half his glass as Warren, Cecil, and Jack sat in silence, not daring to say a word and inadvertently change the subject.

"We were also in a club of sorts some time ago." Doolittle leaned back in his chair and fumbled with an unlit cigarette. "This was again back in our Cambridge days and for some years after."

"Like an art or drama club?" Cecil prodded.

"No, more like a supernatural club. It was a spiritual thing." Doolittle eyed the three aloof yet curious onlookers. "We were, you could say, at the time obsessed with certain mystical pursuits, magic, divination, spells, necromancy, and the like. Obtaining power at any cost. The lustful things all young men crave. Though some never grow out of it."

"What do you mean by 'at any cost'?" Lewis questioned, looking as disinterested as possible as he lit his cigarette.

"It means just what I said," Doolittle snapped. "The members of the club got to where they were capturing small animals for their silly magical ceremonies, saying they were going to offer them up to some strange deity like Bacchus or Mithra, all to gain wisdom or a better grade on an essay, or for the love of a girl or boy. All of it made my skin crawl. I couldn't be part of it any longer, and I left." Doolittle laughed as he remembered. "It was absurd, if you think about it. A bunch of grown men wearing dresses and pretending to do magic. Besides, none of it worked. I gained nothing from the experience except a few years of bad dreams, hangovers, and a depleted bank account. You can thank Crowley for that."

"Do you suppose he still does that sort of thing?" Warren asked. "Cruelty, sacrifices, and whatnot?"

Mortimer shook his head. "I don't know. Crowley wouldn't risk jail. He's too smart and loves his freedom too much. But if not him, maybe some of his followers would partake in things I'd rather not mention. Insane attracts crazy, and I saw it in most of their eyes. Absolutely terrifying, the feeble minds in his grip, especially Baron Huxley. I wanted no part of it. I have vices of my own to deal with."

"Don't we all?" Cecil raised his glass and flashed a dazzling smile. "I suppose we all have our secrets."

"Who is Baron Huxley?" Lewis said, with a practiced quizzical expression.

"A member," Doolittle said with disdain. "I'd rather not discuss him." He swirled his drink. "I do know something embarrassing he'd like to keep secret," Doolittle added. "About Crowley that is." A slight slur was noticeable in his voice as a sly smile began to spread across his reddening face.

"Don't hold us in suspense." Cecil leaned forward over his plate. "Spill it or I'm taking my family's art to Paris."

Doolittle held out his hands in mock surrender, and Lewis's ears pricked. This was what they'd come here for, the little cherry on top to end the evening.

"A year or so ago, Crowley filed for bankruptcy," Doolittle disclosed, with a bit of smugness. "I have a friend who works for a well-known bank in London, and he thought I might be amused. I was, especially after learning that Crowley showed up one day demanding, and then begging, for a personal loan. I was delighted at first but even more tickled when I heard the bank refused and threatened to remove him forcefully. They weren't going to fund his magical experiments and pay for his lustful escapades and drug habits."

Mortimer finished another glass of ale and wiped lazily at his mouth. "And to think, all those years earlier, even before the war, I had ideas that would have made us all rich men, Crowley included. And when I finally shared them, my grand business ideas, Crowley said I would spoil it. That he was about true magic and the pursuit of the divine in all of us." He shook his head. "Imagine that. Crowley claiming to be a purist, and I was the stain on something otherwise beautiful." Doolittle leaned back in his chair and belched loudly. "For all I care, Aleister Crowley can go straight to hell."

{14} The Chalkboard

Thursday, December 17

There is nothing like looking, if you want to find something. . . . You certainly usually find something, if you look, but it is not always quite the something you were after.

—J. R. R. Tolkien, *The Hobbit*

Tolkien rapped on the door three times. He heard voices inside, followed by laughter and possibly a baritone singing. *Dyson must have already arrived.* He knocked again, this time using the bottom of his fist instead of knuckles.

He was soon let in and received warmly by a smiling Warren. "Good to see you again, Tollers." Over Warren's shoulder, Tolkien saw Dyson with his hands spread wide, enthusiastically telling a tale to an enthralled Adam Fox. Jack sat in his second-favorite chair reading a creased trifold letter with a frown while absentmindedly smoking a cigarette.

"How's the boat?" Tolkien asked, taking off his homburg hat and twirling it with his free hand.

Warren laughed and slapped the professor on the back,

nearly spilling his drink. "Everyone is so curious about that blasted boat. May have to wait until the spring thaw to re-paint her. She'll be all tarped up until then."

Lewis's Magdalen room was mildly cramped yet workable, with a small open area now filled with two burnt orange cushioned chairs; a low, tufted, and well-worn chesterfield sofa; and one extra simple chair brought up from a downstairs classroom. A chalkboard on wheels from that same classroom now sat against the far wall, next to a double window that overlooked the dark and empty quad. Curtains were pulled open to reveal the outline of the Great Tower looming at the far end like a sleeping giant. The chairs and small couch had all been arranged to point toward the chalkboard, unironically in a half-moon shape. Jack had moved his bedside lamp nearer, with its shade positioned lateral to cast an orangish incandescent glow on the wiped-clean slate board.

Tolkien made his way over to greet Fox and Dyson. A dry bar off to one side near the lavatory contained a few open bottles and a metal bowl of half-melted ice. The other side of the room held a simple writing desk and, in the corner, a small bed barely larger than a cot, with a thin mattress and a cream-colored wool blanket folded neatly at the foot. On the far wall, a small fire burned behind an iron fireguard.

Despite its modest look, the room was a blessing. Unused student dormitories were usually offered to senior professors, and Lewis, though not that senior, was fortunate enough to cast his lot and secure one. There was far more room with only one person using the space as a residence than the usual two, three, or even four students who would regularly share a dormitory of similar size. The best thing about Lewis's room was that it was completely private, perfect for tonight's function. The rooms adjacent were a broom closet and a faculty lounge that was used only during the day. In the evenings, this became the place for confidential conversation between friends or even the occasional cramming in of seven men.

Tolkien took a chair next to Lewis, who was still reading the letter, perhaps for the third or fourth time. After a minute, Lewis removed his glasses, set the missive on a nearby side table atop a cream-colored envelope with a broken wax seal, and scrunched his unkempt brow.

"Anything interesting?" Tolkien quizzed in a hushed tone.

"Oh very," Lewis replied absently, "very interesting indeed. I may have a busy weekend."

Charles Williams appeared in the doorway just after Cecil. He was the last to arrive, and since it was his first visit to the Magdalen room, Warren felt the need to take him on a protracted roundabout tour, which was completed in under a minute. Williams stood near Lewis and Tolkien, and the three exchanged pleasantries.

After a few minutes of friendly talk, it was time for all to be seated and get down to the business of the evening. Six men sat in a half circle. Tolkien, the seventh, now stood up front. He would lead the evening's brainstorming.

"Thank you all for coming tonight," he began as he leaned over and tapped out his pipe into a pewter ashtray. "And thank you to Jack for letting us all crash your bachelor pad." That elicited a chuckle from everyone. "We have much to discuss, but first I wanted to say that Nevill sends his regards. He could not be here tonight. The stage production will conclude in a few days, and he wishes he could do more."

Tolkien extended his hand toward the sofa. "In his place, one could say, Charles Williams has joined us to complete the seven, and we are glad for it."

All eyes went to Charles, who was squished on the sofa between Warren and Hugo. He saluted once he got his arm free, then adjusted his glasses, which had fallen down the bridge of his nose.

"We have now completed the first week of our investigation," Tolkien went on. "I would like to use this evening to discuss openly four areas of highest priority in the case. The first is corroborating what we know of the victims, the second is listing our current suspects or persons of interest, the third is to discuss the evidence or potential evidence thus far in our investigation, and the fourth and final order of business is simply to give individual assignments to those willing and able to complete them in this week leading up to Christmas."

Tolkien paused and chose his words carefully. "I feel I need to make sure you are all aware of the timetable we are under. Unless we can collectively solve this crime and find the culprit very soon, there is a strong likelihood that there will be another murder eleven days from now on Monday, December 28. And no, we do not know who that victim could be, though we will discuss some possibilities before we conclude tonight."

Tolkien turned in the ensuing silence, a fresh piece of chalk in hand, and wrote the name Baron Huxley in an elegant scroll on the chalkboard. "The first victim was Baron Huxley," he recounted. "He was killed during a full moon, on All Hallows' Eve. His body was found in his bathtub by Aleister Crowley, who says there was an occult symbol carved into his hand." Tolkien held out his palm. "The number 418, which, if you have read my transcript of the interview, you know is significant within this secret Order of the Golden Dawn." Tolkien faced the six onlookers. "So, what else do we know of the first victim?" He shifted his gaze to Dyson. "Hugo, have you got anything for us?"

Hugo Dyson cleared his throat. "A Coventry man," he announced boisterously. "Huxley had known Crowley, Beckworth, MacDougall, Pennington, and whoever else was a part of this blasted Order of the Golden Dawn, for nearly thirty years. I was also able to find out he owed a large sum of money to our second victim, Lord Roger Pennington." That news elicited a few low murmurs between Fox and Warren.

Tolkien wrote the word *debt* next to Huxley, then wrote the name Pennington below that. He drew a curving line between the two.

"We'll come back to Huxley, but for now that brings us to our next murder victim." Tolkien drew a breath. "Lord Roger Pennington was killed nearly three weeks ago on November 29, which also happened to be a full moon. He was found by his housekeeper, whom I will discuss in a moment, and soon after by Lords Beckworth and MacDougall, who were interviewed last Saturday at White's club in London."

Tolkien walked over to where his jacket hung on a brass hook and fished a small leather journal from his hip pocket. He leafed through a few pages until he found what he was looking for. "I interviewed the housekeeper," he continued, "a Ms. Sarah Cornish, and learned some interesting things. First, Roger Pennington has a son, Francis Pennington, who may have been in some financial trouble of his own. He may have had reason to hate his father because, according to the housekeeper, Lord Pennington recently refused to provide him financial assistance. Also, Francis Pennington is the heir to his father's fortune and has already placed the London home up for sale. Each of these actions is highly suspect."

"Very suspicious," Fox agreed, which garnered a few nods of assent.

"I would think money to be a worthy motive for a few of our suspects, which leaves only means and opportunity in those cases." Tolkien consulted his notes again. "Ms. Cornish also informed me that Lord Pennington had not been feeling well for the last few weeks before his death. He'd began experiencing disturbing symptoms of feeling as though his flesh were burning, and he started pulling out his hair. I don't know if these symptoms were psychosomatic or . . ."

"I would suspect poison," Lewis inserted matter-of-factly.

"Would you care to share more?" Fox shifted in his seat to face Lewis.

"Not quite yet," Lewis answered. "Sorry for the interruption, Tollers, but I'm hoping to arrange a meeting that may be able to clear up some of the confusion. I've reached out to an old friend and have only just received a partial reply." He glanced at the letter on the side table. "But we know Pennington did not die of asphyxiation, as the Yard wrongly believes, and I may have an alternative solution, though I'm not yet fully certain. It might all come to naught."

"We all look forward to hearing more on that subject very soon," Fox said.

"Something similar was happening to Huxley," Dyson interjected. "He was unusually sore and losing his hair in clumps. I don't think it a coincidence that both men experienced such strange and acute symptoms before they died."

Tolkien nodded and thumbed through the pages of his notebook. "That is a very interesting development, among others, and one deserving of further pursuit. On the whole, it solidifies, at least in my mind, that these murders are indeed connected and that a single murderer is to blame for both."

"I would agree," Fox stated. "Seems prudent to proceed with that connection in mind."

"Finally," Tolkien told them, "I believe that a young boy I met when I went to interview Sarah Cornish is her son, not her sister's, and I believe the father of that boy is, or was, Lord Roger Pennington himself."

Dyson gasped. The others all started talking at once. Tolkien wrote the word *son* on the chalkboard and stood patiently waiting.

"What makes you think so?" Fox questioned, once all eyes were again focused on Tolkien.

"Well, first of all," the professor began, "the boy looks like him . . . like Pennington, I mean. At least from the photograph I saw. He also looks like his mother and not his aunt. Sarah is handsome and strong, and she looked to be the type a wealthy man might desire as a mistress. Beyond that, she mentioned she needed to help out around the house to earn 'our' keep. She didn't say 'my' keep; she said 'our.' I didn't notice at the time, but it came to me later."

Tolkien scanned the men before him. "I believe the child was and had been staying with her sister in Bath, but I would wager good money that the boy belonged to the housekeeper. And the only reason to keep the child hidden or not make his existence plain would be because of some sort of shame or societal pressure. An affair, most likely, and given the age of the child, Pennington's late wife would've still been alive at the time of infidelity. Ms. Cornish also mentioned Roger Pennington was a good father. This was right after describing to me the way Roger and his elder son, Francis, fought and argued. I got the sense she was saying that Roger had been a good father to their shared son, for what it's worth. She also mentioned that if still alive, Roger would never have dismissed her and cast her out, as the elder son and heir did. No, I think there is a great possibility that she was hiding something, and . . ." He paused. "Possibly hiding even more than the parentage of the child."

"Do you suspect her as a killer?" Fox pressed. "Is she capable of it?"

Tolkien nodded. "She is indeed capable of it. As we all are. Perhaps she truly loved the man and her affections were scorned. Perhaps he meant to cut off the boy and had said as much. Who knows really?"

"Does she have knowledge of the occult?" Charles Williams spoke up for the first time.

"Not that I know of," Tolkien replied. "I didn't see any telltale titles on her bookshelf, though that sort of information could easily be hidden. She was, however, working for over a decade in the household of a man very involved with the Order. Certain things could be picked up by one who has ears to listen through doorways. Nevertheless, I will continue in that vein and investigate the Pennington angle further." Tolkien then looked at Lewis. "Jack, if you would take over from here—I feel you are more familiar with the other lines of investigation."

Lewis stood and accepted the piece of chalk while Tolkien took the open chair. "Where to begin?" Lewis mumbled, more to himself than anyone else. He then drew a line in the middle of the chalkboard from top to bottom and wrote the numbers 1 and 2 just to the right side of the line. "Our list of suspects is as follows. We have the two that were just mentioned: first, Francis Pennington, the angry son who seeks to take the fortune by force that his father would not freely give, and, second, the scorned maid, who is surely hiding secrets and may be hiding more."

Lewis wrote the first name next to the number 1 and the second next to 2. He then wrote out 3, 4, and 5 in descending order. "There is a mutual understanding that perhaps a former disgruntled member of the Order of the Golden Dawn is to blame for both these murders given the details. But it could just as easily be a current member of the Order or an outsider who may have learned enough to shift the suspicion. The housekeeper and older son both fit that bill. Perhaps they learned certain things from Pennington and the company he kept and thought a ritualistic killing would clear them of wrongdoing and instead cast it onto members of the Order."

"But what connection does Francis Pennington have with Huxley?" Dyson frowned. "He was the first victim, not the boy's father."

"Yes, that is true." Fox raised a finger. "And in the same way, what about Sarah and Huxley? I don't see any connection there either."

Lewis cleared his throat. "Just because we don't see the connection doesn't mean there isn't one. It only remains to be seen. This is why we investigate further."

Tolkien then spoke up. "It does make more sense to me that both these suspects would fit somehow with Pennington but not Huxley. We would need to distinguish the means, motive, and opportunity for both murders, not just the one."

Lewis nodded. "That brings up a good question. How were our two victims, Huxley and Pennington, connected beyond the Order? That connection could be the link between the son or the housekeeper and both men."

"Perhaps they had business dealings together," Fox suggested quickly. "Especially since we've already established the exchanging of monies and debt. It would make sense for men in the Order to use that relationship to their advantage in many areas of life. No doubt his son and staff would have met Huxley . . ."

Lewis glanced at Dyson. "Something worth investigating further, and I'd say you're the man for it."

Dyson smiled and inclined his head in acceptance of his extended role.

Lewis paused before continuing with his next thought. "The third suspect is Mortimer Doolittle. He is truly a vile man, as I have now personally witnessed, and his vitriol for anyone currently having to do with the Order of the Golden Dawn is easy to see. This man was hurt or wronged in some way long ago. If our motives thus far are greed from the son and misplaced love from the maid, then perhaps Mortimer's motive would be vengeance for some act yet to be discovered."

"Doolittle is a bit of a fraud," Warren added. "The man doesn't truly know anything about history, though he poses as a student of it. He likes the idea of history—of kings, castles, wealth, and thrones—but in my opinion, that's all it is, a desire to live in a bygone era where all would grovel at his feet."

"I would agree with your assessment," his younger brother said, "but when Crowley and the Order were brought up, there was definite hatred there." Lewis lit the cigarette that Tolkien handed him and continued. "The fourth suspect is Aleister Crowley himself. He found the first body, and he doesn't have a sound alibi for the time of the second since he claims he was home alone in his rented London flat. When it comes to Crowley, lying is a second language, so we don't know what to believe or not. He may have cast suspicion on Mortimer Doolittle simply to take it off himself."

"Whether a murderer or not," Charles Williams remarked, "simply as a witness, the man cannot be trusted. It will be important to have physical evidence or secondary corroboration to confirm anything he says."

"But why would Crowley kill Huxley or Pennington?" Fox wondered. "What would his motivation be? From what I heard, those two men were practically bankrolling Crowley's lifestyle—his trips, his benders, his adventures, his magic, and even his writing projects."

"Excellent question," Lewis noted. "According to Doolittle, Crowley is some sort of magical purist. Money is secondary to the craft. Maybe Huxley and Pennington offended him in some way. Perhaps they wanted the seat of honor in the Order. Either way, murder is in no way beyond him, and the murderer would need to have knowledge of the occult and some personal vengeance to do it. Charles is helping me understand more of Crowley's history and his mindset, but guilty or not, I still think something in his past holds the key to this whole thing."

Warren spoke up. "We also learned from Doolittle that Crowley filed for bankruptcy last year."

"Really." Fox arched a brow and smiled faintly. He always loved a bit of gossip mixed into an investigation.

"It is true," Lewis affirmed. "Not many know this, but the man was in desperate need of money. Pennington and Huxley were two of his main financial backers, so even those wells have now dried up. It is as though the murderer—if it is not Crowley for some motive yet to be discovered—is targeting Crowley indirectly. At least that is one theory."

"I have some London banking contacts," Cecil offered. "I was planning to confirm whether the news of the bankruptcy is true or not after I heard it last night. Just give me the weekend and it will be done."

"Very good." Fox slapped his hands on his knees. "This is all very interesting. Very intriguing indeed." He then turned to Tolkien. "Did you get the sense that Beckworth and MacDougall suspected Crowley in any way of being behind these murders?"

"Good question, but difficult to say," Tolkien responded. "Both had respect bordering on fear of the man. But who knows if that trepidation was and is based on respect for their superior or fear of his violent nature? However, if he were the murderer, it would also make sense that he would want to be in the room when Beckworth and MacDougall told us their story. A way to control the narrative through intimidation."

"Speaking of Lord Beckworth and being filled with fear . . ." Cecil drew out the words. "I am planning to meet up with him tomorrow if one of you would like to join me. I think he's a bit afraid that if we're not able to solve this soon, his life is in danger and he could very well be the next victim. He also asked me to join him the night of the full moon at his country estate and to bring along a hunting rifle if I had one."

"The man could die of fright well before the full moon," Warren quipped, which elicited a few low rumbles of laughter until the seriousness of the topic came flooding back.

"Also," Cecil went on, "as was mentioned, the Pennington house is up for sale. There is a public viewing, but it's Saturday."

"We're going," Tolkien decided quickly. "You and I."

"But Saturday I always spend the day in bed. You know this."

"Not this Saturday," Tolkien replied firmly. "And could you change the date of your meeting with Beckworth to Saturday as well? I'd like to be there and ask him a few questions without Crowley being present."

"Oh, I like it!" Fox grinned from ear to ear. "The professor has a plan."

"Very well," Cecil conceded, somewhat irritated yet seeing the wisdom of the plan. They would be able to question Francis, view the place where the murder took place, and speak to Beckworth all at once.

"There is a fifth suspect," Lewis stated, still standing quietly by the board, chalk in hand. All eyes slowly turned to refocus their attention on him.

"And who might that be?" Fox quizzed.

Lewis drew a question mark next to the number five. "We should not be so naïve as to think it must be one of the four we've mentioned. It could very well be someone we have not settled our gazes on. Someone hiding in the shadows or in plain sight. Perhaps even watching us."

A collective shiver passed through the room as if a window had been left open. In the silence, Warren rose and tossed two small logs on the fire and kindled it back to life with an iron poker.

"We focus on means, motive, and opportunity," Lewis emphasized, tapping the board with chalk. "Stay alert and keep your eyes open. Who has the ability to murder, the knowledge needed, and the driving motive? I have a feeling this is going to get much darker before we see the light at the end of the tunnel."

Before long, the chalkboard session came to an end. Fox and Cecil made their exits soon afterward with handshakes and good wishes all around. Then Charles departed for his hotel room near the train station, followed by Dyson and Warren, who always loved to prolong good company. Warren saluted and began whistling an old Irish folk tune as he made his way down the hall toward the stairwell that would lead to his bicycle. Tolkien stayed back, pretending to leaf through his journal.

"What is it, old boy?" Lewis asked, moving toward his favorite chair. He could feel a familiar exhaustion washing over him.

"We may be looking at this all wrong." Tolkien tapped his finger on the leather of his journal. "We're each pursuing different leads. Only one will lead to anything. The others are only wasting time."

Lewis sighed. "Perhaps all these trails we blaze will come to nothing, and *everything* we do here is only a fruitless waste of time."

"That was encouraging," Tolkien said dryly.

Lewis smiled. "But even more likely, though not all will be fruitful, surely something of substance will come from it. We know not every suspect is a killer, even if they are not moral or likable people. We know not every interview ends with useful information or a viable lead, and not every piece of evidence is evidence at all."

Tolkien furrowed his brow. "This has the makings of being a frustrating and discouraging hobby, I think."

Lewis pinched the bridge of his nose with thumb and forefinger. "What in God's name have we gotten ourselves into, Tollers?"

Tolkien grinned for the first time all night. "Yes, Jack, whatever were we thinking? I never thought our role in the battle of good and evil would look quite like this." He gestured toward the chalkboard.

"Yet here we are," Lewis mused, "scribbling chalk on a board as if it's our only weapon."

Tolkien took his jacket from the hook and put it on, then made his way slowly toward the door. Just before he exited, he looked back through the room and noticed something. Lewis followed his gaze, and both men knew exactly what the other was thinking. Through the window they saw the widening sliver of moon emerging from behind a bank of clouds. The glow was a constant not-so-gentle reminder to both men of the immensely crushing weight they now carried.

{15} The Solicitor

Friday, December 18

> There is no surer or more illuminating way of reading a man's character, and perhaps a little of his past history, than by observing the contexts in which he prefers to use certain words.
>
> —Owen Barfield, *History in English Words*

As the late night drifted into the wee morning hours, Lewis wound down his long day with a snifter of blackberry brandy while staring at the chalkboard now covered with symbols, names, earlier lists that had been mostly obscured by midnight, and a thrice circled number 418 with a question mark next to it. When the chalk became a painful jumble in his mind, Lewis lit his final cigarette of the night, turned off the glowing lamp, and watched the moon peek momentarily out of the clouds only to fall back into shadow.

Lewis was able to get only a few hours of restless sleep before he was awakened naturally by the brightness of the rising sun beaming through the still-open curtains. He groaned and sat up, sliding from under the bed a brown suitcase that held an extra change of wrinkled clothes for exactly these types of situations. He checked his pocket watch, which was laid out on the bedside table, and hurried his pace.

The Eastgate Hotel lay just across the street from the Magdalen College library. The hotel was a simple tan-stoned building with a wall of windows facing the High Street. Its first-level bar and popular art deco eatery were a frequent meeting spot for Lewis any time of day, be it a quick early bite before a lecture or tutoring or a late evening drink with friends who did not yet want to retreat home.

Lewis spotted Owen Barfield already seated at the usual corner table near the window, looking out at a line of robed students nervously making their way in small groupings to the final day of oral exams before beginning their holiday. Barfield stood and smiled as his old friend approached. The lawyer instinctively buttoned the top button of his tailored, dark navy three-button notched-lapel suit, which featured a crisp, horizontally striped tie complete with a silver tie clasp engraved with a scrolling letter *B*. Lewis made his way over the black-and-white checkered flooring, past wooden tables covered with cream-colored linen cloths.

Lewis always felt a bit of a slob compared to Barfield, who, as usual, looked altogether a handsome and clean-cut gentleman, with square jaw on a chiseled face below a perfectly coiffed head of hair. As a former professional dancer, Barfield was strong, athletic, and still in as good of shape as he had been almost twenty years earlier when he and Lewis attended Oxford together. It was strange to Lewis how men so different in upbringing and other aspects of life could be so similar in others. The two were from different worlds, yet they had become instant friends because of shared interests in poetry, fantasy, spirituality, medieval literature, and a general sense of imaginative wonder at the world around them.

Still, despite their similar interests, many of their deeply held views were polar opposites.

After shaking hands, embracing, and each commenting on how the other looked, both men sat, and Barfield used a small spoon to continue stirring his tea with lemon. "Your tea and egg are on their way," he noted, to which Lewis smiled faintly and glanced toward the glossy wooden bar where a swinging door with a porthole led to the kitchen. He sniffed and noticed how much the restaurant smelled of breakfast meats. His mouth watered, but he decided to settle for the egg and not say a word about it.

"It was a long night," Lewis told him. "Chalkboard session."

"Ah yes," Barfield responded, "a fresh mystery, I hear. And if it makes you feel any better, I hardly slept a wink either. Fox sent a page to the port where the ship came in yesterday morning. A letter was handed to me the moment I stepped off the gangplank." Barfield regarded Lewis. "Quite the scrum you and Tollers have gotten yourselves into. I can't say I'm not glad to be sitting this one out."

Lewis sighed and folded his hands on the tabletop. "Well, that's just it. You don't have to be sidelined. We'd love your help, if only in a small way. Do you wish to be brought up to speed, or do you really want to sit out the second half?" Lewis lit his first cigarette of the day. "We could use someone with your mind and connections, and we may need some legal advice before this whole thing is over."

Barfield frowned. "I don't like the sound of either option. Of course I want to know everything, but I also can't get involved. Maud and I are only here for a few days; then we are leaving for Liverpool for two weeks, until well after the new year. I'm afraid I won't be of much use in this, Jack. And before you suggest it, if I bailed on her, I might be the one getting murdered, and it wouldn't take much of an investigation to know exactly what had happened."

Both men chuckled at this as a young woman with red hair brought Lewis a mug of Earl Grey tea and set a hard-boiled egg, placed upright in a white porcelain egg cup, in front of each man.

"How about I give you a quick bite as we enjoy these eggs and we'll leave it at that?" Lewis offered.

"Only a tiny nibble may be enough to get me on the line." Barfield scratched at his chin. "But you already know I'll risk it. How's Janie?"

"Fine, fine," Lewis answered. "Busy as always. Finding things to do. I feel she's less pleasant with each passing year, but it may be all in my mind."

Barfield stifled a laugh as he took a spoon and cracked his egg with a single tap. "You have that to look forward to. The oaths we swore out of the goodness of our hearts."

Lewis reached into his inner breast pocket, pulled out a folded cream-colored envelope, and handed it to Barfield.

"What is this?" Barfield examined the broken red wax seal and pulled out the folded parchment.

"I reached out to Dorothy earlier in the week." Lewis leaned forward in his chair and spoke in hushed tones. "I needed a favor related to the case, and as always, she has a list of demands. Not exactly sure how to take it. She sent back a letter, an invitation really. You'll see."

Barfield read each line of the letter with rising amusement. As he placed it back in the envelope, he smiled widely and shook his head. "That's Dorothy for you. So, I assume you wanted her help setting up a meeting with Agatha?"

"That is correct, and she agreed to set it up, but as you

can see, there are stipulations. I have to promise to do all three, or she will not merely refuse to put in a good word and arrange the meeting but instead use her influence to oppose it and make sure the get-together never happens."

Barfield snickered. "Oh my, that woman is a force of nature and a piece of work. Three nights in a row, *and* a luncheon? Do you even own three jackets? It sounds like she's got you over a barrel and you don't have a choice. Although most men would jump at the chance to attend any of those events. There is a certain level of exclusivity."

"I am not most men," Lewis replied evenly. "I have to work myself up to go out one night on a weekend, and she wants my company three nights in a row."

Barfield continued to look amused at the whole situation. "She admires you, Jack. Though I'm not sure why. You must realize it."

Lewis looked offended. "Of course I do. I consider her a close friend as well."

"You know I'll be at that one"—Barfield pointed to one line from the letter—"the gaudy tomorrow night at the Queen's College. Why do you think I was so keen to get back here so soon from America? We could have stayed an extra week, then gone directly to Liverpool. It was closer . . . But no, I never miss a good Boar's Head Gaudy."

Lewis furrowed his brow. "I don't see the appeal. How did you even get an invite? I thought only alumni and university administration were invited."

Barfield sipped his tea and glanced out the window at students passing with muffled shouts. "Our law firm does some work for the administration. We get a few invitations every year, and every year I claim one. Perks of having my name on the sign. The more important question is how Dorothy got an invite. She went to Somerville College, not the Queen's."

Lewis said enthusiastically, "I hear she's a guest of honor this year. Requested me to come see her in all her feminine glory. Her latest book—*Gaudy Night,* I think it is called—was based in part on the event and the college, and they wanted to honor the book's success and her with it. She had a plus one, and I suppose no one else wanted to go with her, so now I am being forced to attend."

"I haven't read that one." Barfield grinned. "I've never been much for crime novels."

"I've read it," Lewis confided, "and personally, I didn't like it much. But don't tell her that. Some of her writing is quite good. I just didn't like that story."

"All this for the Queen of Crime herself," Barfield mused. "I never thought I'd see you attend the gaudy, let alone a dinner in London and a stage play all in the same weekend."

"It should be exciting, if I survive it." Lewis feigned apathy, then changed the subject. "Tell me, out of curiosity, what do you know of Aleister Crowley?"

Barfield frowned. "I heard he was a part of all this. All the more reason I should stay far away from the case." He pondered for a moment. "If you had asked me this question fifteen years ago, I may have even said I admired the man, or at least some part of his own unique spiritual journey. Of course, now I see that it was all a road leading off a cliff, but at the time, if you remember, it was so very real and different. Almost a counterfeit purity to it all, like fake silk or a wig." Barfield lit a cigarette and pulled gently on it.

"What do you mean?" Lewis shifted his weight and settled into his creaking chair.

"You were there, Jack," Barfield responded, exhaling. "You saw how my mind was so easily corrupted. The new ideas, the new spirituality, a little bit of Eastern thought mixed with Western. We were not so different, he and I, though I never actually met Crowley." He studied Lewis. "You know all about this, Jack, how my pursuits led to a great conflict even between you and me, and that was back when you were an atheist."

"Refresh my memory," Lewis prodded. "What was the basis of your thinking? What was your motivation? What drove you then? It may be important to get into the mind of a killer."

Barfield nodded but eyed his friend Jack curiously. He took another moment to gather his thoughts. "I became convinced that experience was all that mattered. The brain, logic, reason, and truth gave way and were of less importance than the heart and how I felt. Emotions had become my new truth. A sort of spiritual lust I know you are familiar with, though in vastly different manifestations. There were, and still are, striking similarities between all mystery religions and forms of Gnostic thought. They all essentially pointed down a similar road, which is the pursuit of God on our terms rather than His, and when that happens, sometimes the god we find at the end of the road isn't the one we thought we had been seeking. Perhaps it's even just an ugly, twisted version of ourselves."

He paused, waiting for a reply, but Lewis said only, "Go on."

"Well, over time I became convinced that elements I believed to be absolutes in my youth were riddled with fallacies, which I am still wrestling with to this day. I believed that I was doing God's work and that my newfound views were not only Christian but a vital part of what Christianity would and should become. Little did I know that much of it was all a fine-sounding lie, a subtle repackaging of similar heresies of the first and second centuries. I was caught up in the enormous excitement of those days and the mysterious passion waiting to be discovered."

"And of motivation?" Lewis asked. "What prompted your pursuit beyond this spiritual lust you mentioned?"

"I would say I had good and noble intentions if not even a little bit selfish." Barfield answered slowly, thinking and remembering as he spoke. "But in all my steps and decisions, I let my emotions lead rather than the truth. This is well and good if the strongest emotions are love, compassion, and joy. But when anger, envy, and bitterness take hold, that is where trouble springs forth." He shook his head. "I was not alone in this pursuit. The pressures of society and friend groups played a role during that time. Interest in the mystical and interweaving paganism into orthodox faith were all the rage during the last decade, as you are well aware." Barfield looked up and met Lewis's eye.

"Now, how is what you just said related to murder?" Jack questioned plainly.

Barfield raised a brow. "I suppose we are talking about murder, aren't we? And all this would be connected to some motive. When a person is led by their emotions, it is contagious, and sometimes that path includes wrath and hatred strong enough to act on."

Lewis nodded. "An act of anger can be just as pleasurable to one man as narcotics could be to another."

"It's all release," Barfield added. "It could be that these murders are just that—a release of some sort. And I wish you all the best in solving it."

Jack opened his mouth to speak, then closed it.

Seeming to sense what he'd started to say, Barfield preemptively agreed. "Fine, I'll do one small favor related to your case. But it must be something I can complete before I leave Tuesday morning."

Jack smiled. "You know me too well. Perhaps you can use your legal network to dig up something on Crowley and let me know if he comes to town. Knowing Crowley, he'd likely stay in the nicest hotel."

"Consider it done. I'm owed a few favors." Barfield knocked on the table. "One should watch his back with Crowley around."

"Speaking of . . ." Lewis's smile faded. "I truly think I am being followed."

Barfield pursed his lips. His eyes naturally shifted toward the door. "I'll keep that in mind, Jack. And I gather you think Crowley may be behind it? On a happier note, Maud sends her greetings, and also, I feel you'll be pleasantly surprised when you find out tonight who the president of the Detection Club is."

"Who is it?" Lewis pressed, as Barfield slid the letter from Dorothy Sayers back toward him across the tabletop.

"Oh no, I'm not going to spoil this," Barfield replied with a sly grin. "Trust me when I say you'll be more than glad you went."

Lewis made a face. "In that case, I guess I've decided it's worth it for me to agree to her demands."

{16} The Detectives

> Fairy tales do not give the child his first idea of [the dragon but] his first clear idea of the possible defeat of [the dragon]. The baby has known the dragon intimately ever since he had an imagination. What the fairy tale provides for him is a St. George to kill the dragon.
>
> —G. K. CHESTERTON, "The Red Angel"

Later that evening, Lewis stepped off the train at Paddington station for the second time in one week. The last time he'd done anything like that had been fifteen, if not twenty, years ago. The sun had just set as Lewis walked eastward out from under the station's massive arched ceiling. He climbed a set of concrete stairs and emerged onto the busy London streets just as a double-decker bus zoomed past, nearly splashing water on his freshly polished brown shoes.

His destination wasn't far. Only a dozen blocks or so. Lewis had opted to save the money for a cab and instead taken an earlier train to account for the walking time. He wore a dark navy blazer with matching trousers, a minimally rumpled white collared shirt, silver cuff links, and a navy-and-crimson striped bow tie that Warren had lent him. He already felt uncomfortable, and with each step toward the event past flickering streetlamps, he felt increasingly so because of both the suit and the unfamiliar social territory he was walking into.

The annual holiday dinner of the London Detection Club was held in a nondescript yet spacious catering hall on a corner near the Regent's Park. The interior of the rented hall, part of an old Victorian hotel conference room, was well lit by multiple chandeliers and filled front to back with many rectangular tables placed together in a large horseshoe shape for tonight's event. At the open far end, a stage had been set up with a square podium and fixed microphone. *There will be speeches,* Lewis thought. He observed the white-paneled walls that held wired sconces spaced evenly around the exterior, casting a soft glow up toward the ornately molded cove ceiling. Lewis hadn't known what to expect from the event, only that his presence was a necessary condition of Dorothy's assistance, and thus far, it didn't look all that dreadful. Of the guests who had already arrived—nearly half by his count of all the chairs—most had made their way over to a linen-clothed serving counter where drinks and hors d'oeuvres were set out with a sort of Christmas-meets-the-tropics theme. Lewis meandered over and had just dipped a shrimp into cocktail sauce when he heard a familiar voice behind him.

"Jack, it's been too long." Dorothy Sayers spoke in a husky tone, her hand held out toward him. "You look nice, very well put together. That jacket is two sizes too large, though. It must be Warren's."

"Good to see you as well, Dorothy," Lewis responded, frowning, but playfully so.

She smiled widely and winked. A familiar sarcastic grin

formed deep dimples in her pale cheeks. "You, too, Jack, but I am right about the jacket."

Dorothy Sayers had a round, plain face, with thin lips that were held in a sort of continual pout when she was not forcing herself to smile. Her hair was pulled into a bun tightly pinned up high on her head. Large seashell earrings and an emerald necklace comprised her jewelry, besides a single ring on her right hand, which featured an ivory profile of Queen Victoria. Dorothy wore small circular glasses and an almost masculine boxy dark green blazer with a silver brooch pinned over her left breast in the shape of the Queen's College crest.

"You look lovely," Lewis remarked.

"I know," Dorothy agreed. "I feel like I did when I was young and slim and full of energy, back when life lay out in front of me like a buffet." She gestured toward the food and smirked playfully. Out of thin air, she produced a cigarette that had been placed in a brass holder. It would be a rare feat indeed to catch Dorothy when she was not smoking. Lewis took her hand as they both politely bowed to each other. Dorothy then flung one end of an ermine fur wrap back over her shoulder and squeezed up next to Lewis.

She blew smoke toward Lewis out the side of her mouth before starting to walk forward, bidding him to follow her with a curled finger.

"Is this your first time?" she asked over her shoulder. "Of course it is. Why else would you have come? I'm not speaking tonight, so I can sit with you at least for part of dinner. I don't suppose you know anyone else here, though you are a writer, but a much different type." She glanced back to make sure Lewis was still following her through the crowd. "I'm taking you to meet Ronald. He will be speaking tonight. It will be Ronald, Gilbert, and Agatha, in that order: the president, the godfather, and the queen. It's a rare thing for all three to be here simultaneously, though I suppose Christmas brings us all together despite our schedules." She paused again and studied a dark-haired man who was engaged in conversation with another. Lewis guessed him to be their target, Ronald.

"We'll wait," Dorothy decided in a huff, then looked at Lewis. "It's really good to see you again, Jack. I know I'm all frazzled and frantic at the moment, but it's a big weekend for me. I suppose for you as well."

"Yes, it is," Lewis said dryly. "You will hold up your end of the deal, won't you?"

Dorothy fluttered her fake lashes. "Of course I will, darling. I'm not a Welshman."

Lewis glanced around at the conversing crowd. The noise level was steadily rising as more guests arrived and each fought to be heard over the din of conversation next to them. "Who attends things like these, and what is the purpose exactly?"

Dorothy shrugged. "Mostly filled with writers, like you and me. A handful with some real talent. These are your people, Jack. You should fit right in, and you would, if you made any sort of effort outside of a tavern."

"I have enough friends," Lewis objected.

"Yes, but these friends live in London, Jack, not Oxford or Headington."

"Why would I ever want London friends?" Lewis asked. "I would have to travel to London to meet them, at least half the time. I've already hit my limit of visiting this crowded city for the whole of next year."

Dorothy frowned and placed the brass tip of her cigarette holder between her teeth. "And as to the purpose of our meetings, you should know that better than most, Jack. It is a place to converse, talk about writing, play a murder mystery game, hone our skills, swap manuscripts—that sort of thing. Though some don't just write about murder; they consult with the Yard as well."

"Really?" Lewis gave the attendees another once-over through squinted eyes. "Imagine that."

"This is Ronald Knox," Dorothy stated, stepping forward into the conversation that Ronald looked to be done with. "He and I founded this little Detection Club." She then turned to the man Ronald had been speaking with and admonished, "George, go mingle elsewhere. You've taken enough of Ronald's time. He needs to network and not be bothered by your silly grammatical queries." George obeyed hesitantly, his narrow, balding head hanging low. Dorothy turned back and sighed. "Ronald, this is C. S. Lewis, the man I've been telling you about."

Ronald Knox, a handsome man with dark hair and honest eyes, smiled widely and extended his hand. "I've heard much about you, Lewis," he said warmly. "A fellow Oxford man. I graduated from Balliol a decade before your time and served as chaplain at University College, your old stomping grounds, if I'm not mistaken. I'm surprised we haven't met before. I even attended one of your lectures a year or so back when you were working on your book about love. Quite good if I remember." He regarded Dorothy. "I hear you would make an excellent novelist if only you'd put away the notions of poetic verse. Waste of a good crime writer, I'd say."

"Even crime has a sense of poetry to it," Lewis countered. "Don't you think?"

"Oh? How so?" Ronald leaned closer and tilted his ear toward Lewis.

"Take murder, since it is what you crime writers usually fixate on. Well, it's driven by a sense of emotion, isn't it? Anger, envy, jealousy, rage, passion . . . most vices, really. These are the stuff of murder and also of good poetry. I think Poe joined the two rather well."

Ronald looked pleased. He addressed Dorothy. "Get this man a membership card immediately. Waive all dues. I want him here for our January dinner." He turned back to Lewis. "Did you know your friend Dorothy here not only helped to start the Detection Club but also wrote the initiation oath? She really is very naughty, your friend Ms. Sayers. It was her idea that new members be elected by secret ballot with an initiation ceremony that involves taking an oath while one's hand is placed on a real human skull."

"I assure you there is nothing pagan or sinister about the skull, Jack," Dorothy defended herself. "I am a Christian woman. The skull simply represents the convergence and seriousness of death, detection, and devilishness—or if you prefer *m*'s, murder, mortality, and mystery."

"Mayhem," Lewis added.

Dorothy pointed her finger at him. "*Mayhem.* I like that much better than *mortality*. You should be a writer."

"So, are you going to tell him the secret oath or not?" Ronald asked slowly with a grin.

In reply, Dorothy merely smoked with an air of forced agitation.

"So long as I don't have to repeat it afterward," Lewis commented. "Or place my hand on a skull. I'm afraid I would have to refuse."

"It's no secret, Jack. You raise your right hand as one of

the founders says, 'Do you promise that your detectives shall well and truly detect the crimes presented to them, using those wits which it may please you to bestow upon them and not placing reliance on nor making use of Divine Revelation, Feminine Intuition, Mumbo Jumbo, Jiggery-Pokery, Coincidence, or Act of God?' If the initiate says yes, they are then approved and learn our secret mysteries, of which there are few, and each is quite underwhelming." She arched a dark brow at Lewis. "And that is that."

Ronald Knox laughed. "I believe it's time to move on from these appetizers to the real meal. Gilbert and Agatha have arrived, and we mustn't keep the king and queen waiting behind a curtain for too long."

Dinner, served buffet style in steaming chafing dishes, consisted of braised rosemary lamb chops, seasoned mashed potatoes, green beans with chopped almonds, and fresh warmed sourdough bread with rosemary herb butter. Lewis was very pleased with the meal and helped himself to a special spiced cider that had been delivered for the event. He was even more pleased when Dorothy mentioned that both cherry and apple pie would be available after the evening's speeches.

Ronald Knox soon took the stage while Lewis wiped his plate clean with a piece of sourdough. The co-founder of the Detection Club made sure the microphone was working with a few gentle taps before calling for the attention of the freely chattering crowd.

"Ladies and gentlemen of the London Detection Club, I hope your food was to die for," he joked, which elicited a roar of laughter as heads turned his way. "Perhaps if one of you were to keel over dead, we might have some entertainment for the rest of the evening in attempting to solve your unfortunate death." Ronald eyed the still-laughing crowd. "Anyone? Anyone at all?" He pretended to pout. "Pity. One loves a good Friday night murder mystery right before Christmas. It has all the makings of a brilliant story."

Lewis leaned toward Dorothy, who sat on his left. "You people are depraved," he declared, with a hint of a smile.

"Oh quiet, Jack," Dorothy retorted. "I've heard your lectures. You're as bad as any of us."

Ronald continued, "I'd like to thank those who made this night possible, as well as those of you who are current on your club dues." He paused and scanned the audience to a smattering of chuckles. "I also have the honor of calling to the stage our current, duly elected club president, Mr. Gilbert Keith Chesterton."

Lewis nearly spit out the drink in his mouth and stared in disbelief as a young assistant helped a large, portly man with a great mustache to the stage. G. K. Chesterton, one of Lewis's greatest inspirations, especially regarding his faith, was here, in this same room. Lewis couldn't help himself and stood to applaud, which led to those nearest him standing in an unplanned ovation as well. Soon, the whole room was clapping furiously as an aging Chesterton continued making his way to the podium, leaning heavily on his cane. He was noticeably tall, and thick in the middle, even from this distance. He wore a loose-fitting black jacket with a red pinstriped vest and small round spectacles that sat atop his red nose.

"You see his cane?" Dorothy whispered as she and Lewis resumed their seats. "It's a sword cane. The blade pulls out of the sheath—benign but deadly in another's hands." She arched a thin brow and turned her attention back to Chesterton, who cleared his throat and pulled a wad of crumbled papers from his pocket before shoving them back in.

"Don't sit down, Ronald." Chesterton waved the host back toward him. "I've decided my prepared speech was dull and lifeless. Like a corpse." He grinned, a joy-filled expression that, despite his bad teeth, brightened his whole countenance. "I'd like to quickly revisit the ten rules of writing detective fiction, and I may need your help with this since you wrote them and my memory isn't what it used to be."

Ronald smiled broadly and sidled up shoulder to shoulder with Chesterton, revealing that he was a head shorter than the older man.

"Let us begin," Chesterton said playfully. "I know the first rule has to do with revealing the culprit or something of the sort. Would you care to elaborate, Ronald?"

"Yes," Ronald responded, leaning into the silver microphone as someone offstage brought up a second. "The guilty party should be mentioned in the early part of the story but without giving the reveal away too easily."

"That is a good rule," Chesterton affirmed. "And it must be done in a clever way. We must always be clever, or the public will turn on us. The second rule stifled my Father Brown storylines and put some good ideas in the wastebasket: All supernatural or miraculous happenings must not be included as a means of solving the mystery or cause of the crime itself."

"Yes, very good." Ronald prodded, "And the third?"

"Whose speech is this?" Chesterton replied to a roar of laughter. "To save time, I'll quickly give the next four I remember, since you all came here for dessert and plotting murders, not to hear an old man blather on." Chesterton tapped his cane. “More than one secret room or passage is not allowed; there can be no use of new, undiscovered, or made-up poisons, nor means of murder weapons that require a long, drawn-out scientific explanation.” Chesterton held up five fingers. “There can be no stereotypical use of foreigners as culprits or means of murder, and no accident can help our sleuth solve the mystery.”

“Those are all correct, Mr. President,” Ronald confirmed. “Very impressive.”

“Is this a test?” Chesterton quipped to more laughter. “One rule I would add if I could is to keep it simple. That is what we all love about a good murder story—simplicity and seeing how the answer was there under our noses all along. Confusion always leads to boredom, and that is simply bad for business, is it not?”

“Quite so, Gilbert,” Ronald answered. “We’re coming down the home stretch now.”

“What number are we on?” Chesterton thought for a moment. “Ah yes, seven. And perhaps Dorothy Sayers can help us with number seven.” He looked around the tables and settled his gaze on Lewis and Dorothy. “Yell it out, dear girl,” he urged with a flourish of his hand.

Dorothy stood and nearly shouted, “The detective himself, or herself, must not be the one to commit the crime.” She confidently performed a mock bow as the captive audience applauded once again.

Chesterton nodded his large head vigorously. “So, this means I will not be reading a copy of your latest novel and discover that either Lord Peter Wimsey or Harriet Vane are really killers themselves?” He raised a brow and waited for a reply.

Dorothy laughed and shook her head as Chesterton pretended to wipe his brow in relief. He then turned and looked toward the table where he had been seated earlier, unbeknownst to Lewis. "And, Agatha, do you know the eighth rule?"

Agatha Christie stood, and all eyes turned to her. She wiped her mouth with a napkin and cleared her throat. "The detective is bound to declare any clues that he may discover. Nothing is to be kept up his sleeve. The reader should have all reasonable questions answered when they place the book down as finished."

The audience clapped vigorously as Agatha gave her own mock bow and took her seat.

"Very well said, as always." Chesterton turned to Ronald. "I've completely forgotten number nine, but it has to do with a sidekick, I believe."

Ronald nodded. "The partner or sidekick of the main character must also not conceal from the reader any thoughts that pass through his mind. They must be of average intelligence or even slightly below that of the reader and have similar questions or concerns as the average reader would."

"We all love having a friend around who is not quite as smart as we are." Chesterton hooked a thumb at Ronald, and the crowd erupted in laughter.

"Here I thought you were my sidekick," Ronald teased, to even more hilarity.

"And finally, number ten is about twins and doubles," Chesterton explained. "They must not appear in the story unless the reader has been duly prepared for them through viable clues. The alibi of one twin so that the other could commit murder is an overused trope, though some have said that Ronald and I are twins separated at birth."

This received yet another round of applause and laughter,

including from Lewis, whose side had begun to hurt. As Chesterton gave his own mock bow to conclude his speech, Lewis couldn't think of a time he'd enjoyed himself more in recent years. He also felt as though these two men may have just said something that could be helpful in the Inklings' investigation. He just wasn't quite certain yet what it was.

{17} The Queen

> You gave too much rein to your imagination.
> Imagination is a good servant, and a bad master.
> The simplest explanation is always the most likely.
> —Agatha Christie, *The Mysterious Affair at Styles*

After Chesterton exited the stage, Agatha Christie, the Queen of Crime herself, gracefully ascended the steps and allowed Ronald Knox to lend a guiding hand and lightly kiss her cheek. Agatha knew how to be effortlessly elegant when she wanted to be. She wore a dark green dress with a fur mink wrap slung over her shoulders. On her head sat a dark green hat with green peacock feathers jutting up from a band that matched her dress. Her short dark hair curled around her temples in a way Lewis thought made her look like a Hollywood starlet.

She smiled, and her dark eyes surveyed the room, searching like pools of wisdom that Lewis knew saw more than others ever could. She had thick brows, dark red lipstick, and a long pearl necklace wrapped three times around her slender neck with matching earrings dangling from her ears. *Enchanting* was the word that ran through Lewis's mind.

"Ladies and gentlemen of the London Detection Club," Agatha began without notes, "I would like to give you all a lesson in murder." The phrase was met with a chorus of low chuckles, as it was meant to be. Agatha flashed a coy grin and raised a dark brow. "Not about how to murder someone, mind you. That would be inappropriate." She looked at each table in turn as she spoke. "But rather a lesson in how to write a murder so that your reader is yours for life." She paused for effect, and this time it was Lewis who smiled. If she was as good a speaker as a writer, he might enjoy himself more than he'd expected.

"The key to a good murder is what is left unsaid. What is left off-screen or off the page. It allows the reader to fill in the gaps themselves. Perhaps they will match what you, the author, had in mind, or perhaps not. But either way, it is glorious for you the writer because your reader has, in a sense, helped to make your story better. They add the missing parts in their own minds the way they would want those literary gaps to be filled in." Agatha arched her brow again. "Don't you see it? If they want more guts, gore, and blood, then they will close the gaps with more of their proclivity to violence. Yet if they want a clever crime, one to read while snuggled up with a blanket and sherry next to a crackling fire, and a murder that aligns with their religious family values and sense of purity of heart, then by Jove, their minds will fill in the gaps just so. But only if you allow them."

Agatha paused to eye the room and let her words find purchase. She held up her pointer finger. "Don't make the mistake of forcing a Christian woman with an ill-settled stomach to trudge through three pages of your descriptions of evisceration and entrails, or she will never pick up another of your books again. And not only that, but she will also surely tell her book club and high-society friends to keep far away. Bad for business, I say. Also, in the same frame, never leave a blood-lusting reader with an ill-exposed forced coziness that will not satiate them. Leave room for imagination, I tell you! It is your best friend—not only in reading for personal enjoyment but especially for you, the aspiring writer. The reader's imagination is immensely friendly to you if you do not harness it and shove a bridle in its mouth. Let imaginations run free like wild horses in the country. I promise, your readers will return like moths to a flame and your publishers will love you for it. Your bank account will also toast your name."

For a moment, it seemed as though her gaze settled on Lewis, as though she were looking inside him, his heart laid bare.

"Most of my success has come from what I didn't write, not from what I did. I could have explained too much, exposing what was unnecessary and uncared for by the reader. If you are bored writing it, chances are the reader will be bored reading it. A good musician knows when not to play, a good actor knows when to keep silent and stoic, and a good writer knows when less is more." Agatha stopped again, breathing deeply before smiling to signal a coming shift in the tone of her speech. Lewis hung on her every word. He, too, had always believed imagination was an underutilized tool in writing.

"Two years ago," Agatha continued, "my book *Murder on the Orient Express* was released, and thankfully it has been my greatest success to date." The audience clapped furiously as Agatha nodded with gratitude. "I thank you all for the inspiration for the story and also for your support before, during, and after its release. I promise that within this club, which I now see as a sort of brotherhood and sisterhood of writers all combined into one glorious hive mind, we can pledge ourselves to not only pursue our ambitions and desires but also commit to the welfare and benefit of those who would sit beside us with hopes and dreams of their own. After all, this is something we all love and we all share."

This comment was met with a roar of support and applause, to which Agatha graciously bowed and leaned into the microphone. "With that," she concluded, "I will keep you from your pie no longer. Let us stab each with our collective knives and let the cherry filling flow."

Twenty minutes later, Lewis asked, "So, how does this work? Do I meet with her now or later?" He had just eaten his second piece of delicious cinnamon-infused apple pie. He'd avoided the cherry after picturing blood.

"Not yet." Dorothy stubbed out a cigarette in a nearby glass ashtray and leaned back in her chair with a groan from eating too much. "I've arranged a luncheon for you tomorrow at her home in Wallingford. I'll write the details on a napkin for you before you go. However, keep in mind, you still have two events to attend to uphold your end of the bargain. And you'd better not be late for Agatha tomorrow."

Lewis sighed. "I'll show, but only if you give me the right address."

Dorothy smiled with half of her mouth and took a drink from her cocktail. "Did you enjoy yourself?"

"I did," Lewis said truthfully, "far more than I thought I would."

"It only gets wilder from here," Dorothy told him. "The gaudy is a gas. Sorry about the strong-arming, Jack, but I figured it would be the only way to get you out into the world and inject some culture into you."

"I have plenty of culture," Lewis protested. "Heaps of it. I attended evensong a few nights back and listened to a choir sing Christmas carols."

"Hmm," she mused, "Oxford can be a beautiful prison if you let it. I should know, having spent so much of my life there serving time." She smiled. "It's far better to be out and inspired rather than locked away."

"I have my process, and you have yours."

"And Agatha is part of your process now?" Dorothy was fishing for information, no doubt curious as to why Lewis had requested to meet with the Queen of Crime.

"I have questions she may have answers to," was Lewis's only response for the moment. He trusted Dorothy, but he also liked just a little bit to watch her squirm. "What would your protagonist Lord Peter Wimsey do in my situation?" Lewis added.

Dorothy's frown eased. "Oh, if he had Agatha Christie at his disposal, my guess is he'd do the same thing you are. The woman knows more about most subjects than anyone I know. Even more than me, and that is a feat."

Lewis pushed his empty plate away from him. He enjoyed talking to Dorothy. "I have one more request of you."

"Name it." Dorothy traced Lewis's gaze to an area near the stage.

"I wonder if you wouldn't mind introducing me to Chesterton when the crowd disperses from around him. I'd like to personally thank the man for the impact he has had on my life. And after that, I may have another piece of pie."

{18} The Open House

Saturday, December 19

His grief he will not forget; but it will not darken his heart, it will teach him wisdom.
—J. R. R. TOLKIEN, *The Return of the King*

The Pennington home was located just inside the district of Belgravia in central London. The stark white row home loomed three stories overhead with a walkout terrace jutting out over the sidewalk on which Tolkien and Cecil had approached the front steps. A man Tolkien assumed to be Francis Pennington answered the door, since all other household staff had previously been let go, if the former maid was to be believed. The son and heir apparent was small framed, with prematurely thinning dark hair and a face that reminded Tolkien of a German schnauzer. A dark and patchy beard was doing its best to fill out an otherwise narrow, angular face.

Tolkien had been counting on Francis being here, and he smiled both in amicability and internal relief at the opportunity to ask the man questions, hopefully without him sensing an entrapping interrogation.

"Hello, good man," Cecil greeted him enthusiastically, reaching out his hand and gripping the other's as if they were old friends. "You must be Francis Pennington. I am so sorry to hear about your father. My condolences. Didn't know Roger well, but I'd heard good things from the boys at White's. I am Lord David Cecil."

"Yes, welcome." Francis's frown contorted into a plastered smile, an expression Tolkien could tell didn't come naturally and pained the man to hold. "Come inside, gentlemen." He ushered them inside with a flourish of his hand. In just half a minute, Tolkien sized up Francis as a nervous man whose mind moved faster than his twitching facial features could keep up with.

"This is my good friend, John Tolkien," Cecil explained, once they were in the foyer and the heavy door had again clicked shut. "He is a professor at Oxford, Pembroke College to be exact. Were you an Oxford man, Francis?"

"No." Francis's voice held a hint of disdain while he shook Tolkien's hand limply. "Cambridge."

"Ah." Tolkien nodded. "I would have guessed by the look of you."

Francis blinked, not knowing how to take the words.

"Yes, yes," Cecil added with an arched brow. "Just like your father. He was always raving about that place. Beat our boys in crew last year. Well, as I said on the phone, my father, the Marquess of Salisbury, is interested in purchasing property in this area of the city, and I'd hoped to poke around for a minute or two to see if yours would be a good estate investment. Tolkien here is tagging along only as a second opinion and because I don't like to walk alone."

Tolkien had stepped away from the other two and now stood looking at a portrait of Roger Pennington that was hanging over the ornately molded door leading into the front sitting room. He could see the slight resemblance between father and progeny as he flicked his eyes from the painting to the son and back again.

Francis nodded, eyeing the wandering professor but perking up his ears at the mention of the assumed wealth of a marquess. "I can walk with you about the house if you'd like," he evenly, "but I am afraid I have two others stopping by to see the home as well—old friends of my father's."

"Oh." Cecil frowned. "Are you expecting multiple offers?"

"Well, I do hope so." Francis flashed a genuine grin. "Bidding wars would play in my favor, yes?"

"Tell me," Tolkien questioned, pivoting on his heel. "Are you looking for a maximum offer or to sell quickly?"

"To sell quickly would be ideal," Francis admitted. "The less we have to deal with banks the better."

"Oh, I can assure you," Cecil remarked with a placating smile, "my father has enough in his safe not to require the hassle of loan paperwork. We could do this cleanly and quickly. That is, if the tour is satisfactory."

"But not too quick," Tolkien put in, his pointer finger raised. "Where would you stay if not here? You would need time to secure new lodging, no?"

Francis puffed his chest. "Oh no, I haven't lived in this house for quite some time. I have a home in Brighton. I don't like the city. Could never see myself living here. I left as soon as I could. Too many ill-suited memories."

"Hopefully nothing too traumatic." Tolkien tilted his head to one side. "Except for recent events, of course."

"My father's death was not as traumatic as you'd think,"

the son replied evenly. "I wasn't even in London at the time." He shifted his gaze toward Cecil. "Tell me, would your father, the marquess, move here?"

Francis had changed the subject, which was not lost on Tolkien.

"No." Cecil shook his head and squinted, pretending to inspect a nearby molding. "My father is mostly interested in a place he could use as an extra apartment. Somewhere close to Parliament and Hyde Park, with a spacious bedroom and adjoining study with a view that he could use as an office. Is there anything like that here?"

"Yes, the second floor." Francis looked pleased to be able to answer in the affirmative. "It was my father's old room and study. He also used the space as an office."

Cecil smiled brightly. "Yes, perfect. May we go see it?"

"I can take you now," Francis began, but a sharp knock at the front door interrupted him.

Soon, Lord Percival Beckworth entered and took off his hat. "Francis, my dear boy, I hope I'm not too late," he said, smiling and shaking Francis's hand before flicking his eyes quickly to Tolkien and finally to Cecil.

"Lord Beckworth," Francis welcomed him. "I was surprised and delighted to hear from you also. I never thought you'd be interested in purchasing the place."

"Oh yes, I've always liked it here. Many fond memories. I wonder"—Beckworth narrowed his dark eyes—"if you would show me the kitchen. I have certain questions about what would stay in the house at the sale and what would be taken away."

In that moment, Tolkien realized Cecil had personally asked Beckworth to come as a distraction. Tolkien shot a sidelong glance at his friend, who confirmed his suspicion with a quick, knowing smile. The two of them turned and began their ascent to the second floor.

"That was good thinking," Tolkien praised when they were finally alone. He stepped into the wide carpeted hallway at the top of the stairs. "Better to see the scene of the murder and discuss openly without the son present."

"I still have a trick or two up my sleeve, Tollers," Cecil shot back gleefully as he continued to grip the handrail and climb the few remaining steps. "We struck a deal, Beckworth and I. He will offer a suitable distraction in exchange for my company and hunting rifle at the next full moon." Cecil reached the top of the stairway, breathing deeply. "Let's get this over with quickly. I have a bed calling out to me."

Tolkien led the way into the space in question. It was cold—the result of no servants present to light fires. As he walked slowly through the bedroom first, then the office, keeping one visual box in front of him at a time, he looked carefully at each section, being mindful of what exactly he was observing. Tolkien reminded himself that a detective can take in too much at once and miss out on the small things, and he was determined not to let that happen.

First, he inspected an alcove seating area near the window, noting the rug, blanket material, and artwork, which featured a painted castle he didn't recognize but that was most likely Bavarian. The next area was a floor-to-ceiling bookshelf containing many historical and occult titles on alchemy, numerology, Thelema, mysticism, and various benign spiritual disciplines. Tolkien scanned the titles, as well as a handful of volumes written by Crowley in their own bunched section directly behind the desk to be easily referenced.

He then pivoted and observed the desk itself—a large,

dark, wine-colored mahogany piece that would be difficult to move, given both its sheer size and presumed weight. On the desk sat a blank writing pad and ink, a small spinning globe, a bust of Julius Caesar, a crystal paperweight, and a pair of thick whiskey glasses stacked off-kilter next to a half-full bottle of single malt. The bottle bore a small red bow and card attached by wax to the glass side. Tolkien leaned over and read the expensive reserve label as well as the card, which said, *Happy Birthday, Old Man.* It was signed only with a stamped symbol, a triangle with a small cross at the top.

Less than five minutes later, Tolkien and Cecil descended the staircase. Not only were Beckworth and Francis busily discussing the house, but a nervous-looking Robert MacDougall had also arrived and now stood awkwardly, his head nodding along while he stared at his brown leather shoes.

"It's like a reunion of the Order," Cecil called loudly before he reached the bottom. Francis glanced up but didn't react to the words, which told Tolkien that the son was familiar with his father's membership in the secretive fraternity. MacDougall looked at them and blinked. He swallowed hard and shifted his weight from foot to foot—clearly suffering the effects of frayed nerves.

"A lovely home," Cecil commented to the heir apparent with a brisk handshake. His job was complete.

A hopeful Francis Pennington smiled widely and fell into a rehearsed speech highlighting the home's benefits that Cecil may not have seen on his tour, including its overall size, various rooms, and servants' quarters.

"I was curious," Tolkien broke in. "Did your father recently celebrate a birthday?"

"Yes, last month. November 11, to be exact. It was his

sixtieth birthday." Francis pursed his lips. "That may have been the last time I saw my father alive."

There was a momentary silence.

"I noticed a bottle of twenty-year-old Bell's Royal Reserve Scotch Whisky on his desk with a bow," Tolkien continued. "I suppose it was a birthday gift?"

"Hmm, not from me," Francis replied without emotion. "Like every year, I got him a box of White Owl cigars, his favorite."

"Yes, mine too," Cecil remarked. "I have regular monthly deliveries."

"I quite enjoy those myself," Beckworth added lightly. "I believe you sent me a box."

"Then was the scotch from the Order?" Tolkien asked, eyeing Beckworth and MacDougall.

"Not that I'm aware of," Beckworth responded, "though a fine whiskey could have come from anyone. We of the Order have impeccable taste."

Tolkien turned back to Francis. "I noticed there were no staff here today. Yet the home looks as though it has been recently dusted clean."

"I let them all go," Francis explained, almost with a reluctant air of embarrassment. "Much of my father's money is now tied up, and as I said, I'm looking to sell the home as quickly as possible."

"I'm sure that was a difficult decision," Tolkien sympathized, watching Francis closely. "Some of the staff may have even felt like family to you, having been here since your childhood."

Francis clasped his hands behind his back. "I am neither compassionate nor nostalgic," he said evenly. "Some would consider it a weakness, but I know the ability to make difficult choices without emotional attachment is a gift necessary in this world." He then furrowed his brow toward Tolkien while the other three looked on. "You are an inquisitive one, Professor Tolkien."

"Goes with the job." Tolkien chuckled. "I'm a professor and a writer. I can't help but ask questions. A man who ceases to ask questions is a man who ceases to be wise."

Francis frowned and smoothed his mustache with his thumb and forefinger.

Cecil, sensing the interrogation was at its natural end, coughed unnecessarily and moved toward the door. "I'll speak to my father and let you know." He gave Francis one final firm handshake and a wave from over his shoulder as he walked down the steps onto the light gray sidewalk. Tolkien followed, deep in thought.

Then they heard Beckworth yell, "Gentlemen, I wonder if I might have a quick word."

Tolkien and Cecil waited while Beckworth approached. The man wiped a sheen of sweat from his forehead before stuffing his handkerchief back into his jacket pocket. MacDougall trailed a dozen steps behind him, just out of earshot and looking pale and agitated.

"I wanted to catch you before you headed back to Oxford," Beckworth said. "I'll be quick. MacDougall wishes to speak to me about something urgent, probably more family drama or some mysterious illness. For a tough Scotsman, he's a bit of a nervous hypochondriac." He glanced over his shoulder before continuing to his point. "I was wondering how the investigation was progressing?" He held a hopeful, if not desperate, look in his eyes.

"It is moving forward," Cecil assured him. "Leads are being pursued, and new developments are coming to light."

"What new developments?" he asked quickly.

"It's too early to discuss," Tolkien cut in.

Beckworth frowned. "Gentlemen, I don't think I need to remind you that another full moon is approaching."

"We are well aware, and we are moving along as quickly as we can," Tolkien responded. "Now, if you'll excuse us." He turned and began walking, an action that had always helped him think. The two other men kept in step.

Beckworth opened his mouth, then closed it, seemingly to collect his thoughts before attempting to speak again. He ventured, "I wondered if perhaps you both, or even a few other trusted, capable gentlemen, wouldn't mind joining me at my country cottage on Monday, the twenty-eighth. MacDougall will be there as well; it's been settled." He glanced at Cecil. "I know you're already in."

"The night of the full moon?" Tolkien asked.

"Yes, that's right," he confirmed. "Just in case, I'd like to be surrounded by people who I know don't wish me dead." He laughed nervously.

"That seems to be a small list," Tolkien observed. "What about the other members of the Order? Aren't their lives at risk as well?"

"I'm a selfish man, Professor. I'm not as worried about others as I am my own skin. MacDougall is the only other I trust. Known him most of my life."

Tolkien glanced back at the trailing Scotsman. "Do you think the killer would target the two of you specifically?"

"Yes, I do. And I have good reason to think so. There are certain things I share in common with our two brothers of the Order who were killed. We are all in the Order, yes; wealthy men, yes . . . of an age. These are all true. But there is more."

"You all have known Crowley for decades," Tolkien filled in, "going back to the beginning. All Cambridge men as well. You are the inner circle."

"Yes, exactly." Beckworth held up a finger. "And not all members of our order share those traits. Only me and MacDougall that are still living. So, you see my dilemma, don't you, Professor? I fear the reaper is sharpening his scythe even now."

Tolkien nodded slowly. "I do, but I'm afraid I'm not certain at this time if I'll be able to join you that night."

"I'll be there," Cecil said. "I said I would, and I will. My word is my bond."

"If you decide to come," Beckworth told Tolkien, "make sure to bring a weapon if you have one." He eyed Tolkien curiously. "You do have a weapon of some sort, don't you?"

Tolkien smiled. "I fought at the Somme. What do you think? But I just remembered one other question I had for you." Spotting the crossroads up ahead where he, Beckworth, MacDougall, and Cecil would all go their separate ways, Tolkien stopped walking and looked Beckworth in his beady eyes. "Were you aware Baron Huxley was nearly bankrupt and owed great debts?"

"No," Beckworth replied evenly. "But it doesn't surprise me. Probably related to gambling. He loved to throw the dice."

"What about Crowley?" Tolkien pressed. "Were you aware Crowley filed for bankruptcy just last year?" He tilted his head and watched Beckworth closely.

"Yes, I was aware of that," Beckworth admitted. "Crowley has always been quite open with the Order about many aspects of his personal life. The death of his child, his estrangement from the other daughter, the spiral of his wife and her death as well. I know the man can appear deceptive to others, but Crowley has always been trustworthy for those of us closest to him."

Beckworth's response struck Tolkien as honest, reminding him of the concept of honor among thieves, and he wondered if something similar was true of occultists.

{19} Winterbrook House

Instinct is a marvellous thing. It can neither be explained nor ignored.

—Agatha Christie,
The Mysterious Affair at Styles

Lewis hired a car, something he rarely did, and journeyed south from Headington to Winterbrook House in Wallingford. After about a half hour, the driver turned down a surprisingly smooth gravel road past apple orchards bordered by trimmed hedges and pulled up to a brick two-story home.

The house featured a stark white front door surrounded on both sides by white columns that held up a square portico. Lewis paid the driver and walked toward the front door, his hard-soled brown leather shoes crunching on the crushed stone, which was still wet from an overnight rain. As he drew nearer, he felt a strange nervousness rising from the pit of his stomach, the likes of which he hadn't experienced in nearly two decades. He realized then what it must feel like for one of his new students to meet their tutor for the first time.

The front facing windows of the home were bordered with an orangish soldier course of bricks, which immediately reminded Lewis of the Kilns. Perhaps his actual kilns had fired these bricks some decades past. Lewis held that thought as he walked, and it helped calm his nerves. He wiped his feet, cleared his throat, and used the knocker—a bronze piece cast in the shape of a Scottie dog—and waited. Lewis heard a voice calling from the other side to enter. He tapped his foot, feeling a bit uncomfortable as he glanced from left to right, but worked the handle and opened the door a crack, which was just enough to hear more clearly the voice and the repeated call to come in.

Inside the foyer, Lewis looked up and noted a crystal chandelier above his head and the carpeted staircase to his left leading to the upper floor. Without lingering too long, he ambled down a hallway past portraits of the unfamiliar husband and celebrity wife toward the rear of the home, where the voice had come from. The hall passed through an arch into a spacious kitchen attached to an even more spacious living space lined on the far side with a wall of windows looking out to a mature back garden.

Agatha Christie stood at the kitchen counter, cutting small tea sandwiches with a knife and placing them neatly onto a two-tiered serving plate, which could be easily carried by a silver hook sprouting from the top. She looked very different from the night before, almost sweet and much like Lewis's memories of his mother, though he would never dare tell her so. She wore a long cream-colored front-buttoned housecoat that fell to her knees, with a white collared blouse underneath. The matching pearl earrings and necklace from the night before were also gone, and there was now no makeup or lipstick to speak of.

Agatha looked up and smiled as if Lewis were an old friend, though the two had never formally met. "It is a pleasure to meet you finally, Professor Lewis," Christie welcomed him. "I hope the journey wasn't too far from the safety of Oxford."

"It was a pleasant drive, actually." Lewis clasped his fingers behind his back. "I rarely travel out this way, and it was nice to see the countryside—and so much of it so fast. It's incredible how slow walking is. I suppose that is why we are called pedestrians."

Christie chuckled, picked up the serving plate by the hook, and began to walk out into the living room. A low bookshelf stretched around two sides of the space. On the top shelf, about waist high, instead of books sat what looked to be various archaeological and cultural items on display, from a fragment of bone to a figurine, a bust of someone famous, and some sort of medieval weapon—possibly Babylonian. Lewis wondered whether they had always belonged to Agatha or if some were her husband's archaeology finds.

"You were there at dinner last night as Dorothy's guest," Christie noted. "And now you're mine. I'll have to keep an eye on you, C. S. Lewis."

"My friends call me Jack," Lewis offered. "Thank you again for agreeing to meet with me." He followed Agatha as she passed through a separate door and stepped down into a warm sunroom. She set the food in the middle of a small black iron café table, next to a white porcelain tea set, and bid Lewis to join her. "I thought we could have tea and talk out here. It's so lovely when the sun shines right in, even in winter."

Lewis entered and felt as if he were in a jungle, surrounded on three sides by a wide array of potted plants of many vibrant colors, shapes, and sizes. Some were hung from the framing of the glass ceiling, and others were gathered in tiered bunches in the corners. The sun shone brightly through the glass ceiling into the south-facing space, warming the herringbone brick at their feet. It felt humid to the point Lewis shed his jacket and placed it on the back of his chair even before he sat down. The last thing he wanted to do was sit drenched in sweat wishing to get this all over with as quickly as possible.

"Don't mind my husband." Agatha inclined her head toward the backyard. "Max prefers the outdoors and tending the gardens especially."

Lewis nodded. Out the window, he could see a thin man working furiously with pruners, cutting away at dead branches and thorny bushes in the back garden and throwing all the refuse onto a pile that rose taller than he was. "I'd love to meet him," Lewis said truthfully.

"And you shall," Agatha assured him as she sipped her tea and set it back down to cool. "Tell me, what did you think of my speech last night?"

Lewis blinked, then sucked in a long breath. "I enjoyed it. I agree with your take on leaving something to the imagination of the reader."

Christie nodded. "I'm not as funny as Chesterton or Knox. Never have been. I've always been an overly serious person. And my humor is so dry most wouldn't get it anyway, even if I made an effort."

Lewis smiled faintly. He had that in common with the woman. "You provided a good balance for the evening."

"Dorothy asked a favor of me," Agatha went on. "She said

it would be well worth my time and yours if we were to meet. If I heard correctly, you are writing a book, had some questions about poison, and sought out my expertise?"

"Something like that," Lewis hedged, sensing the woman already knew much more than she let on.

Christie flashed an even smile. "Let us dispel the nonsense, Professor," she replied. "You and I both know this is not for a book, though at some point it may very well become useful fodder. My own writing has often stemmed from real-life situations. You are working on a case, aren't you? And for Mr. Doyle, no doubt."

Lewis felt his breath catch. "How did you know that?" He was surprised, but not nearly as much as he would have been if any other person on earth were sitting before him.

"I've worked with the man in the past, before his 'death.' " She made quotation marks in the air with her fingers and flashed a sly smile. "And, I might add, in a very similar capacity to your own current arrangement. I've also refused him of late." She pursed her lips. "Which explains his branching out into fresh recruits. I felt as though I should retire from the field and do a bit more behind-the-scenes consultancy. Which is why I agreed to meet with you, Professor Lewis. You would be my first client in this new capacity, and pro bono, mind you.

"How we met is a fascinating story," Agatha continued. "One that I've told in full only three other times: once to Dorothy, once to my husband Max, and once to a police inspector when I was interrogated. But even then, they did not get the full unadulterated story. But if I tell you here now, you cannot share what I have divulged with anyone. Not even your elder brother or your fellow Inklings. Do you accept?"

Lewis felt strange but nodded. How could he pass this up?

"Yes," he agreed as he watched Agatha sip her tea. "I solemnly promise I will not tell a soul."

There was a sparkle in her eye as she began. "As I'm sure you know, in 1926, I went missing for eleven days. It's all true and well documented in the press. Anyone can look it up easily at the library if you didn't read it at the time. I claimed amnesia and medical reasoning . . . some sort of fugue state, if I remember correctly. But the press nonetheless accused me of faking my death as a publicity stunt."

Christie frowned. "What the press and all other people do not know is that my publicly given story was not what happened, neither was there any amnesia. The real reason for my eleven days of absence could not be divulged at the time, nor will I share all the details here with you now, other than to say I was tracking a killer and it became best for everyone involved that I disappear for a time." She paused to sip tea, and Lewis leaned forward in his metal chair. He was already captivated.

"Drink your tea, Jack," Agatha encouraged before picking up where she left off. "The story in the newspapers was that my then-husband, Archie, asked for a divorce. This was true, though not at all connected to my disappearance as some speculated. Archie had long been tired of my life of criminal obsession and gave me a firm ultimatum of choosing either him or my life of detection. Of course, I knew there was more to it for him than he let on—we don't need to get into that—but he made it easy to absolve himself by putting the blame and decision on me. To choose between my first and second love was torture, but I chose to be a detective, my first love, and let him know it then and there. I wasn't going to be badgered into giving up what I love so dearly. Archie then told me he never wanted to see me again, which was fine by me, though I did miss him dearly after it was all over." Agatha met Lewis's eyes. "This part you may already know. It was in the papers at the time, though I don't believe the gossip pages to be the first choice you would have turned to. You don't strike me as a gossipy man."

Lewis shook his head in response to Agatha's knowing stare.

"I left our home in Sunningdale the following morning and decided to use the break to dive into some undercover work. Archie came looking for me, even though he said he was done, but I was not to be found. He soon became panicked and went to the police, lighting a fuse in the process." Agatha blinked and exhaled slowly. "I had garnered a certain amount of fame due to the recent release of *The Murder of Roger Ackroyd,* and when the press got wind of it, a media firestorm ensued, which at the time, I was not aware of. I didn't even know I was being searched for until it was too late."

Agatha rolled her eyes. "The morning after my departure, my car, a lovely Morris Cowley, just so happened to be discovered at Newlands Corner in Surrey, parked near a chalk quarry with an expired driver's license and a change of clothes inside. It was feared that I may have drowned or taken my own life in a nearby beauty spot known insidiously as the Silent Pool. Fantastic name for a book, by the way." She paused to smile and raised a brow. "See, Professor, I do have a sense of humor. In actuality, I had met an informant at that spot and left my car and extra change of clothes behind, which I'd fully intended to return to—except now the place was crawling with camera-wielding reporters, investigators, and uniformed men carrying billy clubs." She studied Lewis. "Professor, you're not eating any sandwiches."

Lewis helped himself to two and began to eat.

"The disappearance," Christie continued, "quickly became a major news story that even gained coverage in America. The press, no doubt seeking only to satisfy their readers' hunger for scandal, sensationalized the whole affair, as they tend to do. Even the home secretary at the time, a man I knew, William Joynson-Hicks, pressured Scotland Yard to scale up the manhunt to a frothy hysteria.

"Oh yes." Agatha snapped her eyes back to her guest and sucked in a long breath. "After eleven days I was not found, and many had lost all hope. My case had concluded favorably, and I needed to reintroduce myself to society in a way that caused the least amount of damage to my career and didn't reveal too much about the case. Amnesia or some fugue state was my only real answer. I was finally located at the Swan Hydropathic Hotel in Harrogate, Yorkshire, after news of my whereabouts was tipped anonymously by my own publicist. I was registered as Mrs. Teresa Neele and claimed I didn't know who I was.

"I suppose now I can tell you the truth without fear of legal repercussions. I truly didn't mean to cause such a stir, though some good came out of it—a lost child was found and a killer thwarted and brought to justice. Sir Arthur came to visit me later. Through his connections he had discovered what happened, and so a friendship was formed, which has led to many more adventures, many resolved cases, and quite a few good ideas for stories as well." Agatha sipped her tea and gazed out the window in bittersweet thought. "I suppose that part of my life has come to an end."

"It's a fascinating story," Lewis remarked, then cracked a smile. "And I promise I won't press you on all the details you left out."

Agatha flashed a quick smile back. "You wouldn't be a

good detective, or writer, Professor Lewis, if you didn't have at least a dozen questions you were fighting to hold back at this very moment."

"That I do," he affirmed, seeing in Agatha a kindred spirit. "Now, what can you tell me about Aleister Crowley?"

"Ah yes." Agatha nodded. "Not too long ago, in 1930 I believe, Crowley faked his own death. Perhaps I inspired him, though I claim no fault."

Lewis tilted his head to one side. "Where was this?" He had not known this detail before, and even Charles Williams had never mentioned it.

"Outside Lisbon, Portugal, at a rock formation called Boca do Inferno, right on the coast. I only remember the name because it translates to 'Mouth of Hell.' Crowley is a man of theater. No doubt the spot was chosen well beforehand—it's the first clue that this was no accident. He had helped in the execution of his plan, and he was soon presumed to be dead, drowned, and pulled out to sea. At least for the next three weeks, before he changed his mind and reappeared at the opening of his art exhibition at the Galerie Neumann-Nierendorf in Berlin. Quite a stir that whole ordeal created as well."

"Why do you think he did it?"

Agatha raised a dark brow. "One of five reasons, I would think. One, he may have thought it was his best way to get out of financial trouble. Crowley has been known to squander his ill-gotten gains. Two, he may have wanted to separate himself from some who would want him dead. Crowley had contacts with a dangerous crowd: the British secret service, the Mafia, and current or former students of the occult. He has always been well loved and well hated in equal measure. Three, he may have wanted to escape from a relationship. Crowley drifted from partner to partner over the years, male and female, especially since the death of his wife Rose. Four, the event was planned all along as a publicity stunt for the opening of his art exhibit. The reappearance did garner a fair amount of coverage, though not what he had hoped, I imagine, given all the trouble and expense he went through to disappear. And five, because Aleister Crowley is so very self-absorbed. He is also brilliant and a master manipulator. I'm not sure which of those descriptions is worse."

"What do you think happened?" Lewis prodded. "Which is it?"

Agatha shook her head. "I don't know. You can never be sure with a man like that. Perhaps all five are true at the same time—or none. Take from that what you will. I hope it provides some clues to your case." She folded her hands on her lap. "So, how can I be of further assistance?"

Lewis took a breath, gathering his thoughts. "I believe the victims whose deaths I am investigating were both poisoned. I had suspicions at first, but now I'm fairly certain. However, I don't personally know a great deal about poison. This is where a certain crime writer living nearby who once worked in a hospital dispensary and gained a thorough knowledge of poisons comes into the story." Lewis flashed a smile.

"I have lived a very interesting life—many lives, some have said. I am unapologetically a collector of ideas, as are you surely, and among them, I have indeed amassed a knowledge of poison." She met Lewis's gaze and then asked, "What were the symptoms?"

Lewis looked up and to the left as he recalled from memory, "Nausea, loss of hair, hot feet and hands. One victim fell a few times prior and lost most use of his arms and legs. There were also mentions of stomach pain, tremors, headaches, loss of balance, insomnia, seizures, and skin lesions present at death."

Agatha closed her eyes and nodded as Lewis listed the symptoms from memory. When he finished, she pursed her lips. "Interesting," she muttered just above a whisper. "I suspect low doses of thallium, given over a few days or weeks. If it were a high dose, hair loss could not have occurred before death. There would exist all the symptoms you mentioned: nerve damage and numbness in the extremities. The eyes can bleed after the hair falls out. The skin has an intense sensation of burning, like walking on or handling hot coals. These men you describe did not die peacefully if it was indeed thallium. Some have said the poison is like experiencing the fires of hell on earth, with only death to look forward to. Not at all a pleasant way to go."

"Why would someone use this particular poison? Why not arsenic?" Lewis wondered.

Agatha sniffed. "Thallium is colorless, odorless, tasteless, slow acting in low doses, very painful, and with wide-ranging symptoms that are often suggestive of a host of other illnesses and conditions, making it ripe for misdiagnosis and incorrect treatment. I would suppose the discomfort of it all may have been why it was chosen. This sounds to be a vengeful killing, stemming from a very real hatred of the deceased. Slow and painful. And I would guess that the killer was quite intentional and careful not to administer too high of a dose and end the misery too quickly, until the right time."

"How would the poison be administered?" Lewis had pulled out a pad and was jotting down some simple notes.

"Inhalation in gaseous or powdered form. Or direct contact in liquid form. Put the poison on food or in a drink, or drip some on a glove you know the intended victim will wear. The poison can be absorbed through the skin, but ingested would cause much more rapid symptoms, similar to inhalation if the concentration was strong enough."

"Where would one procure thallium?"

"Most pharmacists would have access. It has its beneficial uses, though not many, and access is very restricted even when there is a supply, which is, as I mentioned, rare. I suppose it could be stolen or purchased alternatively given the right contacts. There are much more deadly and fast-acting poisons that could be obtained far easier and at a lower cost. In fact, if I were to make you a tea using the dried leaves of nearly half a dozen of the plants in this room, you would be dead within the hour."

"That is a disturbing thought." Lewis's throat felt momentarily dry before he took another hesitant sip of chamomile.

"Isn't it, though?" Agatha's grin was coy.

"I fear another, a third victim, may be killed next Monday night," Lewis told her. "Though I know not who, where, or how."

Agatha narrowed her eyes. "Knowing when can be useful. Most likely, whoever it is may already be poisoned. That is, if the modus operandi holds true. The date you speak of could be a culmination of sorts, a final stronger dose. Are you certain it will be Monday?"

"Yes, as certain as we dare to be," Lewis said. "On the full moon, as part of some twisted pagan ritual."

"Or someone trying to make it look like one," Christie suggested.

Lewis's expression turned grim. "Exactly my thoughts. A mystical smoke screen."

Agatha nodded as if she had suspected some ritualistic

component. "So dark and macabre. And now I see how Crowley fits in." She thought for a moment. "If that is the case, do you mind if I begin working on brewing you an antidote to thallium poisoning? It's called Prussian blue. I believe I have everything I need right here with me in my apothecary, though it may take an hour or two to get right. Do you mind waiting?"

Lewis's eyes widened. "Yes, of course I'll wait. It may prove useful before this is all over."

Agatha rose and made her way toward a dark, glass-fronted cabinet full of boxes and vials. She pulled out a small key from a drawer and slid it into the cabinet lock. "Better to have an antidote and not need it, I say, than not have it and die a horrible and painful death." She glanced at Lewis over her shoulder. "Don't you think, Professor?"

"Oh, I very much do," Lewis asserted.

While she worked, Agatha occasionally looked back toward where Lewis sat. "You know," she mused, "poison is typically thought to be a woman's murder weapon of choice."

"Yes, it is," Lewis agreed.

Agatha arched a brow. "Or a man trying to make a detective think the culprit is a woman."

"So, not helpful in the least." Lewis smirked.

Agatha laughed. "It is all maddening, isn't it, Professor? Puzzles upon puzzles. Who's the cat, and who is the mouse?" She added three drops from a pipette into a larger vial. "The murderer either runs away or stays close enough to move the pieces around the board. Either way, we follow the evidence, but we must also trust our gut, our God-given instincts. They won't hold up in court, but they have been known to lead us to what will. I trust you have a good gut." She winked at Lewis, who looked down at his stomach.

"Warren tells me mine is expanding as of late."

Agatha tilted her head to one side. "And what is your gut telling you?"

"My gut is telling me that the answers I am looking for will be found in Scotland."

"Boleskine?"

"Thereabouts."

"Why?" she asked with a slight squint.

"It's where this story all begins," Lewis said evenly.

"So, what is stopping you?" She spoke as if she'd known the conversation would eventually end up in this place.

"If I cross a line, I may not live to see the new year," Lewis confided.

"Are you being followed?"

Lewis nodded.

"Never let the threat of death keep you from being a good detective," she advised. "There are far more important things to lose than your life."

"Like what?"

Agatha smiled faintly as she stirred the vial's contents. "Like your self-respect."

{20} The Gaudy

Still, it doesn't do to murder people,
no matter how offensive they may be.
—DOROTHY L. SAYERS, *The Five Red Herrings*

The Queen's College was located just off the High Street in the heart of Oxfordshire. A graceful baroque façade separated the college grounds from the busy cobbled sidewalk where passersby braved the cold this final Saturday before Christmas. Lewis entered the college grounds through an arched stone doorway, above which sat a prominent dome-covered statue of Queen Caroline, her abdomen exposed, looking down over all who entered. He nodded politely toward two male students dressed in dark dress robes who acted as sentries, checking names off a written list.

Lewis glanced back over his shoulder and caught the eye of a man staring at him. The man quickly broke his gaze. He was unusually large, looming a full head and shoulders over those around him. He wore all black with a bowler hat pulled low just above his eyes. Lewis didn't like the look of him and felt a familiar shiver pass down his spine as he turned back the other way.

As the line moved forward, Lewis could hear the rumble of brass and stringed music spilling out through propped-open doors at the other end of the quad. There was an almost palpable excitement in the air as the press of guests hurriedly pushed forward past the porter's lodge into the dining hall, which already smelled of ham enough to make Lewis's mouth water, despite the lingering anxiousness at the back of his mind. He turned and looked again over his shoulder just before he entered the Great Hall, and sure enough, the looming figure was only a half-dozen people behind him. Lewis could feel the man's eyes on the back of his neck.

The Great Hall featured a collection of oversized portraits of past queens all staring down on whoever dined. Most in attendance wore their Queen's College gowns, both current students who had not yet returned home for Christmas and former students who, despite their gray hair, regarded their alma mater with youthful pride.

Lewis made his way past long dining tables decorated with twisted evergreen boughs, sprigs of holly, and a mass of candles running their length. More candles lined the upper eaves, which cast an ominous dancing glow off the timber-framed ceiling. Lewis settled into a corner for the moment and peered out to get his bearings. He didn't like crowds. They always seemed to press down on him and squeeze the breath from his lungs. He especially didn't like crowds that could be concealing some nefarious character who looked as though he could crush a man with his bare hands.

By this point, hundreds of attendees milled about, gravitating en masse toward an open bar at the far end that had been set up underneath a prominent portrait of Queen Philippa, the wife of Edward III, for whom the college had been named. Meanwhile, a three-piece minstrel band featuring a trumpet played upbeat instrumentals of Christmas hymns alongside a bearded herald, who repeatedly called out that a special Boar's Head ale had been made for the event and was readily available.

Scanning the crowd, Lewis spotted Owen Barfield, looking every bit the solicitor and scholar that he was. He had risen from his place on a bench and enthusiastically waved for his friend to come over. Next to Barfield sat his demure wife, Maud, and across from the couple sat Adam Fox, who scooted down on the bench and made just enough room for Lewis to squeeze in and take a seat next to him.

"What have we gotten ourselves into?" Lewis questioned with a raised voice as he sat. Barfield slid a glass of ale across the thickly lacquered table with a red-faced grin. The drink was cold and delicious and instantly made Lewis's shoulders relax. He wiped foam from his upper lip, glad to be among friends for many reasons.

"You're in for a real treat, I'd say." Fox smiled and returned to humming along with the music.

"Is this your first gaudy?" Maud asked, meeting Lewis's eyes. She was a kind woman with straw-colored hair that had been curled for the event. Lewis had always liked her.

"Yes, it is." Lewis shifted on the bench to search for the man in black and to take in the room, which seemed to be growing louder with each passing minute. This made the Detection Club dinner look more like a tea party. "I had no idea what I'd been missing all these years," Jack commented to no one in particular.

"There is our guest of honor." Barfield inclined his head

toward a raised dais, on which sat a table lined on one side with chairs facing out toward the room. A duo of students had just shown Dorothy Sayers to her seat. Lewis raised a brow when he saw her. She wore a tight-fitting green dress that fell to her ankles, and again her hair was done up under a floppy black hat that sparkled in the candlelight.

"She looks like a Hollywood starlet!" Maud exclaimed with glee. "I've never seen the woman in lipstick. It suits her."

"Dorothy's book was based in part on this very event," Barfield said. "In case you are wondering what all the fuss is about. The school wanted to show their gratitude for the influx of applications."

Lewis nodded. "Yes, I was the one who told you that, Owen. Though it still strikes me as strange, since Dorothy never attended the Queen's College. But I suppose the book's success made all that nothing to thumb one's nose at."

Barfield lifted his glass in a mock toast. "A nod is as good as a wink to a blind man."

A sudden blast of a trio of trumpets got the whole room's attention, and everyone soon wrapped up conversations and took their seats. After a pregnant pause, the trumpeters began a rising melodic tune, ending with a single long blast that echoed off the rafters.

In the silence that followed, a set of twin doors leading to the kitchen creaked open, and the onlookers, starting with the eldest alumni, began clapping their hands. Others rhythmically pounded their mugs of ale on the tables, while also stomping their feet and shouting, before finally coming to a crescendo and then falling quiet once more.

Through the doors stepped the first of several in what would be a very strange parade. The procession began with another familiar tune, to which a choir in another part of the room started singing. Afterward, a gowned man carried a flag with a silver Queen's College crest on it, followed by four men, alumni in black formal gowns, each holding one part of a large silver platter over their heads, who made their way down the aisle between table rows. On top of the platter, now fully raised for the whole room to see, sat a blackened boar's head—teeth protruding and tusks intact.

Lewis regarded the strange brown mound with interest as the four men continued marching in step to the sound of some ceremonial dirge that every Queen's College student was familiar with but Lewis had never heard. The parade moved slowly down the aisle, passing behind Lewis, and came to a full stop near the raised head table. When they had ceremoniously placed the oversized silver tray atop a decoratively carved wooden stand, the four ushers bowed and took their seats. The room burst forth with another round of enthusiastic, ale-fueled applause.

It was then that Lewis spotted the man in black, little more than a shadow standing on the far side of the room, a head and shoulders above all those around him. The man was not looking at the boar on the stand. His eyes were fixed on Lewis, and again Lewis felt his breath catch in his throat and his heart start pounding. He wondered for a moment if he should mention the potential threat to Owen and Fox, but the clapping was too loud.

The provost of the Queen's College, a short man with bright white hair, stood up from his seat at the head table and waited for the room to quiet down. To his right sat the guest of honor, Dorothy Sayers, who had just spotted Barfield, then Lewis, and inclined her head toward them.

"I welcome all students, alumni, old members, and honored

guests to the annual Boar's Head Gaudy." The provost spoke slowly in a deep voice that in no way matched his slight demeanor. "Ours is a tradition that dates back hundreds of years, and you here tonight have been selected to bear witness to this great honor." He paused while applause once again filled the room. The man gestured with his hand toward Dorothy before saying, "Our special guest of honor tonight is Oxford's very own Dorothy Sayers, whose most recent bestselling novel is lovingly based on our little yearly soirée here. Let us bestow upon her some Queen's College gratitude."

The room erupted in more cheering, to which Dorothy stood, waved, bowed, and joined the provost shoulder to shoulder in a preplanned toast. She held her glass high without a word, and soon the audience stood and joined the pair, eager for another reason to sip deeply. Lewis held his glass of Boar's Head ale high over his right shoulder and smiled, even as his eyes wandered toward his watcher.

"Thank you all!" Dorothy acknowledged, her glass outstretched. "I am delighted to be here with you tonight. A true honor. I will now quote from Shakespeare's *Antony and Cleopatra*. Let us all remain standing and recite the words together if you know them: 'Let's have one other gaudy night,' " she quoted boldly as the crowd spoke the words partially in time with her. " 'Call to me all my sad captains; fill our bowls once more; let's mock the midnight bell.' " With that, she tilted her head back and drank, as did Lewis, who finished half his glass before setting the mug on the table with a thump and joining yet another round of rising applause, which fell into whistling and bawdy singing.

A clanging bell rang and was quickly swallowed up by more clapping, shouting, stomping, and pounding of mugs on wooden tables. It was enough to give Lewis a headache. He looked at the hulking shadow again and thought for a moment of making his escape, until he saw a line of robed student waiters carrying plates filled with potatoes, vegetables, bread, pudding, and, of course, steaming pork.

"I may need to loosen my belt if I keep eating like this," Lewis declared, again to no one in particular, before using the provided knife to slice into his very own slab of roasted pork.

After the meal was finished, Lewis excused himself to use the lavatory. He made his way out of the Great Hall, down a series of long hallways of checkered stone floors, past signage that pointed the way. It was on the return journey that Lewis heard the tapping sound of footsteps on stone behind him. He turned, and his blood ran cold when he saw the man in black coming around a corner and into view. Lewis hurriedly rounded the next corner, his mind racing through a series of options in a flash. He could make a run for it back to the Great Hall or try to exit altogether through some side door. But the fear within him was suddenly replaced with anger and indignation. He was never a man to run from danger, and he resolved not to do it now.

Lewis reached out and gripped the brass handle of the nearest door, labeled a custodial closet, and jerked it open. As he heard the clacking footsteps grow closer, he grabbed hold of the first thing he saw that resembled a weapon. Lewis spun on his heels and held up the wooden broom just as the man came into sight. The two were now face-to-face in a sense, though Lewis's wide eyes were even only with the man's broad chest.

"Don't come a step nearer!" Lewis yelled. "I will hit you." His knuckles were white as he prepared to strike.

What happened next surprised Lewis. Instead of advancing with raised fists or a menacing sneer, the giant of a man stepped back, cowered in fear, and put both arms up in front of his face in a defensive posture.

"D-don't hurt m-me, m-mister," the man stammered in a high-pitched voice. He sounded like a child. "I didn't m-mean anything by it. He t-told me to f-follow you. Don't hurt m-me."

Lewis lowered the broom halfway. "Who told you?" he demanded sternly.

"The m-master m-made me," the man answered, his voice shaking.

"Crowley?" Lewis guessed.

The man nodded vigorously while still cowering.

"Compose yourself, man," Lewis ordered, his own fear having vanished. "What did Crowley want you to do?"

"Just for m-me to w-watch you," the man replied, finally able to look up and meet Lewis's eyes. "And report back. Nothin' m-more, m-mister. Honest. I swear."

"There you are," a voice echoed down the hallway from the direction of the Great Hall. It was Fox, walking toward the pair of men with a curious look. "I wanted to tell you about something, Jack. Are you busy? Who is that man, and where is he going in such a hurry?"

Lewis turned back to see the man running in the opposite direction as fast as his large legs could carry him, soon darting around a corner and out of sight. *Too bad I didn't get the chance to ask more questions.*

"That was strange," Fox remarked.

"Yes, it was." Lewis leaned the broom against the wall. He'd think more about this encounter later.

"I had an epiphany just now." Fox clasped his hands behind his back and leaned toward Lewis's ear. "Do you know where the legend of the Boar's Head Gaudy comes from?" He rocked back and raised a bushy brow while a knowing smile played on his lips.

Lewis shook his head. "I haven't the slightest idea, Fox. Though I'd imagine there is a pig involved." He glanced over his shoulder again, but the man was long gone by now.

"Yes, yes," Fox acknowledged. "All the pageantry, the horns, the speeches, the choir . . . Where does it all come from? How is it that this ridiculous affair exists today in all its pomp and revelry?"

"I have a feeling you're about to tell me," Lewis said. "Though I am confused as to why exactly I need to hear this now." Over Fox's shoulder, he saw a lit trophy case filled nearly full with the Queen's College crew awards.

"I'm getting to it." Fox waved a hand in front of his face, which was reddened, no doubt from the Boar's Head ale. "The legend goes that many centuries past, a student of early medieval Oxford was walking through the forest of Shotover, reading Aristotle as he went, when out of nowhere he was attacked by a wild boar." Fox bared his teeth. "The boar was vicious and wild, but the student, with great presence of mind—or perhaps an element of luck—rammed the very book he was reading into the open mouth of the advancing animal and thus choked it to death."

"Doubtful," Lewis inserted, to which Fox nodded vigorously.

"I, too, doubt it actually happened," Fox agreed. "At least not the way it's been told—whispering down the lane and all that." He held up his pointer finger. "But the fact remains, Jack: All you see here today stems from that single incident or fabled telling of the incident." He paused and puckered his forehead until his eyebrows nearly connected into one over the bridge of his nose. "I was thinking about it just now and had an epiphany of context within literary criticism."

Lewis tilted his ear toward Fox. "Go on," he prompted, though his wandering mind could pay attention only in part.

"You start with the macro and narrow your focus to the micro." Fox glanced up at Lewis. "I know you are aware of this, but bear with me. Or should I say 'boar with me'?" He laughed at his pun before straightening up to continue. "It is the same as with literary criticism or a hermeneutical approach. You move from the wider context down to the minute jot or tittle. What is the passage in question within the culture, geography, and time period? Then you analyze the speaker or writer and the intended audience. After these considerations, the study moves further down to the actual words, their placement, interpretation, and contextual meaning." He hesitated.

"I know you are going somewhere with this," Lewis commented, amused. "Please do try to arrive soon."

"Well, it's the same with murder, don't you see, Jack? Or with solving any mystery really. We start with a macro of the event and the suspects—the city, region, house location, room where the murder took place, and the position of the body—then move down to evidence of small things like a colored hair, fingerprints, or some trace the killer left behind. But in all of it, there is a source—not the murder itself but the thing that gave birth to it. Not the evidence but what led to that evidence being left. It is that small thing that leads to everything else. A single act, even a thought or idea. The zero event."

"I see what you're getting at," Lewis mused, now more intrigued.

Fox nodded and swirled his hands in front of him. "Then that small thing begins to spiral outward, a ripple to countless ends. The key in all of it is to get back to the center, to the core of where it all started, like the book and the boar. If you find the center, you will solve the crime, but to do that, you need to stop looking at the spiral and instead focus on the spot in the middle where everything else radiates from." He stared Lewis in the eyes. "Do you understand what I am telling you, Professor?"

"I believe so," Lewis said. "Look for the source that led to this chain reaction of progressively horrible events."

"Precisely." A smile slowly worked its way across Fox's face. He leaned forward and put his hand on Lewis's shoulder to steady himself. "And this can happen only by asking the right questions. Perhaps you are asking *why* when you should be asking *where*. Or perhaps you are asking *how* when you should be asking *when*." He stopped suddenly, blinking his eyes. "My head is spinning. I think I need to sit down."

The evening continued for another hour with a series of toasts and choral songs, accompanied loudly by well-lubricated students, both former and current. Lewis spent the time thinking about his encounter in the hallway, as well as what Fox said and how it fit with the case.

As if on cue, as soon as it was announced that the ale had run dry, the room began emptying and spilling out into the cold streets to be continued in a dozen smaller establishments.

"Thank you for inviting me." Lewis approached Dorothy,

who had momentarily freed herself for what seemed like the first time in hours from an onslaught of mostly male well-wishers.

"Don't mention it." Dorothy smiled as she watched her admirers depart. "My characters are mostly men," she explained. "I need to spend time with them to know what they say and how they say it. At times, it's a bit like Darwin studying a strange new species."

"I've never really cared for Darwin's work," Lewis remarked.

Dorothy laughed. "I'm so glad you didn't stand me up, Jack."

"Did I have a choice?"

"No, you didn't," she admitted quickly, flashing a grin as they began walking toward the coat check. "Two down and one still to go. I know you'll love the theater best of all."

"I am looking forward to it," Lewis said truthfully, almost surprised at his own words.

Dorothy raised a brow. "I'll make a man-about-town out of you yet. And how was your luncheon with the Queen of Crime? I hope it was worth all this trouble." She gestured flippantly to the room around her, though Lewis knew she had loved every minute of it.

"It was a very rewarding and fruitful conversation," Lewis replied with complete honesty. He could feel the small vial in his right breast pocket. "I walked away with a pocketful of wisdom, in more ways than one."

Dorothy squinted. "What strange phrasing. But you keep your cards tight to your chest, Jack. That way you can bluff, and none will be the wiser." She nudged his arm. "What are you doing now? Are you up for an after-party? Completely optional."

"I don't think I would survive it." Lewis could feel his eyelids drooping, a telltale sign of the exhaustion washing over him. "Sorry to disappoint. I've had more excitement for one evening than I was built for. I need to race to the nearest bed, get some sleep, and prepare for whatever adventure tomorrow brings."

{21} The Letter

Sunday, December 20

> It does not do to leave a live dragon out
> of your calculations, if you live near him.
> —J. R. R. TOLKIEN, *The Hobbit*

After church, Tolkien said farewell to his family, as they were off to spend the day at the Covered Market for some late Christmas shopping. With a weary sigh, Tolkien shoved cold hands into the hip pockets of his overcoat and set off south toward the Martyrs' Memorial. The gusting wind tried to steal his hat from his head, where troubling thoughts awakened and fluttered like swirling leaves. He soon found himself mumbling under his breath, replaying conversations he'd had over the previous two days. He resolved to set the case aside; he had work to do, and it was not the kind he preferred. A final set of papers and exams needed to be graded and posted early Monday morning to the student boards before his three-week holiday officially began. One last push and he would be free to shift his full and undivided attention onto solving murder. Decision made, he continued past the memorial in the direction of Pembroke College.

Tolkien had just opened the frosted-glass-paneled door to his office when he nearly stepped on an envelope. Most likely, the college porter had shoved it under the door. Written messages were often passed to a gate guard, porter, or head student with access to the hallway, to be delivered on trust in exchange for a coin. The professor wiped his nose with a handkerchief as he turned the cream envelope over. There was nothing on it besides *Tolkien,* written in dark blood-red ink.

"How odd," he said out loud as he closed the door behind him and spied his name in such strange script. The ink had been smudged from not being allowed to dry properly.

He flipped on an overhead light and found his monogrammed silver letter opener in the top drawer of his chestnut desk. Once he unfolded the letter, he discovered it held only a few words: "Need to talk. I have a confession. Blackwell's. Philosophy section. Sunday at sunset." It was signed by Robert MacDougall.

"MacDougall is in Oxford?" Tolkien questioned under his breath, turning the paper over to make sure nothing else was written on the back. He quickly reasoned that the Scotsman could have come on a late train after seeing Tolkien the previous morning at the open house in London. Not knowing the professor's home address, MacDougall had likely made his way to Pembroke to find a way to convey his message.

"What does MacDougall have to confess?" Tolkien whispered, curiosity beginning to take hold. He squinted his eyes and read the message again.

For the next few hours, Tolkien worked at his desk, but his

mind frequently floated back to the letter that lay open facing him, as if calling out to be read over and over. It was quite a nuisance, and since it wasn't even yet noon, he still had a long time to wait until sunset, Blackwell's, and any sort of answers.

His work finally done, Tolkien picked up the phone to connect with Lewis at the Kilns. However, realizing the time just before the operator picked up, he set the phone back into its receiver and tapped his foot nervously. Jack, Warren, and Janie would be at church in Headington Quarry. He contemplated making the walk, then glanced out his window and thought better of it. No use getting a cold or pneumonia walking into the wind for nearly an hour when such an important week lay ahead for him. Instead, Tolkien leaned back in his creaking chair, pinched the bridge of his nose with thumb and forefinger, and rested his tired eyes.

The professor realized he must have fallen asleep when he awoke to the waning, low winter sun casting an orange glow through his office window. After a telephone call home to Edith, telling her he would not be back for dinner, Tolkien locked up his office and walked briskly to Blackwell's in as straight a line as possible, cutting through narrow back alleys and taking whatever shortcuts he remembered. Quickly realizing he was still far too early, he took momentary refuge from the cold by sliding into a booth at the sparsely occupied Turf Tavern.

When he smelled food and his mouth watered, he realized he hadn't eaten yet that day and reasoned an early dinner on his own was called for. He ordered a cottage pie and hot cider and idly looked out the window as hurried shoppers, bundled against the cold, whistling wind, moved past in either direction. Tolkien sighed, pulled his sketchbook from his pocket, and set to drawing a character in charcoal while he waited for his food. What started as just a furry-footed hobbit soon turned into a sketch of a dragon.

After a hearty meal, Tolkien checked his pocket watch and reluctantly scooted out of the booth. He soon caught a glimpse of the bookstore entrance and found the nearest street crossing. The front façade was so simple and nondescript that a tourist might mistake it for a small shop, but inside, Blackwell's spacious bookstore rivaled the world's largest libraries. Floors of books, some even below ground, were proudly displayed nearly as far as the eye could see. Tolkien loved the way it smelled best of all. Something in the aromas of leather, paper, and binding glue made him feel strangely at home. He made his way through the aisles to the philosophy section, a place he knew well and would need no help finding.

Tolkien waited patiently at an open table and tapped his foot. The bookstore was surprisingly empty. To pass the time, he pulled a volume on Greek thought off the nearby shelf. A half hour passed before Tolkien anxiously looked up, frowned, and set about reading another chapter he didn't particularly care for.

After many more chapters and a sore backside, Tolkien scowled when he heard the clocks strike seven. He realized the bookstore had already been closed for an hour. Tolkien worked his jaw in frustration and tapped his fingers on the table before reluctantly concluding that MacDougall would not be showing up and that no confession or resolution of any sort would be heard this evening.

"What a waste." He got up to leave, gathering his jacket. As he moved toward the entrance, he spotted a familiar face—or at least a portion of a face—buried in a leather-bound book somewhere near the mythology section.

"Charles, is that you?" Tolkien asked, making his way over.

Charles Williams furrowed his brow until recognition brought a smile. "Professor Tolkien," he acknowledged, standing to shake his hand.

"What brings you to Blackwell's at this hour?" Tolkien said.

"I do a lot of work with Blackwell's and Oxford University Press," Charles responded. "However, this evening I am following up on something Professor Lewis asked me to look into."

"Ah, you're here for the case as well." Tolkien looked down at the academic volumes set out before the man. "Speaking of, can I talk to you privately for a moment?"

He paused and swept his eyes over what he could see of the nearby stacks. Besides a familiar employee and an older woman a few aisles over, they were sufficiently alone. Satisfied, Tolkien slid the unfolded letter in front of Charles.

Williams read it slowly. "I take it he didn't show," he said, refolding the letter and handing it back to the professor.

"No, he did not," Tolkien confirmed, frustration plain in his voice. "Any guess as to what he would be confessing?"

"To murder?" Williams said evenly.

"That's what I thought, but why would he do that?"

"Clarity of conscience," Williams offered. "The tone of the letter, though short, suggests a weighty burden. Confession is good for the soul." He adjusted his glasses and leaned closer. "Perhaps he was involved in one or both of the murders and wishes to confide in you. Or perhaps he only knows more than he was letting on and wishes to clear the air."

Tolkien nodded. "So, either he is the murderer, or he knows who is."

Charles returned the nod. "Those would be the two strongest options. Or a third may be that this is a confession of something far older—perhaps how this whole set of affairs was put into motion."

"That could also be true," Tolkien agreed, again reading the letter for himself. He frowned. "Which makes his absence all the more frustrating."

"Did you speak to Lewis about this?" Williams asked. He stepped back and pushed his round wire-framed glasses onto the bridge of his nose before gathering up his briefcase and coat.

"No, I was hoping to have something to tell him first," Tolkien replied. "You know how Jack feels about people who bring problems with no solutions."

"I see," Williams said. "But now the absence may be saying something as well. MacDougall may have changed his mind and gone on the run."

Tolkien tapped the table with his knuckles in silent thought. He then snapped his fingers and made his way toward a clerk's desk near the front of the shop. Williams, seemingly curious, followed at a distance. After asking to use the phone, Tolkien again made the connection to the Kilns. Janie Moore answered, and the two spoke for less than a minute.

"Where's Lewis?" Williams said when Tolkien had disconnected.

"He's not far from here," Tolkien answered. "Only a few blocks. Jack's gone to see *Doctor Faustus* at the playhouse." Tolkien put his jacket on and popped his hat back on his head. "I'll be off, Charles," he said. "Thank you for your insight. If I hurry, perhaps I'll catch him on the way out."

{22} The Stage

When once your point of view is changed, the very thing which was so damning becomes a clue to the truth.

—Arthur Conan Doyle,
The Case-Book of Sherlock Holmes

The brand-new marquee of the Oxford Playhouse was lit bright white with crisp black lettering telling the name of the play—*Doctor Faustus*—with the notice Final Showing after it. The not-yet-officially opened Oxford Playhouse was located off Beaumont Street, just south of the Ashmolean Museum in the heart of the city. Lewis had walked past often during the previous spring and summer construction phases, but never when the place was lit up and accepting guests. It was the final night of the short-run stage play, which had served as a soft opening for the highly anticipated performance venue, set to open to the public the following year.

Lewis took his place in a short queue leading to a glass-walled booth that jutted out into the newly paved sidewalk. Dorothy had left instructions that a ticket was waiting for him at will call. Looking around, Lewis instantly felt underdressed in simple trousers, the same borrowed dark jacket and shoes from the dinner two nights earlier, and a tie with a mostly hidden stain from said dinner. He spotted distinguished gentlemen in black-tie and semiformal attire, three-button tailored suits with notched lapels and colorfully printed pocket squares.

Lewis noted many glamorous women in attendance as well, their gloved arms clinging closely to their dates in the cold. He saw silk dresses with glittering jewelry to match, and hair done up in the latest trends, accented with stylish hats and hair clips. Like the gaudy event the night before, this was proving to be some sort of major occasion, of which Lewis would have had no idea if not for Sayers's insistent prodding and arrangement.

It was the first time Lewis had been out three nights in a row in decades, and in his mind, he blamed Dorothy for the slight pain in his lower back. He sighed and longed for a warm fire, an oversized mug of tea, and a good book. But that would come later. He owed her, and deep down he appreciated her nudging him to the other side of what his world had to offer besides a pub and a conversation, keeping in mind that Dorothy Sayers enjoyed those things too. He chided himself for being petty and selfish in the face of what most presumably was an expensive and hard-to-come-by theater ticket.

"One for Jack Lewis," he said into a small brass circle with holes cut for sound. The smiling old gentleman in a bow tie rifled through a box on his desk and handed Jack an envelope that contained one ticket and a puzzling note that just said, "Don't keep him waiting," signed "D."

An usher directed Lewis up two sets of maroon carpeted

stairs; through a dark mahogany door; down a dimly lit, carpeted hallway; through a similarly colored fringed curtain; and finally into a private balcony box that jutted out and overlooked the stage and orchestra pit from an angle Lewis had never experienced before. Only it wasn't Dorothy sitting in the box's other seat—it was the burly frame of a bearded gentleman wearing a top hat, with a cane resting on his lap. The man shifted and watched Lewis, who hesitantly pointed to the padded chair that matched his ticket. "I am in the right area, am I not? I was told . . ."

"Have a seat, Professor Lewis," the man said. "We've not yet met in person, though I have met some of your fellow Inklings. You were under the weather, if I recall. My name is Sir Arthur Conan Doyle. Though I admit the disguise I am wearing is not a very good one."

Lewis sat fully and looked at the man in amazement. He was wearing a glued-on fake beard, and up close, his nose seemed to have some sort of prosthetic addition.

"It's dark in here," Doyle explained. "I don't plan to stay long."

"Sir Arthur," Lewis said, still surprised, "it is an honor to meet you, though I was told you would be in contact after Christmas when—" He stopped, his eyes narrowing. "Dorothy," he muttered, half to himself.

"Yes," Doyle confirmed with a sly smile. "I see you are working it out. Dorothy Sayers is my most promising protégé. She works with me closely as my apprentice and has been keeping an eye on you, as well as Tolkien, over the past weeks and even months leading up to my approaching your charming literary group. Ms. Sayers has helped and will help when needed, a gentle nudging at first—though connecting with Agatha was the right decision, and you made it all on your own. Thallium poisoning. Now we just need the who and why."

Lewis sat dumbfounded. His thoughts swirled, then settled again on Dorothy. It made sense, given her penchant for crime writing coupled with her naturally sleuthing, puzzle-solving mind. He had just opened his mouth to speak when another thought struck him, but Doyle spoke first.

"Agatha as well," Doyle said as if sensing the question forming in Lewis's mind. "Though we have no formal partnership. She's a bit of a recluse really. The Detection Club has flashes of talent for the real thing, though most just have a wild imagination and a liking for good food, free drinks, and rubbing shoulders with those they aspire to be. Still, there has been a rich pool of recruits in the past. Knox, too, to an extent. Agatha rang me not long after you left yesterday."

"Sir Arthur . . ." Lewis began, his mind still racing. The small musical ensemble in the pit below tuned their stringed instruments and sounded low wails.

"Call me Arthur," the man said. "And I trust you will keep all this between us."

Lewis nodded. "Yes, of course. Is there anything about the case I should know?"

Doyle snorted. "I was about to ask you the same question. Pressure brings the best out of us, in my opinion, and no doubt the pressure is building with each passing day." He checked his pocket watch, then gripped his cane. "I should be going."

The seats were nearly full, and the overhead lights flashed. The musicians stopped playing as the start of the performance drew nearer.

Doyle stood and buttoned his jacket. "I only wanted to meet you, Professor Lewis," he said. "I'll be in touch soon.

Continue with urgency." He touched his forehead with the crystal ball of his cane and was off through the curtain.

No sooner had Doyle gone than Dorothy Sayers slipped into his seat, fanning herself while smoking. "So now you know," she said. "Do you hate me, Jack?"

"Why on earth would I hate you?" Lewis questioned.

"For keeping secrets from you," she responded. "I'm too good at it, though I don't like to. I respect you too much to have hidden it for much longer, no matter what Doyle said."

"Why would I be angry with you about that?" he asked. "In a way, I was doing the same thing, wasn't I? I never told you about any of it. Yet you knew it all along."

Dorothy arched a brow, relieved. "It does my heart good to hear it."

Lewis felt himself relax a bit as well, now that one mystery had been solved, leaving only a dozen to go. He cracked a smile. "Is it like being mentored by Sherlock Holmes?"

"Oh, far more intense," Dorothy replied, a sly grin playing across her face, "though a lot less deduction and cocaine and more procedural detection. He is good at what he does. Doyle has much to teach, and I have much to learn."

"May I call you Watson?"

"Don't you dare!" she exclaimed with a side-eyed glare. "You wouldn't make it out of the theater alive."

Lewis sighed. He looked over the printed playbill that contained a list of scenes, the cast, and some notes of thanks to the sponsors and significant members who made the play possible. "I'm exhausted, Dorothy," he said lightly. "I was supposed to be on holiday now, but three nights in a row you've kept me. I could sleep through Christmas." He turned toward her, reached out, and squeezed her hand.

"Couldn't be helped," she said and squeezed back.

The lights went down as a hush fell over the at-capacity theater. Curtains opened, and Nevill Coghill walked onto the stage into the shine of a single spotlight. He held up his hand to quiet the enthusiastic crowd.

Dorothy leaned over. "There is your boy. The Inkling himself, enjoying his nightly single minute of fame. They add up to fifteen over the long run."

"Thank you all for coming," Nevill addressed the audience. "Tonight is the final night of our performance."

A roar of applause erupted. It was strange to see Nevill in the spotlight, since he preferred to do most of his work in the background; yet with this first play now under his belt, he seemed comfortable and in his element.

"Did you bring Nevill flowers?" Dorothy asked as Coghill began to thank a list of mostly unfamiliar names for their patronage and support.

"No," Lewis answered, reaching into his inner breast pocket for his cigarette case. "Was I supposed to?"

"Never mind," Dorothy said with a smile. "I did. Perhaps I'm just a better friend than you are."

"And with that," Nevill concluded, "Merry Christmas, and I hope you enjoy tonight's performance of *Doctor Faustus*."

The lights went black as the ominous thrum of a cello rose like an auditory wave. The stage lights soon came up dimly for the opening scene, which took place in the doctor's library. Faustus, the lead character, stood up from a comfortable chair and spoke his opening monologue in a heavy German accent.

For the next hour, Lewis watched a story he was familiar with, but through a new lens of performance. A talented German doctor and scholar, having reached the limits of human knowledge, believes the next evolution of his mind must be found outside conventional means. He turns to the supernatural and is offered a choice. A benevolent angelic being guides and encourages the doctor toward goodness, while a malevolent spirit guides Faustus down a path that surely will lead to damnation and destruction. As Lewis observed the play unfold, he could not help but see the story's similarities and parallels with recent events regarding the case and Aleister Crowley.

When the lights came on for intermission, Lewis found himself almost startled from his depth of thought. He sat for a moment in silence trying to make sense of what the deep recesses of his mind were attempting to bring to the conscious forefront.

Dorothy excused herself and slipped away to speak with some friends she had seen from the balcony. After smoking for a bit, Lewis felt as though he should use the restroom before the third act started. As he made his way out into the hallway, past opinionated conversations and couples staring lovingly into each other's eyes, he saw a large-framed man with a piercing gaze walking purposefully toward him. It was Crowley himself, and his wild eyes were focused on Lewis.

Lewis could not help but think that the devil was coming to have a conversation.

{23} The Curse

Indeed the safest road to Hell is the gradual one—the gentle slope, soft underfoot, without sudden turnings, without milestones, without signposts.

—C. S. Lewis, *The Screwtape Letters*

"Have you looked at the moon lately?" Crowley demanded, his mouth twisted in an arrogant sneer. His right hand was half hidden under the lapel near his left breast pocket. He appeared to Lewis a bit like a mortician.

"I have, often as of late," Lewis replied evenly. "One more week until the full moon."

"And . . ." Crowley prompted, tapping his black walking stick on the carpeted floor. "Where are we in the investigation?"

"Did you hire a man to follow me?" The words came out more forcefully than Lewis intended.

Crowley smirked. "I heard about your run-in with Jasper. He was more frightened than you were, I suspect."

"Was he supposed to be some sort of threat?" Lewis asked.

"He's harmless," Crowley said dismissively. "A man with the mind of a young boy. Does what I tell him to without question. A useful tool yet, as you saw, with limitations. But I would be a fool if I didn't keep an eye on you, and Tolkien as well."

"Do you not trust that we are pursuing leads relevant to the case?" Lewis shifted his gaze around the room to make sure no one was within earshot.

"I have looked into your past," Crowley responded, just above a growl. "I wanted to know more about you in particular, since we weren't able to speak privately in London. I have a curious desire to know the way your mind works, and I'm certain I am not alone in my curiosity. You have been looking into my past as well. You and that odd fellow who came to White's with you and Tolkien."

"That I have. As any investigator worth his salt would." Lewis met the magician's eyes and held the stare.

Crowley sniffed, almost appeased that he would be worthy of special interest. Lewis saw him visibly relax. "Well, now that's out of the way," he said lightly. "How are you enjoying the play? It's a favorite of mine, though I've seen it done better in Berlin. I see a lot of myself in the character of Faustus and his noble pursuit of greater knowledge and power, don't you?"

"I've read the book," Lewis noted. "It ends badly for the doctor."

"We all die, Professor Lewis. I will spend my eternity with my master, and you with yours."

"As long as your eyes are open," Lewis said. "Then there is nothing more I can say."

Above their heads, the electric lights flickered as Lewis inspected Crowley's profile. He could never feel at ease around the man. There was a lingering sense—perhaps a spiritual intuition—that something was indeed very off with him, like a piece of fruit gone bad beneath the peel.

"I suppose it's time we got back to our seats," Crowley said with a smile. "Mine are down front."

"Yes," Lewis remarked, "wouldn't want to miss how this one ends." Lewis started to turn but Crowley reached out and caught him by the shoulder. His hands were strong, his grip firm yet not aggressive.

"Are you sure there is nothing you can tell me about the case? Is it because I am a suspect?"

Lewis nodded. He felt a boldness within him, coupled with the thought of never showing this man weakness or timidity. "In my mind, you are still a suspect in that you have not been eliminated," he replied. "That and also the fact I don't work for you or report to you or even like you as a person."

Crowley grinned, revealing his large teeth. "I am not a likable man, and I am admittedly not a moral man. But I am no murderer, Professor. You may think me a beast, but your energies would be better served looking elsewhere."

"I feel as though everywhere I turn," Lewis said carefully, "there are people who are not telling me the whole truth, you included. Beckworth and MacDougall as well. I'm not sure if anyone connected to this mystery has told the whole truth or is even capable of it."

Crowley let his smile fade and tilted his head to one side. "How did Pontius Pilate put it? 'What is truth?'" Crowley clenched his jaw. "Even when you know it, will you accept it?" He paused, then added, "What will you do next?"

"I would be a fool to tell you, yet I will say that sometimes, the best way to get to the truth is to go right to the source."

Crowley raised a brow. The lights flickered again as he

reached into his breast pocket and pulled out what looked to be a business card with writing in pen scribbled on it. "If you change your mind, Professor, I can be reached at this number until the full moon. I can be a powerful ally." Crowley turned on his heels and left without another word, his dark cape trailing behind him.

Lewis felt his heartbeat slow as if a venomous snake had passed by and was now out of striking range. He swallowed and felt reality return, as if for the past few minutes he had been in a kind of trance or hypnotic state. With a shiver, he turned back toward the private box, forgetting entirely his need to use the restroom.

"I saw you speaking with Crowley," Dorothy said when Lewis had retaken his seat.

He thumbed at the business card he hadn't yet looked at, now in his pocket. Lewis was lost in thought but nodded at her unspoken question. Dorothy didn't press.

The third act opened with a supernaturally empowered Faustus riding in a chariot drawn by dragons. Lewis was impressed by the theatrically creative feat and would be sure to mention it to Nevill at the next opportunity. As the scenes progressed, Lewis's mind drifted to thoughts of the supernatural realm and how evil poisons and influences the hearts of men. Despite what Faustus had gained in ill-gotten knowledge and abilities, when the clock struck twelve, the doctor was dragged off to hell in an unsettling and nightmarish final scene.

Once the performance came to a close, the actors came out from behind drawn curtains to take their bows to thunderous applause. Lewis could not help but think of something the play had sparked in his mind: how one is influenced not only by the supernatural but also by events that occurred much earlier in life. In the end, Faustus faced a horrifying fate, yet this harvest was simply the result of a seed that had taken root with a single decision made decades earlier. Lewis's thoughts shifted again to the horrors of these murders, and he pondered the likelihood that the seed of vengeance and wrath in this case had also taken root many years earlier.

Lewis caught Dorothy watching him as he sat silently until well after the applause had died down. She waited near the entrance to the balcony, smoking and sweeping the emptying auditorium with her observant eyes.

Lewis sighed, stood, and placed his hat on his head. He felt the weight of exhaustion yet, at the same time, an invigorating spirit of resolve deep within him. In that moment, he knew what he needed to do next. It had been staring him in the face for the better part of a week. Something who was it had said? Charles Williams? Or perhaps Fox or Agatha or Crowley himself, or a combination of all four.

"Congratulations," Lewis said as he and Dorothy made their way through the throng toward the theater doors that would lead them out into the cold December night.

"Whatever for?" Dorothy asked as she fiddled with her handbag.

"I hear you helped write the stage version of the play. It was very well done. A much better version than I remember."

Dorothy smiled. "Be sure to congratulate Nevill when you see him next. He's been working on this for the better part of the year. Lost a bit of hair too, I'm sure. Far more time invested than anything I did."

When they exited the playhouse and walked down the steps toward the street, Lewis saw a familiar figure approaching, though the man's face was red with cold and he was out of breath.

"There you are, Jack," Tolkien said, pausing to catch his breath and wiping a sheen of sweat from his forehead with his embroidered handkerchief. "I've just come from Blackwell's. Janie told me you were here. Glad I could catch you. Listen, I received—" He stopped and looked at Dorothy.

"It's all right," Lewis assured him. "She is aware."

"I'm in it up to my eyeballs, darling," Dorothy stated with a flash of a smile.

The three of them took a few steps away from the lines of exiting people where they could speak in hushed tones.

"I received a note from MacDougall to meet with him," Tolkien explained. "He said he had a confession to make, only the man never showed."

Dorothy sucked in her breath and eyed Lewis. "Do you think he's on the run?"

"Possibly," Lewis replied. "If he wanted to confess to his crimes, then he changed his mind and ran scared."

"Could be." Tolkien nodded. "Or could be that something else kept him. I just thought you should know sooner rather than later."

"This only confirms what I had in mind to do next," Lewis said, his eyes unfocused. He then looked around and lowered his voice. "I am going to take a trip for the next few days."

Tolkien frowned. "Good heavens, Jack. Where are you going?"

"I am going to travel to Scotland. Inverness, more precisely," Lewis answered.

Dorothy blinked. "Why?" Her eyes then brightened. "Oh, you think MacDougall fled there? It is where he is from. That's how he met Crowley."

"Not exactly," Lewis said. "There are answers in Scotland

that I need. A decades-old piece of the puzzle we're missing. Though I'll keep my eyes open for him as well."

Tolkien raised a brow. As the professor looked up over Lewis's shoulder, Lewis saw his eyes go wide. In turning to see what he was looking at, Lewis spied Crowley standing just off the curb, waiting a moment to snuff out a cigarette and slip into the back seat of a '32 Morris Cowley. "He's here?" Tolkien said. "In Oxford?"

"Yes, we had a little chat earlier," Lewis responded, remembering the ill feeling. "It was not pleasant. That is why I'm going to Boleskine." He looked at Dorothy. "It's the place, along the shores of Loch Ness, where Crowley took control of the Order nearly thirty years ago. Whatever happened there at Boleskine House way back then may have set these murders in motion. I believe the key to all of this lies with Crowley. I cannot explain it. I don't know what I will find, if anything, or even what I'm looking for, but I need to go. It is the zero—the epicenter that the spiral traces back to."

Dorothy grunted. "Crowley won't like you visiting Scotland and poking around. He's had people watching you, and he won't like you spending the holiday in his old stomping ground."

"I'm not holidaying in Scotland," Lewis said. He cracked a smile. "Warren and I are going to Ireland for a few days to visit family for Christmas . . . only we're getting there by way of Scotland."

{24} The Journey

Monday, December 21

The love of knowledge is a kind of madness.
—C. S. Lewis, *Out of the Silent Planet*

On the shortest day of the year, Lewis, Warren, and Janie set off in the dark from their home in Headington Quarry in the back seat of Hugo Dyson's green Vauxhall Cadet. They arrived at the Oxford railway station in well enough time to take the early train north from Oxfordshire toward Leamington Spa. The brothers would spend most of the day sitting, reading, talking, eating, stretching, and being lost in thought before they finally arrived at Inverness station the following morning. Even then, their journey would not be complete, as they would need to find lodging and hire a car to take them to Boleskine House.

Janie hugged Lewis and Warren in turn before going her own way at Manchester station. She wished to spend Christmas with her daughter, Maureen, who had been visiting her father for the past few months at his home near Leeds. When Lewis had told Janie and Warren about his travel plans the night before, after returning from the playhouse, she had decided then and there to pack a bag and come along for part of the trip. The last thing she wanted was to spend Christmas alone in that old, drafty redbrick house.

The train had just jostled into movement when Warren asked, "So, tell me again, Jack—what in God's name are we doing in Scotland?" He leaned forward and lowered his voice. "Didn't these killings happen in London? Seems to me we're going the wrong way."

Jack could tell the question and coming conversation had been burning within his older brother for hours. He smiled knowingly, appreciating that Warren dared not ask and discuss an open case, or any past case for that matter, around Janie. The poor woman already had trouble sleeping, and the impending frightful nagging would not be helpful to anyone.

"You know why we are going," Jack replied, adjusting his jacket and leaning back into the thinly cushioned bench seat. "But beyond that, I have no special insight or answers that would satisfy you. I have reason to believe—that is, I have faith—that a missing piece of this puzzle can and will only be found where we are going. I'm nearly certain something happened at Boleskine House more than twenty years ago that set in motion what has recently taken place. I don't possess any solid evidence to support that fact, only a lingering instinct and reasonable suspicion that may prove a complete waste of time for us both."

"Wonderful," Warren said with a grim expression. "I'm glad to be spending Christmas on a potential waste of time." He slid a flask from his breast pocket and unscrewed the cap without looking.

"Nonsense, Warnie." Jack frowned. "You love to travel, and Christmas in Scotland is beautiful. Besides, you and I both needed a change of scenery, if only for a few days. We will share a walkabout and explore the city and lakeshore. Then in the evenings we will have spiced ale and ham, and you will close your eyes and pretend you are home in Belfast or wherever your imagination takes you."

Warren raised a brow. "Hmm." He set his lips in a thin line, then said, "So, tell me again why I, of all people, needed to come along. Why not Fox or Nevill?"

"Three reasons," Jack answered, sitting up straight as the train whistle sounded outside. He grabbed hold of one finger with his other hand. "First, to sell the idea that this was only a family holiday; second, because I enjoy your company above all; and last, because I need your help. And I know you enjoy a good mystery paired with sightseeing as much as I do."

"Exactly what type of help do you need?" Warren waved at a passing porter but couldn't get the man's attention, which brought a sullen frown. "I'm a bit in the dark as to what we are looking to find."

"As am I," Jack admitted with a laugh, "but two sets of eyes and ears are better than one. You also share a quality with Dyson I lack—the gift of loosening lips and getting people to talk. It is simply astounding the amount of quality information that can be gained from a gossipy spinster or a lonely local who wants only to share a pint or three with an interested tourist."

Warren scowled, his brow raised, then curled one side of his mouth into a dimpled smile. "I do enjoy dark beer and interesting conversation, stranger or not."

The train whistled again and passed into the darkness of

a tunnel. Both men used the moment to pause and feel the gentle rocking and rhythmic rattling of the train on its steel tracks. Each was lulled into a state of calm, which soon led to a contagious yawn.

"I'm going to take a nap," Warren said with finality. "There is plenty of time to talk later. And I do still have questions."

"So do I." Jack closed his own eyes and exhaled slowly. "So do I."

The train arrived in Inverness on schedule the following morning. Both brothers were stiff and longed for fresh air and a brisk morning walk, which was exactly what they did after a station luggage porter informed them that, to his knowledge, they could book a hired car for the day or a more extended period at the desk of the nearby Abertarff House. Warren recognized the name of the oldest residential building in the city.

Jack and Warren walked toward the River Ness, suitcases in hand, just as shops were opening for the day. The smell of fresh bread made their mouths water for scones. They arrived at the lime-white historic house, a classic example of sixteenth-century Scottish architecture, complete with crow-stepped gables looming overhead. After stepping inside, they were soon greeted by an older woman with long white hair twisted into a braid who was sweeping the stone floors. Jack made arrangements for a room while Warren smoked his pipe and inspected the inner character of the old building.

"Dinner service begins at five," the woman said as she paused to write their names in a ledger. Jack noted her accent sounded English, not Scottish. "All guests are welcome to join, and it is included in the price." She quickly added,

"I'm making a roasted duck stew, which is a family recipe going back hundreds of years. You won't find anything better in the city, so there's no need to bother looking."

"Oh, I believe you," Jack responded, smiling. "That sounds delightful. You don't sound as if you're from around here?"

She cackled loudly. "Married for forty years. Trust me when I say I'm an honorary local now." After snatching a key from a hook on the wall behind her, she took up both suitcases in her arms like they weighed nothing and began a quick ascent up the turnpike staircase. Jack left Warren behind and tried to keep up.

"Did you know that this very house was once owned by the Fraser family of Lovat?" she called back over her shoulder. "Their clansmen fought on the Jacobite side in the Battle of Culloden."

"I was not aware of that," Jack replied. "My brother is more versed on the subject than I. Are you a historian?"

She cackled again. "Not me, young sir. My husband is the one your brother would want to talk to. I've just picked up a thing or two."

"My brother and I are interested in hiring a car," Jack mentioned when they reached the top landing.

The woman nodded while she worked the skeleton key into the lock and opened the door. "My husband and my son have the car now. They will be back in the evening for dinner in the common room. You can make arrangements then to use it in the morning."

"Nothing today?" Lewis asked, moving his eyes around the simple room and finding it adequate.

"I'm afraid not, young sir," she said. "Only the one car, and in the evenings, it's spoken for—a taxi for the old drunks."

Jack and Warren decided to spend the morning walking

the city on foot, seeing sights like the Cameron Highlanders statue, and the towering brownstone of Inverness Castle, complete with dry moat and leftover cannons.

"There are many people here over the age of forty," Jack observed over a bowl of vegetable soup at lunch. "Someone saw something. Someone knows something. We just need to ask the right questions, then close our mouths and listen." He glanced at Warren, who nodded while shoving a buttered biscuit in his mouth.

"Got it," Warren finally said once he had swallowed. "Find old people, buy them drinks, and spark their stories of yesteryear, especially ones involving Crowley or Boleskine from around 1910 to 1913."

"Exactly," Jack said with a quick smile. "Though don't be too pushy. You may make a good private detective after all."

"Here I thought I already was one."

After lunch, the brothers took the Market Brae Steps to an upper street, cutting through a row of glass-front shops and modest row homes to reach a newer, more modern part of the city. While perusing a quaint bookstore, Warren chatted up the oldest employee to no avail. The gentleman only seemed to wonder whether the brothers were in town to snap a picture of Nessie. Warren replied that he was on a historical sightseeing tour, which wasn't far from the truth.

"You think he's a murderer?" Warren asked, once they had left the bookshop and found themselves walking a deserted street.

"Who? Crowley?" Jack answered. "Possibly. He's capable of it. The man's heart is black. But even if he is not, he is still the key to the lock."

"What makes you so certain of that?" Warren demanded.

"He is the lynchpin," Jack said matter-of-factly. "He is

what connects all the people of this case together. I also find it strange how he up and sold Boleskine House back in 1913 in such a hurry. From what I hear, he loved the place. Called himself the Lord or Laird of Boleskine."

Warren stopped to inspect a placard on a lichen-covered historical building. "He was running out of money?"

Jack pursed his lips. "Perhaps, but he had wealthy people he could ask for money."

"If his pride would let him," Warren pointed out, with an arched brow. The brothers walked on.

"It just seemed sudden," Lewis said. "I think something else happened. He didn't just sell the house; he left the country and moved to Paris."

"You think he was running from something?" Warren wondered.

Jack smiled and kicked a stone. "That's what I hope to find out."

At five o'clock sharp, Warren and Jack were seated at a table back at the Abertarff, and within a few minutes, each had a pint of dark ale, a large wooden bowl filled to the brim with duck stew, and a round stump of bread. Despite dinner being so similar to lunch, the meal far surpassed their expectations.

The owner of the Abertarff, whose name was Duncan, was hard to miss. A tall, older man, he walked from table to table in a circuit asking the same few questions with an honest smile and nod of his head before moving on. Warren attempted to engage him in extended conversations a few times, only to be interrupted by regulars with empty glasses.

When the brothers had finished eating, Jack gave Duncan his compliments and asked about a car to drive them around the following morning. Duncan was more than willing to rent out his car for the day, minus the driver, who was needed for other errands. Jack, who had never possessed a driver's license, was again glad he'd brought Warren along.

The warm common room didn't empty after dinner; it filled even fuller as a new group of what appeared to be older locals, most wearing colorful kilts, entered and took their places at the bar. Duncan took up his post as barkeep, pouring drinks and sharing stories the locals had most likely heard many times prior. As Jack sat watching the seven men laugh and take turns telling tall tales or somewhat dirty jokes, he wondered whether it was a picture of what the Inklings would become in time. He sighed and lit a cigarette.

Soon after what Warren promised would be the final round, two of the elder men passed by the brothers' table on the way back from relieving themselves, and one stopped to speak to them. He had a full head of gray hair with coarse red still in his beard. The way he spoke suggested he was asking a question, though the thick brogue accent made it nearly impossible to decipher what exactly he was saying.

After a second try and more confused smiles, the friend nearest him, a fellow Scotsman with bowlegs and flaming red hair, cleared his throat and asked in a low voice, "Ye come tae see Nessie? That is wha' he's askin'." He smiled widely and swayed from side to side while stroking his forked beard. "Everyone comes now tae see Nessie. Since tha' picture a few years back. Everyone comes tae spot the monster or snap a photo o' their own. Is that ye as well?" His speech was slurred, and the two Scots held on to each other to steady themselves.

"Oh," Jack said. "Not exactly. Though I believe Loch Ness is in the direction we will be heading in the morning."

The man winked. "Whatever ye do, don't go for a swim in

Loch Ness. Ye might get pulled down into the dark by yer toes. Those who go into the depths of darkness ne'er come back up."

"Thank you for the advice," Warren called after them, as the two men stumbled back toward their stools. He was about to stand and attempt to further engage the men in conversation, but the group suddenly burst into song.

It wasn't a loud, bawdy sing-along but a low, thrumming dirge that Jack could feel resounding in his chest. He was taken by the emotion of the singing, despite having no idea what the lyrics said. When it was over, Jack couldn't help but wipe a tear from his eye, though the song had nearly put Warren to sleep.

"I suppose we should go to bed." Jack took the final gulp from his mug. "We'll try again tomorrow."

Warren blinked his eyes open and glanced at the group of men who had begun singing again. "I'm sorry, Jack. We didn't get much."

"But that's why they're called regulars," Jack responded as he pushed out his chair and got to his feet. "They'll be in those same seats tomorrow."

Warren looked one final time at the group of older men at the bar. "I wonder . . ." he said slowly. "I wonder if that will be us in thirty years."

{25} The Jumble

Tuesday, December 22

> Faithless is he that says farewell
> when the road darkens.
>
> —J. R. R. TOLKIEN,
> *The Fellowship of the Ring*

"They've gone where?" Fox said loudly once Tolkien had relayed the full events of the previous two days. The Magdalen dean glanced around the space and lowered his voice cautiously, though Charlie Blagrove had kept the two tables nearest the Rabbit Room empty and all other patrons of the Bird out of earshot. "It's a fine time to take a sightseeing journey."

"You know it's not like that," Tolkien answered. He puffed his pipe and blew smoke out the side of his mouth. "I trust Jack's judgment, and I know you do too."

"We all do," Cecil affirmed. "And he's taken Warnie along, so that at least makes me feel better, though I am curious as to Jack's state of mind." He glanced sidelong at Hugo Dyson, who raised a brow, uncrossed his arms, and shrugged.

"I drove to the Kilns yesterday morning before sunrise," Dyson finally offered. "Jack was already awake and out front with bags packed when I arrived. He seemed eager to depart. Warnie was not as perky. I drove them to the station, and Janie tagged along as far as Leeds." He squinted at his pocket watch. "With no delays, they should have arrived in Inverness by now. Couldn't ask or say much with Janie in the vehicle, but I got a short snippet on the platform from Jack before the train departed. I've been instructed to tell you all that it has been all but confirmed that Pennington and Huxley were poisoned with thallium, but exactly how is still a mystery. Do with that knowledge what you will."

Fox stood and began pacing the room, his eyes fixed in concentration on nothing in particular as the floor creaked underfoot. He stopped by the fire to warm his hands, then paced again while shaking his head. The other three Inklings present at their regular Tuesday morning meeting sat silently, absorbing this new information.

"No use allowing our minds to float north with the brothers," Tolkien finally said. "We have a job to do here in the meantime."

"Find MacDougall?" Cecil asked.

"If we can," Tolkien replied. "Though Jack and Warnie are just as likely to stumble upon the man before we do."

"If he is indeed a man on the run," Dyson pointed out. "But more likely, he's buried in a shallow grave somewhere."

"Don't speak like that," Fox said sharply. "We're the holders of hope, not pessimistic defeatism."

Dyson frowned and crossed his arms again.

"We also now know Crowley is here in Oxford," Cecil noted.

Tolkien pointed at Cecil with the stem of his pipe. "Thank you for the reminder. I called around during the day yesterday. Crowley is staying at the Old Bank Hotel. Checked in on Saturday."

Fox stopped pacing. "No doubt it is odd the man shows up the same day the Scotsman goes missing, if indeed that day was Saturday."

Cecil narrowed his eyes and blew out smoke. "Are we insinuating Crowley may have had something to do with MacDougall's disappearance?"

"It is not beyond the realm of possibility," Tolkien said. "Perhaps Crowley wanted to keep the man quiet from whatever he wished to confess. Desperate men do desperate things if backed into a corner."

"Not to complicate matters further . . ." Cecil began, snuffing his cigarette into the nearby tabletop ashtray. "But in other news, I convinced my father to donate three seventeenth-century Dutch paintings to the Ashmolean after our dinner last week. Doolittle was thrilled but expected more, I think. Perhaps he is holding out hope for more donations in the future. However, he did call and leave a message that he is in Oxford currently and that this week would be good to set delivery. I rang back to tell him it wouldn't be possible until the new year, but it did strike me as odd he was here as well."

"Oh bother!" Fox exclaimed. "Everyone we want to be in Oxford is leaving town, and everyone we don't want has come flocking to our fair little city of spires."

"It would seem that way," Tolkien mumbled. He tapped his foot. "With Jack and Warnie out of town, and with Charles Williams leaving a note with Charlie saying he is headed back to London, for now, it will fall to us to pull the weight here. We'll need to keep an eye on Doolittle, Crowley, and Beckworth . . . not to mention Sarah Cornish, the maid. We'll want to follow up with her."

"And keep an eye out for the missing MacDougall," Fox noted.

"And also continue to investigate both Baron Huxley and the Penningtons, father and son, and make sure our Christmas shopping is complete," Dyson added.

Fox let out an exasperated sigh. "We mustn't forget to keep our wives happy, or this whole thing goes away. This is the part of any investigation where things get all jumbled. Too many strings, some needing to be cut."

"Much like a story in a book," Cecil said with a faint smile. "Hopefully we've come to the jumbled part right before everything comes together."

"We'll see about that." Dyson sounded skeptical. "Some stories end up in the wastebasket."

"What did I tell you about curbing your pessimism?" Fox asked, casting a sidelong glance at Dyson, who lifted both hands in mock surrender.

"I hope I'm not interrupting," a familiar voice called from the doorway.

The four men turned to see Owen Barfield, looking like a dapper gentleman in a three-button blazer and matching pants and vest. All of them stood and shook hands with him, genuine smiles on their faces. It was good to see him after his many weeks away.

"Have you come to lend a hand?" Fox questioned with a hopeful smile. "It seems as though we're barely treading water here."

"Sadly, no," Barfield replied. He held his hat in his hands and spun it between his palms. "Maud is waiting in the car actually. Just popped by to say hello and goodbye since I knew you'd all be here."

"See what I mean?" Fox turned to look at everyone dourly. "Those we want to stay always have somewhere to go."

"I do have one tidbit," Owen said. "Lewis asked me to keep my ears open for any news involving Crowley. Seems he's in town and checked into the Old Bank Hotel."

"We know," Cecil told him. "Checked in Saturday."

Owen nodded. "That's right. But did you also know he's been searching for the past three days for a man named MacDougall? Crowley along with a simple-minded giant called Jasper and another . . . Lord Beckworth."

"Oh, that is interesting!" Tolkien sat up straight in his chair. "So, Crowley doesn't know where the man is either."

"Could be a ruse," Cecil said. "He surely knows we're watching him the same as he is watching us. Especially after the altercation."

"By the way," Owen wondered, glancing toward some open chairs, "where are Jack and Warnie? And what altercation?"

"Jack and Warren have gone—" Fox began.

"No, no," Barfield interrupted, raising a hand, palm out. "On second thought, don't tell me anything. I really can't get any more involved. Too much going on right now. I have a client to interview at the office, then it's off to the station. I promise in the new year I'll be back in the thick of it, ready to listen to readings and lend a hand in any extracurricular activities."

After firm handshakes, Barfield departed with a tip of his cap. It was back to the four of them, and it felt as though the morning's meeting had drawn to its natural conclusion.

Tolkien spoke up just as the men gathered their coats and reluctantly prepared to face the winter cold. "I've had an idea just now," he said, still working out some details in his mind.

"Oh, and what is it?" Fox asked, taking the bait.

"What do you say we cut some strings of this mystery and put our best effort toward eliminating a suspect or two this week? After all, it is our final official meeting of the Inklings before the full moon. What say you three?"

Fox, Dyson, and Cecil nodded.

"Whatever it takes," Fox declared. "Though my wife expects me home at seven most nights."

"I will need help from all of you on this." Tolkien turned to Cecil. "You wouldn't by any chance need the services of a currently unemployed housekeeper?"

Cecil frowned. "I already have a cook, a housekeeper, and now a nurse to pay for. I'm afraid my royal allowance is tapped."

"You don't need to hire the woman," Tolkien said, tapping out his pipe into the ashtray. "You'll just contact her, let her know you're in the market, and set up an interview with her. Get her to come to you at your place. I want to speak with her away from her sister and son. There was something I missed the last time that needs to be righted."

"Oh bother," Fox muttered, shaking his head. "What have you got in mind, Tollers?"

"A ruse of our own," Tolkien responded confidently. He flashed a smile and put his hat on top of his head. "I'm trying my best to unjumble the jumble."

{26} The Loch

Wednesday, December 23

I say also this. I do not think the forest would be so bright, nor the water so warm, nor love so sweet, if there were no danger in the lakes.

—C. S. Lewis, *Out of the Silent Planet*

Lewis was eating an oat muffin at one of the inn's tables when he heard the car horn sounding out front. He called for Warren to hurry with his biscuit and took the last swallow from a mug of tea thick with honey to soothe his sore throat. The many hours of raised voices, laughter, and haze of thick tobacco smoke the night before had left it raw.

Lewis and Warren emerged into the chilly morning air, thick with fog, the latter still rubbing at dark circles under his eyes after a night of restless sleep on an unfamiliar and lumpy bed. A blustery wind blew eastward off the nearby loch, causing Jack to pull the collar of his hunting jacket up around his neck and slip the wool cap from his pocket onto his head and over his ears.

"I could have slept another hour or two," Warren remarked.

"What, and miss the beautiful morning?" Lewis said.

Warren gestured at the mist around him. "I can't see past my nose, Jack."

A young man with bright red hair and an equally red and freckled face emerged from the driver's seat and saluted. The car was an early-thirties dark blue Austin 12 whose rough appearance made it seem as though it had served as a taxi far longer than it actually had. The car did boast spacious front and back seats with a metal rack on the roof for luggage.

"My da says she's all yers for the day," the young man said, his accent and facial shape similar to his father's. "Engine's warm too. The name's Rory. I'll be back here around sundown tae get the car . . ." He paused and looked the two brothers over. "Hopefully she'll be in the same condition she's in now. If nae, I'll expect payment for any dents or scratches." All three men looked at the car. "Well, any new dents or scratches," Rory amended. "I know what's there and what's nae."

"Agreed," Jack said, not wanting to waste time. He bent down to grab a small waxed canvas day bag before walking toward the rear door to stash it on the seat.

"Ye've come for the beast, haven't ye?" Rory asked, hands on hips.

"No," Warren answered, a bit grumpily, "we're not here for this Loch Ness Monster. And we've brought no camera, as you can see."

Rory smiled knowingly. "I was nae speaking of Nessie. It's the Beast of Boleskine I mean. People come tae the loch tae see one monster or another, I'd think."

Lewis eyed the lad. He was more perceptive than he looked. "In a sense, then, yes we have."

"The manual crank is a wee tricky," Rory said, pointing to the car. "If I were ye, I'd just leave it running." He turned, yelled "Good luck!" over his shoulder, and gave another salute before slipping inside his father's inn.

The drive south from Inverness took over an hour, especially since Warren kept the speed low in the sputtering and backfiring car. They passed through the village of Dores, then hugged the coastline of the long, narrow lake known as Loch Ness as the fog burned off. Jack kept his nose buried in a small printed map for most of the way, glancing up only to squint at crossroad signs or to note the distinguishable landmarks Warren pointed out.

A while later, the elder brother slowed the rattling car to a crawl. Across the glimmering expanse of water were some stone ruins surrounding a central square tower that jutted up impressively from the opposite coastline.

"It's Urquhart Castle," Jack announced, finding it on the map and tracing their route with his finger. "Which means we're not far."

"That's right," Warren said with newfound enthusiasm. "I've heard of Urquhart. It's nearly nine hundred years old. That castle was involved in the Scottish Wars of Independence in the fourteenth century, with the Bruces and all of that."

"How interesting." Jack took a second look across the water to admire the upper bailey, which he thought must be much more impressive up close.

"Isn't this place rife with folklore?" Warren asked.

"Yes," Jack replied, still looking at the map. "I prefer Norse, but there are some interesting characters that supposedly lived in the lochs as well."

"Like what?" Warren glanced over, prodding his brother for some imaginative tale to pass the time.

Jack thought for a moment. "The baobhan sith is a monster that takes the form of a beautiful woman and roams the Highlands looking for a victim."

"What about the horse one?" Warren wanted to know. "I've heard of some legend with a horse."

"Oh, the kelpie," Jack said. "That is a water spirit said to change its form into a horse on occasion."

Warren squinted. "Doesn't it also turn into a man or something and lure people to their deaths in the lochs?"

"Two very similar legends," Jack explained, lifting his eyes from the map and turning toward his brother. "The kelpie turns into a horse, though it is only spirit, whereas the each-uisge is a water horse that disguises itself as a man, or sometimes a pony, to lure people into the lochs."

"How very strange." Warren shuddered. "I'm glad I was born in Ireland."

Lewis laughed. "You know Irish folklore is far stranger than what I described."

"True, true," Warren conceded with a grin.

The car finally pulled to a stop near a low stacked stone wall. The driveway continued on, but there was a gate with a chain and lock. Warren set the brake yet left the car running as instructed. After exiting the vehicle, the two men walked toward a clearing in the trees, their shoes crunching on crushed stone. Warren lifted his hand to shield his eyes from the midmorning sun as they scanned the property.

Boleskine House was large but rather plain from this angle, with white walls and a series of chimneys jutting up from the roofline. The ground sloped down and away from the front of the house toward the lake. Further up, the hillside behind the home showed glimpses of the ancient Farigaig Forest.

"What are we looking for?" Warren asked, slipping his hands into his pockets and rocking side to side in the cold wind. "Are we going to knock or break in?" He frowned at his brother. "I'm not good at picking locks. Detectives should be good at that sort of thing, don't you think?"

Jack shook his head. "We don't need to get inside the house. I just wanted to get a feel for the place." He turned on his heels and began walking back toward the car.

"Is that it?" Warren said, following behind and kicking a baseball-sized stone.

"The answer I seek is not here, though it is close by." Jack pulled the map from his hip pocket and unfolded it. "There is one more place I'd like to stop."

Serving the local parish of Boleskine was a small stone church that looked like it could hold only a little more than a few dozen people at a time. A cemetery surrounded the main building on nearly all sides, except for a small garden and stone walkway that led to the front door. Upon entering the church, the brothers were soon greeted by an elderly gentleman, wearing his clerical collar, who looked surprised to see anyone. His face was kind and gentle, and he reminded Jack of a neighbor in Belfast when he was just a boy.

"We wondered, Reverend, if we might ask you a few questions about the area," Jack ventured.

The man's pale face fell for a moment. "I'm not a tour guide," he said evenly, with a trace of a Welsh accent. "If you want to know whether I believe the monster in the lake is some sort of demon, I haven't the foggiest, and I don't want to say any more about it."

"We're not here about the monster in the lake," Warren

answered. "It's something else entirely. And we'd be willing to give a donation to the church for just a few minutes of your time."

The man stood a bit taller and scrutinized Warren and Jack in turn. "Very well," he said at last. "We can talk informally in the manse. You look like you could use a spot of tea and a scone."

Soon the three men were sipping chamomile tea from matching porcelain cups. The minister, who told them his name was Peter, spooned preserves into scones and set them before the brothers.

"How long have you served the parish?" Jack wondered.

"For nearly fifteen years," Peter said. "Before that, I served with the Presbyterian Church of Wales in Cardiff."

"Lovely place," Jack commented. "I attended a conference there once."

"I miss it." Peter paused, then asked, "How can I be of service?"

"We're here because of the Boleskine House," Jack told him. "Do you know about it?"

"Yes, of course. It's just up the road," Peter responded. "I've never been inside—wouldn't want to. But I've performed a handful of graveside services just down the hill from it at Fraser Cemetery. And yes, before you ask, I know a bit of the history of the house by reputation."

"What can you tell us about it?" Warren said.

Peter pursed his lips. "Let's see . . ." He thought for a moment, leaning back in his chair. "It was originally built by Colonel Archibald Fraser in the late 1700s as a hunting lodge on the site of the original church. Sadly, legend says that the church caught fire and burned down." The minister opened his mouth to continue speaking, then closed it. He looked suddenly uncomfortable.

"What is it?" Jack questioned, sensing the tension.

"Well . . ." Peter took his time replying. "Not sure if this is the information you're after, but when the church caught fire, it burned the whole congregation alive. No one was able to escape."

"That sounds a bit like murder," Warren observed, uncrossing his legs. "Like they had all been locked in."

The older man nodded. "That's how the legend goes. Over a hundred years ago now, but there is some truth to it, I'd expect." He studied the brothers again. "Not to speak ill of where I've chosen to live and serve the Lord, but there are a lot of strange happenings around here, beyond the monster in the loch. And the strangeness of it only works to attract more strange people who then do more strange things. It seems as though we're caught in a bit of a downward spiral."

"Can you elaborate?" Jack leaned closer.

Peter exhaled slowly as if bringing it up were an exercise. "I forget the year exactly," he said, flicking his eyes up toward the low, wood-beamed ceiling. "Sixteen something, not quite three hundred years ago, the minister at the time—Thomas Houston, I believe—kept detailed church records. He wrote about hurrying to rebury corpses in the Boleskine graveyard on the estate after a local wizard raised them to life." The reverend shrugged. "Whether or not anything supernatural happened is to be determined. As I said, this area is so rife with stories and myths, it's difficult to separate fact from fiction."

"What do you believe happened?" Warren pressed.

"Well, I do believe in the supernatural and the miraculous." The minister raised a brow. "These things are possible from a Christian worldview. But I also know how stories get embellished the more they are told and passed down from generation to generation, until they are little more than myth. Regardless, even the stories, whether true or not, attract a certain type of person to venture to our now mythical shores."

"Which leads me to my next question," Jack said. "What do you know about Aleister Crowley?"

The priest frowned. He blinked as he thought. "Case in point. The strangeness of this area attracts those who are equally strange, or perhaps insane. I never met the man personally. He left before I came north to Scotland, and if I had known where I was coming, I may have refused. But I've heard stories from locals who know much more than I do." He sipped his tea. "Called himself To Mega Therion of all things. It means 'the Great Beast' . . . Latin, I think."

"Greek," Jack interjected. He couldn't help himself. "I'm sorry, Peter. Please continue."

"Yes, Greek," the older man said without offense. "Crowley moved here and bought the house in 1899 because of the ley lines or something about the strange mystical energies of the place. I know he and his followers set out to practice some kind of magic called Abramelin, though I cannot pretend to understand it or know what it means."

"It comes from the name Abraham," Jack clarified. "Crowley sees himself as the father of a new religion."

"Hmm." Peter eyed the younger Lewis. "You are smarter than you look. All I know is that the purpose of Crowley's plans here was to bring himself and his handful of disciples into direct contact with their guardian angels, or so they thought, who would then give them supernatural powers. If you ask me, that would more than likely result in the summoning of evil spirits and signing your name in blood, if you know what I mean."

"We get the idea," Jack said.

"What happened then?" Warren prompted, now more than interested in what the minister had to say.

"Well, legend has it . . ." Peter began, then paused to scratch at his nose and study the brothers in turn. "Mind you, I would not tell these stories to fantastical men. But you seem to be of sober and academic minds that can parse what needs to be." He stopped again to collect his thoughts. "Legend has it that after half a year of strict preparation for a magical ceremony, Crowley and the others summoned twelve beings from the depths of Sheol, which were released into our earthly, physical realm but never sent back from whence they came. And since that time, these twelve malevolent spirits have roamed free around Loch Ness, causing havoc wherever they rest."

"What was Crowley's purpose?" Warren asked.

Peter answered, "The way I heard it, the otherworldly powers harnessed and bound in this ceremony were supposed to have granted the operator, Crowley himself, some form of spiritual authority."

Jack frowned. "How could these malevolent spirits be both bound and roaming free?" He reached for a scone and bit into it.

"Ah, you caught that as well." The reverend smiled. "And that's just it, isn't it? The local story goes that Crowley left Scotland midway through the process, which was supposed to take two years, to take care of some pressing estate business in Paris. He left his disciples behind to wait for him. Many folks believe that when he abandoned the site, a curse was bestowed on the house because it had all been improperly done. Some even go so far as to claim that sightings of the original version of the Loch Ness Monster began not long afterward. This is why some believe the monster in the lake is some evil spirit taking physical form in various ways." Peter paused before continuing, "Though as I said before, I don't believe all that, at least not the way the pagans tell it."

"Something tells me you believe more of it than you pretend to," Jack remarked.

The minister smiled faintly but said nothing. He finished his tea.

Warren broke the momentary silence. "You've been most helpful, Peter. I feel we've taken up enough of your time . . ."

"Earlier you mentioned locals who may know more about these stories and legends," Jack inserted quickly. "Perhaps more of what happened at Boleskine and in the area."

Peter's eyes lit up as he lifted and wagged a finger. "I've just remembered . . . if it's Boleskine you're interested in, then the man you'd want to speak with is Hugh Gillies. Hugh has lived here most of his life, before and after Crowley. He was a groundskeeper and tended the lodge when Crowley was away. A bit of a recluse, though. A strange man, but understandably since he's had a very difficult life. His only son died very young. The boy's body is buried right here in the cemetery. A real life of tragedy."

"Do you know where we could find this Hugh Gillies?" Jack asked.

Peter stood up and began collecting the now-empty cups. "He's the groundskeeper for a local lord . . . MacDougall. Donald MacDougall."

Jack and Warren stared wide-eyed at each other. "Did you say 'MacDougall'?" Jack finally managed.

"Oh yes, the MacDougall clan is a name that goes back

many centuries in this area. They have a castle of sorts, slowly crumbling over the last thirty years, just holding on for another generation. The grounds are just outside Inverness." The older man paused and stood up straight. "But it's gated and walled. No doubt you'd spend hours out front without any luck of entry. You'd be better served to speak to MacDougall himself first and have him get you in touch with Mr. Gillies, if that is what you want."

"Do you know where we can find him?" Warren helped himself to a scone and put it into his jacket pocket.

"Yes, I do." Peter smiled. "He spends most of his time in Inverness, drinking at a local watering hole, the Abertarff House."

"That's where we're staying!" Warren exclaimed.

"Then it should be easy," Peter said. "From what I've heard, he's there most nights. But you'd better find him early before he's too drunk to stand."

{27} The Uncle

> A book, a good chair, my pipe, and a good bed to go to when night falls, and I'm as happy as one can be in this very trying world.
>
> —Warren Lewis

Prior to returning to Inverness, Jack and Warren ventured from the manse to the nearby village of Foyers. They stopped first at a petrol station, then enjoyed a late-afternoon fish sandwich at a lakeside shop. The morning cold had given way to milder temperatures, so they ditched their heavy coats after the meal and threw rocks into the sparkling waters of Loch Ness before heading northeast up the coastal road the way they'd come. As they drove on, mostly in silence, the low sun began to set behind them, drawing a very short day to a close. Jack pondered what the parish minister had told them, jotting down a few random thoughts in his notebook while Warren focused on keeping the sputtering car running and on the road.

Later that evening, Jack slumped into a creaking chair at

the same round table they'd occupied the previous night and dug into his pocket for his cigarette case. This time he chose the chair facing the bar in hope of soon spotting Robert MacDougall's relative, who had been described to them by the innkeeper's wife. Warren, meanwhile, searched for the inn owner's wife to ask about a pot of tea, preferably Irish. Neither the owner nor his wife could be found, but Rory soon came through the door, tipped his cap at the brothers to officially signify their rental period was complete, and went behind the bar to help himself to a triple whiskey in a water glass.

Warren approached him and persuaded the young man to pour the same for him and his brother too. Jack didn't much like Scotch whisky, but it paired well with a sore throat on a cold winter's day.

The room soon filled with customers just as it had the night before, and without the Lewises even ordering, they were served a meal of potato and sausage soup with shallots and dark rye loaves. The food was quite good, and both Jack and Warren used the stumps of bread to wipe the last dredges of soup from inside their wooden bowls.

An hour after dinner, as Jack could feel his eyelids growing heavy, the uncle of Robert MacDougall arrived. He walked bowlegged and swayed alongside a short, stout man in a kilt who helped him up onto his regular stool at the end of the bar. A mounted cuckoo clock hung just above his head. MacDougall was hard to miss, with his curly, flaming-red hair and a white speckled beard that forked into straggly points. The reverend had been right about where he would end up, although from the look of him, this was his second or third stop of the night. Jack and Warren, surprised to recognize the man from the night before, waited to approach until the inn owner, Duncan, had placed a mug of dark liquid in front of him.

"Good evening, sir," Warren said. "Do you remember us? We spoke to you last night. You helped us interpret your friend's question."

"Why wouldn't I remember tha'?" MacDougall replied. "It was only a wee bit ago." He smiled and gave a slight raise of his now nearly empty glass. "Ye fine gentlemen can call me Donald if ye wish. How can I be of service?"

"We were wondering," Jack began, "if we could ask you a few questions." He gestured toward a table. "Could we sit for a moment where we can face one another?"

"Can ye buy me a drink?" Donald asked, lifting his cup again with a hopeful look.

"Of course we can," Warren said with a grin. "As many rounds as you'd like."

"Don't tempt me, laddie." Donald snorted. "I'll drain yer pocketbooks faster than I drain a keg."

Once the three men were seated at the table and well supplied with drink, Jack mentioned, "I believe we know a relative of yours." He was thankful the hour was still early enough that there were no boisterous drunks and raised voices.

Donald MacDougall regarded both brothers and frowned. "How do ye know Robert?" He rolled the *R* excessively.

"My brother here was in the Royal Army Service Corps," Jack responded, "and I am a professor at Oxford. We met Robert recently in London. I admit we don't know him well, but we did wish to speak with you about him."

"What's he done now?" MacDougall spat. "Robert is my nephew, the only son of my older brother, deceased several years ago." Without prodding, he added, "Tha' boy has been a great disappointment. A weak boy. He follows the foolish crowd, always has, and allows himself tae be manipulated and swindled. That's why his father passed the estate on to me, his younger brother, instead of his own son as would be customary."

"I see," Jack said. "Have you heard from Robert recently?"

"Ha!" Donald exclaimed with force. "Nae for years. Lives in London now, as ye know. Doing his lordly thing, though it's all an act. The fool didn't inherit a thing besides a small allowance." He furrowed his brow over his raised mug. "Why ye be asking about Robert? Is he missing?"

Jack considered lying, if only to assuage the old man's possible worry, but thought better of it. "Yes, in fact, he is. Must be four to five days now. He failed to show up to a meeting and . . ."

"And ye thought maybe he came back here?" Donald finished Lewis's thought. He drank the rest of his beer in a single gulp and raised his arm in the air. When he caught Duncan's attention, he pointed to his cup and put up three fingers. He then turned back to Jack and quizzed, "Wha' sort of trouble has the fool got himself into?"

"There may be people who want him dead," Warren said evenly.

"Aye, that sounds like Robert, always heaping trouble on himself. He's yet a boy in a full-grown man's body."

"We believe," Jack explained, "the trouble he's in may have something to do with Aleister Crowley."

Donald MacDougall pretended to spit on the floor, his face twisted in sudden disgust. "Tha' man is a menace. He'll burn in the lowest part of hell, he will."

"We may be able to help Robert," Jack went on. "And I know this might sound strange, but it may be very helpful if we were able to speak to Hugh Gillies."

"Hugh?" MacDougall flicked his eyes between the brothers. "My groundskeeper? Why on God's green earth would ye need to speak tae him?"

"He served at Boleskine," Jack answered. "He may have witnessed things he wasn't even aware of."

"Does this have anything tae do with his boy?" Donald leaned forward, his lower lip quivering.

"Possibly," Jack said, though he wasn't sure. "If we could speak to him, it would be most beneficial."

"You won't upset him?" Donald's eyes betrayed his sincerity. "He's a kind man. But a bit like a pot that's been broken and glued back together, if ye catch what I'm sayin'."

"I can't promise our questions won't upset him," Jack replied. "But I won't dredge up anything that isn't absolutely necessary."

MacDougall leaned back and thought while Duncan brought over three new glasses and took away the old.

"Where are ye two staying?" Donald asked.

"Here, at the Abertarff." Warren took a sip of fresh ale.

"Nonsense!" Donald bellowed, frowning. He waved a hand, gesturing to the establishment at large. "This place is only good for ale and a good story, not tae lay yer head at night. Ye will both come and stay with me at MacDougall Castle. Ye can meet with Gillies there."

"I'm afraid we already paid for the second night and our bags are in the rooms already," Jack noted.

"Hmm." Donald frowned again, then belched. "Tomorrow, then, ye will both come tae my home as guests. Rory knows it well. I'll unlock the gate, and Rory can drop ye by in the afternoon."

"We don't want to impose," Warren lied.

"Nonsense," Donald countered. "I have plenty o' room.

And I know how ye can pay me back in kind. I'd like tae hear more about the south, a good story about London and Oxford. Ye look as though ye both could spin a good tale. I haven't heard one of those in quite some time, and it would do my old heart good."

A group of men at the bar started singing a low dirge. Donald winked before rising to join them. "As my father used to say, '*Lang may yer lum reek.*' "

Warren and Jack stared at each other in confusion.

Donald snorted and slapped Warren on the back as a new round of drinks was set in front of them. "It means 'Long may your chimney smoke.' " He reached down to grab hold of one of the mugs and was gone.

Not until later that evening, when Jack had laid his head on the thin pillow, did he realize he would be spending Christmas Eve in a Scottish castle.

{28} The Castle

Thursday, December 24

What you see and hear depends a good deal on where you are standing: it also depends on what sort of person you are.

—C. S. Lewis, *The Magician's Nephew*

After a morning exploring Inverness in the opposite direction from their earlier excursion, Jack and Warren ate lunch at a local café with a bubble glass window facing Inverness Castle. The brownstone castle sat high on a hill, drawing the eye and imagination to what must have taken place on those ancient grounds. Warren couldn't help himself and soon launched into a lesson on Scottish history while Jack enjoyed his Scotch broth soup. Once the brothers returned to the Abertarff, bellies full and hearts hopeful, they checked out of the inn and waited out front for Rory to arrive, brown leaves swirling around poetically.

The drive took them outside the city limits, just far enough for homes, roads, and businesses to give way to wooded forests and rising Highland pastures filled with stacked stone walls, shaggy-haired cows, and overly fluffy sheep. The car came to a sputtering stop soon afterward at the property gate, which was difficult to make out from the road. It had been propped ajar as promised, in expectation of their arrival. The gate itself was an old, rusted iron piece with spikes on top and the letter *M* in ornate metal scrollwork. It was likely impressive at some point in history, but now, rusted and sagging, it spoke of a golden age gone by.

Rory hopped out and wrenched the gate open further, the iron squeaking and squealing in protest. No doubt Donald MacDougall did not have guests often. Once Rory climbed back in, the car lurched and sputtered to life and made its way on a gradual incline up the overgrown and winding entry drive. Jack noticed a stacked stone pillar off to the right topped by the bronze head and neck of a proud stag with one side of its antlers broken off.

The driveway soon widened, leading into the grounds of the castle, which itself loomed impressively through the front windshield. The brothers craned their necks to gaze up and take in the towers' height on approach. At first glance, Jack noted the gray castle was of medieval style, typical of the time and place, with twin spires that mirrored each other rising out of a central bailey and stabbing skyward into an embankment of fog. The dark stone of the central keep was covered in lichen but stood like a monument to enduring strength and resolve. The outer walls featured rounded corners where staircases led to the upper walkways that, at one point in the past, had looked down over some enemy below. Both brothers leaned forward until their necks ached, then slumped back into the rumbling bench seat.

"I've ne'er been inside," Rory remarked, glancing at them over his shoulder. "Not sure I'd want to. A word of advice—keep yer head on a swivel when walking out in the courtyard. Roofing has been known tae come loose. Could kill an unlucky man."

"Thank you for your warning." Jack tried not to picture his brother's skull being smashed by a falling slate tile.

"I'm having second thoughts," Warren said with a flash of a smile.

The closer the car came to the castle, the more maintained the exterior looked, at least on the ground level. No doubt the work of Hugh Gillies. Fronting the castle was a circular drive with a crumbling monument at its center. Again, it featured a stag, but this one had antlers intact. Donald MacDougall himself had emerged and now stood proudly on the top step, framed by the home's grand entrance, which had iron-clad arches that met in the middle and a large door inset with a smaller one.

Rory dropped them at the front, unloaded the bags, and accepted a generous tip, doffing his flat cap toward the brothers and Donald. He hastily set off back the way he'd come, with a shrill double *beep* from the car's horn that caused Warren to flinch.

"A quick walkabout before ye lads go in," MacDougall called out, smiling as he made his way slowly down the stone steps toward his guests. "It's been a wee bit since I've done this. Used tae give tours all the time. Let's see wha' this old mind remembers."

MacDougall walked slowly in front, his bowlegs causing him to rock and waddle as he moved around the circuit. He talked back over his shoulder loudly while waving his arms, gesturing at points of interest as if it were his first time seeing them in years. Jack found it strange and difficult to explain, but as he listened, he couldn't help but sense how the old castle was both impressive and sad at the same time. A monument to strength yet also emanating a sense of impending doom—the crumbling frailty and atrophy of something once resolute.

MacDougall stopped the tour and pointed up toward a crenellated tower, now free of the fog. A Scottish flag, a white cross on a field of blue, rose from the highest point and flapped in the breeze. "Tha' tower was built in the late thirteenth century," MacDougall told them, "right before the First War of Scottish Independence. Robert the Bruce once stayed the night there." He pointed to a spot midway up the tower that presumably contained a spacious bedroom behind its thick stone walls. "The position of the castle made it easier tae defend against the bastard English." MacDougall winced and looked back at his guests with a half smile. "Sorry," he apologized.

"We're actually from Ireland originally," Warren reassured him. "Born and raised in Belfast."

MacDougall beamed and snorted. "Ye don't say?" he said almost in a shout. "I knew I liked ye lads. I'd love tae hear a story of the Emerald Isle over a drink or three."

"Thank you again for hosting us," Jack added, to which MacDougall grunted and concluded his tour.

"That's the main keep." MacDougall pointed ahead toward a wide, low building—at least low compared to the surrounding towers. "A banquet hall is what's behind the stone, and guest rooms are on the second floor."

Having come full circle, the brothers found themselves walking up the front steps where they had been dropped off. On the tour, Jack had kept his eyes peeled for any sign of Gillies, but he saw only a small groundskeeper cottage near the gardens. It had looked empty, with not even a hint of gray smoke coming from the chimney.

"Can we meet Hugh Gillies soon?" he asked as they all entered through the door-within-a-door.

"Yes, yes," MacDougall answered. "I'll have him come right round. Let's get ye settled first."

Inside the castle, the three men were greeted by a tall, pale woman who appeared to be little more than a frowning skeleton with skin on. Her eyes were mostly closed, and wrapped around her head was a dark blue cloth that gave thready evidence of being a Scottish flag past its prime.

"This here is Bonnie," MacDougall said. "Her name means 'pretty' and 'charming.'" He smiled and paused as the woman glared back at him. "She is one of my last remaining staff, which has sadly fallen from thirty to three over these past decades." He glanced over to Warren. "Bonnie doesn't say much unless she needs tae, but she's the best cook in the Highlands, and she'll take good care of ye fine gentlemen. Hugh and I will see ye both at dinner at dusk. Ye lads should prepare yourselves for food, drink, and revelry—after all, it's a holiday!"

Bonnie didn't speak. She only turned, and her long legs propelled her quickly forward over wide plank floors polished to a high shine in the corners and worn dull in the higher-trafficked areas. She reminded Jack of a giraffe he'd seen once at London Zoo, and the thought made him chuckle.

A spiral staircase wound upward to a second level that featured a series of tapestries hung in front of ebony wall panels. The brothers followed the narrow shadow of the housekeeper down a dimly lit hallway to their rooms, which lay across from one another.

"Dinner will be served in the banquet hall in one hour," Bonnie announced in a raspy voice that rose just above a whisper. "I have drawn each of you a bath in your rooms, so you'll be expected to be clean and dressed for dinner to the standards of this fine house." With that, she spun on her heel and left.

Each room was twice the size of their shared room at the Abertarff and, though spacious, smelled of dampness. Jack's room had a simple bed, a wardrobe with carved designs, and a desk and chair that sat near a pair of arched windows overlooking the courtyard. His room was cold despite a fire being lit in the hearth, but he was hopeful that it just needed time to warm up. The chill air caused steam to rise off the water that filled a copper bath, which had been placed right in the middle of the bedroom floor. After taking one of the candles off the bedside table and walking in a circle to inspect the room, he set the candle back down and began unbuttoning his shirt.

Jack and Warren entered the banquet hall, taking in the simple rectangular room with large wooden beams on the ceiling, which bowed in the center from centuries of unyielding weight. A single black iron candelabra in the shape of a wagon wheel was lit and lowered by rope over a table that ran half the length of the room. The table could easily seat twenty or more people but had been set for only four. Jack pulled out the chair to the left of the head of the table, his back to the blazing fireplace. Above a mounted caribou head were two side-by-side portraits—one of a man who looked like Donald MacDougall, only a bit skinnier, and one of a younger version of Donald himself. Another Scottish flag hung from the ceiling rafter and swayed in the waves of heat radiating from the fire.

"If ye're cold, drape an animal skin over ye," MacDougall suggested as he entered the hall from the kitchen. Until then, neither brother had noticed the various animal hides, all unique, draped over the backs of the dining chairs.

"Oh, very nice." Warren seated himself and pulled a wolf skin over his shoulders while grinning and eyeing his brother. "I feel like a Viking."

"We cannae afford tae heat the whole castle like this all winter," MacDougall explained. "Tonight is a luxury I, too, will enjoy. Once again, I am indebted tae my guests." He pulled out his chair, and the three men sat to dinner.

"Gentlemen, I have good news, more good news, and some bad news as well," MacDougall continued with a mock grim look. He then smiled and pounded the table with a fist. "The good news is tha' a special roast has been prepared by Bonnie the beauty and will be brought out momentarily. The other good news is tha' before we eat, we must celebrate this holiday with a drink of my late father's prized homemade peat whiskey."

He set a half-filled bottle on the table and popped the cork. After pouring two fingers' worth into each of three heavy glasses, he slapped the cork back in the bottle with his palm and handed the glasses around. The smell of smoky bog peat filled their nostrils. When they tasted the alcohol, it was like liquid smoke on the tongue—and not at all enjoyable. All three men coughed, then snorted and laughed to clear away the thick taste.

"It's horrible," MacDougall admitted. "But as a Scotsman, it's a necessary tradition tae savor the strongest batches with honor and gratitude tae those who have gone before us and who, though not perfect and smooth on the tongue, will be remembered long after tonight."

"Well said," Jack agreed.

"And the bad news?" Warren prompted, with a glance toward his brother.

MacDougall tilted his head. "I'm afraid I spoke too soon about Hugh Gillies. The man's not here at the moment. I'm afraid our fourth setting will go unused. He went tae visit his cousin for Christmas just north of here. Only two days a year do I let the man go and just so happens tae be when he is needed most. I forgot about it." He paused, then added, "He'll be back Saturday, and ye're welcome tae stay and wait if ye gentlemen are so inclined."

Jack sighed, but there was nothing to be done about it. He wondered for a moment if the old man was telling the truth yet decided it didn't matter either way. They would wait.

After a delicious dinner of tender roasted meat and boiled herb potatoes, Jack and Warren retreated from the table under the direction of their host to take seats in three chairs that surrounded the fireplace, which had now burned low. MacDougall served more whiskey in heavy glasses. This time the amber liquid was smooth and enjoyable on the tongue, especially with a splash of water and a dash of bitters.

"I wonder if you wouldn't mind telling us a bit more about Hugh Gillies," Jack said as soon as a pregnant silence hung in the air.

MacDougall nodded slowly. "I'll say what I can. Though I'm nae gossip." He arched a brow.

Jack held his hands out in a placating gesture. "Of course. You mentioned before that Gillies's son died. Was it an accident?"

"Aye, he drowned in the loch. Down below the manor." MacDougall leaned forward in his chair. "They found what was left of the boy a few days later near the shore."

"'What was left of' him?" Warren questioned.

MacDougall sniffed and nodded again. "A body in the loch won't stay whole. There are monsters below the depths. They take a bit of whatever they can. Razor-sharp teeth." He looked up from his glass. "The loss hit Hugh especially hard. It cast a long shadow over the whole region. He was a good lad. Even Crowley up and sold the place and left."

"That was when it happened?" Jack asked quickly. "The boy dying? It was the same year?"

"Aye, the same month," MacDougall confirmed. "Couldn't get out fast enough."

"Could Crowley have been involved?" Jack wondered.

MacDougall squinted his eyes. "In the death, ye say? Are ye saying the boy's death was nae an accident?"

"I don't know," Jack replied. "But it does strike me as strange."

MacDougall shook his head. "Could nae have been Crowley," he decided. "From wha' I remember hearing, he wasn't even here when it happened. Came home a few days after, packed up, and left. No one ever saw him or any of his disciples around here again."

"Could one of his students have been involved?" Warren ventured. "It was said that many stayed there for long periods of time."

Jack glanced from his brother to the aging Scotsman, suddenly aware of what could be implied.

"They'd come and go," MacDougall said. "My nephew was one of them. I told him tae stay away from Boleskine. Strange stories. But the boy was pigheaded like his father. I hope you're nae suggesting that my kin had anything tae do with any mischief."

"We're not suggesting anything," Jack assured him. "Only

asking questions. Listening to stories. And we thank you for your candidness."

MacDougall frowned. "This isn't what I had in mind for Christmas Eve. Speaking of stories, would ye tell me a story? Ye promised me a good one in return for room and board."

"What would you like to hear?" Warren took the lead as Jack fumbled with his cigarette case.

The Scotsman stared into the fire, then smiled. "You mentioned the RASC. Did you both serve in the army?"

"Yes, in the Great War," Jack responded.

MacDougall's smile faded. He nodded solemnly. "Yes. 'The Great War.'" He lifted his glass in a wordless toast. "That's what they say, though I ne'er thought it all tha' great." He drank the entire contents of the glass and set it down on the side table with force. "Let's hear a story from the war then."

Warren began by sharing a somewhat humorous story of a series of pranks his fellow soldiers played in the barracks while stationed in France. Jack followed with the only story he could think of. He told of his good friend Paddy Moore, of the vows they made to each other should either not make it home from the war, and of his fulfillment of that vow in taking care of Paddy's mother.

"Good stories, good stories," MacDougall pronounced when they were done. "Deserving of a fitting toast to honoring our vows." He raised his glass, and the brothers reciprocated.

MacDougall then began to sing in a low, wavering voice. He closed his eyes as the familiar words rose up:

O holy night, the stars are brightly shining;
it is the night of the dear Savior's birth.
Long lay the world in sin and error pining,
till He appeared and the soul felt its worth.

Soon Jack and Warren joined in.

A thrill of hope, the weary world rejoices,
for yonder breaks a new and glorious morn!
Fall on your knees! O hear the angel voices!
O night divine! O night when Christ was born!
O night divine! O night, O night divine!

MacDougall stood to his feet in the thick silence that followed. "I've decided I do nae want tae get drunk tonight," he told them. "It's nae good nursing a hangover on Christmas Day. Ye're welcome tae stay here by the fire as long as ye'd like . . . but I'm going tae bed."

After the man left, Warren said, "I got you a present," while fishing a small package from his hip pocket.

Jack took it and unwrapped a notebook encased in leather. On the lower right-hand corner of the front cover was the inscription *C. S. Lewis*.

"I noticed on the train yours was nearly full," Warren explained. "And it just so happened that on our walkabout in Inverness I spotted a shop selling them. You had your nose in a book in the nearby bookstore when I slipped away." He beamed. "The man used a monogram punch right there. He had all twenty-six letters and even grammatical symbols. Took only a few minutes. You were none the wiser. Not a very good detective."

Jack laughed and flipped open the blank pages. "Thank you, but I'm sorry, Warren. I'd forgotten all about gifts, and I haven't gotten you a thing."

Warren waved a hand in dismissal. "Just write me into one of your stories. Hopefully, I'll be a wise old man or something. Merry Christmas, Jack."

"Merry Christmas, Warren."

{29} The Call

Friday, December 25

> You have been chosen, and you must therefore use such strength and heart and wits as you have.
>
> —J. R. R. TOLKIEN,
> *The Fellowship of the Ring*

Just as the Christmas ham was served, the phone rang, which elicited a frown from Edith. Christopher Tolkien answered the second ring eagerly and soon called out that it was for his father. Tolkien felt his heart race but was more than disappointed to hear Cecil on the other end of the line.

"You would not believe who I've just been speaking with," Cecil said through the earpiece.

"Tell me." Tolkien eyed the small corner of the dining room table he could see from the other room.

"Lord Beckworth. And calling on Christmas Day, if you can believe it." Cecil paused, then continued when Tolkien didn't respond. "He seemed very agitated, frantic almost. Even more than the last time. I told him I would visit him Sunday after my Sabbath and not before, certainly not on

Christmas Day. But it was no use trying to calm the man or reason with him."

"What did he want?" Tolkien asked.

"He was notably panicking, breathing heavily, and not making a lot of sense. He feared for his life, and by the end of our conversation, he said he was leaving immediately for the country and would be there for the duration."

"Did he say anything else?" Tolkien fumbled with the flap of his jacket's hip pocket to take out his notebook and pen. "Did he mention MacDougall?"

"This is the strangest part," Cecil answered. "He did. I didn't hear quite clearly. I had to keep asking the man to repeat himself, but he said he knew that MacDougall had been murdered and that he was next. He also mentioned he had stopped searching for MacDougall. Said he didn't care what Crowley said. Though he was surprised when I brought it up. I don't think he knew that we knew that MacDougall was known to be missing, which makes sense. Why would he? When I asked him how he knew he was the next target, he had no real answer for me, just a few stutters saying he was certain of it and that hell was coming for him."

"That sounds familiar," Tolkien mused. "Do you think he's already been poisoned? It could explain his erratic behavior."

"Hard to tell for sure unless we could get Dr. Havard to examine him," Cecil replied. "It would also be difficult to tell if his hair is falling out when the man didn't have any to begin with." Cecil snorted, then caught himself.

"Is that everything?" Tolkien questioned as he jotted down a few notes.

"That's about it," Cecil said. "Though I'll be seeing you tomorrow, I thought you should know now. As I said, Beckworth is driving himself out to the country, to his family's cottage in the Cotswolds. I know where it is, but the house is quite cut off and secluded from the outside world. I know why he picked it. Only a single long driveway and marshlands all the way around. He plans to hole up there for the next few days, probably armed and extremely paranoid."

"Will you go on Sunday?" Tolkien asked.

"I hadn't planned to go until Monday, but plans change. He wants me to join him sooner than later . . . though I have no idea why I should be a bodyguard. I can hardly defend myself. But I did agree to it, and I'm not one to welch on agreements." Cecil sniffed proudly over the line. "I'd like it very much if you would join me, Tollers, as a personal favor to me. I've been looking up at night, and the moon is a bit too full for my liking. We could take my car."

Tolkien paused in thought. "You think the murderer will actually show up? Seems to be a high risk of exposure."

"I don't know one way or the other," Cecil responded. "It's all a guess, but I'd certainly feel better if you were there either way. I'm likely to get shot coming up the driveway. I need a second set of lungs crying out reasons to hold fire. And besides, you've always had more courage than I do."

"So, you admit I'm a better bodyguard than you?" Tolkien teased with a faint smile. He closed his notebook.

"You were a soldier," Cecil said quickly. "You know how to shoot far better than me, I'll admit. I prefer a sword. But mostly I want you to join me so I don't murder the man myself. I could barely stand spending a few hours with him, let alone a couple of days. I know this much excitement will ruin my rest day tomorrow. Especially with an added housekeeper interview. A fake one, to boot. I might ask my nurse to give me a sedative so I can sleep before such an adventure. And now I'm rambling."

"I'll come with you." Tolkien regretted it as soon as the words left his mouth. "Get your rest. We'll leave from your house early Sunday morning."

"Please come prepared," Cecil stated. "And you know what I mean."

After the call ended, Tolkien didn't immediately return to dinner. Instead, he walked straight to his office and closed the door. He flipped on a light and inserted a small key from his pocket into the top-drawer lock. Inside the drawer sat a wooden box. Tolkien opened it to reveal a carton of bullets alongside an Enfield No. 2 pistol.

{30} The Groundskeeper

Saturday, December 26

To love at all is to be vulnerable.
—C. S. Lewis, *The Four Loves*

"I was told to notify you when Mr. Gillies arrived," Bonnie the housekeeper said dourly. Her gray eyes stared unblinking as she stood silently in the doorway of Jack's room. Her blue hair wrap nearly touched the top of the frame.

Jack thanked her, then quickly strode across the hall to rouse Warren from his sleep, informing his confused brother that he was off to interview the groundskeeper and that there was no need for Warren to join him.

The morning fog had nearly lifted by the time Jack made his way out to the groundskeeper's cottage, a small square hut built with stacked granite stone from the property. Garden tools were lined in a row against the stone on either side of the front door, which looked barely more than a few vertical slats of wood with cracks wide enough to peer through.

Jack cleared his throat as he stepped up to the door and knocked.

"Come in, come in," Mr. Gillies invited.

Lewis stepped into the cottage, taking in his first impression of the one-room shack's inhabitant. Hugh Gillies was a thin man, hunched over at the waist, with wispy gray hair. He stood at the stove—a small iron potbelly with a chimney that curled and popped out through the stone at the back. Gillies warmed one hand at a time while the other held on to a twisted bentwood cane.

"Hello, Mr. Gillies," Jack greeted him. "Thank you for seeing me."

"I was told I may have a visitor," Hugh said, "though I don't know why anyone would want to talk to me." His voice was soft and frail, full of air and riding on a whispering wheeze. He made an obvious effort to look up and meet Lewis's eyes before letting his gaze fall again to the worn wooden floor. Yet Lewis saw enough to notice a deep sadness in the man's light blue eyes.

"Sit, sit." Hugh pointed to an upturned barrel that served as a table on which a single lit candle sat.

Jack settled onto a creaking bentwood chair he was surprised supported his weight.

"Lord MacDougall says you wish to speak with me and that it is a very important thing you are wanting to know." Gillies bobbed his head up and down as he spoke, carefully making his way down into his chair with a grunt. The cane wobbled before he leaned it against the barrel.

Lewis noted that the man did not have a strong Scottish accent, and he was pleasantly surprised to be able to understand him so clearly. "Yes, that's right." Lewis said. He didn't want to dive right into his questions. He felt the need to build some kind of rapport with the man. "How was your Christmas?" he asked lightly.

Hugh reached out and began to pour hot water from a black kettle into two wooden cups. The steam smelled familiar.

"It was lovely," he answered, bobbing his head again. "Went north to Dingwall to visit my cousin for a few days. She's the last kin I have left." He smiled faintly and set one cup in front of Lewis. His hand shook. "Not long for this world, I'm afraid. Hope you like anise. It grows wild here. I dry some and steep it in hot water. Good for the throat and lungs during the cold months."

"Smells like licorice," Lewis observed as the steam lifted to his nostrils.

"That's right," Gillies confirmed with a single nod. "Anise is used in the recipe for that." He wrapped his cup with his hands, which were rough and calloused, his skin worn and weathered from years of working outdoors in the elements.

"I wondered if I might talk to you about a job you used to have," Lewis ventured. "You were the groundskeeper at Boleskine House."

Hugh Gillies looked down at his hands and shook his head. "I was, sir, and I don't care to talk about that place or that time in my life. But if Lord MacDougall invited you here as guests, and if he said I should and that it may be important, I'll do it."

"I understand your reluctance, Mr. Gillies," Lewis assured him. "I want you to know that my brother and I have traveled all this way just to speak to you. It is as if God Himself has set up a divine appointment between you and me, and I believe that your memories may hold the key to a very serious mystery." Gillies looked up and met his eye as Lewis spoke. "It is a mystery I am determined to solve and one that could save lives. So, anything you could share would be very much appreciated."

Hugh nodded slowly, then asked, "How old is your brother?"

"He is my elder by about three years," Jack responded.

Gillies's expression brightened. "That was the same with my boys, three years apart." Then the deep sadness returned to the man's glistening eyes. He reached up and wiped at them with the back of his hand.

"Tell me about your time at Boleskine," Jack said. "When did you first come there?"

Gillies took a deep, labored breath. "I was hired to come and care for the lodge . . . It must have been around the turning of the century. Men would go there to hunt in the forests above the loch, so when it was offseason, the place was empty and needed tending, inside and out. That was my business, and God has blessed me to be good at it."

"When did Mr. Crowley purchase the home?" Jack wanted to know.

"Oh, not long after I came is when Mr. Crowley bought it. I thought I would be sacked, but he kept me on, which was good because I had just gotten married and we had our first son. Oliver was a beautiful boy."

"What was your job exactly?" Lewis took a sip of his tea.

"Mostly outdoor work. After Crowley moved in, I had to give back my key," Gillies explained. "The master of the house gave strict orders not to come inside any longer, under any circumstances. I tended the gardens. Fed the animals. I also maintained the graveyard next door. But the house itself was forbidden, and I'm glad of it. I don't want to know what went on there at all hours of the night."

"What type of things do you mean?" Lewis pressed. He felt his heart race.

Gillies worked his jaw. "Do you mind if I smoke?"

"Not at all," Lewis said.

Gillies leaned over far enough to grab a wooden box, which he set on the table. He took out a corncob pipe with a long, swooping stem, pulled a generous pinch of tobacco from a small leather pouch, stuffed it into the pipe's bowl, and inserted the stem with a series of twists.

After striking two matches together, Gillies finally spoke. "Every year things got a little stranger. Mr. Crowley had many visitors, both men and women. They would stay up all night. Some would live there for months. The noises and the stories . . . It all seems like a dream now or maybe a nightmare."

"What type of stories?" Lewis asked, hoping the man would speak freely without prompting.

"Aye, many legends are born of purity. The head of a Jacobite rolling around the halls. Strange voices, deep and low and inhuman. Languages shouted into the night sky that I'd never heard before. Screams either of pain or ecstasy rolling over the loch and up the hillside. After a few months, I began to have strange dreams myself. My wife and son did as well. Oliver had trouble sleeping. But we grew used to it over the years. We knew when to make ourselves scarce, and when the full moons came, we'd stay away from the house altogether."

"And why is that?" Lewis quizzed. "Why the full moons?"

"That was when everything I mentioned seemed to be at its peak."

Jack wrote in the notebook he kept in his pocket. "How long were you there?"

"Nearly a decade." The old man shook his head. "My wife died of the pox a couple of years after our second son was born. Edmund died soon after that of the same thing."

"I'm sorry to hear that," Lewis sympathized.

Gillies cleared his throat. "It was just me and Oliver then. There was a small outbuilding we moved into for a time. Just a gardener's shack no bigger than this here. But my Oliver loved it there. He helped me tend the garden, trim the hedges, cut the grass, and feed the animals. He befriended the Crowley girl, my Oliver did. Swam in the loch. Explored the graveyard."

Lewis tilted his head. "Excuse me, Mr. Gillies, but what Crowley girl are you speaking of?"

"Lily," Gillies said. "They were about the same age. Thick as thieves, the two of them . . . before the accident. Every day they played together outside from dawn till dusk. Couldn't keep them apart, though Crowley tried. Apparently, he thought my Oliver wasn't good enough for his Lily. He kept the girl hidden away like she was Rapunzel."

Lewis held his pencil above his notepad as his mind raced. Now came the part he had been dreading. He sipped his tea, taking time to gather his words, and studied Hugh Gillies. The man must have sensed what was coming because his hands visibly shook. "What happened to Oliver?"

"Ahh." Gillies's voice wavered. "Oliver went missing. They told me maybe he was a runaway, but even Lily insisted that wasn't true. The girl was worried. She said she would help me look for him and bring him back, but I never saw her after that either. Three days later, my Oliver was found floating in Loch Ness, pale and lifeless." Hugh paused and took a series of deep breaths. He wiped at his nose with a dirty cloth and nodded slowly. "I lost myself for a few years after that. I don't remember much from that time. So thick was my grief that it washed over me like a tide and left me hollowed and dead inside."

"Could it have been an accident, as they say?" Lewis asked.

"He was a good swimmer," Gillies replied. "Oliver was strong and determined. But even the strong get pulled under by the currents or by the monsters who peer up from the dark."

"I'm so sorry you had to face that." Lewis sighed. "It's unimaginable."

"I wouldn't wish that sort of pain on my worst enemies." Gillies's shoulders began to bounce in a silent sob.

Jack couldn't think of anything to say, so he set his pencil down, reached out, and grabbed hold of the older man's hand, gripping it tightly as a prayer soon spilled out of him. By the time he said amen, the gardener's trembling had stopped.

Jack said goodbye, and as he walked back from the cottage to the castle, his mind raced again with what he'd just heard. He knew a handful of additional pieces had just been thrown on the puzzle table. He just needed a moment to put them in the right place.

Later that evening, Warren sat at the banquet hall table, with his shoulders wrapped in the pelt of a stag, sipping tea and poring over what looked to be a very old book. Jack entered, pulled up a nearby chair, and spoke quietly over the roar of the fire. “I’ve been mulling it over, Brother, and I think I know who killed those men and why.”

Warren looked up, wide-eyed.

“We’re leaving in the morning,” Jack stated. “We’ve got to get back as quickly as possible if we want to stop another murder.”

{31} The Follow-Up

Oft hope is born when all is forlorn.
—J. R. R. Tolkien,
The Return of the King

While Lewis was speaking with Hugh Gillies, Tolkien had arrived in the morning gray at Lord David Cecil's home and been ushered in by Morley the butler. He drank tea with Cecil, who sat up in his bed and complained that his day of rest was ruined because of all this agitation and anticipation about both Beckworth and the soon-coming housekeeper.

Thankfully for Tolkien, he had to endure only ten minutes of Cecil's whining before Morley announced that Ms. Sarah Cornish was here, expecting to be interviewed about a possible job. Tolkien made his exit with a promise to return and take the lead momentarily.

When Ms. Cornish had been escorted into the room, Cecil addressed her from his place on the bed. "Tell me about your qualifications," he said, though he didn't care.

She began to recite them in a rehearsed way, her hands folded neatly, one on top of the other. She wore a blue dress with a dark gray hat tilted and pinned with coils of hair beneath. Tolkien sat in the next room over and listened through the door while Cecil's nurse folded towels, sorted medicines, and went about her duties in indifferent silence.

After a handful of general questions, Tolkien made himself known. "Ms. Cornish, would you have a seat, please?" he asked as he stepped into view. In stunned surprise, the woman ignored his request and remained standing, squinting in confusion. Tolkien continued, "Do you remember me?"

"Yes," Sarah said after a few blinks. "You came to my sister's house. You're the professor."

"Quite right. I met your sister and your son," he confirmed.

The woman froze, and the blood drained from her face. She tried to right herself, but her reaction to being caught off guard gave her away and, at least in Tolkien's mind, proved him right.

"I . . ." Sarah closed her mouth. She looked down at the floor, then back up at Tolkien, flicking her eyes toward Cecil, who watched with great interest. "I am the boy's mother. That is no crime."

"But you hid it. Why?" Tolkien pressed.

Her face twisted in anger. "I don't have to stand here and answer anything."

"No, you don't," Tolkien agreed. "And I'm not here to expose you or threaten you, but you may be the key to justice being found for those men who were murdered, including Roger."

Her mouth quivered, and Tolkien waited.

"You need to answer this man's questions," Cecil put in. "And you need to be completely and totally honest. It's as simple as that, dear. We will know if you are misleading us. No harm will come to you and yours if you answer honestly. I promise you that much, as a man of honor."

She stared blankly before shifting her gaze back and forth between her interrogators.

"I'll go first," Tolkien said. "I'll share a secret before I ask you to divulge any of yours."

The woman didn't respond. She was obviously in a state of complete fear mixed with confusion.

"I introduced myself to you as an author and professor, which is true. But here today and when I met with you earlier, I was working in the capacity of a private investigator of murder."

"Roger . . ." Sarah began, more a statement of revelation than a question.

"That is correct." Tolkien nodded. "I was hired to solve the murder of your former employer, who also happens to be your former lover and father of your son."

Again, Sarah froze and then recoiled. "That is a lie!" she exclaimed quickly, as if that was what she was supposed to say. "He is not. Roger wouldn't . . ."

"Ms. Cornish," Tolkien admonished, "remember the stakes. You need only to admit the truth." He paused while Sarah shifted nervously from foot to foot, no doubt a flurry of thoughts racing around her mind like a blizzard. He continued, "I know you will keep my secret because I know this secret about you. See, we both hold things we don't want the public to know. I also know you want to protect Lord Pennington. Somewhere inside, you still love him, even if that love was spurned. You cannot protect him now, because he is already dead, murdered savagely by a hate-filled individual. I wish to put together the pieces to make things right, and I believe your cooperation in this puzzle would be most helpful if only you could come to trust me."

"Why would I trust you?" she spat. "You lied to me and my son."

"True," Tolkien conceded. He took a step toward her. "But another may want you dead. Which is worse, to be misled temporarily by potential allies or be murdered by a sadistic killer who wants what you know to be buried with you? Besides, I spoke with your sister's neighbor a few days ago—a nosy woman who doesn't like you or your son. She told me that a fine-dressed gentleman who looked like a lord came to visit you soon after the child was born." He paused to let her quandary take root.

She worked her jaw, swiped at her eyes, and finally broke. "Roger is the father," she murmured, barely loud enough for John and Cecil to hear.

"We know," Tolkien told her. "And frankly I don't care. It means nothing. I just wanted to hear you admit it."

"Of course it means something!" Sarah shot back defensively. Her eyes were filled with tears now, and her chin trembled.

"Why?" Tolkien asked. "The older son, Francis, inherits the wealth regardless of the boy's existence. He is no threat to anyone, only a measure of embarrassment in certain circles. My question is whether or not the boy serves as a motive for murder."

Her eyes went wide as understanding dawned. "You don't think *I* had anything to do with his death?"

"The thought had crossed my mind," Tolkien said evenly. "But no, I don't. At least not on purpose, though you may have handed Roger the murder weapon that took his life."

"What do you mean?" She leaned forward, her head tilted to one side.

"Now that we're being honest, I have a few more questions." Tolkien took out a notebook and flipped it open to a recent page. "The bottle that arrived by courier . . ." he began. "Exactly when did it come?"

"What bottle?"

Tolkien referred to his notes. "A bottle of Bell's Royal Reserve Scotch Whisky. There was a card attached saying it was a birthday gift. When did it arrive? Was it on his birthday?"

"No," Sarah answered. "That was an early gift, a couple of weeks before. He drank two fingers' worth every night in front of the fire. Said it was his favorite bottle. Difficult to come by since it's made in limited batches."

"Yes, that's right." Tolkien tapped his notebook. "I think he was poisoned. His killer put the poison into that bottle, and Roger slowly killed himself over the next two weeks, two fingers at a time."

"He drank himself to death," Cecil mused, more to himself than anyone. "How interesting. I hadn't thought of it before, the killer using the vices of men to seal their fate. I wonder what it was with Huxley."

"Baron Huxley," Sarah muttered, coming to a realization. "Do you think he was murdered as well?"

"Oh, we know it," Cecil told her. "Poisoned as well."

"Dear God," she blurted. Her hands began to shake, and she looked ready to collapse.

"Dear girl, sit down before you crack your skull," Cecil suggested. Sarah obeyed and put her head into her hands.

"You may not want to know this," Tolkien said in a low voice, "but we believe Beckworth, MacDougall if he is not already dead, and Crowley, if he's not behind it, will also be killed if the murderer is not stopped."

Sarah sat up, placed her hand over her heart, and breathed in short little gasps. "I think I'm going to be sick."

"Who else knew about the child?" Tolkien questioned. "Crowley?"

Sarah nodded. "Y-yes," she stammered. "Probably. Roger confided in that man like he was making confession to a priest."

"What about the others?" Tolkien asked. "Beckworth and MacDougall?"

"No," she responded. "I don't think so. MacDougall was only a low man on the totem pole. He'd come around and tell dirty jokes and get his fill of drinks. Borrowing a book or filling his pockets with cigars all the time. But Beckworth was always eager to learn a secret. Something to hold over his fellow members. He may have found out." She paused and then continued, "He hates children. Beckworth, I mean. He sees them as only a distraction or an obstacle to getting what a man wants in life. I heard him once talking about it many years ago, saying they were just brats who can't help but put their noses where they don't belong."

Tolkien stepped closer to where Sarah sat and leaned over her. "Do you have a key?"

"A key?" Sarah repeated, almost in a mental haze.

"You know what I mean." A smile played on Tolkien's lips. "A house key."

Sarah glanced over at Cecil. "Yes, but only because I forgot to give it back when I got sacked."

"Oh, don't do that," Tolkien urged. "If you want to see justice for the man you once loved, I need you to sneak back in and get something for me."

Sarah shook her head. "I cannot. If I'm caught, I won't be able to work in the country. I'll be arrested. My son . . ."

"If you do this," Cecil promised, "I'll personally reference you and make sure you are set up in a fine house. Think of your son and do as this man says."

Sarah looked back and forth between the men before making up her mind. "What do you need me to get?"

"Get me the bottle," Tolkien said. "It's on his desk, unless Francis drank it. In which case we'll soon have another corpse on our hands. Within that liquor lies the evidence we need that this was murder and not some random suicide."

{32} The Train

Sunday, December 27

> Love anything, and your heart will certainly be wrung and possibly be broken. If you want to make sure of keeping it intact, you must give your heart to no one.
>
> —C. S. Lewis, *The Four Loves*

The train whistle sounded its call, and soon the brothers were off from the station, making their way south toward Edinburgh and then on to Oxford, scheduled to arrive Monday morning with time to spare to set things right.

"We'll gather everyone together as soon as we get back," Jack decided. "I'll phone Hugo to meet us at the station. We need to get this right, or else the killer will take to the wind and we'll be looking over our shoulders the rest of our lives."

"Do you think MacDougall is dead?" Warren set the folded newspaper down beside him and watched his brother with steadiness despite the jostling train.

"Yes, I do," Jack said matter-of-factly. "Killed because of what he knew or what he was about to confess. I highly doubt the man would remain in hiding this long without surfacing and making some sort of contact."

"Do you actually know who is killing these men?" Warren asked.

"Yes, I think I do. At least . . . I have a strong feeling."

"Are you going to tell me or let me ride for hours with a nagging tension, like the end of a good book?"

Jack smiled faintly in amusement, causing his brother to frown. "Oh, all right," Jack gave in with a roll of his eyes.

He recounted what he suspected, including who, why, and how. Warren nodded along, wide-eyed, as if the answer had been under his nose the whole time.

Afterward, the brothers sat quietly for a while, the landscape streaming past the windows in a continual blur. Warren was too stunned to speak, and Jack was diligently planning out his next steps for when they arrived in Oxford. His heart thumping wildly already, he forced himself to close his eyes, take a series of deep breaths, and say a prayer. He pulled out a worn paperback to at least attempt to finish reading a chapter to pass the time.

Many hours later, after the evening had given way to night, their next train departed Edinburgh just as heavy snow began to fall. The brothers could feel the tension tightening the muscles between their shoulder blades with each passing hour. This time they sat shoulder to shoulder on a bench seat backed with striped fabric, facing an empty seat. On the mounted side table to Jack's right was an attached ashtray, which already held half a dozen cigarette butts. Jack found it impossible to read or sleep. His mind kept drifting back to images of the young Gillies boy—an unblinking pale ghost, with lifeless, hollow eyes, pleading with outstretched hands while floating in the otherworldly depths of Loch Ness.

Jack jerked his eyes open and looked toward the seats on the opposite side, where a map of the train line was tacked just above the curtained windows. Only a few more stops, though there were hours between each.

Warren snored softly, his head resting on his folded-up jacket pressed against a metal pole. Jack watched out the window as large snowflakes continued to swirl in the glowing light cast outward from the train cars. About that time, a hiss of steam was followed by a grating sound. The train slowed dramatically and came to a sudden stop, jostling Warren from his sleep and prompting a semi-coherent question.

"Are we there?" Warren yawned. "It's not yet even morning."

"No, it's not." Jack sighed, dread rising within him. "It's barely after midnight, and we've still many more hours to go." He heard voices outside the train car and watched as uniformed men ran past, their legs sinking into drifts of snow past their knees.

"Drat!" Jack exclaimed. "I fear the weather may delay us."

Warren blinked and looked out the window at the flurry of activity. Not knowing what else to do, he prepared his pipe and took a long drink from a flask pulled from his jacket's breast pocket.

Jack eyed his brother. "I've noticed lately you've been drinking more than you usually do."

Warren took another sip. "Only trying to enjoy life. It is short."

"Perhaps you are making it shorter," Jack countered with a frown. "And I would suggest there are other joyful pastimes. Just make sure the bottom of a heavy glass or flask is not where your search ends."

"We all have our journeys, Jack. Our memories to blot out, our pains to numb."

"Is that the end-all?" Jack said more sharply than he'd intended. "To simply live numbly? When we avoid the pain, we also miss out on so much that could just be the stuff of life."

"Like this?" Warren gestured glumly to their surroundings. "Like a daylong train ride? Being stranded in the snow? Is this the joy you speak of, Jack?"

"Of course not," Jack replied. "You know I am not a judgmental man. You live your life as you think best. It is only that my love for you cannot remain silent when I see a thing that prods my spirit to roar. I worry about you, as I know you do for me."

Warren flashed a quick smile and took another defiant swig.

Jack shook his head but smiled back. "You are stubborn, Warnie. May I have a drink? I think we may be stuck here for quite some time."

A passing porter apologized for the delay and explained that a drift had slid down from a nearby hillside, covering the track, and that they were lucky to have seen it. The workers spent many hours digging through the drift by hand, while the dark sky turned gray and then pink. Soon after the train started moving again, the porter announced that they would arrive at Manchester station within the hour and, after that, on to Oxford.

The next stop was scheduled to be a short one, but there was much to be done. Jack gave Warren the task of phoning around for Hugo, suggesting a few places to check, although Jack felt confident his brother already knew where Dyson would be holed up. Jack then attempted to contact Tolkien, but a confused Edith said he had gone to the Cotswolds with

Cecil the day before. Something about helping a man or interviewing a man who had a country house out that way. Jack felt his heart sink when he realized there would be no way to contact his two friends. Beckworth's country home had no phone. Hugo would have the address, but until someone arrived, Tolkien and Cecil would be on their own.

The whistle sounded just as Warren approached the call booth and knocked on the glass. "We've got to get back on board," he urged. "I got in touch with Hugo. He'll meet us at the station, though by that time the moon will be well and up. Hugo says he thinks he's figured out how Beckworth has been poisoned. Something about cigars and men's vices."

Jack started toward the train, then stopped. He felt the card still in his pocket and pulled it out. "I need to make one more quick call," he told Warren, dreading it deep within him. "I need to speak with Crowley."

{33} The Cotswolds

Monday, December 28

> The world is indeed full of peril, and in it there are many dark places; but still there is much that is fair, and though in all lands love is now mingled with grief, it grows perhaps the greater.
>
> —J. R. R. Tolkien, *The Fellowship of the Ring*

Tolkien walked a slow circuit of the grounds of the Beckworth country home. The full moon shone overhead and cast such a strong bluish glow over the entire property that Tolkien blew his lantern out and let his eyes adjust to the eerie strangeness of the night.

The cottage itself had a simple layout, with windows on nearly every side that displayed the interior like an aquarium. Even from the yard, Tolkien could see Cecil and Beckworth sitting in high-back chairs near the brick fireplace. Cecil was most likely doing his best to keep the man calm, as he'd done since they'd arrived the day before.

Every hour on the hour since night had fallen, Tolkien had made his rounds along the edge of the property. He checked outbuildings through windows and followed a path at the bottom of a shoulder-height berm that stretched around as a circular dam, keeping the damp marshes on the outside.

But this time he climbed on hand and foot to the top of the grade for a full panoramic view. Only a single driveway cut across the wetland like a land bridge. The wrought iron gate had been securely locked, and the trio of men could think of no other way onto the property, other than hiking miles across a bog and over the berm Tolkien was standing on. He scrutinized the two cars parked near the front entrance of the home—Beckworth's dark green Bentley and Cecil's black Lanchester Ten Saloon. The moon glimmered off the bonnet of each, a small scene of modernity in the otherwise ancient time capsule of the estate.

Tolkien turned and looked out into the cold winter's night. He heard frogs croaking, which surprised him because of the time of year. A distant owl hooted, then a scraping sound caused him to jerk his head around and scan the grounds again. When a cold breeze whipped over the marsh, Tolkien realized just how much the berm had blocked the wind and how much colder it was up here than down below. He pulled his jacket and scarf tight and hurried down the hill to complete his inspection and get back to the fire.

Just as he passed the cottage's back outbuilding, not more than a small lean-to shack, Tolkien noticed that the lock, though secure in itself, was not looped through the door latch. "How did I miss that?" He pulled the squeaking door open and looked inside.

The only thing the shed contained was a wooden trunk about the size of a coffin sitting on the dirt floor. Tolkien relit his lantern with a match and held it in front of him as he slowly reached toward the chest. His heart beating faster, he raised the lid. But all it held was a pile of rusted work tools—

rakes, a few shovels, and an axe. He was about to reclose the lid when he noticed the residue of a dark substance, almost black in the glow of his light, on the sharp end of the axe. Tolkien felt his breath pull from his lungs. He touched it and felt a hint of stickiness. The shovel also showed signs of being recently used, which sent adrenaline pumping through the professor's veins.

He aimed his light low to the ground and immediately saw what he'd hoped not to—disturbed soil, recently upturned. Tolkien set the lantern down and dragged the wooden box clear of the spot. He dug and chipped down into the half-frozen soil with the shovel until he found what he was looking for. First, a human arm, then fingers curled tightly, a leg pointing in the wrong direction, and soon red hair on a face, though badly disfigured. Tolkien sucked in his breath when he recognized Robert MacDougall.

"Dear God!" Tolkien exclaimed. Hesitantly, he pulled free one of MacDougall's detached hands, which bore the familiar ring the Scotsman had worn at White's. Tolkien held the lantern as close to the flesh as he dared. He stared at it for a moment, almost disbelieving what he was seeing as his mind raced. *Perhaps it is only another nightmare from the war.* He had just turned to leave when he saw the silhouette of a figure in the doorway and felt a cold steel blade press against his throat.

"I wondered if you might come in here." Beckworth's outline swayed from side to side, but he held the American Civil War–era saber tight to Tolkien's pulsing neck. "Forgot to lock it. Where is my mind?" He glanced down and said, "The gun, now. I've not gone so far to have forgotten that."

Tolkien slowly pulled the Enfield No. 2 from his waistband and reluctantly handed it over. Beckworth pointed both the pistol and sword menacingly toward Tolkien. He flicked the wrist holding the gun, signaling for Tolkien to exit the shed and walk in front of him.

The two made their way around the front of the house, walked through the door, and entered the living room, where Cecil sat up suddenly wide-eyed, a cigar in one hand and snifter of brandy in the other. His expression was a mixture of shock, bewilderment, and confusion at what he was witnessing.

"Take a seat, Professor." Beckworth's voice shook as he swiveled the gun back and forth from one man to the other. "Don't either of you try anything heroic, or I will not hesitate to pull the trigger. We're going to be here for some time, the three of us, until I can figure out what to do with you."

"He killed MacDougall," Tolkien said flatly while ignoring the request to sit. "I found the body hacked up and buried in the shed out back."

"You did what?" Cecil yelled. He shifted in his seat toward Beckworth. "How barbaric! How could you? We've shared brandy, cigars! How could you murder someone?"

"Oh, shut up," Beckworth retorted. "It was an accident."

"When?" Cecil blurted. "When you murdered the man in cold blood or when you chopped him up in little pieces like a savage?"

"He was going to confess." Beckworth's face twisted into a sneer, his brow sweating profusely. He steadied himself by leaning against the doorframe. "I couldn't let the fool do it."

"Good God, man." Cecil narrowed his brow. "You don't look well at all. You'd better sit down, or you'll fire that thing accidentally. How about we all have another cigar and brandy? It will calm your nerves and settle your stomach. We'll talk this out." Cecil was ever the diplomat.

"You just keep quiet and try not to move suddenly," Beckworth responded, blinking rapidly. He leaned the sword against the wall and wiped his face with a handkerchief, which he then shoved back into his hip pocket.

"What was he going to confess?" Tolkien pressed, his hands still half raised. He knew he needed to keep the man talking instead of thinking about how to get rid of two inconvenient witnesses.

"He was going to spill the beans about the Gillies boy all those years ago." Beckworth switched hands with the pistol and pulled the hankie out to wipe his face a second time. "It was eating him up inside—MacDougall, I mean—and then he thought the grim reaper himself had come for us all." Beckworth put one hand on the doorframe and blinked his eyes. "Perhaps my old friend Robert reasoned that he would be spared vengeance as long as he confessed. A clean conscience would equal a clean slate or some such foolishness."

"What happened with MacDougall?" Tolkien questioned. He took a half step closer to Beckworth and glanced at Cecil.

"Well, since I'm going to kill you both anyway, I'll tell it quick. It was soon after the open house at Pennington's," Beckworth explained. "You saw what state the man was in, and it only got worse. An hour after you left, he was dead set on going to Oxford and finding you, and nothing I said would sway him otherwise. I thought he wouldn't go through with it, but after he caught the train, I got in my car and followed. Later that evening, I finally saw the man walking determinedly down the High Street of all things. I confronted him about his planned confession, and he said it was settled and there was nothing I could do about it."

"So, you killed him then and there?" Cecil was horrified. "Good God, you were in the middle of town."

"That's not how it happened," Beckworth countered. "I knew then I would have to kill him, so I feigned my relief at the thought of finally coming clean of my crimes. MacDougall was always such a gullible fool, so ready to do whatever would make others approve of him. I invited him to ride with me to a local pub for a drink and then on to the police station. But when he was about to get in the back seat of my car, I clubbed him over the head with my heavy cane and shoved him inside."

Beckworth smiled as he lurched from side to side, the gun's barrel drooping toward the floor. He seemed almost proud of what he had done. "I then drove out here and had to use what was available to dispose of the body."

"I still can't believe you chopped up another human being," Cecil muttered, half under his breath.

"I did what I had to," Beckworth spat. "And I'll do it again." He raised the gun.

"What happened with this boy you spoke of?" Tolkien asked quickly. "What was Robert going to confess?"

Beckworth leaned back against the doorjamb and took a few deep breaths as if deciding whether to tell the story. "We were in over our heads—that's what happened," he finally said. "There was a magical ceremony performed involving an innocent. A boy was killed." Beckworth swallowed with difficulty.

"You murdered a young boy?" Cecil looked paler than usual.

"Again, it was only an accident," Beckworth asserted, showing no remorse. "But still, we had to get rid of the body. We tied rocks to the legs and heaved him into the loch, though we're not much good at tying knots either. But the lake covered our tracks, with all that lurks below, so it was chalked up to a great tragedy. Crowley—who was supposed to be there, I might add—got wind of what had happened after the body was found, and he closed down our magic shop. Took his daughter away and left. The party was over for a good many years, and even when it started again, everyone acted like the deed never happened, like it was all some horrible fever dream that no one ever talked about. Even Crowley never once brought it up."

"Then why kill the others now?" Tolkien wanted to know. "Why kill Huxley and Pennington?"

"Me?" Beckworth's eyes grew wide as he pointed the pistol at his chest in a gesture of confusion. "Of course I didn't do that. Full moons and all that. I have no more need for theatrics. That was surely not me. MacDougall yes, but not Huxley and Pennington."

"Then who?" Cecil asked.

"I haven't the foggiest," Beckworth replied, and Tolkien believed him. "The ghost of Oliver Gillies come to exact revenge," Beckworth guessed, then laughed at himself in the way of a madman.

"Who was Crowley's daughter?" Tolkien wondered. "You mentioned a daughter."

"Lilith Crowley," Beckworth answered absently. "We don't talk about her either, before or after the incident. She's a ghost herself. Supposed to be dead." He eyed both Tolkien and Cecil and took a step forward. "Enough of this. I'm not on trial, and I have the gun. What to do now? I suppose I'll need to go on the run, perhaps to South America. But first, I'll need to make sure I'm not followed."

He shifted his gaze back and forth between Tolkien and Cecil and took another step toward them.

Tolkien lunged as soon as he saw Beckworth's eyes move

toward Cecil and the gun barrel rise. He saw Beckworth twist as if in slow motion, heard the shot ring out, and felt a burning sensation near his shoulder. Tolkien plowed into the thin Englishman and knocked him down, clunking his head onto the hardwood floor and sending the man into a daze.

Cecil leaped from his chair and grabbed the saber while Tolkien used his left hand to retrieve his gun, which had gone skittering and clattering across the planks.

"Good show, Tollers," Cecil praised, pointing the tip of the sword down at the murderer.

Tolkien wrenched Beckworth up by one arm and shoved him onto a chair, where he collapsed. Blood dripped from a gash on the back of the man's head down onto his collar and neck.

Tolkien backed up and felt a burn flare up on his shoulder. He grimaced as he felt warm blood trickling down his arm under his sleeve and dripping from his numb and dangling fingertips.

Just then Cecil wobbled and fell to one knee. "I don't feel so well, Tollers," he murmured before slumping down on his side and letting the saber fall with a clang.

Tolkien knelt next to him, unsure of what to do. "I'll take the car," Tolkien decided. "I believe you both have been poisoned. I'll go get help and return."

Cecil's eyes went wide, and he struggled to speak. "Behind you!" he cried, but it was too late. Tolkien had just begun to turn when he felt the crunch of metal on the side of his skull. His world flashed, spun for an instant, and then faded to darkness as he dropped to the floor in a lifeless heap.

{34} The Dead Man's Walk

> I slept with Faith, and found a corpse in my arms on awaking; I drank and danced all night with Doubt, and found her a virgin in the morning.
>
> —ALEISTER CROWLEY, *The Book of Lies*

Jack watched as Warren and Hugo sped away from the station in Hugo's car. He turned on his heels, exhaled a deep breath, and walked eastward from Park End Street to New Road, and then south on St. Aldate's Street where he turned east again at Christ Church College. He needed information, and there was only one place to get it. As he walked, Lewis could almost feel the weighty stares of stone gargoyles from the rooftops. There was a strange stillness in the air, as if night was holding its breath. Lewis's moon shadow darkened the ground in front of him, and steaming breath poured from his mouth when at last he turned onto Dead Man's Walk.

Staring at the old city wall was Aleister Crowley, unmoving in the glow of an oil lamp even as Lewis approached.

"Surely you know how this place got its name," Crowley remarked, his voice low, just above a whisper. He turned and stared at Lewis with eyes so dark they looked almost like pools of black.

"It was a route of medieval Jewish funeral processions that moved along this path from synagogue to cemetery."

"Yes, but why call it Dead Man's Walk?" Crowley prodded. His black hat was pulled low, and a black scarf was wrapped high around his neck, allowing only his ghostly face to peer out.

"Because even those alive," Lewis answered, "those bearers who carried the body, knew it was only a matter of time before their own walk would come."

"Precisely." Crowley bared his teeth like a wolf. "We never know when death comes for us. We only know it comes for us all eventually."

"I do not fear death," Lewis stated. "Not anymore. I know you pretend not to either, but deep within you, I think I hear a faint scream."

"Have you figured it out?" Crowley questioned, ignoring Lewis's comment.

"I have," Lewis confirmed. "It's Lilith, your daughter, back from the dead."

Crowley narrowed his eyes. "I knew you'd come to it. Cannot keep a good man down."

"When did you realize it was your own daughter killing these men?" Jack asked.

"It took far longer than it should have to figure out," Crowley said evenly. "I first thought of a wide swath of people who despise me, and rightly so, but after Roger's death I began to suspect she'd finally returned to England. It is as if I'm being saved for last—sacred and set apart to watch as my daughter's cruel hand plays an instrument of death. And who would hold on to that much hatred?" Crowley glared at Lewis and jutted his jaw defiantly. "I am a man famously hated, it is true, but there is only one who holds that much abhorrence. It didn't take long after White's for my mind to work it out. I still didn't know where she was, though I do now, and right under our noses for the duration." He smiled, as if all of this would only increase his prestige.

"I just hope we're not too late to prevent more deaths," Lewis put in. "Warren and Hugo are on their way now."

Crowley barked a laugh. "What use is hope? Events have been set in motion that cannot be stopped, like a runaway train or the sinking *Titanic*. It's too late. The iceberg has already been struck, the midnight bell has rung, and the angel of death will not be thwarted."

"Why now?" Lewis wondered. "Why did Lilith wait so long to act?"

"Who cares?" Crowley replied, indifferently. "There are a hundred nonsensical reasons it could be. I suppose it would be hypocritical of me to advise her to stop or to stand in her way. I am known for espousing that all should do what they want, after all. If revenge is what the girl wills, who am I to keep her from it? Even if it tears apart my kingdom?"

"It's a good thing others don't stand by so idly," Lewis argued. "There is still an arm of justice that flexes."

"Oh yes, the Inklings." Crowley smirked. "I had almost forgotten. As if my blood could be foiled. Her determination will not be fruitless. Mark my words, Professor. By sheer force of will, she will complete whatever she has begun, if she is any daughter of mine, and I will not shed a tear over any of it."

Lewis set his jaw. "When good men stand by in apathy, you would be correct. But that is not the case here."

"We shall see, won't we?" Crowley pivoted and began walking slowly away.

"What happened at Boleskine?" Lewis called out after him. He stayed back a few paces but followed as the large man lumbered into the night.

Crowley paused, breathing heavily. "For years we worked. Years we wasted. We prepared ourselves—our bodies, minds, and spirits—in the most strict and disciplined ways I was taught. We were even celibate for an entire year. All five of us. We were the pentagram, and my disciples and I would soon summon angelic beings who would grant a release of significant magical powers. Or at least that was the Egyptian working theory I saw in my visions." Crowley snickered. "The day of the ceremony was set. All we would need was a little blood from an innocent and willing participant. I promised the boy Oliver a generous payment for his service, and he was eager to prove his bravery, especially in front of Lily. It was only to be a small cut on his palm and a few drops of blood, nothing more and nothing less. He would only experience minor discomfort and walk away with a pocketful of notes."

Crowley resumed walking. It had started to snow lightly. Steam rose from his lips.

"I'd guess that's not what happened," Lewis pressed, keeping pace.

"You'd be correct." Crowley growled. "Unfortunately, I wasn't able to join in the ceremony as originally planned. I had no choice but to leave Scotland at the very worst of times. I was asked to travel to the mainland and take control of the Ordo Templi Orientis, which was in disarray. One week turned into a month away. My mind was not focused on my home, and Boleskine, too, had fallen out of order. While I was away, the four who remained—Beckworth, Huxley, Pennington, and MacDougall—foolishly took it upon themselves to attempt the ceremony the following full moon on their own without me."

"They took it too far." Lewis's mind pictured some version of the horrid scene.

"That they did," Crowley conceded. "These men didn't know what they were doing, like I would have, and they cut too deeply. There was too much blood." He shrugged. "The boy went to sleep and never woke up. It was an accident, I suppose. No use crying over it. But nonetheless, an accident that could never be made public."

"What about Lilith?" Lewis asked.

"Oh yes," Crowley said, "she is the point of this little story, isn't she? To make matters worse, my daughter, whom I had left behind at Boleskine, happened to see those fools casting the Gillies boy into the loch on that moonlit night. She had been in love with young Oliver, her first love, and that night her world broke and a beast of vengeance emerged." He stopped and turned back toward Lewis, his mouth curved in a strange smile. "The things we do for love."

"Lilith," Lewis mused. "How was she still living? It was said the girl died at a young age."

"It was the only way I could get her away from her mother," Crowley responded. "Rose was an addict. An alcoholic, cruel, among other things. Abusive both verbally and emotionally and, from what I could see, would soon be lashing out in physical abuse, if she hadn't already."

"A bit hypocritical," Lewis commented. "Weren't you an addict as well?"

"Yes." Crowley nodded. "I still am, but I could always control it. I can function and am my best self when under the influence. I like all types of influence—I like to exude it, and I like to be possessed by it. But sadly, Rose could not." Crowley folded his gloved hands behind his back. "I knew I was going to divorce the woman, but how could I manage to take my daughter with me and not leave her with her horrid mother? She was to be my greatest student. The answer hit me one day while I was in an opium stupor. I waited until one of Rose's drunken binges where she blacked out for days on end. Then, when she awoke, I told her Lilith had fallen ill and died. People owed me favors. I had witnesses to her supposed illness, receipts from the hospital, a certificate of death, and even a headstone above an empty grave."

"She believed you?" Lewis was incredulous.

"Tell someone something enough times and in enough ways, and they will believe anything." Crowley shifted his weight before pivoting and walking again, his shoes crunching softly on the thin layer of snow. "The grief was too much to bear," he called back over his shoulder. "I used the grief of Lily's death as a way to finally be free of Rose. Sadly—not to me but to some—I later heard she had drunk herself into oblivion. I guess the grief was too much for her to bear. Oh well, the world is better off without Rose Crowley in it."

Lewis felt a chill run up his spine but kept pace. This man was clearly a sociopath, but Lewis needed to gather as much information as he could while Crowley was speaking. If Lilith should get away, any details he gleaned could be helpful in tracking her down.

As if sensing Lewis's thoughts, Crowley spoke. "Did you know I grew up in a Christian home? Very fundamentalist. So righteous and good were we, yet I rebelled. The prodigal who never returned home. Lily ran away soon after we left Scotland. She would write me letters every year around All Hallows' Eve to let me know she was alive and to remind me of what she saw that night and how she blamed and hated me for it. Beckworth is the only one of the four left now. Then her vengeance will be satiated, and she will disappear into the night once again."

"Will she come for you?" Lewis wondered.

"No." Crowley shook his head. He drew up near a single lamppost and turned back to face Lewis again. "My punishment is to live, not die. Lilith knows that. She has my mind and my blood coursing through her veins. She wants me to watch as my world crumbles, as my minions are swept away and I am left with nothing."

"Is that why you came here to Oxford?" Lewis asked. "You knew she was close by?"

"Yes, I came here looking for my daughter. I knew if she were responsible, she would be nearby keeping watch and moving the pawns around the board. I wanted to find her first, perhaps to save her life. Men in the Order would not hesitate to string her up if they knew what she's done. And perhaps I would be next. They may have even thought I put her up to it."

"Did you?" The thought had been nagging at the back of Lewis's mind.

"Not directly, but I suppose in a way I am to blame," Crowley answered. "I took her away from her mother. I made her witness things she shouldn't have, at least not at that young age. I allowed her to be broken, and I did nothing to put the broken pieces back together. I am a proud man, I admit it. But even I am not proud of what I did to my daughter." Crowley shook his head. "I'm afraid I am responsible for having released yet another beast upon this world."

{35}
The Full Moon

So comes snow after fire, and
even dragons have their ending!
—J. R. R. Tolkien, *The Hobbit*

Tolkien slowly blinked awake. The room was still spinning. Blurry light from the incandescent bulb hurt his eyes, and he pressed his eyelids together tightly. A pulsing throb at the back of his head matched his beating heart. At least he was alive, for the moment. His shoulder burned, and he dared not move it. Tolkien attempted to open his eyes again and blink away the blur. After some time, he could see the outline of a figure standing over him, and with each passing second, the indistinguishable voices became clearer.

Someone grabbed him forcibly by the collar and hoisted him up to sit with his back pressed against a bookshelf. His entire body flared in pain at the movement. Tolkien clenched his teeth and looked down to see a dark pool of blood where his head had been just a moment before, a clear outline of his ear imprinted on the wooden planks. His vision still spun, but he noted it was a woman standing in front of him, staring down with eyes so dark they looked almost black. She wore a dark robe that covered her from neck to floor. The woman was familiar to him, but it hurt to rack his brain as to how. Then he heard Cecil speak, and suddenly the lights of familiarity flickered on.

"What in God's name are you doing, Beth?" Cecil cried. He, too, had been propped up against a table, his hands now tied behind his back. "Why are you here? And what is that you're wearing? What is happening?"

"You know her?" Beckworth mumbled, his voice faint. He was lying on his back, or as much as his bound hands would allow him, and a look of shock had fallen across his narrow face.

"She's my nurse," Cecil replied. "Brings me towels and medicines . . . fluffs my pillows and such."

"Tell him who I really am," the woman said evenly. Her hair was down, long and black, spilling around her pale face and wild eyes. "Go ahead, Lord Beckworth." Her words dripped with disdain. "Surely you of all people should remember me."

With effort, Beckworth tilted his head to one side. His face was pale and twisted in pain and disgust. "Am I supposed to know you?" he questioned.

"It's been over twenty years since we've last seen each other, or at least since you've seen me," she answered. "I've been watching you closely for quite some time. You and all your lordly friends. You are an evil little urchin. No repentance in your heart at all, never a care for anyone but yourself. It will be a blessing to watch you breathe your last."

Beckworth furrowed his brow curiously and swallowed

with difficulty. He looked more unwell by the minute; his eyes were glassy, and a sheen of sweat formed on his forehead. "Lily, is that you?" The realization and horror washed over his face in a fresh wave.

"Yes." Lilith glanced at Cecil and Tolkien. "My name is Lilith Rose Crowley. You know my father. I was there at Boleskine when the four horsemen murdered Oliver Gillies and, instead of owning up to what they did, threw his body in the loch. He was the only good thing in my life." She looked back at Beckworth. "And you all cared not for the pain it added to his father's life. You cared only for yourself. For all these years, you tried to cover it up. To bury your sins. But I won't let you." Lilith smiled for the first time as she paced in a circle. "Isn't it ironic that you all devoted your life to lies and make-believe, but that night you did release a power—one of vengeance."

She glared down at Beckworth. "I have been biding my time hunting four men, and now three are dead, one killed by this man's hand." She pointed at him with the barrel of Tolkien's pistol. "MacDougall died far too quickly and painlessly. I never got a chance to poison him and watch him suffer. But there will be a fourth very soon." She glanced toward the window. "The moon is just about in place, and then my work will be complete."

"You are insane," Beckworth spat.

She pressed the gun to her breast. "Me?" she questioned mockingly. "You are a killer of the innocent. And for what? A little power? Power that is nothing more than an illusion. Just another counterfeit fraud and web of lies spun by my father, the ultimate con artist."

"The power is real," Beckworth argued defiantly. "I've felt it."

"Do you feel it now?" Lilith bent over him. "Do you feel powerful?"

Tolkien tried to speak, but his throat was sore, and what emerged was a round of coughing, which sent fresh shooting pains across his body.

The sound got Lilith's attention. She shook her head and walked over, grabbing Tolkien by the hair and pulling his head back so she could look him in the eyes. "Don't worry, Professor. This will all be over soon. Your death will make the papers." When she let go, his head fell back against the bookshelf. She then pivoted and crouched down near Beckworth. "I really can't tell you how giddy I am to be this close to the end," she said, barely above a whisper. "How are you feeling?" She stood up straight. "You've been poisoned with thallium, and even now it's killing you from the inside, though it won't be the poison that will end your life. I'll do that in a special way, a message to my father." She leaned closer and whispered to the petrified lord, "Do you want to know how I did it?" A smile played at the corner of her dark red lips. "You remember that box of cigars Cecil sent you the day after your interview at White's? They were laced with poison."

"I sent no cigars," Cecil blurted from the other side of the room.

"No, you didn't, my dear employer," Lilith responded without looking. "But I did. They came from your private reserve stash, in the glass-front hutch—the one with the key you leave in the lock. A very expensive brand, complete with a card from your own stationery and your own wax seal. It was all too easy to access as you lay in bed that Saturday when Professor Lewis stopped by. He was a suitable distraction. You two should learn to be more discreet and speak more quietly about your cases, by the way."

She pointed to the coffee table on which sat another box of cigars. “I poisoned that box as well. I’m afraid, dear Cecil, that you will also die along with Beckworth. You’re probably feeling it now, the poison flowing in your veins. It wasn’t my intention, truly, but unfortunately, you and the professor won’t be able to live as witnesses. At least you won’t survive long enough to suffer the horrible side effects. You’ll keep your beautiful hair, dearest Cecil.”

“Good heavens,” Cecil mumbled as the finality of the situation began to set in.

Lilith turned and looked at Tolkien. “I heard your telephone call when Cecil rang you. I knew you two were planning to drive here yesterday morning to meet Beckworth, so I hid in the back seat of Cecil’s car under a blanket and nestled up to a set of luggage. You brought the murderer to the safe house.” She laughed. “It couldn’t have happened any better.”

“What are you . . . going to do with us?” Tolkien asked, finally able to string words together. His mind raced as his fingers felt the rope at his wrists.

“That is a good question.” Lilith’s eyes danced as she circled the living room, even skipping joyfully at times. “What sort of ceremony shall we re-create?” She pressed a finger to her lips. “My father loves Egyptology, so I think I know what to do with the three of you. I’ll arrange you in the shape of a pyramid on the floor and bleed you out one at a time. That should get my father’s attention in a poetic way, wouldn’t you all agree? He’ll think it’s a masterpiece.”

Not long after that, Lilith walked to the nearest window and gazed out at the moon. “Oh, I think it’s time,” she said excitedly. She grabbed each man by the ankle or wrist, dragged them helplessly to the middle of the floor, and arranged them head to foot in the shape of a pyramid as she said she would. She stood in the center of the triangle, turning and inspecting her work while nodding in satisfaction. "Yes, that will do." She left the room momentarily, only to return with a small leather roll that she laid on the floor, unbuckled, and splayed out.

"We can get you help," Tolkien urged. "You don't have to go through with this. There are good psychiatric hospitals in London."

She laughed at the professor's words. "Do you think I'd enjoy electroshock therapy? Besides, I'm not insane, just highly motivated." She set the pistol on the floor and, from the leather roll, pulled out a glimmering ceremonial dagger with a red ruby worked into the handle, which had what looked to be a metallic snake coiled around it. After inspecting the blade, Lilith tapped it against her lips as she walked slowly around the three men, pretending to decide which man would die first.

"I'll start with you." Lilith bent over Beckworth, who began to wriggle and kick. "But I want you to watch the others die first; then I'll come back around. You'll need more pain." She grabbed his bound hands and pulled them closer to her. He fought against her, but too much of his strength had left him. With quick flicks, she cut deeply into both of his wrists, and a spray of blood misted the wooden floor.

Beckworth let out a whimper as she let go and moved around the circle again. She then stalked over to stand above Cecil. "My dear former employer, I'm afraid I will pierce your heart. It will be quick, I promise." She leaned down and raised the dagger over her head.

Just then they heard the sound of crunching stone at the front of the house. A quick smash, followed by another, and the front door flew open, wood splintering at the deadbolt.

The first to come barreling into the room was Hugo, with Warren on his heels. Without hesitation, Hugo ran toward Lilith and dove at her just as she stood to her feet, swinging the blade and slashing at him.

The two rolled on the floor. Lilith came up, eyes wide with rage, and readied the blade for a deathly blow. A single shot rang out, spinning the girl in a circle and sending the dagger skittering across the floor. Warren stood at the entrance to the living room, holding the Enfield No. 2 pistol, a look of horror washing over his face as he took in the scene and what he'd just done.

Lilith cried out in pain, clutching her shoulder where she had been shot. She fell back against the bookcase and slumped to the floor.

"Looks like we got here . . . at just the right time," Hugo noted breathlessly, his hand pressing against his slashed arm.

Tolkien felt himself drifting, but he let go. Despite his world fading to black, he knew his friends were here and they would take care of everything.

{36}
The Quiet

Tuesday, December 29

> If you look for truth, you may find comfort in the end: if you look for comfort you will not get either comfort or truth—only soft soap and wishful thinking to begin with and, in the end, despair.
>
> —C. S. Lewis, *Mere Christianity*

Lewis had barely entered the Eagle and Child when he was pelted with a series of questions.

"How is Tollers holding up?" Fox nearly shouted.

"Will Cecil be all right?" Nevill Coghill added, concern visible in his eyes.

"Don't leave us in suspense, Jack," Hugo urged. His arm was wrapped in gauze to cover a half dozen stitches, and he sported a cream canvas sling for the shoulder he'd dislocated when tackling Lilith Crowley.

Jack unwrapped the scarf from around his neck and nodded vigorously. "Yes, yes, Tollers has already been treated and released." He closed the front door to a jangle of bells and lowered his voice. "It was only a grazing wound and a gash. He'll be quite all right. He's at home now, and Edith says no visitors are allowed—so don't bother stopping by; she won't let you in. I don't believe she is too pleased with this entire ordeal . . . too dangerous." He continued, "As for Cecil, he is being kept for observation, a day or two at most. He ingested a good portion of poison, so they want to be sure the antidote Hugo administered was effective and anything in his system has passed. Our friend is lucky to be alive. Though Beckworth wasn't so lucky. I'm afraid the poison was well on its way to working and too much blood had been lost."

The men spent a protracted moment in silence before Fox voiced the next burning question. "Where did the bloody antidote come from?"

Jack brushed past without responding, and the other three men followed close at his heels until they reached the Rabbit Room lair of the Inklings.

"It was Jack," Hugo divulged. "He gave it to me at the train station."

"And where did Jack get it from?" Fox pressed eagerly.

"It was Agatha Christie, if you must know," Lewis answered in a lowered voice as he pulled out a chair. "A concoction she called Prussian blue. Mixed it up right in front of me in her kitchen apothecary. I thought Hugo might need it."

"Remarkable woman," Hugo put in. "And Cecil will live and have all his hair, from the sound of it. I don't know what he would find worse, to die of poison or for his beautiful head of hair to fall out."

Lewis couldn't help but chuckle despite the seriousness of the subject matter. Glancing around, he noticed that his brother was not in attendance. Warren had been quiet since the event, barely speaking a word. It was not surprising he did not show, since he'd then be forced to relive and retell the story. Jack understood it wasn't an easy thing to shoot with the intent to take a life, even when necessary, and especially when it was a woman.

The other men were eager to hear some of the missing parts of the puzzle, but they all settled into chairs and took a moment to stare at the fire, appreciating familiar comforts amid circumstances so new and strange.

"Tell us how you figured it out," Nevill finally said. "If you hadn't sent Warren and Dyson out to the Cotswolds when you did, this may have ended much differently. The woman would have surely killed all three and taken to the wind as free as a mad bird."

Jack shook his head. "I don't think she was as mad as one might make her out to be. Lilith simply viewed life differently. A great pain, like the one she experienced early in life, can do that to a person, break them beyond mending. At least not mending in a natural sense." Jack held a faraway gaze for a moment before coming to himself and noticing the others staring at him intently. "Oh, sorry. Solving it was a combination of many things, really—a hundred pieces of the puzzle all set before me. It just took time to put them all in the right place." Jack held out a hand toward his captive audience. "You all helped even more than you might realize. It ended up being simply a string of logical conclusions and a bit of deduction."

"Well, get on with it," Fox prompted as Charlie brought a round of cider on a tray, which he left on the table.

"First of all," Jack began, "as we've discussed, I knew the murders obviously had to do with the Order of the Golden Dawn. I also knew that it all was linked to Crowley in some way. He was the person connecting all the players and events together. It made sense to focus my primary efforts—and some of yours—on investigating him and the Order. Next, I knew it had to do with some event or trigger in the Order's past. There was nothing recent of note, besides the murders themselves, and Doolittle didn't feel right."

"I was just thinking about him," Hugo interjected, adjusting his sling. "He's not as vile as we thought. After all, he did leave the Order when he felt things were taking a dark turn. Not the actions of a murderer."

Jack nodded. "That's right. He's arrogant, yes. But I believe he was more of a red herring that Crowley threw in our path. Perhaps to slow us down, perhaps to test us. I get the feeling Crowley wanted to be the one to find his daughter."

"So, you went to Scotland because it represented the past?" Fox quizzed.

"Yes," Jack said. "And you yourself were part of that gentle prodding, at the gaudy. You encouraged me to not get caught up in fruitless details and to find the epicenter, or zero, as you put it. Even the Faustus play inspired the idea that something so out of control may have begun much earlier from just a seed. So, I went back to the beginning to find the seed, as one should when they are confused. The beginning of the Order was Boleskine House, so off we went, Warren and I. Hugh Gillies would be the final piece, but certainly not the first. He told me about his son Oliver and how the boy had turned up dead. He also told me about Crowley's daughter and how the two of them had been inseparable. Of everyone we talked to about Crowley, no one else ever mentioned the daughter living with him at Boleskine. Only Gillies did, and he said it because he was one of few that knew Lilith was alive."

"What clued you in that it was this girl who was dead set

on killing these men?" Nevill asked. By this point he had begun jotting down notes to keep track for himself.

"Again, it was a myriad of influences at different times," Jack replied. "Separate bits waiting to be put together to form a coherent picture. Agatha mentioned that poison was a woman's murder weapon. She also reminded me that a murderer often either runs away or stays as close to the investigation as possible to move pieces around the board. The first of the ten rules of investigation I heard at the Detection Club dinner hinted at something similar. Who we are looking for may be closer than we thought and revealed earlier in the investigation. I thought of young Lilith, witnessing what she did when she did. She would have motive, and it fit that these killings were done in some sort of vengeance. She also would have the needed knowledge of her father's work to pull it off. I thought about what she might look like and what she might do to stay nearby. Then it hit me as I was walking back from Gillies's hut to the castle—it was Beth, Cecil's nurse. She was around the right age, and there was something about her eyes. They're her father's eyes. I can't believe I didn't notice it earlier."

Fox cleared his throat. "Why do you suppose Lilith Crowley waited for twenty years before exacting her revenge on those men?"

Lewis sighed. "Perhaps she couldn't. She was a very troubled girl. Her mother also had a troubled mind, and we are all aware of the mental state of her father."

Everyone nodded in agreement and breathed deeply in the momentary quiet before further explanation.

"No," Lewis amended, shaking his head. "I think Lilith bode her time, hiding in the shadows, patience and cunning being her virtues. And finally, twenty-three years later, at the exact same full moon on All Hallows' Eve, she aimed her first blow at Huxley, who by all accounts may have been the one who held the knife. Then, a month later, Pennington, followed by Beckworth. MacDougall would have been the last. Most likely the least guilty of the four, if there is such a thing. But the Scotsman threatened to come clean and confess, and Beckworth took his life for it and buried the body at his Cotswolds cottage."

"Do you think Lilith meant to poison Cecil?" Nevill wondered.

"I don't think she thought about it much." Lewis folded his hands together and rested them on the table. "He was a means to an end. But from what Tolkien and Cecil told me, she was solely focused on exacting revenge in a sort of mock ceremony, just like how the Gillies boy died so many years ago. I can only imagine what that much distorted, festering hatred and revenge could do to a person's conscience. That type of pain eats away at a person, and if we allow it, we become that which we hate the most."

The men stared at the fire while Charlie came in with a fresh platter of clinking glasses, though the others had remained mostly untouched. Sensing the somber mood, he again left the tray without a word.

"So, in the end," Lewis went on, after reaching for a glass. "By sheer force of will, I suppose Lilith accomplished her life's mission of revenge, just as she said she would. Crowley was right when he said she wouldn't be stopped from completing her mission. Though now she'll likely spend the rest of her life in prison, or face hanging."

{37} The Debrief

Wednesday, December 30

> Even darkness must pass. A new day will come. And when the sun shines, it will shine out the clearer.
>
> —J. R. R. Tolkien, *The Two Towers*

Owen Barfield stood and flashed a half smile and wave when Tolkien entered through the doors of the Eastgate Hotel. The professor's arm was in a sling, similar to Hugo's, though his face now had color, and he even managed a smile in return. Along with Barfield, Lewis and Dorothy were seated at their usual place by the window for a celebratory luncheon of sorts.

"There he is—the man of the hour," Barfield greeted him, using his left hand to shake Tolkien's. "Back from the dead."

"Well, back from under the scrutinous eyes of my wife," Tolkien remarked. "She only let me leave the house because Scotland Yard demanded I come and make a statement."

"How are you feeling?" Dorothy asked. "A bit sore, I'd

imagine." She stirred a Bloody Mary clockwise three times with a piece of celery.

"Tollers is fine," Lewis answered for him with a slight grin. "Ready for the next adventure, I'm sure."

"Our dear friend was shot and nearly killed," Barfield pointed out, as Tolkien took his seat. "There is no making light of it, Jack. My plans were cut short when I learned of it." He looked over to Tolkien. "Maud and I arrived only this morning."

"You didn't have to come back on account of me," Tolkien protested. "It was only a bullet graze and a gash on the head. Cecil's situation was far more dire."

The waiter, a young red-haired man Tolkien recognized as a student, set something clear and bubbling in a highball glass in front of him. His friends had gone ahead and ordered for him.

"I spent the morning with Doyle," Dorothy said to both Lewis and Tolkien. "He was impressed. Mistakes were made, but overall, I'd imagine you'll have more opportunities in the new year if you want them. Though he'd be cross if he knew I'd told you. He wanted to say it himself. The man is a grown child."

"Doyle?" Barfield looked confused. "As in Sir Arthur?"

"You'd have been brought into the loop sooner or later," Dorothy responded. "Didn't you know that while you were on vacation, your little literary club became a full-fledged detective agency working for a man with the highest connections in the land?" She eyed Barfield and smirked, loving her role of telling this man, who knew just about everything, something he didn't.

"You're kidding!" Owen looked from Tolkien to Lewis and back again, incredulous. "I leave for a few weeks and the world goes mad." He then opened a leather folio on the table in front of him and scanned a few notes he had previously jotted down.

"I spoke to a contact over at Scotland Yard as soon as I got in," Barfield went on. "Despite the myriad of crimes committed, there are no more looming arrests to speak of. Two living witnesses heard Beckworth confess to the murder of Robert MacDougall. The body has since been exhumed and will be examined, though the findings are to be expected. Beckworth has passed due to loss of blood combined with severe thallium poisoning. Tolkien and Cecil are witnesses who also heard Lilith Crowley confess to the murders of Huxley and Pennington, as well as Beckworth's involvement in the death of the Gillies boy. The poison was successfully recovered, thanks to Ms. Cornish. Lilith has been arrested, and time will tell what is to become of her." He sighed. "Other than that, Crowley might face some legal quandaries for faking his daughter's death all those years ago, though he has friends in high places and I am confident it will all go away quietly. No doubt he will be investigated and vindicated—it wouldn't be the first time. And as for Oliver Gillies, Crowley was out of the country when the boy died, so given that alibi and his connections to the home office and British secret service, even whispers of his involvement will be put to pasture."

"The magician will come out unscathed," Lewis stated matter-of-factly.

"That's quite a trick." Dorothy shook her head.

"I was questioned by Scotland Yard," Tolkien told them. "There was no way to avoid it. They took mine and Cecil's statements, as well as Hugo's and Warren's. I said what needed to be said but left out some of the more sordid details about the Order and our detective agency. Crowley arrived just as I was leaving." He looked at Jack. "He knows your brother Warren was the one who pulled the trigger. That won't be easily forgotten."

"He's right," Dorothy agreed. "No matter the circumstances, I'd imagine it would be a slight Crowley would hold on to. We'd better keep an eye on him. I fear we may have created a bit of a nemesis in that man—our very own Moriarty."

After a meal consisting of hard-boiled eggs and lukewarm bean soup, Barfield and Tolkien said their goodbyes while Jack insisted on finishing his second mug of tea, which had only just arrived. Dorothy stayed back as well to keep her friend company.

"And what is next for Professor Lewis?" she asked lightly, her head tilted to one side as she lit a cigarette.

"Well, there is an old man in a castle who needs some answers about his nephew," Lewis replied. "And another old man, the groundskeeper at that same estate, who might like some closure about what happened to his son all those years ago." Lewis stirred and sipped. "And I also need to finish my book."

"Ah yes, there's always a book to write," Dorothy said. "It's not real unless it has been splashed in ink on a page."

"If there is no record of it"—Jack raised a brow—"did it even happen?"

"What a secret to keep." Dorothy exhaled while gazing around the restaurant. "Crowley kept that poor girl a secret for nearly all her life. Only a few people ever knew she was even alive. What a thing."

"I guess we all have secrets," Jack commented.

"I have some of my own," Dorothy said as she gathered her things. "Perhaps one day I'll tell you about them."

Jack saluted her with his mug. "I suppose the greatest puzzles and mysteries in our lives are the people we choose to surround ourselves with."

{38} The New Year

Thursday, December 31

The game is afoot.
—ARTHUR CONAN DOYLE,
The Adventure of the Abbey Grange

Most of the others had already arrived by the time Tolkien entered Lewis's Magdalen room. He spotted Hugo, arm still in a sling, sharing the story of his heroism for perhaps the dozenth time with wild one-handed gestures. Tonight, his audience was Charles Williams, who squinted behind thick spectacles while nodding along vigorously. On the couch, Warren held a worn leather Bible by the spine in one hand and nursed a thick glass of what looked to be a triple whiskey in the other. Dyson, Fox, and Coghill sat in a half circle of chairs with Jack facing them.

They all stood and turned to applaud Tolkien as he stepped through the doorway.

"Hello, old chap!" he heard over his shoulder. Cecil entered behind him and slapped him on the back.

The others soon gathered around both of them with well wishes and questions about wounds and what it was like spending nearly three days in the hospital due to poisoning. Cecil looked a bit worse than usual, paler with darker circles under his eyes. Otherwise, all were in good spirits.

"One hour until a new year is upon us," Dyson bellowed. He took a drink before continuing, "What shall we do to pass the time? Anything besides conversations about elves."

"I have an idea." Nevill held up a finger. "Perhaps we should read a passage from Amanda McKittrick Ros, and the first to burst out laughing will be forced to tend bar the remainder of the evening." All the men chuckled at this, except Charles Williams, who did not yet understand the inside joke.

Jack leaned over toward the confused man. "She's a writer," he explained. "And not a very good one at that. We all agree."

Charles smiled and nodded. "Ah yes, I think I have heard of her."

"I'd like to know everyone's resolutions," came Hugo's booming voice.

"To finish my book," Jack called out quickly with a grin.

"To lose a stone." Fox rubbed his stomach.

"To spend more time with my children," Tolkien noted, "and to finally publish *The Hobbit.*"

"To begin a new book," Charles Williams stated. "I just had an idea only this morning."

"Oh? What is this idea?" Hugo asked, pointing at his newfound friend.

"It will be called *Descent into Hell* and will feature a character who is slowly being transformed into the evilest version of himself." Charles looked around to nods of approval.

"Sounds heartwarming," Tolkien said to laughter.

"Would you like to come to Oxford and read it to us when the time comes?" Jack invited.

"I would be honored," Williams replied with a quick nod of his head and the flash of a rare smile.

"I, too, have an idea for a book after I've completed the current one," Lewis put in. "And it is also a darker subject matter than what I'm used to. I haven't worked it all out yet, but it will have to do with temptation. I've toyed with the idea of writing the book from the perspective of a demon sent to tempt a man and the conversations this demon might have with a more experienced tempter."

"Oh, how dark and delightful!" Fox exclaimed. "No doubt Crowley was an inspiration for both."

"No doubt," Williams and Lewis said together.

Just before midnight, there was a knock at the door. When Jack cautiously answered it, Sir Arthur Conan Doyle entered the room without any sort of disguise. "I hope I am not intruding," he began, surveying the larger group. "Sorry to show up like this at the eleventh hour." He pulled an envelope from his jacket pocket and handed it to Fox. "There is money in there—quite a lot of it actually—for a job well done. That should help with medical expenses." He looked pointedly at Tolkien.

"Here I thought solving the mystery was payment in itself," Tolkien commented.

Doyle removed his jacket. "If I may get a drink of something, and you all as well, I'd like to make a toast before midnight strikes. And then I must be off, back into this mad world."

They hastily prepared their drinks and held them high, as all nine men stood shoulder to shoulder in a tight circle.

"A toast to the Inklings Detective Agency," Doyle said loudly. "Here's to fellowship. May this new year bring new books to write, new adventures to step into, and new mysteries to solve!"

And with that, the Inklings responded together, "Hear, hear!"

Historical Notes of Interest

The Eagle and Child: This pub, nicknamed "the Bird and Baby," was one of the real-life meeting places for the Inklings from 1933 to 1949. The pub can still be found in its original location on St. Giles' in Oxford and is expected to reopen to the public in 2027. In the back room, a.k.a. the Rabbit Room, there is a small plaque on the wall commemorating these meetings of the Inklings.

Sir Arthur Conan Doyle: Though he is best known for his famous character Sherlock Holmes, most aren't aware of Doyle's extracurricular pursuits, which included investigating supposed paranormal activities or lending his expertise to help solve crimes. One notable case involved the murder of an eighty-three-year-old woman named Marion Gilchrist on December 21, 1908. A petty crook named Oscar Slater was arrested for the crime, but Doyle applied his techniques of deduction and convinced Scotland Yard they had the wrong man.

The Cambridge Ghost Club: This club traces its origins to 1855, when fellows at Trinity College, Cambridge, began meeting to discuss ghosts and psychic phenomena. It was formally established as an organization in London in 1862 and continues to operate today as the world's oldest paranormal research and investigation society. Among its notable members was the author Charles Dickens, whose involvement encouraged the club to take a more active, investigative approach to its work.

The Staplehurst Rail Crash: The rail crash was a fatal train derailment that occurred in Staplehurst, Kent, on June 9, 1865, at 3:13 p.m. The accident happened when the train crossed a viaduct where a section of track had been removed for maintenance, resulting in the deaths of ten passengers and injuries to forty others. The author Charles Dickens was among the passengers and survived the disaster.

The Order of the Golden Dawn: The Golden Dawn, as it was commonly known, was a secret society devoted to the study and practice of the occult, hermeticism, and metaphysics during the late nineteenth and early twentieth centuries. The Order was known to have connections with many powerful nobles and royals in Great Britain and would become one of the largest single influences on twentieth-century occultism and its spread around the world. Some of its members included well-known writers like Evelyn Underhill and William Butler Yeats. One member who rose to positions of power and founded an occult society of his own was Aleister Crowley.

Aleister Crowley: Aleister became infamous during the early twentieth century because of his exploits and teachings. Crowley claimed to have been visited by an angel named Aiwass who dictated to him *The Book of the Law,* which would later become the central text of a new religion called Thelema. Aleister did have his first wife, Rose, committed to an asylum after they divorced, but she remarried and passed away years later in 1932. Crowley did in fact fake his death in Portugal in 1930, and he and Rose had a daughter who died at the age of two that he named Nuit Ma Ahathoor Hecate Sappho Jezebel Lilith Crowley.

The Detection Club: The Detection Club was formed in London in 1930 by a group of nearly thirty British crime writers that included Agatha Christie, Dorothy Sayers, Ronald Knox, and G. K. Chesterton. Knox wrote the ten rules of detective fiction, and the initiation process for joining the club, written by Sayers, really did involve placing one's hand on a human skull. It is also true that, on occasion, Scotland Yard consulted with this brilliant collection of crime writers.

Agatha Christie: One of the most well-known mystery authors of all time, Christie wrote sixty-six detective novels, fourteen short story collections, and many more literary works. Her most well-known characters are Hercule Poirot and Miss Marple. What most don't know about Christie is that she once worked in a hospital dispensary and became known as an expert on poisons. She also really did go missing for eleven days in 1926. Included in the massive manhunt was Sir Arthur Conan Doyle, who gave a medium one of Agatha's gloves in the hope that she would be able to find Agatha spiritually. It is also notable that Agatha was good friends with Dorothy Sayers, who was a good friend of Lewis's, so the two likely met in real life.

The Boar's Head Gaudy: The gaudy is an annual festive tradition at the Queen's College, Oxford. It is typically held on a Saturday just before Christmas, the same day it happens in this book, and involves a procession of the boar's head, the singing of "The Boar's Head Carol," and a celebratory meal. One of Dorothy Sayers's most well-known books,

Gaudy Night, was inspired by and loosely based on this event as well as a gaudy event at her own Somerville College.

Oxford Playhouse: The playhouse opened to the public in 1938, with private shows leading up to the grand opening. One of the plays that ran during those first years was *Doctor Faustus*. Also, the Inkling Nevill Coghill was a stage director for the playhouse and Dorothy Sayers would often work on scripts for the stage, including one called *The Devil to Pay,* which was based on *Doctor Faustus*.

Boleskine House: This former home of Aleister Crowley sits on a hillside overlooking Loch Ness. Crowley owned Boleskine from 1899 to 1913, when he suddenly abandoned the place and eventually moved to Moscow and then Paris. Some accounts state that he held ownership of the home until 1918. The area had a history of strange happenings long before Aleister Crowley moved in. The parish of Boleskine was formed in the thirteenth century with a graveyard added soon after. Minister Thomas Houston (1648–1705) was reportedly charged with the strange and grim duty of returning reanimated corpses to their graves after a mischievous local wizard had "raised the dead" in Boleskine's churchyard. This strange history is perhaps why Crowley bought the place as a hub for his occult ceremonies. There is even a tunnel leading from the house to the graveyard. What's more, Crowley's groundskeeper, a man named Hugh Gillies, had two children who tragically died young. Boleskine was later bought by Led Zeppelin guitarist Jimmy Page, who lived there from 1971 to 1992.

Readers Guide

1. Who was your favorite Inkling character and why? In what ways did their personality on the page match what you had in mind?

2 What scenes or conversations stood out in your mind as memorable?

3. What real-life character cameo was most surprising and fun to you?

4. Which clues caught your eye early on and what plot twists caught you by surprise?

5. How did the spiritual background or beliefs of the different characters come into play during the story?

6. What modern issues are touched on and addressed in this story?

7. What were your initial predictions for who might be the killer(s) leading up to the final reveal?

8. What is a moral lesson or takeaway from the story you find relevant to your life?

9. How important was setting to this story and how did the locations play into your reading experience?

10. What is a favorite passage or quote?

11. What did you like most about the book, and what would you like to see more of in future Inklings stories?

About the Author

JOHN R. KELLY has studied history and spirituality for most of his life, which led to a career teaching church history and biblical studies at True North College, including courses on the occult, history of world religions, and also the real-life Inklings. He lives in New Jersey with his wife and eight children.